THE FIRE KING

NICK STITLE

BOOK TWO OF
THE STORMLESS SERIES

ISBN (eBook): 979-8-9878962-4-2
ISBN (Paperback): 979-8-9878962-5-9
ISBN (Hardcover): 979-8-9878962-6-6
ISBN (Jacketed Hardcover): 979-8-9878962-7-3
Library of Congress Control Number: 2023923774

Cover Artwork & Design by Jeff Brown Graphics

Title Production by The Book Whisperer

Published by Blazecrest Publishing, LLC

For Lukas, who is both my brother and my best friend

AURIS
FREYFALL
ORRINSHIRE
THE ICE FIELDS
UTRYA
ELOS
TELENARIS
HIRANE
CELES
ELAN TAESI
THE HIGHLANDS
FAIRFROST
HYTHE
THE WASTELANDS
ETHERUS
ARVENDON
THE SALARIN SEA
GOLDENLEAF
SUCHARA
ASARI
THE DUNES OF DESPAIR
CYFALION
JASKYE
AYRIA
ASHOS
THE BLAZING CIRCLET

PART I

The Fire King

CHAPTER ONE
CONSEQUENCES

Waves washed against the sand. Sunbirds—complete with their resplendent, crystalline feathers—chirped and cawed overhead. Divebrisks splashed in the distant water. It was... dark. Yet there was light somewhere. Wisps hissed by, swarming the currents with their strange energies.

Castien Varic twisted, or he tried to. He was squished between two jagged rocks. He groaned, blinking his heavy eyes. His vision cleared, revealing the dark stone he was pressed up against. Castien squirmed, trying to wiggle out of whatever crevice he had fallen into.

Pain shot through his left arm. He cried out, reaching for his arm. He looked down, able to make out the burned skin in the dim light. *Wait...*

Images of Ilyana, running through Summerglass, materialized in his head. Thoughts of the Prince... the King... a Shadow-Swift? Castien rubbed his eyes with his right hand, noticing his splitting headache for the first time.

"It's about time you woke up," a familiar voice said from somewhere close by.

Castien turned to look behind himself. The gap in the rocks

widened there. He let out another grunt of pain as his left arm scraped against the rocks.

"Let me help you," Ilyana said. A hand appeared in the gap.

Castien took it, using his right arm to pull himself out of the small crevice. He slid out of the rocks, his face landing in the damp sand of the shore. He laid there for a few moments, trying to discern reality from dreams. *It couldn't be real... This can't be real.*

"Unless you're content with lying face down in the sand for the rest of your days, I'd suggest getting up," Ilyana said.

Castien's eyes snapped open, heat suddenly trickling into his damp and cold body. He shoved his right arm into the sand, pushing himself to his knees. Waves crashed in the background. Wisps danced by, weaving in and out of Castien and Ilyana's figures.

"Wait..." Castien muttered, rising to his feet. He carefully held his left arm out to the side, making certain that it didn't brush against anything. With a glance down, he looked at his arm, getting a better view of the warped and ruined flesh.

"We're going to have to wrap that," Ilyana said, stepping forward.

Castien stepped back. His thoughts were still a mess. *If only this damned headache would go away!* "You killed the King," he said, narrowing his eyes. The previous night was somewhat foggy, but he was certain of that fact.

Ilyana paused, her gaze falling. "I did." She lowered her head.

"You were the spy?" Castien breathed, taking a step forward. He reached down to his side, fumbling at the shortsword at his waist.

Ilyana backed up, drawing her dual butterfly-blades in an instant. "Don't try this with me, Castien. I could've left you up there."

Castien managed to draw the blade. He raised it shakily, gripping the blade tightly in his hand, the soggy leather feeling damp and slick. "You lied to me," he croaked. "I trusted you, and you lied to me."

Ilyana lowered her gaze once again but kept her weapons ready.

"I also saved your life, mind you. You'd think that would be worth something." Ilyana grunted.

"I only needed saving because you made me an accessory to the murder of the *King* of our country! You betrayed us!"

"*Don't* try to play the victim!" Ilyana snarled. "Arvendi assassins killed King Brennan Nightingale of Celes four days ago. Your people *shattered* the peace between our nations, not mine!"

"Wha—" Castien blinked. "What are you talking about?" Castien locked eyes with Ilyana, though neither lowered their blades. Castien winced, his arm burning with a sudden shock of pain.

"Arvendon betrayed Celes," Ilyana said. "If I didn't make my move last night, Titansworn would've gotten away with it too."

"You've been a spy this entire time." Castien blinked.

Ilyana's eyes flickered.

"I don't understand," Castien said. "Why were you even on that expedition in the first place? Why... Why were you even in Arvendon at all?" Castien paused, his arm flaring. "Was this your inten—"

Pain shot through his left arm. Castien cried out, dropping the sword in the sand and falling to his knees. Trying to support the sword had even been too much for it.

Ilyana knelt down, but didn't sheath her blades. "If you don't let me help you, you're going to get an infection, and you're going to *die*, Castien," Ilyana said.

Castien hesitated.

"What do I even care anymore?" Ilyana said, rising to her feet. "Sit here and rot, this is a waste of time." She strode past him, leaving him in the sand.

Castien started, still recovering from the spike of pain. He wasn't a waste of time. He was just... Everything had blown up in his face, and he didn't know what to do.

"Wait," he called out, turning over his shoulder while clutching his arm. "Please."

She paused.

"You're right," Castien said. "I need your help." Castien swallowed, trying to compose himself. "Please help me with the burn. I... I don't know what to do."

Ilyana sighed, turning around. "Promise you won't try to kill me?"

Castien looked down at the sword in the sand. A wave ventured up the shore, washing over the blade with a gentle brush. He nodded, suppressing his anger. If he didn't let her help him, he wouldn't survive much longer.

"Let me see," Ilyana said, kneeling beside him.

Hesitantly, Castien raised his arm to show her. Another wave dashed across the shore, lapping at the backs of his shoes.

Ilyana examined the burn. She delicately turned his arm, surveying the underside.

Wisps dashed by, hissing and whistling through the air with their strange white energy.

She gently probed the warped flesh, sending a flash of pain through Castien's arm.

He winced, pulling his arm back. Castien eyed Ilyana, then hesitantly reached back out.

Ilyana examined it once again, taking a few moments. "I don't have the supplies to treat it properly, and Zephyr knows we can't go to Arvendon to get them," Ilyana said.

Castien tried to meet her gaze, but her eyes were still fixed on his arm. "What can we do?" He winced again as he shifted his arm.

Ilyana furrowed her brow, her Elosian features twisting. "I should wrap it," she said. "We were always taught growing up to loosely wrap Scorcher burns—not too tightly to where it puts pressure on the skin, but enough so that we can protect the blisters while they begin to heal." Ilyana looked around as if searching for something. She reached her hand up to the fabric of her robe and drew a knife with her other hand. Slowly, she started cutting off the arm of the robe.

Castien winced again as Ilyana started wrapping the gray fabric against his arm. Twists of blue decorated the cloth, making for a strange mismatch against his vermillion vest.

Moments later, the makeshift bandage was secured.

"Are you ready to talk now?" Ilyana asked, raising her gray eyes to meet his gaze.

Castien looked away, clenching his good hand. He should punch her right now. She murdered the King. Did she really expect him to just let that go?

Ilyana took his silence as a yes and began speaking. "My last name isn't Xirel," she said. She spoke slowly, carefully, as if she were trying to keep it as simple as possible. "It's Nightingale."

"You—" Castien started, blinking. Nightingale... That name was familiar. The fog over his mind lifted slightly. Castien's eyes widened. *Nightingale...* The King of Celes was Brennan Nightingale, which meant... "You're one of the Celesian Royals?"

"I am," Ilyana said. "I was sent to Arvendon to infiltrate the royal court and act as a spy for my father, King Brennan Nightingale of Celes." Ilyana lowered her eyes. "A few years ago, the King held a competition to determine his next agent. I entered as a way to prove my skill and hopefully gain a position of influence in the court," Ilyana said. "I made it to the finals, and I should've let Delmorian win... I *should've*, but damnit I couldn't." Ilyana paused. "When I won the fight, the King wanted to appoint me as his agent, but I couldn't accept—the role would've had me outside of the city more often than not, preventing me from gathering information.

"I truly had no intention of doing this much damage to Arvendon," Ilyana continued. "For over a year now I have simply been feeding information back to Celes, telling them of Arvendon's courts and explaining the workings of their armies."

"Yet... you killed the King," Castien whispered.

"I had no choice," Ilyana said. "After Titansworn betrayed my people... After he *killed* my father, I had to do something."

Castien paused. He didn't remember hearing anything about an assassination in Celes. Granted, he wasn't highly ranked enough to be informed about such things, but something like that would've likely reached the public ear by now.

"I never intended to kill the King," Ilyana said. "I did, however, have a plan to assassinate someone in Arvendon's ranks, though my father would decide who. Celes has its fair share of enemies in Arvendon's court, and one of these was meant to be my target—my father sent another spy ahead to ensure we chose the right one. The goal was to kill the noble and plant evidence to make it seem as though I had killed a Celesian spy, thus deepening the King's trust in me.

"That was why I brought you into the plan in the first place," Ilyana continued. "You seemed so helpless and lost on the expedition that I figured you could benefit from gaining the favor of the King." Ilyana paused. "By the time that I knew my target *was* the King, you were too involved in the plan."

"But..." Castien said slowly. "Why did Arvendon order your father's death?"

"I don't know, but I intend to find out," Ilyana said.

Castien stared off toward the horizon. "Why hasn't news of your father's assassination reached the public yet?"

"My contact was the only one in Arvendon who knew before today," Ilyana said. "He told me the news the night before the Solstice, and together we decided that the only way forward was to assassinate Titansworn." Ilyana paused. "The only reason the rest of the world doesn't know about my father's death is because the Elosian borders were locked down; only my contact was allowed through."

Castien blinked a few times. *So Arvendon did assassinate the King of Celes?* He looked around, scanning the Wisp-covered beach. Boulders dotted the sands, damp with the crashing water of the waves. Castien turned back to Ilyana.

Ilyana looked up, her eyes brightening a bit. "I'm sorry, Castien," she said. "I didn't mean to bring you into this, but I had no choice. If I had tried to do this alone, I would have failed. I needed your help with the distraction, but you wouldn't have helped me if you knew the truth."

The sun shined brightly overhead, glaring into Castien's curious eyes as he scanned the sky. Sunbirds and blazecrests soared overhead, flaunting their majestic beauty for all the world to see.

"How long was I unconscious?" Castien asked after a moment.

"You slept through the rest of the night and most of today," Ilyana said.

Castien looked up, scanning the cliffs—which were several hundred feet tall. He noted the remnants of a rope hanging halfway up, swinging slightly in the breeze. "What happened?"

"After you were burned by the Prince, you passed out," Ilyana said. "I had attached a series of ropes and carabiners to the cliffside the night before—that's why I was out so late. I had planned for you and me to climb down, but obviously, that couldn't happen. Instead, I was able to create a makeshift harness out of the spare ropes and carabiners and lower you down next to me," Ilyana said. "It took hours, and we had several close calls, but we made it—clearly."

Castien looked back to the cliffs that rose impossibly high overhead. *We went down that?*

"Once we reached the bottom, I knew they would come looking for us, so I found the crevice and hid you there. Then, I walked out from the beach toward where the grass began, leaving behind my footprints. I walked back backward so that it would look like there were two sets. When I got back to these rocks, I found a crevice of my own to hide in, and waited. A squadron of guards came looking for us—I assume that they spotted the ropes from above and knew that we had climbed down. They passed these rocks without looking twice. They probably think we're miles away by now."

"But..." Castien trailed off. She had saved him, again. She could've easily left him behind to be killed by Faelyn, but she hadn't. Ilyana had once again found a way to save his life. *No,* Castien thought. *She was the reason my life was in danger in the first place,* he reminded himself. The King was dead, and Ilyana was to blame.

Castien sighed. He closed his eyes, finding his heartbeat, then took a deep breath, syncing his breathing to the rhythm of his pulse. Opening his eyes, Castien felt part of the haze lift.

Ilyana was staring at the sand as the waves washed up beside her blood-stained blue and gray dress.

Looking down at his own vermillion vest, Castien felt shame. How could he wear the colors of the country that he had just doomed? The entire left sleeve was missing—burned away by Faelyn Titansworn. Many other holes were beginning to form in the vest, as well as in his black pants.

But he had bigger things to think about, like... like...

Calida's Claws! The Starburner Crystal! Castien's right hand instinctively snapped toward his pocket. He halted sharply, his eyes slowly shifting to Ilyana.

"If you're trying to be subtle about reaching for that Crystal, don't bother," Ilyana said. "I already know about it."

"What?" Castien gaped.

Ilyana glanced at him, flashing a half smile. "I went through your pockets looking for anything that might help us once we reached the bottom of the ropes."

Castien glared.

"Oh, don't give me that look. You would've done the same thing."

Castien looked down, pulling the small, fragmented Crystal from his pocket.

"Is it what I think it is?" Ilyana asked after a moment.

Castien looked over to her once again. "Yes," Castien said quietly.

Ilyana grunted, nodding to herself. She walked over to one of the nearby rocks and sat down.

Castien moved his arm slightly, testing the tightness of his bandage. It was sufficient.

"Where did you find a Starburner Crystal anyway?" Ilyana asked. "I know that the Blood Sorcerers are returning, but I can't imagine where you would've found a Crystal like that."

"The Blood Sorcerers gave it to me," Castien said. "...kind of. The

Crystal that you hit when you threw a knife at them to save me back in The Highlands, it was a Starburner Crystal."

"Hmmm," Ilyana said, sitting back on her heels. "Strange that the Blood Sorcerers would have a Starburner Crystal on hand," Ilyana said. "Although there seem to be empty Skin-Shaper Crystals popping up all over now, so who knows what's going on."

"What?" Castien asked. He rubbed the outside of his arm lightly, feeling a slight sting of the nerves as he did so.

"Skin-Shapers—shapeshifters," Ilyana said. "Their Crystals were always depicted as green in the ancient texts and paintings, and the guards have found more than a few of them around Arvendon over the past few weeks."

"What does it mean?" Castien asked, releasing his arm and rubbing his shoulder.

Ilyana raised an eyebrow. "The Crystals obviously mean that a Skin-Shaper must be in Arvendon—likely impersonating someone else—though trying to find out who would be a nightmare, so nothing has really been done about it."

Nyghtmaere, Castien thought. His eyes closed, flickering back to the night before. *A wall cracked in half. A Shadow-Swift crashing through the rubble, killing a dozen men in mere seconds.* "What was the Shadow-Swift doing there last night?" he asked.

"I don't know," Ilyana said. "My contact told me that he had set up a distraction, though he didn't say what it was. After the Shadow-Swift showed up, I figured that was what he meant." Ilyana paused. "Though I did see something strange as we were descending. It almost looked like two Shadow-Swifts were fighting in the night."

Two? Castien thought.

"Of course, given that there are said to be no more than three Shadow-Swifts on Auris currently, that doesn't make any sense. Why would they be fighting each other?" Ilyana said.

The steady beat of the waves seemed to sync with Castien's heart. The fog in his head lifted slightly, and he realized how foolish he was being. "How do I know you're not lying to me about all of this?" Castien asked. "How am I honestly supposed to believe anything you say, given that you've been lying to me all this time?"

Ilyana looked toward the sea. "I understand your apprehension," Ilyana said. "I wouldn't trust me either right now."

Castien followed her gaze, staring out at the Salarin Sea. The waves were shrouded in Wisps, whose white tails screeched and whistled through the waves with delight as the water rolled in. "Why did you save me last night?" Castien asked.

"I don't know," Ilyana said quietly.

"You could've left me behind," Castien said. "It would've been easier to descend the ropes alone, and it would be easier to flee Arvendon's lands without me."

"I'm aware," Ilyana said, still facing the sea.

"Yet you still saved me," Castien said, watching the waves roll in. "Why—"

"Look, maybe I felt sorry for you, okay?" Ilyana interrupted. "I'm the reason you got into that mess... It didn't feel right to not at least *try* to get you out of it."

Castien looked at her, watching her glazed-over eyes.

"Listen, I don't expect you to trust me, but I can get you to safety," Ilyana said. "You can't go back to Arvendon now—they'll kill you on sight—but you can come with me to Celes."

"Who's to say that I couldn't just turn you in to Arvendon and hope that I'm set free as a reward?" Castien asked.

Ilyana snorted. "Even if you could somehow incapacitate me and take me back to the city, are you really willing to bet your life on how the new King will react?" Ilyana asked. "Faelyn's father is dead, and as far as he knows, you are partially responsible... I think that regardless of what kind of trade you try to make with him, you're not going to leave that city alive."

Castien looked down, feeling his breathing increase again. She was likely correct. He couldn't return to Arvendon, even if he somehow managed to bring them Ilyana as a prisoner. "This is great," Castien grumbled. "Just great."

"I can guarantee that you'll be safe in Celes," Ilyana said. "As Princess, I can find you a place to stay for a little while."

Castien didn't respond.

"With that arm, you won't be able to survive in the wilderness on your own," Ilyana said. "I hate to put it this way: But you don't exactly have a lot of options, Stormless."

Castien winced at the name. It still stung, even after all that she had done to him. The worst part was that she was right. He doubted he could even shoot a bow because of his burn. Heading south would require circumventing Arvendon... And the only thing north of Etherus's border was Celes and the rest of Elos.

"When do we leave?" Castien grunted.

"So you're coming with me?" Ilyana asked, sounding surprised.

"I don't have a choice," Castien said. "If I stay here, I die. If I return to Arvendon, I die. If I go anywhere but north, I die." Castien looked at his bandaged arm again, feeling a tingling sensation in his skin.

Ilyana fell silent for a moment. "When a monarch in Celes dies, the royal family votes on who should inherit the throne. It could even be me, though I doubt it. Either way, I'll need to be there for at least a few weeks." Ilyana paused.

Castien looked down, staring at his bandaged arm. "When do we leave?" he asked quietly.

"We should go under the cover of nightfall," Ilyana said. "We'll leave after dark tonight and travel as quickly as our feet will carry us. With any luck, we'll be to the Elos-Etherus port of Fairfrost in a week. From there, we can steal a ship to Celes."

"And then what?" Castien asked, rising to his feet. "You get to live happily ever after in your home, leaving me as a criminal who can't even return to my city without losing my head?"

Ilyana paused. "We'll figure something out. I can provide you a place to stay in Celes for as long as you need it... But you're free to go wherever you please. I suggest you stay in Celes long enough for your arm to heal, but it's your choice." Ilyana turned away, seemingly ending the conversation as she gazed off into the sea. The two of them were well in the shadow of the cliffs, and spotting them from above would be impossible.

Castien glanced to the side, spotting the twin trails of footsteps leading down the beach that Ilyana had made. He shook his head. She was good at what she did, he had to admit. He had no choice but to follow her to Celes—it was the only place he would be safe.

But he would come up with a plan. He needed Ilyana's help to get to Celes, but after that, he would be able to make it on his own. He could even sabotage Celes from within after the war broke out... Perhaps if he helped Arvendon enough he could find a way to be allowed back in the city.

It wasn't much, but it was something. Ilyana had just turned his life upside down, and he had no choice but to try and turn it right side up once more.

CHAPTER TWO
FOUND

Night fell, and under the cover of darkness, Ilyana and Castien began their journey. Castien had to walk with his arm held awkwardly out to the side so that he didn't accidentally bump it with his body. It was as sensitive as a baby blaze-crest, and when he peeked beneath the bandage, the white-red skin almost looked wet.

It was strange—and painful. Ilyana had theorized that there would be a handprint where Faelyn had burned him once the injury healed. She had said that it would take several weeks—if not months—and that it would likely leave a permanent scar.

Castien grumbled as he walked along the soft sand, his shoes sinking with each step. His bow lay comfortably on his back, though he knew he wouldn't be able to use it. He still carried his simple shortsword—he would at least be able to use that.

"We're going to need to keep a lookout for search parties," Ilyana said. "I wouldn't be surprised if Faelyn still has this place crawling with soldiers."

"Great," Castien muttered, walking on.

Ilyana glanced back at him, a strange look on her Elosian face.

She said nothing and turned back to the beach on which they walked.

Lotius's silver glow clashed strangely with Oria's turquoise light, weaving an almost surreal tapestry of color across the open sea. Castien would've found it beautiful if he wasn't walking with a traitor and a burned arm.

"My footprints led around to where the grass began, and I stopped there," Ilyana said. "I would assume that they've figured out that we're going to Elos, given my heritage. But I can't imagine that they'll go all the way to Celes to find us. Once they hit the border, they'll probably be stopped by my people."

"You killed the King, Ilyana," Castien said. "Once they get confirmation that you were acting on behalf of Celes, I doubt the Arvendi will stop at anything to capture us."

"We'll be safe in Celes," Ilyana said steadily. "My father may be dead, but I still have strong ties with my family, and I can't imagine that they'll be upset with me." Ilyana continued walking in the moonlight.

Waves crashed quietly against the sand, washing away Castien's steps as he walked. He looked to the side as they began to come out from the shadow of the cliffs. The land started to level out here, and once they were completely away from the rocks, they would be able to start up the incline—toward the open Wastes beyond the wards.

Another wave washed up on the shore, lapping at Castien's boots. Castien looked down pitifully, cursing the waves back. He continued walking, his face locked in a frown. His King had been murdered, and he had helped the culprit. *Why shouldn't I be pissed off?* Castien thought to himself. He had every reason to be upset. But what could he do? Shouting at Ilyana could make her reconsider her offer of safety in Celes, and then he would have nowhere to go.

As much as he hated to admit it, she was right about that much. He was trapped, and without any other options. He had to go to Celes with Ilyana to seek refuge, and maybe, if he was lucky, he could find some answers about the Starburner Crystal.

A corner lay up ahead where the cliffs dropped off, leaving a sharp turn toward the grass beyond. Castien stayed a few feet behind Ilyana, his mind flashing to the Shadow-Swift and the guards on the night of the Solstice. *Zephyr's Watch...* Castien thought. *That was only last night.*

"We're going to have to move quickly once we reach the end of the beach," Ilyana said. "If we don't want to get—"

"I shouldn't be surprised," a voice said.

Castien jumped back. His arm rubbed against the bandage, sending a bright flash of pain through his burned skin.

A figure stepped out from behind the corner, holding a crossbow in his hands. "I told you it was worth waiting." The man stepped forward, his gray robes and gloved hands becoming visible in the twin moonlights. He pulled back his hood, revealing short hair and a familiar face—Arthion.

Another figure trailed him, this one wearing the long jacket of a Cloudwalker. "You were right, Arthion," the Cloudwalker—Elric—said. "I thought you were wasting my time... But they were hiding down here all along."

"Arthion? Elric?" Castien gasped. "What... How did you find us?"

"The guards reported that both of you had been seen breaking out of the Palace last night. They found your ropes in the morning and determined that you had already left the beach—according to the footprints at least," Arthion said. "I knew better than that. I know the two of you well enough to surmise that you would've misled the guards somehow... And a false escape with the footprints in the sand seemed like the most likely answer," Arthion said, keeping his voice even. The wooden crossbow seemed heavy in his untrained hands.

Castien eyed it carefully before shifting his gaze to Elric.

"Ilyana Xirel, Castien Varic, you are both under arrest," Elric said. A gust of wind blew, and his blades rose out of their sheaths. Elric raised a hand, his two daggers levitating beside him. "You will answer to the new King for your crimes against Arvendon. I am giving you thirty seconds to surrender yourselves—if you do not, you will be taken by *force*."

"You don't understand what's going on here—" Ilyana started.

"Don't try to sway me with your words, *traitor*," Elric growled.

"Elric, please." Castien stepped forward.

Elric shifted his emerald eyes to Castien. "I'm disappointed in you, boy," Elric said. "You had a bright future, and now you've thrown it all away."

"You won't take us," Ilyana said firmly. "Your people have already killed my King. I won't let you take my life as well."

"*Your King*?" Elric growled. "You killed your own King! What in Niventia's Light are you talking about?"

"I am loyal to the King of Celes," Ilyana snapped. "And Avenos Titansworn had him killed but a few days ago!"

"By the Six," Arthion cursed. He turned to Elric. "I told you she was lying to us from the start!"

"I—" Elric stuttered. He looked to Castien, then back to Ilyana. "I don't know what your motives are, but Arvendon did not kill King Nightingale."

"Then why did my informant say otherwise?" Ilyana challenged.

"Perhaps your informant lied," Elric glowered. "But Arvendon has committed no crimes against Celes. The only criminals here are *you two*."

Ilyana did not falter. "We know the truth! Why won't you admit to Avenos ordering King Nightingale's death?"

Arthion lowered the bow slightly. "The late King Titansworn did no such thing; we are speaking the truth."

"I—" Ilyana started. Her face grew red. "The only reason I killed Avenos is because your people killed King Nightingale," Ilyana said. "I wouldn't have done it without good reason, you know I am not that foolish."

"It seems that we don't know you at all," Elric growled. "Why are we even still discussing this? You killed King Titansworn unprovoked. What more is there to say?"

"Your assassins killed King Nightingale," Ilyana seethed. "Your emissaries just haven't made it back to Arvendon yet." Ilyana paused, taking a breath. "Give up the ruse. We know that Avenos ordered King Nightingale's death."

Arthion raised the crossbow once again, giving her a warning look.

Castien remained silent, tense. He made note of the fact that Ilyana was yet to mention that Celes's King was her father.

"Listen to me," Arthion rumbled. "Our King sent no such order." Arthion's amber eyes sparkled in the moonlight. "I'm in the King's inner circle—as is Elric—if anyone would know about this order, it would be us."

"But..." Ilyana trailed off. "Why would... You're lying." Ilyana narrowed her eyes.

Arthion raised the crossbow to eye level and readjusted his grip. "Believe whatever you want, but if you don't tell me why you really killed Avenos, then I'm just going to go ahead and pull this trigger."

"She's telling the truth," Castien blurted. He blinked a few times, the shock wearing off. "I promise, she's telling you the same thing she told me."

"Then who's to say that she isn't lying to all of us?" Arthion challenged.

"I—" Castien looked to Ilyana, then back to Arthion and Elric. "I don't know. But you know I can't go back to Arvendon because of what she's done. Just..." Castien took a deep, shaky breath. "Just please listen to me. I... I don't want to die today."

Arthion looked to Elric for a moment, then lowered his crossbow.

"How in Tarathiel's Stones did you even get involved in all of this, boy?" Elric asked, his voice hard.

"Ilyana offered me a way to elevate my standing in Arvendon," Castien said. "She claims that her plans then changed, and she was tasked with assassinating the King. She never told me who her target was... I thought I was helping Arvendon, I swear!" Castien said desperately. "By the time I knew the truth, it was too late."

"So she betrayed you too! Why on Auris are you still defending her?" Arthion exclaimed.

Castien stepped forward, trembling. "If you take me back to Arvendon, the new King will have me killed," Castien said quietly. "Ilyana is promising me safety in Celes, and right now, sticking with her is my only hope of living through the next few days."

"How do you know she isn't lying to you?" Elric asked. "How do you know she'll truly protect you in Celes?"

Castien hesitated. "She could've left me to die in that Palace last night, but she didn't," Castien said. "So please, for my sake, give us a chance." Castien felt a familiar warmth at the back of his eyes. His thoughts accelerated, skipping ahead to the death he might face in Arvendon. He would likely be burned by the new King himself, perhaps even tortured. And after what Castien had done last night... Who's to say where he would even end up after his death? "Please," Castien pleaded, a tear surfacing. "I don't want to die today. If you take me back, he'll kill me," Castien's voice broke. "And I'm so scared —" Castien stopped, choking back tears.

What could he do? They were going to kill him. Gods above, they were going to kill him. He was going to die.

Ilyana stepped forward. "I know you may not believe me, but I was told that Avenos killed King Nightingale. If what you say is true—if King Nightingale is still alive—then I was tricked... And right now the two of us are your best chance at finding out who's really behind all this."

Elric stared at them, eyes narrowed.

Arthion, however, seemed to consider her words. He watched Ilyana carefully, then shifted his eyes to Castien. "Elric," Arthion said, turning slightly. "Perhaps there is something to discover here." Arthion stepped back, motioning for Elric to do the same.

The two began quietly whispering, Elric keeping an eye on Ilyana and Castien while he spoke.

Castien's lips quivered as another tear rolled down his face. He rubbed his eyes with his right hand, wincing as another shock of pain ran through his left arm. With a deep breath, he began syncing his respiration to his heartbeat.

Five beats in. Six beats out. Hold for three. Repeat.

Arthion and Elric continued talking, seemingly debating how to proceed. Arthion looked back to Castien, then turned to Elric.

Watching anxiously, Castien waited for the two to reach a decision. He figured he was lucky they were even considering letting him and Ilyana go.

Arthion was choosing to give them a chance, and for that Castien was grateful.

Elric stepped back, seemingly frustrated with Arthion. He looked back to Castien and Ilyana, arms folded. With a sigh, he said something back to Arthion, shaking his head.

After a few moments, Elric turned back and approached Castien and Ilyana. "You said you're going to Celes?" Elric grunted, looking at Castien.

Ilyana nodded.

"What about the Blood Sorcerers? The Blood Sorcerers we found in the cave on the expedition said that Celes was already under their control," Elric said.

Castien blinked. He was right. Elric had overheard such information just before he ambushed the Blood Sorcerers' outpost over a week ago.

Ilyana paused. "It doesn't matter," Ilyana said. "Celes is the only home I have left. Even if what we heard is true, I doubt I will be barred from entering my own city."

Elric looked to Arthion, then back to Ilyana. "My opinion? I think we should turn you in. You killed the King and you need to be held accountable." Elric paused. "*But,* Arthion believes that there might be more to this than I assume. He tells me that his Whispering has confirmed that the two of you are telling the truth, and if that's the case... then I want to ensure that those who are truly behind this answer for their crimes." Elric paused.

Castien blinked. He hadn't even noticed Arthion probing his mind. *Strange.*

"Arthion *and* I will accompany you—as your captors," Elric continued, begrudgingly. "We will see if your claims about your King's assassination are true... And you will lead us to the true masterminds behind King Titansworn's murder." Elric sighed. "And perhaps we can get an idea of what the Blood Sorcerers have planned for Arvendon. *Then*, Arthion and I will ensure that the two of you answer for your own part in this mess."

"Thank you, thank you." Castien fell to his knees, trying to hold himself together.

"*But*," Elric growled, "I am going to return to the Palace and inform the Council that Arthion and I are leaving for Celes to investigate Avenos's assassination," Elric said. "If I do not return, Celes will pay the price, understand?"

Ilyana looked to Castien, then nodded.

"Try anything and I won't hesitate to kill either of you," Elric snarled. He waved a hand and lifted into the air. "I'm going to go inform the Council. I will meet the three of you on the hill," Elric said, motioning to the incline behind him. "And if you even lay a *finger* on Sir Arthion while I'm gone, you'll soon find your heads separated from your bodies, understood?"

"Understood," Ilyana said.

Elric glanced at Arthion.

Arthion nodded, sliding his crossbow into the holder on his back. "I think this is the right way to proceed." Arthion nodded. "Regardless of whether or not the King of Celes is truly dead, there is ample evidence of foul play. If Avenos did not lie to us, then someone on Miss Xirel's side lied to her... Either way, we need to get to the bottom of this before war breaks out."

Elric grumbled, rising higher into the sky using his Cloudwalker abilities. "Keep an eye on them. I'll be back soon."

Castien watched as Elric floated away, praying to the Six Divines that the Cloudwalker wasn't simply going to call for reinforcements.

"How would Arvendon not know about King Nightingale's assassination by now, if what you heard is true?" Arthion asked, turning to Ilyana.

"Elos locked down their borders. The only emissary they let through was the one coming to me," Ilyana said. "That's why no one in Arvendon has heard the news yet."

"If Elos started locking down their borders, then we would've heard about it by now," Arthion said. He paused, thinking. "Do you really think that they would've been able to keep *everybody* from crossing the border? What if a Cloudwalker had tried to cross? How would they have stopped one of them?"

Ilyana paused. She turned to Castien, then back to Arthion. "You think I was lied to?" Ilyana stepped forward. "My contact was a childhood friend—I trust him with my life."

Arthion furrowed his brow. "Something strange is truly at play here," Arthion said. "Who knows if the contact you met with was even the man he claimed to be... With all the Skin-Shapers and Illusomancers running around, who knows what truly happened?"

Castien started. "Wait, Illusomancers?"

"Ah, yes," Arthion said, frowning. "After Faelyn was found unconscious, an elderly man stepped forward claiming to be an Illusomancer—and Faelyn's secret advisor."

"*What?*" Ilyana gaped.

"He created light out of thin air." Arthion nodded. "Thus proving his claims to be true."

"How is this possible?" Castien asked. "Are all of the Sects coming back?"

"I'm not sure, but it certainly is starting to look as if the Resurgence is upon us," Arthion said.

"You said the Illusomancer is an advisor to Faelyn?" Ilyana asked.

Arthion nodded. "Eithor—as he calls himself—claims that he has been guiding Faelyn's decisions for several weeks now... He has already tried to assume a position of power in Arvendon's court."

"See! Who knows what else the Titansworns have been keeping

from you?" Ilyana said. "Who's to say that Avenos didn't order the murder of King Nightingale?"

"My thoughts exactly," Arthion agreed. "Why do you think I convinced Elric to accompany you, rather than turn you in?" Arthion trailed off. "Although there is much that makes me question whether Nightingale was truly killed. I can't help but wonder if there was a plot that Elric and I were unaware of."

Castien looked to Arthion, then to Ilyana, then out to the grassy hill behind them. Turning back to Ilyana, he spoke. "Are we not even going to acknowledge the most troubling appearance of last night?" Castien asked, rubbing his shoulder carefully.

She stared at him blankly.

"The Shadow-Swifts?" Castien said, motioning. "They haven't surfaced in such a public way for centuries from what I understand."

"Castien brings up an interesting point," Arthion said. "Perhaps they are involved in this madness."

"It would make sense," Ilyana said. "Strange things start happening with no explanation... The Shadow-Swifts always seem to be involved somehow."

"Point is, dear friends, that I think the two of you are onto something," Arthion said, smiling. "I'm not sure where the future of Auris is heading, but I am certain that I will not find answers in Arvendon any longer." Arthion looked to his right, staring up toward the top of the cliff. "Elric will likely return within the hour, we should start moving," Arthion said.

"Agreed," Ilyana said. "We have no time to waste." She started walking up the grassy hill leading away from the cliff, slightly inland.

Castien followed, brushing past Arthion.

Arthion laid a gloved hand on Castien's right shoulder. "Castien, wait."

Another headache started to come on as he turned to Arthion.

"I have something to give you," Arthion said, unhooking the crossbow from his back. He looked to Castien's bandaged arm, then back to his eyes. "I see that you've been injured... You can hardly shoot a bow with that arm, I assume?"

Castien nodded softly, feeling the warmth in his eyes once again.

"Try this," Arthion said, turning the crossbow around so that Castien could take it. "I'm not a very good shot anyway." Arthion chuckled softly, offering a warm smile.

Castien took the crossbow with his right hand, testing out its weight. It was heavier than an ordinary bow, but it *seemed* that he would be able to use this one even with his burned arm.

"You're giving me your weapon?" Castien asked. "Elric just said you would be acting as our captors, why would you—"

"If you wanted to kill me, you would've done so already," Arthion said, smiling. "Accept the gift, please. I hate seeing one so bright as you stuck like this."

Castien looked back up to Arthion, allowing the warmth in his eyes to come forward. A gentle tear rolled down his cheek. He wasn't sure why he was crying. Perhaps it was all that had happened over the past few days. Perhaps it was yet again because he could never return to Arvendon... Or perhaps it was Arthion's simple act of kindness that brought tears to his eyes. Regardless of what it was, it felt good. At least with Arthion here, there was someone who trusted him.

"Oh," Arthion exclaimed. "And you'll need these too." Arthion unhooked a quiver of bolts from his back, along with a light, hooked harness that would hold the crossbow in place when Castien wasn't using it.

Castien tried to reach out to grab them with his left hand before remembering the bandage.

"My apologies." Arthion laughed again. "Allow me to help you." He strained, reaching over Castien's head, gently lowering the harness into its place. Arthion helped Castien fasten the quiver to the harness, then stepped back and smiled.

Castien lifted the crossbow up, glancing at Ilyana as she walked a few hundred feet ahead.

"It suits you," Arthion said, smiling once again.

"Thank you, Arthion," Castien said. "You're a kind man." Castien smiled.

"Ah, you flatter me, Castien. But you're more worthy of that weapon than I am." the Whisperer waved his hand. He lifted his hood over his head once again. "Now come on, we need to catch up." Arthion turned and started after Ilyana.

Castien reached over his shoulder and hooked the crossbow into place on his back, then followed Arthion. As he started walking further and further away from the cliff, he began to see the tip of Summerglass Palace far above.

The white marble castle was beautiful even in the night, despite missing one of its spires—which likely fell due to the damage the Shadow-Swifts had done.

Castien wondered if he would ever be inside that Palace again. A part of him feared that he wouldn't, but he couldn't let that be true. He would find a way home... he *had* to... he had to.

CHAPTER THREE

THE NATURE OF GRIEF

lood... Fire... Shadows.

Death.

Faelyn Titansworn slowly opened his eyes. His head hurt, as did his chest, and his legs. Energy slowly trickled into his veins, a slight warming sensation drifting across his body. He tried to look around.

Judging by the thick gray curtains and the sturdy cot, he was somewhere in the Palace's hospital. Calida's Claws... He felt as if he had been asleep for an age—almost long enough for him to forget...

Father.

Faelyn's pulse quickened, his eyes scanning the dim room for any signs of life. Nothing moved, though he could hear sounds from beyond the curtain. It was almost like... none of this was real. Nothing felt real, nothing *could* be real. What he remembered was... impossible. It must've been a fever dream of some sort, an elaborate construction of his imagination to entertain his drifting mind while his body healed from...

Something moved to his right.

Faelyn tried to move but found that he was unable to. Crystals clinked against one another somewhere close, but Faelyn kept his eyes on the shadow. *No.*

"I was wondering when you'd wake," a voice said quietly. The shadow moved again, taking shape this time. "The doctors said it would be today, and they were right." Eithor stepped into the dim light of the room, coming out from the shadow of the corner.

"You—" Faelyn stuttered. His tongue felt heavy and dry. His head pounded. Scorcher Crystals lay on either side of him, the steady flow of energy into his body meant to accelerate his healing. The light of the Scorcher Crystals hurt his eyes, amplifying his headache. The room felt like it was spinning.

"You must have many questions," Eithor said. He pulled a chair out from against the wall and sat down beside Faelyn's bed.

"I—" Faelyn could hardly speak. *Where... Where do I even begin?* He closed his eyes, letting darkness take him once again. "Is my father dead?"

"Yes," Eithor said. "The doctors did what they could, but by the time they got to him it was clear that he had been departed for some time."

Faelyn took a deep breath, feeling a pooling shame in his stomach. He wanted to vomit. He wanted to scream, he wanted to cry, he wanted to *kill.* But he couldn't do anything. All he could do was sit here.

"Who did it?" Faelyn rasped.

"Two of the members of your father's expedition: Castien Varic and Ilyana Xirel," Eithor said. "The Stormless and the Dexteris."

The Stormless? Faelyn rolled over, his fragile ribs aching in protest. He didn't care. Nothing mattered anymore. *No.* Faelyn felt the warmth behind his eyes once again.

"And the Palace?" Faelyn croaked.

"The central wing as well as the upper floors have suffered extensive damage," Eithor said. "And one of the spires has fallen... Though workers have been starting on repairs since the moment the Palace settled." Eithor paused. "It will likely take several months—if not longer—to restore the Palace to its prior state."

Faelyn groaned, the horrible ache in his chest and legs seeming to grow stronger. His head throbbed, impeding even the most basic thoughts from truly processing in his mind. It was impossible. It still seemed impossible. He wasn't truly here. This was all a trick, or a dream, or a… Faelyn felt a steady tear flow from his closed eyes.

It was real. It was all real.

A terrible heat flooded his veins, threatening to release as his despair washed across his conscience. He screamed, a horrific, blood-curdling sound. He didn't care. Why should he? His father was dead.

His father was dead.

His head exploded with pain, sending tremors through his entire body. Faelyn shook, groaning and screaming as his body convulsed.

Doctors rushed in from behind the curtain.

Faelyn didn't care. He felt strong hands holding him down, but he continued screaming. Fire burned somewhere, igniting the cot. Heat marred his legs, striking through his broken body. Water poured onto his legs, and then his chest, putting out the flames, his anguish silenced.

Something sharp poked his left arm, sending a wave of pain through Faelyn's thrashing body. He threw his body in any way he could move, doing anything to satisfy this horrific urge within his mind. It was like an itch that could not be scratched, a thought that could not be killed. It was rage. It was something Faelyn had never known—not like this. It was terror, and anguish, and despair, and anger, and fear, and… and…

A heavy blanket covered his mind. Undulating waves of exhaustion danced across his body, visions of shadows and blood replacing the terror. Faelyn, despite himself, despite *everything*, smiled. *Relief.*

Faelyn took a long, heavy breath. His eyelids closed once again, as if sealed by a lock whose key had been thrown away. His arms went limp, and the pain in his legs and chest went away. Finally, as if in a dramatic final show of resistance, the throbbing in his head faded, and Faelyn surrendered himself to the darkness.

The relief was gone. Faelyn felt it as he awoke... That pain. That dread... It was back, stronger than ever. Faelyn's heavy eyes opened once again. He was in this cursed corner room still. The heavy gray curtains were drawn, and his bed was filled with fresh, frustratingly bright Scorcher Crystals to aid his healing.

A shadow moved in the corner once again, the shape of Eithor forming from the darkness and stepping forward.

Faelyn closed his eyes, letting out a pained groan. His head hurt again, as did everything else. He was sweating, yet he was cold. Bandages scraped against his wounds, sending violent pricks of pain all throughout his body. His throbbing headache made it hard to think.

"May we speak? Or shall I call the doctors to deliver another anesthetic?" Eithor asked, the sound of his chair scraping against the stone floor bringing Faelyn's attention back.

Faelyn lay still, falling silent. *Father...* He wanted to scream, and thrash, and burn. But he could not. His mind still felt so, so heavy. Whatever they had given him must still be wearing off. *If only it would last longer...* Faelyn's hands twitched, craving that relief once again.

"We are still investigating the involvement of the Shadow-Swifts in the assassination," Eithor said. "I have ordered several teams to track down your father's killers and bring them back here, to answer to *you*," Eithor said. "Despite our efforts, I fear that those teams will return empty-handed. The assassins escaped over the edge of the cliffs and fled the beach before daybreak yesterday morning.

"Elric believes he and Arthion might have a lead in Celes," Eithor said. "They have already departed for the Elosian Capital, but I estimate their chances of success to be... low."

"How long have I been out?" Faelyn whispered.

"By my count, roughly forty hours," Eithor said. "From what we can gather, the Shadow-Swift broke several of your ribs, though the real damage was done by the strike to your head."

"What?" Faelyn asked, trying to block out the bright light of the Crystals.

"You were found unconscious in one of the northern hallways with a growing bruise on the back of your head," Eithor said. "I presume one of the assassins struck you before escaping."

"I..." Faelyn tried to say. His headache impeded his thoughts once again.

"The hit gave you a severe concussion," Eithor continued. "You will likely suffer headaches for many weeks to come, but you should feel well enough to walk within a few days. Your body has been absorbing energy from the Scorcher Crystals while you've been asleep; they should accelerate your healing nicely." Eithor fell silent.

Faelyn groaned, wincing as a pang of hurt shot through his chest. "Was anyone else hurt?" Faelyn rasped.

"A few squadrons of guards have been found dead," Eithor said. "Some of the nobles were injured, as well as several Lesser Summoners—likely by the collapse of parts of the Palace."

"And the rest of the guards?"

"Rattled—to say the least—but they are alright," Eithor said.

Faelyn closed his eyes, his mind drifting into the darkness. Thoughts of the Blood Sorcerers came to him. *Perhaps they were involved in this,* Faelyn thought. But what could he do? In less than four weeks, Velarus would return with an army of Blood Sorcerers. Even if Faelyn managed to piece the city back together by then, it would simply be torn down again.

Faelyn could feel the Illusomancer's eyes on him, though he did not care. Let him stare. Let all of them stare at the broken Prince: the boy who had long been heralded as the one who may remake

Arvendon into something better than it had ever been before. Let them stare and see the broken child who lay before them now. What was the point in hiding it? There was no point in anything—not anymore.

Another tear slipped from his eyes, sliding down his cheek. Faelyn felt cold, despite the heat coursing through his veins. He felt angry and scared, and... and... *Izara's Shadow, what's the point?*

"You will need several days to heal," Eithor said. "It is my suggestion that you do not rush this process—moving too quickly could set you back even further."

Faelyn cracked his eyes open. He wanted to scream again, if only to feel that sweet relief of numbness once again. But he couldn't. He couldn't even find the strength to fight.

"I'm not sure how much you remember from the night of the Solstice," Eithor started. "But Etenae Hallan—the Cyfali Ambassador—caused the distraction that led to your father's death."

Faelyn's eyes cracked open, a memory flickering across his mind.

"The assassins may have escaped, but we have captured Hallan," Eithor continued. "We haven't extracted any useful information yet, but he was likely a part of the plot that killed your father."

Faelyn said nothing, his head throbbing.

"While you heal, I can personally interrogate him on your behalf," Eithor said. "Through him, we may be able to capture those responsible for your father's death. We can—"

"Has he been burned?" Faelyn rumbled, closing his eyes. His throat ached, stinging with every word he spoke.

"I..." Eithor started. "Pardon?"

"Has my father's body been burned yet?" Faelyn asked, his voice hard. He felt the flames beneath his skin simmer.

Eithor swallowed. "No, Your Majesty," Eithor said. "We will wait until you have healed before we proceed with the process."

Faelyn cracked his eyes open, wincing at the light of the Crystals. "Tell the Council I wish to hold the funeral tomorrow evening."

Eithor scoffed. "Your Grace, you can hardly speak... You can't expect to be able to attend—"

"Tell them," Faelyn growled. He coughed, his voice weak.

Eithor stared. "Yes, Your Grace." Eithor bowed.

"After the proceeding is finished, I will visit Etenae Hallan *personally*," Faelyn wheezed. He lost himself in a fit of coughing.

Eithor started to say something, but fell silent. "As you wish," Eithor said, bowing again. Moments later, he slipped around the curtain, leaving Faelyn alone.

Faelyn stared at the ceiling. His father was dead, and the crown was now his. Arvendon was doomed, Faelyn was sure of it. But if Arvendon fell, Faelyn would ensure that the rest of the world fell with it.

Faelyn closed his eyes, and dreamt of burning the world.

CHAPTER FOUR
MOURNING DAWN

Faelyn Titansworn awoke again several hours later. He slept poorly, likely due to his head injury. He blinked a few times, the glory of unconscious wearing off, giving way to the influx of memories that Faelyn had been trying so hard to escape.

Faelyn tried to move his legs. He prodded them with his fingers to search for tenderness. His white robe was thin and airy; he would have to find his actual clothes. New Crystals had been placed by his bedside, their painfully bright light still giving Faelyn a headache.

Or did I already have a headache? Faelyn thought. He grumbled, feeling a little unsteady as he tried to swing his legs over the cot.

A nurse came bustling through the heavy gray curtain and lightly grabbed Faelyn's legs, keeping him from moving. "Easy there, Your Majesty," the older woman said. She wore white surgical clothes and had graying hair. "No walking until you're off the Crystal Drip." She sat him back down on the cot.

"Wha..." Faelyn mumbled. His thoughts were still thick, and he could hardly form words. *Crystal Drip.* That was the treatment he had been receiving. A constant flow of Summoning energy into the body to help it heal.

"Lie back down, dear," the woman said softly, helping him readjust.

"I'm fine," Faelyn grunted, waving the woman away.

She lingered.

"I'm *fine,*" Faelyn repeated firmly.

The woman nodded quickly. She turned away and slipped behind the curtain without another word.

Faelyn groaned, helplessly falling back into his cot and closing his eyes. His body ached everywhere. His ribs still hurt, and his head constantly throbbed. He wasn't even sure why he was trying to rush to get up. All he knew was that he didn't want to be in this cot any longer.

He knew he wanted to lay his father to rest. He knew he wanted to kill Hallan for his part in the plot that killed his father. But what then? What next? Arvendon was in disarray, and the looming return of the Blood Sorcerers made reconstruction seem pointless.

Father would know what to do. Faelyn's stomach opened again, the endless pit of despair overtaking his senses, giving him that *horrible* feeling of shame and fear. He felt the warmth behind his eyes return.

"Faelyn?" a voice asked from behind.

Faelyn did not answer.

"Faelyn, are you awake?" the voice asked again. The curtain swished, and footsteps followed.

Faelyn cracked his eyes open and tilted his head ever so slightly.

Reluraun stood over his cot, the black vest he wore gently reflecting the light of the Scorcher Crystals.

"Why are you here?" Faelyn whispered, wishing his friend would go away rather than see him in this state.

Reluraun paused, his face twitching. "Why am I here?" Reluraun started. "Why am I here? Faelyn, by Izara's Shadow, you've been in bed for days! Your father is... gone, and you can't even get out of bed! Why would I not be here?"

Faelyn groaned, rolling back to face the wall once again.

A krellin scurried across the wall, its tiny legs clattering against the stones.

"Faelyn," Reluraun said. The cot squealed as Reluraun sat down. "I'm not even going to bother to ask how you're doing because I think I know the answer," Reluraun said. "And I won't begin to tell you how sorry I am because you already know that." Reluraun fell silent. "Eithor told me of your wishes."

"And?" Faelyn rumbled.

"Do you really think that this is the right decision? It seems you can hardly stay conscious," Reluraun said.

"My father is dead," Faelyn said quietly. "Don't tell me that I should wait to see him laid to rest."

"I know you want to proceed with the King's cremation as soon as possible, but I cannot help but advise against holding the ceremony so soon," Reluraun said softly.

"Curse you," Faelyn grumbled.

"That's right, curse me all you want. I don't care so long as you listen to me," Reluraun said. "If you are seen in this state, you will only make the people of Arvendon more afraid than they already are."

"Why?"

"Because you look like shit, Faelyn," Reluraun said. "If you rush this healing, you'll only make this harder for yourself *and* everyone else." Reluraun paused. "I'm not going to tell you what to do, Faelyn," Reluraun said. "But I think you need to take your time and *rest*."

Faelyn looked up to meet Reluraun's emerald eyes; they were warm, strong, and hopeful. "We have less than four weeks before the Blood Sorcerers return," Faelyn said, his throat dry. "I don't have time to *rest*." Faelyn rolled over, turning away from Reluraun. "Besides, all we can do for the city at this point is tell the people to start saying goodbye to one another."

Reluraun laid his hand on Faelyn's shoulder. "I know you don't believe that, Faelyn," Reluraun said softly. "If we rebuild Summerglass, fortify our defenses, and prepare our army, we might stand a chance against the Blood Sorcerers."

"So what?" Faelyn snapped, twisting. "It wasn't a Blood Sorcerer that killed my father!" Faelyn shouted. "I don't know if you've noticed, but the whole damn world is turning against us!" Faelyn turned back to the wall. "What's the point of putting ourselves back together if we're just going to fall apart again?"

"So that's your plan?" Reluraun asked. "Just roll over and die?"

"My *plan* is to take as many of those bastards down with us as we can," Faelyn grumbled. "Because... What else can we do?"

"I know you're angry, and I know you're mourning, but you're better than this," Reluraun said after a moment. "Please, come back to me. I've already lost my King... I don't want to lose my best friend too."

Faelyn twisted, looking his friend in the eyes. Reluraun was just as scared as Faelyn—perhaps even more terrified. Faelyn pulled his friend into a tight embrace, feeling the warm tears dribble from his eyes as he held Reluraun tighter.

"I just miss him," Faelyn whispered. His voice cracked, and he buried his face in Reluraun's black vest. *Worn in honor of my father,* Faelyn realized.

"I do, too," Reluraun breathed, his voice shaking. "I do too."

They sat there for several minutes, holding one another in a brief moment of relief cast somewhere in a vast expanse of fear and despair. Faelyn pulled Reluraun tighter.

Reluraun did the same when Faelyn's tears quickened once again.

Faelyn finally pulled back, staring at his friend for a moment.

"I wish that things were different," Faelyn whispered, realizing that he had never meant anything as much as he meant that simple phrase.

"Me too," Reluraun said, meeting Faelyn's eyes once again. "...But they're not. Wishing that we could change the past will only worsen our future." Reluraun lifted a hand to turn Faelyn's face back toward him.

Faelyn locked eyes with him once again.

"I know that you're scared—I am too. But, Faelyn, we have an entire *city* counting on us. Hundreds of thousands of people are relying on you and me to *fix this*," Reluraun said.

Faelyn closed his eyes, taking an unsteady breath in. He released it, feeling another tear slip down his cheeks. His muscles still ached, and his head still hurt, but he was alive. "How bad is it?" Faelyn whispered, looking toward the closed curtain.

"Bad." Reluraun bowed his head. "The Council is in disarray, the people are hysterical, and the Palace is practically destroyed. Perhaps even worse, we are right back where we started: Our three most powerful Summoners are out of the city, leaving us vulnerable to the Blood Sorcerers and whoever else might suddenly decide they want to see Arvendon fall."

Faelyn looked down. "I just wish there was some way out of this."

"We'll find one," Reluraun said. "We have to."

Faelyn lowered his aching head, feeling empty. He didn't know what to do. There was no way out of this. Yet even still, his father would've known what to do.

"The funeral is tomorrow evening," Faelyn said.

"Faelyn, I thought—" Reluraun started.

"The city is in shambles right now," Faelyn said. "The longer I lie here, the less time we have to fix things."

Reluraun met his gaze. "The Illusomancer Eithor has claimed that you will appoint him as your Chief Advisor," Reluraun said, standing up. "The Council has been considering his suggestions— but hesitantly. Are you sure we can trust him, Faelyn?"

Eithor, Faelyn realized. *He will know what to do. He might be our way out of this,* Faelyn thought. *He's the only one who saw this coming.*

"He tried to warn me about what would happen on the Solstice, and I didn't take him as seriously as I should have," Faelyn said, closing his eyes. "I didn't listen to him before, and it led to my father's murder. I won't make the same mistake again."

"But..." Reluraun trailed off. "How did he know that something was going to happen on the Solstice?"

Faelyn blinked a few times. "I—" Faelyn started. *How did he know?* "I'm not sure."

"Could he have had something to do with the assassination?" Reluraun advanced.

"Why would he have warned me about something he was a part of?" Faelyn asked. "Rel, I know you don't trust him, I didn't for a while either. But if he was working against us, he would've hit us while we were down, not start trying to help us rebuild." Faelyn paused. "If he wanted to destroy us, he would've already done so."

Reluraun still seemed hesitant, but Faelyn brushed the concerns aside. He couldn't worry about this. Not now.

"I need to think," Faelyn said. "Tell the others not to disturb me, please," Faelyn said. "Not until I lay my father to rest."

CHAPTER FIVE
THE STORM GALE

astien Varic cautiously peeked out of the small beachside cave they had stopped to rest in. The sun had risen just above the eastern horizon when the rain had started. The winds had picked up soon after, and the thunder and lightning had been quick to follow.

Storm Gales were the most dangerous of the Tempests. Traveling in one was a death sentence unless you were a Voltarian, so it seemed that Castien's crew would not be able to continue toward Fairfrost until nightfall.

Castien stared out at the violent rains, watching with fascination as countless bolts of lightning arced through the clouds. *I can't even imagine being able to call a Tempest my own,* Castien thought. Of course, as a Stormless, he had no Tempest. All seven storms still seemed alien to him, even after spending his whole life living among them. As a child, he used to dream of a world where the sun would shine softly, so softly that it wouldn't burn any who went out in it like it did on a Blazeday.

His mother had told him that such a world was impossible, and she was right. The forces of nature were not of the tame sort, and Castien realized now just how absurd his dream had been.

Thunder cracked and lightning struck somewhere above, causing Castien to jump. The strike had been close, but they were safe within the cave. He could easily see the ocean from here, though the heavy rains obscured his vision slightly. The Salarin Sea was violent today, naturally. He knew that Storm Gales seemed to upset the sea, but he had never truly observed how powerful of an effect the Tempest had on the water until today.

Castien turned around, shifting his eyes to where Ilyana had started a small fire in the back corner of the cave. In the dim light, Castien could read her absent expression.

She was staring off, a strange sadness over her Elosian face.

Castien wondered what it must feel like. A part of him even wanted to pity her...

He stopped himself. His arm pulsed with pain as he became aware of his bandage once again. She was the reason he couldn't go back to Arvendon, and she was the reason he got hurt. He didn't owe her anything, especially not sympathy.

Elric sat a good distance away from her, toward the other side of the cave. He leaned forward slightly, almost as if he were still trying to feel the warmth from the fire despite the distance. Castien supposed the Cloudwalker could move closer, but, then again, that would put him closer to Ilyana. Elric had hardly said a word to any of them throughout their night of travel. It was clear that he still didn't believe either of them.

Elric and Arthion had even decided to trade off sleeping shifts so that one of them was always awake and on watch.

Arthion had laid down nearly the moment they settled—which was roughly an hour ago. Though he now rose from his spot in the corner and patted Elric on the back.

Elric took it as a signal that it was his turn to rest, and he gladly laid down on the hard rock floor of the small cave.

Arthion strode past Ilyana, his gray robes whispering across the ground. He glanced at Ilyana, then continued walking toward where Castien sat at the edge of the cave.

The wind was blowing to the east—as was the rain—so Castien was able to remain dry.

Arthion sat down next to Castien and followed his gaze to the outside world.

"There's a sort of beauty to it, isn't there?" Arthion said, staring out.

A dozen arcs of lightning shot across the dark gray sky. Seconds later, deafening thunder rumbled overhead. Not a moment after, Castien could see a few bolts of lightning strike out in the raging ocean.

"It's just so... violent," Castien breathed. Storm Gales were the rarest of the Tempests, and Castien had only seen a few outside of Arvendon's wards.

"Sometimes I wish I could know what it's like to be up there," Arthion said. "You know, during one of these."

"I doubt anything could survive up in the clouds," Castien said.

"Voltarians can," Arthion said. "Have you not heard of Stormriding?" Arthion asked. "No, I suppose as a Stormless you wouldn't have heard much about it..."

"What's Stormriding?" Castien asked, turning to Arthion.

"It's the greatest ability of the Voltarians," Arthion said, smiling softly. "A Voltarian can launch themselves into the sky during a Storm Gale and use the lightning to continuously slingshot themselves across the sky... It's incredible, truly."

"Have you ever seen someone do it?" Castien asked.

Arthion paused, thinking. "Once, from a distance," Arthion said. "Although my eyes struggled to believe it."

"Sometimes it's hard not to wish I was a Summoner," Castien said, lowering his head. He shifted slightly, careful not to move his burned arm too much.

"I can imagine," Arthion said. "Believe me, I understand."

Castien looked back out to the storm, watching as another explosion of lightning illuminated the sky. "You don't use your Whispering very often, do you?" Castien asked.

"Oh," Arthion said. "No, I don't. I prefer to allow my friends to keep their thoughts private. I know that some of my associates do not share that mindset, but I think that my gifts are exactly that: gifts. To abuse them would be to abuse Niventia's power," Arthion said.

Ah, Castien realized. *So that's why.* "Are you a strict follower of the Path?" Castien asked.

Arthion looked down. "I suppose I am. There is some comfort to be found in the words of those above us."

"I guess," Castien said. He had never been too interested in religion—nor had his parents. They had said that if the gods of Auris truly existed, then no one would be Stormless. Unless, of course, the Stormless were simply *meant* to act as servants and soldiers for the Summoners.

Castien agreed with his parents, for what cruel god would create a world where half of humanity possessed divine powers while the other half had *nothing?*

Not necessarily nothing, Castien reminded himself, thinking of the Starburner Crystal. He debated telling Arthion about it, but decided against it. If it were still up to Castien, Ilyana wouldn't even know about it. He would've preferred to keep it a secret from everyone... for who knows what it meant? The implications of Castien's experience were frightening enough. A Stormless that suddenly developed ancient powers... How would the Summoners react? Were there others like Castien?

He still yearned for answers, though he knew that with his present situation, it would likely be some time until he found them.

Footsteps sounded behind him.

Ilyana approached, settling down beside Castien and Arthion. "Watching the storm?" Ilyana asked, her voice soft.

"It's beautiful," Arthion said. He stared off into the sky, watching as lightning struck the ocean once again. "So we're heading to Celes, eh? I've never been. What's it like?"

"Cold," Ilyana said, her voice hardening once again. "Though it's pleasant enough."

Arthion nodded. "I assumed as much."

"We rarely get storms like this that far north," Ilyana said. "Not more than a few times a year, and even then, having snow instead of rain makes it seem a little more... tranquil. Though the lightning doesn't help, I suppose."

"There's still lightning even when it's snowing?" Castien asked, turning.

"Of course," Ilyana said. "The Voltarians command lightning, so of course every Storm Gale is going to have a little lightning..." Ilyana trailed off. "That's the only way we can tell Storm Gales from Frost-falls and Slick-Days, for both of those include snowfalls as well."

"I've always wanted to see Celes with my own eyes," Arthion said. "Is the grand library truly as magnificent as they make it out to be? I've heard a lot of things, but I don't know—"

"I spent a lot of time there as a child," Ilyana said. "And yes, it's beautiful. I remember my father..." Ilyana trailed off, her voice faltering.

Castien shifted uncomfortably, then winced as his arm rubbed against the bandage. Watching Ilyana mourn her father still hurt him, especially given his own past, though he kept himself from offering her any comfort.

His arm throbbed again, and a thought struck Castien. *Will I be in history books?* Castien wondered. Once the thought materialized, it was impossible to stop it from running ahead. *I was involved in the assassination of an Arvendi King... What does that mean for my legacy?*

Castien ran his right hand through his dirty blond hair, which was slowly getting longer. It had originally been far above his eyebrows, yet now it easily hung over them if he didn't brush it back. He had a bit of a stubble as well now.

"We're still a few days outside of Fairfrost if I've tracked our progress correctly," Arthion said, breaking the silence. He had quieted after Ilyana had stopped talking, seemingly reading the room—or cave, Castien supposed.

"Yeah," Ilyana said, rubbing her eyes.

"What do you plan to do once we reach Celes?" Arthion asked.

Ilyana leveled her gaze. "Find the truth," Ilyana said firmly. "Someone has fooled some very powerful people, and I intend to discover who."

"You still think Avenos ordered King Nightingale's death?" Arthion asked.

"I do." Ilyana nodded. "But I suppose we'll see once we reach Fairfrost."

"What do you mean?" Castien started.

"News of King Nightingale's death would've reached Fairfrost by now," Ilyana said, looking ahead. "Whoever is managing the port would've been told to keep any Celesian ships from entering, if I'm correct."

Castien looked forward as well, thinking. "Right..." Castien said. *Niventia's Light, what am I doing?* Castien thought. *Sitting here with a Whisperer and a spy-turned-assassin...* But he had a plan, he reminded himself.

And besides, perhaps if Celes's library was truly as magnificent as Arthion and Ilyana claimed it was, Castien could find some answers about himself as well. Maybe there were others like him—Stormless who could connect with Ancient Crystals. He needed answers, and he knew that his best shot at getting them was going to Celes.

Castien glanced at Ilyana. *But I need to get there alive first.*

CHAPTER SIX
EMBERS

It was dark when the lightning of the Storm Gale finally settled. The rain had subsided, leaving the procession in an eerily quiet state. A candle burned softly on the iron coffin. Crystals lined the edges, enigmatic orange light drifting within.

Clouds parted to reveal Lotius's pale gray light, and then Oria's turquoise glow. Lights began appearing in the windows of every building of Arvendon with the fourth strike of the Palace bell.

Faelyn Titansworn stood silently. The small group had gathered on the edge of the cliff on which Summerglass sat—as was tradition. Only a few others were allowed to attend: the Council and four high-ranking Scorchers.

Faelyn had risen from his cot in the medical wing a few hours earlier. He found himself surprisingly dizzy, even now, as a result of the concussion. His head still throbbed. His ribs had healed quickly thanks to the Crystal Drip, but they were still very sore—which was especially bothersome earlier when he was changing into his black vest.

But none of that mattered right now. All that mattered was ensuring his father's spirit safe passage to the Afterworld.

Tears stained Faelyn's face. He had been scared that he would feel nothing. The last few days had felt like a nightmare. Nothing had felt real, not until this very moment. Faelyn had wondered when it would finally hit him... It was now.

It was here, on this warm summer evening.

Faelyn stood at the base of the iron coffin, waiting for the Paladin's signal. It would happen soon. The burning would proceed the same as it always had throughout Arvendon's long history. The Scorchers would lay their hands on the coffin and burn the body, then the coffin would be carried to its final resting chamber beneath the Palace.

Idris stood to his right. To his left stood a pair of the strongest Scorcher officers. Beyond them stood more Scorchers, and standing on the opposite side of the coffin was the rest of the Council: General Falx, General Derius, Estmar the Whisperer, and Reluraun—in place of Elric. They stood quietly, heads bowed as the Paladin began to speak.

He was uttering one of Niventia's prayers, though Faelyn didn't listen. What was the point? Faelyn still believed in the Afterworld... How could he not? If his father was not there, where could he be? Yet even so, Faelyn couldn't bring himself to listen. Hearing the Paladin say his father's name within this prayer would only worsen Faelyn's pain.

His father... Gone. Not lost, *gone*. Gone forever. Which meant that Faelyn was alone. He was alone, for the rest of his life.

Never would he be able to live a *single* day without this grief plaguing his thoughts. Though he was glad for that. He was glad that he would never be the same.

The pain would serve as a memory. Perhaps if he had been there, things would have been different. Perhaps if he hadn't argued with his father and been banished to his room, that night wouldn't have ended the way it did.

It didn't matter. It was too late now. It was far too late.

A soft summer breeze drifted across the group, brushing across the simple black vest Faelyn wore.

The Paladin finished his prayer and began to deliver his instructions to the Scorchers.

They stepped forward in unison, as did Faelyn. With a hesitant hand, he reached out.

As the Paladin gave his final instructions, Faelyn laid a hand on the coffin. He reached deep within himself, pulling heat from the Crystals at the base of the coffin.

The other Scorchers did so as well, and the Crystals began to glow even brighter. Slow tendrils of orange light started drifting from the Crystals, passing through the Scorchers' bodies before being channeled into the iron coffin.

Faelyn *pushed*, directing heat into the metal tomb. Iron hissed as the other Scorchers did the same. He closed his eyes. A tear rolled down his cheek as he began to feel the heat rise within the iron. It grew hotter, and hotter, and hotter. Faelyn's hands began to simmer, tingling from the heat.

The coffin heated further, now glowing a soft orange in the warm night. He began to hear the crackling within. Faelyn grimaced, closing his eyes. His mind went blank for several moments, void of all thought as he continued with the deed.

It was over as soon as it started.

After what felt like an eternity, the Paladin reached forward with thick gauntlets and slowly heaved off the glowing coffin lid.

Faelyn opened his eyes, struggling to see through the painful tears as he gazed upon his father one final time.

A part of him expected to see his face, maybe even his smile. A part of him thought that maybe this had all been some horrible trick. Maybe he would sit up in the coffin and wrap Faelyn in an embrace. Maybe he would tell him that it was alright.

The iron lid crashed to the ground. And when Faelyn peered over the edge, he saw nothing but embers.

CHAPTER SEVEN
THE PRISONER

Faelyn Titansworn stood in the torchlit dungeon hallway, deep in the bowels of Summerglass Palace. He still wore his black vest and pants; he wanted Hallan to see him in this attire. Perhaps a reminder of what the Etenae had caused would get him to talk.

A pair of guards stood beside Faelyn. He had insisted on going alone—save for the guards to ensure his safety. He wanted this to be a very *personal* interrogation.

Faelyn stepped forward, still feeling dizzy from the concussion. The throbbing in his head was merely a reminder of what Hallan had caused. Eithor was certain Hallan knew something, and Faelyn was going to find out what it was.

The guards trailed Faelyn, quiet save for the clinking of their armor and Crystals.

Faelyn turned around and held out a hand. "Your Crystals, please," Faelyn said. "Just one of you." Faelyn motioned to the Crystals that hung at the left guard's waist.

Without hesitation, the guard unhooked the Crystals and handed them to Faelyn.

Faelyn took them and attached them to his belt. This would be a night that Hallan would not soon forget.

The iron door at the end of the hall looked small to Faelyn. Behind it was the man who was responsible for the death of Faelyn's father... Strange how Faelyn felt almost nothing at the thought.

His pain had morphed into a cold, calculated anger. Reluraun was right: There was no time to waste. The city needed to rebuild and recover, and bringing his father's killers to justice was the best way to accelerate that process. The assassins themselves were being pursued by Elric, and they would be captured in due time... But Hallan was a nice place to start.

Faelyn advanced, approaching the door with a cool sense of calm. There was a small, barred window at the top, allowing a trickle of light through. Faelyn motioned, and the guards unlocked it.

With a push, the heavy iron door squealed open, revealing the small room within.

Hallan sat against the dark stone wall, chained to the floor in his dirty, torn green robes. He raised his eyes to Faelyn, his dark skin shimmering in the dim torchlight. His pained expression slowly took on an air of fear.

"Hello, Hallan," Faelyn said. He took a step forward, still a little unsteady from the dizziness. "I've been looking forward to speaking to you."

Hallan's eyes went wide with terror. "Please, I've already told your people everything I know," Hallan said, his voice desperate.

Faelyn looked the man over, spotting bloody bruises on his legs and arms. It appeared the guards had already done a number on him. *Good,* Faelyn thought. "Let's start from the beginning," Faelyn said, pacing out of Hallan's reach. "When did you first learn of the plot to kill my father?"

"I told you: I *never* knew about it!' Hallan whimpered. "On the night of the Solstice, an Elosian woman told me that she was going to help lead a rally against the King in an effort to pressure him to tell the truth," Hallan said. "She wanted me to start the rally, as she claimed I would be able to attract more support than her."

"And then your 'rally' ended up being the distraction that led to my father's death," Faelyn finished, cutting him off. "I suppose you mean to tell me that this was all coincidental?"

"I swear by Zephyr's Watch that it was!" Hallan started. "Just please, don't hurt me anymore. I don't know anything else!" Hallan pleaded.

Faelyn sighed. He stopped pacing, turning to Hallan. "Let's try again," Faelyn said, leaning down to meet Hallan's gaze. "When did you first learn of the plot to kill my father?"

"I never—" Hallan started.

Faelyn conjured a small flame in his hand, curled his fingers into a fist, and punched Hallan in the face.

Faelyn's knuckle cracked, his hand stinging from the impact.

Hallan cried out, falling to the side. He held his jaw, which was simmering from the heated punch.

"It doesn't have to be this hard," Faelyn said. "Tell me the truth and I won't have to do that again."

"I *am* telling you the truth!" Hallan shouted. "I don't know why you don't—"

Faelyn raised his hand, threatening to send a blast of flame toward Hallan.

"I don't know what you want," Hallan said, lowering his head to the ground and raising his hands. "I don't know where the assassins went, and I don't know why they killed your King. I swear by it, I know nothing else."

The guards had already beaten Hallan, and that had gotten them nowhere. The Whisperers had reportedly tried to extract more information at Eithor's direction, but their powers were imprecise. Finding specific information that one was consciously hiding was incredibly difficult, even for the most skilled Whisperers. Hallan wouldn't tell them anything.

But Faelyn was different. He would make Hallan talk, and even if he didn't, at least Faelyn would get the pleasure of punishing Hallan for what he had done.

Faelyn raised his hand, conjuring another flame. He approached, the fiery rage within him rising to the surface. Hallan had helped kill Faelyn's father, and now he was going to pay.

Hallan whimpered, shying back.

Faelyn lowered himself, strengthening the flame. Thoughts of his father passed through his mind. Tears began to pool in Faelyn's eyes. He soon found himself crying. None of this was fair. His father was dead, and Hallan was still alive. The *assassins* were still alive. Shouldn't there be justice? Would the gods not force it upon them?

He reached forward, growing the fire in his hand to a terrifying blaze. And then, he hesitated. His hand still stung from the punch.

There was no reason to stop now. Hallan should pay for what he had done. And yet, Faelyn remained still.

Faelyn grunted, trying to move his arm forward. His body disobeyed him, and his mind soon followed. Faelyn lowered his hand, extinguishing the blaze. He stepped back.

Hallan raised his head, his frightened eyes looking confused.

Faelyn rose to his feet, Summoning another flame. Yet he soon extinguished this one as well, his mind frozen. Another tear rolled down his cheek, sizzling against his burning skin.

He couldn't do it.

Hallan sat back, breathing heavily.

Faelyn raised his eyes to the Cyfali Ambassador. "I—" Faelyn's voice gave out. He closed his eyes, bringing a hand to his mouth. More tears fell from his eyes, a whimpered cry escaping his lips. He slipped out the door quickly and commanded the guards to close it.

As the heavy iron door squealed shut, Faelyn looked down at his still-stinging hand.

Faelyn sighed, and turned away.

Faelyn lay on his bed, staring at the ceiling, forcing his mind to stay blank. What else could he do? There was no point in trying. Hallan was partially responsible for the King's death, and Faelyn didn't even have the stomach to punish him for it. Even that simple punch had left him with an ache of guilt.

He was numb. Empty. Tired. Scared. He was everything that a King shouldn't be.

Faelyn rolled over, longing to hear his father's voice. It was something that he would never hear again, he realized. Never again would he see his father's warm face twist into a smile. Never again would he hear that booming laugh from across the ballroom. Never again would he get to stand proudly behind his father while he delivered a powerful speech.

Never again.

A knock at the door pulled him from the haze of his semiconscious mind back to reality. He grumbled, feeling an overpowering weakness as he tried to find the will to stand.

"Come in," Faelyn rumbled. Whoever it was had likely arrived to deliver more bad news and tell him how poorly everything was going.

The door creaked open.

Faelyn remained still. He didn't dare look out the window; he would only see one of the now-ruined courtyards. *A perfect backdrop for my misery*, Faelyn thought.

"Unsurprising," Eithor muttered from the doorway, surveying Faelyn's state.

Faelyn closed his eyes, sinking further into the soft sheets of his canopy bed.

"I was a bit... shocked to hear about what happened in Hallan's cell, though," Eithor said.

"What do you want?" Faelyn grumbled, rolling to face away from Eithor. He heard Eithor take a few steps on the carpet.

"I want to check on you, Faelyn," Eithor said.

"Check on me?" Faelyn wheezed a laugh. "You wanted to see how I was doing... How do you think I'm doing?"

"That's... not quite what I meant," Eithor said.

Faelyn tilted his head ever so slightly. *Father used to always laugh at me when I did that... Until mother told him that it was hurting my feelings and forced him to stop.* That had been almost ten years ago. Faelyn closed his eyes even tighter, sealing the tears inside as he savored the memory.

It was all he had. They were all he would ever have now: memories.

"I want your permission to try another interrogation tactic with Etenae Hallan," Eithor said. "I thought that you might want us to try something that didn't involve hurting him."

"Why would you think that?" Faelyn grumbled, rubbing his tear-streaked face.

"Because you could hardly lay a finger on him without breaking down, Faelyn," Eithor said. "I only heard of your interrogation secondhand, but if I may ask: What changed, Faelyn?"

Faelyn stared silently. He wasn't even sure himself. "I don't know," Faelyn said. "I punched him," Faelyn said, rubbing his bruised hand. "And then I wanted to punch him again, but I couldn't."

Eithor said nothing.

"That man deserves to die for what he did," Faelyn said, his voice shaking with anger. "He should be burned for his crimes but... But I can't hurt him."

"Why?" Eithor asked.

"Because I'm too weak," Faelyn said softly, closing his eyes. "I'm too weak to do what needs to be done." Faelyn could feel Eithor's eyes on him.

"You're not ready for this, are you?" Eithor asked. "Being King, I mean."

Faelyn shook his head.

"Unfortunately, these things often don't wait until we are prepared to handle them," Eithor said.

"Do you think I should've killed him?" Faelyn asked, turning his head.

Eithor paused. "I think you should've gotten him to admit the truth about his involvement in your father's assassination—whatever that truth may be."

"And then?"

"Yes, I think you should've killed him."

Faelyn blinked. "How do you know?"

"The same way I knew that the Solstice would turn deadly for your family," Eithor said softly.

Faelyn's ears perked involuntarily.

"I have created enough false realities for myself to know how each player in this game behaves... And I know that if you don't kill Hallan for what he did, then you will be viewed as a King who is too weak to punish those who hurt us."

Faelyn closed his eyes, keeping the tears in. "How do you know that he's lying?" Faelyn asked. "I mean, are you sure that Hallan really was involved in this plan?"

"Knowing Hallan—and the Cyfali—I would assume that he had something to do with the assassination," Eithor said. "The Cyfali have been waiting for a chance to strike at Arvendon for years now, and it can only be assumed that Hallan relayed knowledge of the Blood Sorcerer's threat to the Council of Jaskye... Upon hearing this, I'm all but certain the Jaskyan Council would try to find ways to further weaken our country—such as killing our King, for example."

"But how do you know?" Faelyn asked. "I mean, one of the assassins was Elosian! How can you be certain that the Cyfali did this?"

"They did," Eithor said. "And what better way to cover it up than by hiring assassins from other nations to do the job?"

"But this is all just speculation!" Faelyn snapped, sitting up.

"I can prove it," Eithor said, continuing to pace. "You see, I had an idea... If you recall, I was just about to tell you my idea regarding Hallan's interrogation."

Faelyn tracked him with his eyes.

"If we play this correctly, Hallan will admit it all on his own," Eithor said, a slow smirk creeping across his face.

"How?" Faelyn asked.

"I will stage a rescue," Eithor said, raising his hand. Turquoise frost sparkled at his fingertips as his Illusomancer powers surfaced. "I will create an illusory Cyfali rescue team, and then we will steer the conversation in a way that forces him to admit what he knows."

"A rescue..." Faelyn started. "That might work."

"It will work, Faelyn. I'm sure of it," Eithor said. He paused. "And after we get him to admit that the Cyfali helped organize the murder of your father, you're going to kill him."

Faelyn quivered, falling back into his bed. "You know I can't," Faelyn whispered.

"Yes, you *can*," Eithor said firmly. "I know you're angry at him, somewhere down there... I know that you have the strength to punish him for his crimes, Faelyn," Eithor said. "Killing the King is the greatest crime one can commit; if he admits to it, killing him wouldn't be murder, it would be *justice*."

Faelyn closed his eyes once again. Eithor was right. If Hallan truly did help organize the plot to kill the King, then he would be sentenced—by law—to death. Faelyn knew it was the only way to proceed if Hallan confessed... He just wished that hurting Hallan made him feel better about himself, not worse.

"If you knew my father was going to be murdered, then why didn't you save him?" Faelyn asked, remembering his discussion with Reluraun. "You knew that my father was going to die, and you let it happen."

"I knew that your father may be in danger." Eithor continued pacing. "But my predictions are limited: I had nothing more than a premonition that one of our enemies would send assassins on the night of the Solstice. Some of the things that slipped past my predictions, however, include your grounding and the efficiency of the assassins... and the fact that the killers came from your father's own ranks." Eithor paused. "Despite how it may seem, Faelyn, I cannot predict the future. I can make fairly accurate guesses—from time to time—but I cannot see that which has not yet come to pass."

"That still doesn't explain why you didn't try to stop this from happening."

Eithor paused for a long moment. "I believed that the King would be able to protect himself," Eithor said. "I was almost certain that Arvendon would come out of that night unharmed. When I finally realized that the danger was far greater than I had imagined, I went to retrieve you from your rooms... But by then it was too late." Eithor sighed. "I realize my mistake, now. I assure you, Faelyn, all I wanted was for you to trust me. Do you recall the scene I conjured for you prior to the Solstice, the vision of Arvendon under attack?" Eithor asked.

Faelyn nodded.

"I still fear that such an event may be in our future. Just look at how Cyfalion has turned against us already," Eithor said. "I knew I couldn't help if you didn't trust me, and I knew you wouldn't trust me unless you had a reason to." Eithor paused "If I were truly working against you, we would not be speaking right now. If I were your enemy, I would be destroying what little of Arvendon is left, not trying to put it back together." Eithor took a deep breath. "I had originally tried to win your trust by proving my skills as an advisor. Now I will simply ask directly: Will you trust me, Faelyn Titansworn?"

Faelyn didn't answer.

"With myself as your Chief Advisor, I could lead you away from this dark path and down the road of *justice*," Eithor continued. "Let me interrogate Hallan *alone*. I will use my abilities to stage the rescue, and we will listen as he confesses the truth to those he thinks to be his own men," Eithor said. "You can even stand outside the cell and listen, if you wish. But if this is going to work, I need to be in there alone."

Faelyn remained silent.

"If I prove unsuccessful, or if my suspicions about the Cyfali are incorrect, I will leave this city and never return," Eithor said. "*But* if I am correct... it would be in your best interest to make greater use of my counsel."

"I don't care anymore," Faelyn said. "Even if we do find that the Cyfali did this, what then?" Faelyn asked. "It's not like there's anything we can do about it, so what's the point?"

"We still have over three weeks before the Blood Sorcerers return," Eithor said. "If Hallan confesses, we can sail to Cyfalion, exact our revenge on their leaders, and sail back with time to spare! If the Tempests are favorable, we will even have several days to prepare our city's defenses before the Blood Sorcerers arrive," Eithor said.

Faelyn rolled over. He still didn't care. Even if they went all the way to Cyfalion, burned the city, and sailed back, they would just be destroyed by the Blood Sorcerers anyway. What was the point?

"Faelyn—" Eithor started.

"*Stop*," Faelyn groaned. "Just *stop* talking, please. I don't care anymore, okay? Just leave me alone."

Eithor quieted, but did not leave. "I know what it feels like," Eithor said, his voice hard. "I understand why you do not care."

Faelyn shifted, staring at the wall.

"Because you know that if you start caring, then everything will come crashing down again." Eithor nodded. "Your mind is numbing your emotions so that you can handle the pain, I understand. This is something that happens to many."

"Then why do I feel like this? If everything is numbed, then why does it still hurt?" Faelyn asked, his voice weak.

"Because you were happy, and the things that made you happy have been taken away from you," Eithor said softly. "You are upset— just as you have every right to be. And while your mind is doing what it can to make the pain manageable, you still feel the inherent *wrongness* in the air."

"Yeah," Faelyn whispered, his voice breaking. His eyes snapped shut. Everything seemed to quicken, to *worsen.* His thoughts raced, his heart thundering. Pain flooded his mind. He couldn't put words to it, for it was a feeling so simple and terrible that it was nothing more than sheer distress.

"It's alright, Faelyn," Eithor said, laying a wrinkled hand on his back.

Faelyn flinched at the warm touch.

"I promise you, it will be alright," Eithor repeated.

"I just—" Faelyn took a deep breath. He couldn't hold it in any longer. He didn't care that Eithor was here, he just needed to get the words out. "I feel *nothing* for hours and then everything just crashes into me all at once and I feel like... like..."

"Like you won't be able to get back up again." Eithor started tracing lines in Faelyn's back. "I understand." Eithor paused, continuing to trace the lines.

Faelyn took a shaky breath in, feeling the markings sketched lightly into his robes.

"Do you know what I'm drawing right now?" Eithor asked.

Faelyn shook his head, keeping his eyes shut as another tear rolled down his cheek.

"It's called a glyph," Eithor said, making a circle, and then adding a line through it. "I use them to conjure my illusions," Eithor continued. "It helps me build and store my tricks so that I can readily use them at any time. You know how I always snap my fingers before an illusion?" Eithor asked.

Faelyn nodded softly.

"That's what I do to transform the stored glyphs into illusions. I've never met another Illusomancer, so I don't know if we all do it like that... But it's always been my method," Eithor said, withdrawing his hand.

Faelyn hung onto his next breath, trying to steady his thoughts. The surge had passed, and his mind was moving at a manageable pace once again. *So quick...* He felt like he was going insane. It wasn't even about his father anymore—though he did occupy a great deal of Faelyn's thoughts—it was the simple fact that Faelyn could feel himself losing his desire to care.

He had nothing left.

Eithor snapped.

Faelyn's eyes slowly cracked open, and he found himself still in his rooms.

Something was different. It was darker. Beyond the glass windows lay a vast expanse of mountains, with snow drifting slowly across the landscape. A large fire burned behind Faelyn.

He shifted in his bed, finding that the illusory fire gave off no heat. Faelyn looked back to where the snow fell gently beyond the window, then back to the large fireplace that had replaced the tapestry on the empty wall.

Eithor sat on the edge of the canopy bed still, hands folded as a slight aura of turquoise frost hovered around his wrists. Faelyn met the old man's warm eyes.

"What is this place?" Faelyn asked, his voice raw.

"I grew up in Utrya," Eithor said, smiling. "This was always what it was like when I was most comfortable, as a child... A gentle Frostfall and a warm fire. What more could a little Utryan boy ask for?"

Faelyn looked out through the illusory window, watching the mountains in the distance as Lotius and Oria slowly rose. Stars began to light up the sky. Hues of blue and green began populating the air above the mountaintops, warping the heavens with a strange beauty.

Faelyn had seen these lights before—on his excursion to The Highlands. They were beautiful, even from afar. Yet now... Now it was like he was seeing them up close. It was almost as if they were more real than reality.

Eithor smiled. He walked over to Faelyn's nightstand, where Faelyn's water cup sat. Eithor reached out and waved his hand, picking up the cup. With a wave of his hand, the water turned a deep, opaque blue. "You see, everything I do is merely theatrics, and I give you this now because you desperately need a change of scenery... And I've found that simple effects like this can help ease the transition." Eithor handed him the cup.

Faelyn stared into the blue water, then looked back to the large hearth and the Frostfall beyond the illusory window. "Thank you, Eithor." Faelyn nodded, feeling that emptiness within once again.

"It's been an honor, Your Grace." Eithor bowed. He backed toward the door. Faelyn took a deep breath and closed his eyes as he gulped down the water.

When he opened his eyes, Eithor was gone, and his room was dark. No change of scenery. No change at all. Faelyn leaned back into the folds of his bed, snuggling up against the warm blankets.

Eithor has a plan, Faelyn thought. It wasn't much, but it was something... something to hold onto.

Strangely enough, Eithor's illusions had eased Faelyn's pain—if only slightly. Odds were Faelyn would wake up feeling horrible once again, but even now he realized there was nothing he could do about that. He needed to move forward.

Eithor was right. Faelyn needed to kill Hallan if he confessed to organizing the assassination. And if the Council of Jaskye was truly behind all of this, then Faelyn would need to ensure that they did not go unpunished.

And one day, he would make things right.

One day...

CHAPTER EIGHT

THE HARBOR

Fairfrost lay just below the ridge where Castien Varic crouched. The journey here had taken several days, and it had been painfully tense. Yet they had arrived. They had made it here alive, and for that Castien was thankful.

Fairfrost was smaller than Castien had expected. He had imagined a harbor like Arvendon's, with row after row of docks and ships and dozens of warehouses and homes alongside the water. Instead, Fairfrost was composed of a few stone bunkers carved into the ridges and hills nearby. They had been built that way so that they could be protected, for Fairfrost was not within the wards. In fact, Castien was decently certain that the ridge they were standing on was a bunker as well. They had arrived under the cover of a Mistveil a few hours ago and were still watching quietly.

A single ship was docked at the small pair of stone landings. It hadn't moved in hours, and it didn't seem to be going anywhere anytime soon. It was small—likely a merchant's ship. Though it seemed unattended, for Castien hadn't seen anyone in Fairfrost during the several hours they had spent scouting the area.

It was an Etheri port, technically speaking, although it was close enough to the border of Elos that it was considered to be neutral ground—or at least it used to be. Castien leaned back, sliding down the small hillside and arriving at the setup that the others had made.

Elric had to stop and hunt for food, which consisted of choking the life out of a passing divebrisk while they were walking along the water. He had done the same thing to a few krellins as they walked over The Wastelands.

Elric had been in a particularly sour mood, so Castien was fortunate that he *couldn't* use his mind to suffocate Castien and Ilyana at will. Castien himself hadn't been in a much better mood, but at least he wasn't tempted to murder half of the party.

Although would it really be considered murder? Castien and Ilyana had killed Avenos. He blinked a few times, staring at the ground. Thinking about the assassination felt so normal now. It was almost like he didn't even care anymore.

There were times in his past when his pulse would increase, and his breathing would quicken for no apparent reason. He would get panicked at something as little as daily training. Yet, since the King's assassination, he felt nothing.

I'm not sure what I should make of that, Castien thought. His anxieties seemed to be selective, though depending on what, he couldn't be certain. He glanced at Elric.

The Cloudwalker was rubbing his arms, seemingly trying to fold his jacket to give himself extra layers of padding. Elric had originally proposed that Castien start meeting with a Whisperer to talk about his struggles, though obviously that deal was now forfeited. Elric had said that he overcame a similar difficulty, meaning that Castien was not the only one in the world who felt like this sometimes.

"It's your shift, Ilyana," Castien said, looking to the Dexteris.

She looked up, staring at the ridge just above them, then nodded, and wordlessly stood up, making her way over to it.

"Anything yet?" Arthion asked from his spot on the ground beside Castien. The Whisperer looked up, his amber eyes hopeful.

Castien shook his head. "No."

"They've probably locked down the port, considering that the other user of it is the nation that's responsible for King Avenos's death," Elric grunted.

"We made it to Fairfrost without any trouble," Arthion said. "All we need to do is figure out how to talk our way past the guards and get them to open up the port again."

"Do you think you'd be able to convince them to let a ship leave?" Castien asked, turning to Elric.

He looked up, his emerald eyes dark.

Castien got a flash of Reluraun's face, seeing it in Elric's eyes.

"Given that I'm traveling with Avenos's killers, probably not," Elric grumbled.

"It still doesn't make sense as to why there's not a single person out here right now," Arthion said, craning his neck as if to look over the ridge.

Ilyana crouched above, most of her body hidden behind the rocks.

Arthion didn't say anything and instead reached for his bag.

"What are you doing?" Castien asked, sitting up.

"I'm hungry," Arthion said. "And given that we're about to restock our food storages here, I think I can afford to eat a little over what we agreed." He fumbled around with the straps for a few moments before finally coming up with a stormroot; the white-gray root was wrinkled and ugly, made of a hard—yet somehow edible—substance. Arthion took a bite of it.

Castien wrinkled his nose, imagining the bitter taste in his own mouth as Arthion ate. The pale, cracked skin of the stormroot was strange... almost looking a bit like Luka's skin. Castien thought back to the Cryostalker, wondering where he was now. Luka had continued north, heading toward Freyfall to seek answers regarding the Blood Sorcerers' occupation of the city.

Castien never had gotten an answer as to why Luka's skin was so strange. Nor had he figured out why Elric was suddenly making a fuss over the padding of his jacket the last few days. *Could it be related?* Castien wondered. Summoners surely had limits, though Castien couldn't imagine what they were. *Maybe I can ask Arthion,* Castien thought.

At a certain point, the body *must* start to break down, though Castien had never heard much about anything like that. Then again, he never really did pay attention to the science of Summoning.

The Starburner Crystal's weight was now a regular presence in the pocket of his vermillion vest. The moment with the Blood Sorcerers continued looping in his mind, playing over and over. He wasn't sure what had happened, or if his memories were even accurate. But the Crystal was real, that much he could verify—and that was enough, for now.

"I'm tired of waiting," Ilyana said. "It's almost nightfall, and we haven't seen a soul," Ilyana turned around, sliding down to where the others sat. The fog of the Mistveil densely covered The Wastelands, though it was slowly beginning to thin.

Castien looked over to the west, where the sun would be setting behind the jagged mountains of The Highlands.

"She's right," Arthion said. "There doesn't seem to be anyone home, not on the outside at least."

"So what? Are we just going to steal the ship and head north?" Castien started. "Do any of us even know how to sail?"

"Elric could push wind through the sails," Ilyana suggested.

All eyes turned to Elric, who rubbed his arms once again.

"No," Elric said firmly.

Ilyana raised an eyebrow, her Elosian features twisting. "Ah," she said, looking at his arms. She nodded and turned to Arthion. "We're going to have to find someone to captain the ship for us. Would it be worth looking in the bunkers?"

"I don't know where else we *would* look," Arthion said, standing up.

Castien nodded. He stood up as well, his left arm brushing against his chest as he rose. Castien grimaced, but kept his pain hidden. It had been several days now, and his arm still burned like

Helionn's Sun when it touched something, though if he kept it away from other surfaces the pain was manageable. Ilyana had unwrapped the makeshift bandage a few days back and flipped it inside out, claiming that switching the bandages was necessary for the wound to heal properly.

The skin was white and red, looking like a stew of flesh and blood. Castien had nearly vomited when Ilyana took off the bandage. It looked worse than it was, but somehow, staring at it made it hurt more. Sure enough, a handprint was visible about halfway up Castien's arm—courtesy of Faelyn.

"So what's our plan?" Elric asked as they climbed the ridge.

"Hopefully, we peacefully convince the captain of that ship to take us to Celes," Ilyana said. "If we can't do that, well, we may have to find another way to get them to take us."

"I won't let you hurt anyone else," Elric said, stopping. "If they say no, then we figure something else out."

"Fine," Ilyana said, glaring at Elric.

He glared back.

"Alright, be careful on the way down," Arthion said as he sat down, lowering himself. He slid slowly down the somewhat steep decline, stopping softly at the bottom. He turned around. "Ah, there is another storage bunker under here." The Whisperer pointed to the other side of the ridge.

Castien slid down next, careful to avoid getting any of the black pebbles in his bandage.

Ilyana followed.

Elric stayed up above for a moment, but finally shook his head and slid down slowly.

Once Castien reached the bottom, he surveyed the door. It was comprised of what appeared to be several layers of thick wood from ghost trees, and the door had one handle with a lock attached.

Ilyana eyed the lock curiously, kneeling before it. The door was no more than four feet tall, and probably only three feet wide. It was small, to say the least, but the cavern inside was surely larger.

Arthion knocked on the door.

No response.

"What do you guys think?" Ilyana asked after a moment. "Pick the lock or just break it?" She turned back, her hand sliding down to her boot where Castien knew a knife waited.

"It would probably be wise to *not* add breaking and entering to your list of crimes against Arvendon," Arthion said. "Although at this point, you're probably supposed to be executed on sight, so it's up to you I guess."

"Hmmm." Ilyana turned back. She pulled the knife from her boot and opened up a part of her robe. She pulled out a small pick, flipping open a small portion of it and extending a sharp, firm tip.

Ilyana leaned closer to the lock, sliding the knife in first and following it with the small pick. She twisted the knife a little, finding its place before moving the pick. After sliding it in a bit deeper, and seemingly finding what she was looking for, Ilyana started turning the pick.

The lock didn't move much at first, but as Ilyana fished around with the pick, it started to twist slightly. Ilyana paused, a flicker in her eyes signaling that the pick had caught on something. Delicately, she started turning the knife, moving it alongside the pick.

A firm *click* sounded, and the door unlocked. Ilyana stood up, pulling her instruments from the lock and slipping them back into their respective spots. "And there we have it," she said, reaching for the handle. She pushed open the door, revealing a short, dimly lit passage beyond. Ilyana slipped inside, followed by Arthion.

Castien took a step forward, kneeling down when he felt a hand grip his shoulder. Castien turned around.

"I expected more from you, boy," Elric said.

"I—" Castien stuttered. The Cloudwalker's emerald eyes bore a sense of intensity and disappointment that Castien hadn't seen since... *since...*

"You could've been so much more..." Elric motioned to the picked lock. "So much more than this."

Castien looked back at the Cloudwalker, feeling his face warm. "I didn't know," Castien said softly. "And with all that's happened, it's not like I have many options other than sticking with Ilyana." He shrugged off Elric's hand.

Elric grunted. He looked past Castien, staring into the torchlit cavern. "Try to keep her from killing anyone else," Elric grumbled. He released Castien and turned around. "I'll stand watch."

Castien stumbled slightly, staring after Elric as he looked off into the night. The sea washed silently against the shore, rhythmically crashing into the bow of the merchant ship. Light was beginning to fade from the evening sky. Night was fast approaching, and the mists were beginning to disperse. Castien looked back to the open door and slipped inside.

The small passageway inside was dim and dusty. Castien peered down the small drop before him, seeing a larger opening beneath. Ilyana and Arthion shuffled around within, sounds of containers opening and closing filling the small chamber.

"Is it empty?" Castien asked, placing his good hand on the overhead rock and sliding down. He winced as his left arm skimmed the rock, but he held his composure.

"Of people at least," Arthion said. The room was somewhat small, and obviously meant for storage. There were upwards of fifteen crates scattered about, as well as several barrels and chests.

"What's in them?" Castien asked, nodding toward the containers.

Ilyana slid the lid off one of them, setting it down beneath a nearby torch stone. "Mostly just iceblooms," she said, picking up a few of the light blue plants and putting them in her pack.

Castien took a step closer, picking up one of the strange, hard flowers to examine it himself. They were native to Elos, north of Celes mostly. Only the petals were picked, though they were ice-blue and painfully hard. Castien raised it to his mouth and bit a chunk of it off.

It was bland, unsurprisingly. He knew that food to the south supposedly had spices and flavors that could make one's tongue feel as if it were set afire, but he was used to the dull and uninteresting flavors of central and northern Auris. Maybe someday he would make it to the southern parts of Auris, and see the Dunes of Despair and The Archipelago for himself.

Of course, the odds of such things happening were much lower now that the most powerful nation on the continent wanted him dead; that thought still hadn't truly struck him, strangely enough. It was almost as if he had been so distracted with the current journey to Celes that he had forgotten about the situation at hand. Well, that of course, and the fact that whenever he thought about never returning to Arvendon he began to get lightheaded, so he simply averted his thoughts from the topic.

"Why won't Elric use his Summoning to help us sail to Celes?" Castien asked, forcibly taking his mind off Arvendon.

"Because something's happening to his body," Ilyana said. "The same thing that's happening to Luka, and I can't say I'm surprised," Ilyana said. "It'll probably happen to us too, before too long." Ilyana motioned to Arthion and herself.

"What will?" Castien asked, standing up. He looked to the container of iceblooms and began picking them off the top, sliding them next to the stormroots he had been carrying.

"Breakdown," Ilyana said.

"It's different for every Sect, but we all have our ways of deteriorating," Arthion added.

"Elric seems to be experiencing what's called Breezebone," Ilyana explained. "If I remember correctly, his bones are becoming lighter, which is good for Cloudwalking, but not good in general, as they are much easier to break."

"And that's why he doesn't want to use his powers to push the sail?" Castien asked.

Arthion nodded. "Breakdown happens when one either expends a tremendous amount of energy at once or when they go through a period of several weeks without giving themselves much of a break from Summoning," Arthion said. "Now you see part of the reason why I try to avoid Whispering unless I have to."

"Whisperers have it the worst, don't they?" Ilyana asked.

"Indeed they do," Arthion said. "Mindmelt, it's called. Essentially, your senses go into overdrive, and you're unable to differentiate between others' thoughts and your own. It sounds *quite* troubling."

"Luka is going through Permafrost," Ilyana said. "That's why his skin is pale and cracked. If he keeps up with this usage of his power, he could quite literally freeze himself to death."

"Oh," Castien said. His voice sounded quiet. He looked up, watching as Arthion and Ilyana started shoveling more iceblooms and stormroots into their packs. Castien hadn't realized that being a Summoner could lead to such things.

In a weird way, it was comforting to hear about Breakdown. Summoners were not immortal, nor were they indestructible. They had weaknesses, and even their powers had limits. It made him feel better. Summoners may be more powerful than the Stormless, but they were not invincible.

Which means, regardless of what becomes of that Crystal, I will always have weaknesses too, Castien thought.

Castien opened his mouth to ask another question but thought better of it. The subject seemed to be fairly sensitive to the Summoners, and Castien knew better than to push them on such topics.

"I've fit about as much as I can," Arthion said.

"Me too," Ilyana said. "At least in terms of food storage." She started rifling through the other barrels, searching for something.

"Oh, come on, Ilyana," Arthion grumbled. "You've already killed the King of Arvendon. Do you really need to rob Etherus's ports of their gold as well?"

"We may need money to get to Celes," Ilyana said. "I know that this cavern was vacant, but there have to be people somewhere in Fairfrost."

"I still can't believe that someone bothered to name this place,"

Castien said, buttoning his pack up and making for the passageway out. "It's not much more than a pair of small docks and a few holes in the ground."

"Welcome to most of Auris, Stormless," Ilyana said, leading the way out of the storehouse.

Elric stood outside, arms folded. He didn't look at them as they exited.

Ilyana climbed out of the door first, followed by Castien and then Arthion. The waves washed against the shore a few hundred feet away, and the seemingly unoccupied ship sat bobbing in the water, just as it had before they left.

"If it makes you feel any better, we didn't kill anyone," Ilyana said as she passed Elric. "We didn't even see anyone, actually."

"Ah, well at least your thievery is not coupled with murder—this time," Elric said, shaking his head. "Now come on, we need to find whoever lives here," Elric said. "We can't leave until the chain is down anyway."

"What is he talking about?" Ilyana turned back.

"The chain," Arthion said, pointing out toward the small extension of land to the left. "There's a chain that blocks ships from entering unless they have a passage to make shore here."

Castien squinted, seeing a thick black mass stretch across the small harbor in between bouts of waves. He looked to the tiny peninsula on the right and saw a large chain extending out of the water and into the rock.

"Is that where it starts?" Castien asked, pointing.

"I'd reckon so," Arthion said.

The chain was distant, but even from here, Castien could tell that it was at least a few feet in width. *Too large to simply cut or sail through,* Castien thought.

"The only way to lower it is to get the Portmaster to do so," Elric said, his arms still folded. "And good luck getting him to do that, considering how you've ransacked his storage room. Oh, and let's not forget that you killed his King as well."

"We get it, we get it." Ilyana waved her hand as she walked back. "Trust me, I want to uncover the truth about this whole situation just as badly as you do."

"The difference is you actually *killed* a man and now want an excuse as to why. I just want to know so that I can correctly exact justice," Elric said.

"Enough," Arthion said, stepping between the two. "Arguing will do us no good. Elric, you've already decided that you're going to travel to Celes with us. You made us that promise, now stick to it."

"Oh, so you're on her side now?" Elric asked, raising his voice.

"I'm not on anyone's side! I just want to find out why Avenos is dead!" Arthion exclaimed, tossing his hands up and making for the other door set into the ridge across from them.

Ilyana looked at Elric and shrugged, then started following Arthion.

She is the reason I'm in this whole mess, Castien reminded himself. It was true, but if she hadn't saved him from the Blood Sorcerers—and later Faelyn—then he might not even be alive right now.

"Hello?" Arthion started knocking on the other door.

Ilyana stepped to the side, leaning against the ridge a short distance away in the dark night. It would probably be better if an Elosian *wasn't* the first thing someone saw.

Castien approached the door, Elric staying behind.

Arthion was kneeling beside it, listening. Castien listened as well, hearing a soft set of footsteps.

"Who's there?" a voice called out.

"Arthion Aldrich, sir," Arthion said. "Whisperer of the King's Court in Arvendon. I'm terribly sorry to bother you, but I'm afraid that I have need to make sail here, and head north."

"One moment," the man said. A clicking sound vibrated through the door, shaking it slightly. The door cracked open, revealing a pair of eyes peeking out. The man surveyed Arthion, taking in his robes, then nodded, and disappeared.

The door opened all the way, revealing another small entrance hall within. The man stood in the small chamber, his dark brown beard and bald head making for an interesting sight. Castien synced his breathing to his heart, centering his mind as the man started talking.

"I received a letter this morning saying not to let anyone enter or leave the harbor, I'm sorry to say," the man said. "Something about an attempt on the King's life, or something."

"It wasn't an attempt," Arthion said. "King Avenos Titansworn was killed, and we need to sail north and find out why." Arthion paused, looking back to Ilyana.

"Has there been any news from Celes, may we ask?" Castien said, thinking of Ilyana's father.

"The border's been shut down," the man said. "No one crosses either way—whether through this port or on the road—not even emissaries." The man looked at Arthion, then back at Castien. "Who's that?" the man asked, nodding to where Elric stood a few dozen feet away.

"A member of the King's Council," Arthion said. "Someone who wants to know why the King is dead, you see."

"Hmmm," the man grunted. "Well, even if I wanted to let you have that ship, it's not mine to give away. An Elosian merchant was stopping here to restock when I got the order, and he's been stuck here ever since. Come in," the man said, waving them inside.

Arthion slipped in first.

Castien followed Arthion into the chamber, glancing at where Ilyana remained off to the side.

"The name's Byrne, by the way. I'm Portmaster of Fairfrost," the man said as he climbed down into the chamber. It looked very similar to the other one they had been in, though instead of barrels and crates, this one had a bed and a campfire with a small hole for ventilation in the ceiling.

"It's wonderful to meet you, Byrne," Arthion said. "This is Castien."

Castien nodded, offering a slight smile. An older man sat in the corner of the room, seeming to look over some papers. He wore blue and gray—Celes's colors.

"That there is Sebol," Byrne said.

Sebol glanced at them, holding up a hand in greeting. He had tired eyes and a short gray beard. His blue and gray robes were simple, though they seemed fitting for a merchant.

Byrne paused, looking to Arthion. "I will need to see your writ of passage, please."

Arthion hesitated. "We left in haste, my good man," Arthion said. "We do not have one, but I can assure you that we are true members of the King's Court, and it is imperative that we get to Celes."

"Well, then I can't let you sail out. Orders is orders," Byrne grunted. "Come back when you have a writ of passage." He motioned back toward the door.

"If I may," Arthion started, raising a hand. "This mission is the most important in Arvendon's recent history. And, I might mention, we have been given the right to use force to complete our task, if necessary."

"Are you threatening me, Whisperer?" Byrne growled, stepping up to Arthion.

"Not threatening... Just informing," Arthion said, raising his hands as if in surrender. Arthion turned to Sebol. "We need safe passage to Celes. Can you take us there?"

"Hmmm," Sebol grunted. He leaned back. "Can I take a writ-less Whisperer and a Stormless? I don't think so. Besides, even if I wanted to, this one won't let anyone leave the port." Sebol motioned to Byrne.

"Perhaps we could make a deal," Arthion started.

Sebol watched Arthion carefully, seemingly intrigued.

"An Elosian woman has assassinated the King of Arvendon," Arthion said. "And until this conflict is resolved, no one will be allowed to leave this port. Now tell me: Does that sound like the sort of issue that will be taken care of in a timely manner?"

Sebol laced his fingers together, leaning forward. "Go on."

"Taking us to Celes will allow you to return home as well," Arthion continued. "So I ask again: Will you grant us safe passage to Celes?"

"Now just wait a minute, you can't—" Byrne started.

Arthion held up a hand, silencing him. "Will you?" Arthion asked again.

Sebol's gray eyebrows furrowed in thought. "You say no one's allowed to leave?" Sebol asked Byrne.

"Not under my watch," Byrne said firmly.

"And them?" Sebol motioned calmly to Arthion and Castien.

"Not under my watch," Byrne repeated, sharper this time.

"I see," Sebol said, folding his arms. "Well, gentlemen, if you can find a way to convince Byrne here to let us make sail, you've got yourselves a deal."

Arthion looked to Sebol, then back to Byrne. "You really aren't going to let us go, are you, my friend?"

Byrne folded his arms.

Arthion took a deep breath. "Niventia forgive me," Arthion muttered. "Listen here, Mr. Byrne: I am a Whisperer. Now, I can use my Whispering and force you to do as I please, but... I'd rather not do that. So, for the sake of maintaining your autonomy, will you please do as we ask? I assure you that we are not trying to mislead you. We truly *just* want to help the crown." Arthion paused. "So, what do you say?"

Byrne looked down, then released his grip on his weapon. "You say you're here on orders from the new King?"

"In essence." Arthion nodded.

Byrne looked down, thinking. After a moment he spoke. "I'm gonna get hell for this," Byrne grumbled, pushing past Arthion and making for the door.

"Thank you, gentlemen," Sebol said, smiling softly. "I've been trying to convince him to let me leave all day."

"Pleasure's all ours." Arthion bowed. "Now, I must inform you we have two other passengers. I assume that won't be a problem?"

Castien didn't listen to the rest of the conversation. He started out the way Byrne had left. Castien reached the door quickly and exited the small bunker.

Ilyana was waiting in the shadows, and Elric was standing off on the dock.

"How did it go?" Ilyana asked. "I assume well," Ilyana said, motioning to where Byrne walked across the shore toward the large contraption where the chain met the land.

"The merchant who owns the ship is going to take us to Celes," Castien said, his eyes shifting to the small ship. "Apparently we just helped him find a way back home—he's been stuck here."

"See, not everything I have us do is bad," Ilyana said, smirking.

Castien grimaced. She still frustrated him. Castien perked up as he heard Arthion and Sebol making their way out of the bunker behind him. "Ilyana," Castien said.

She turned her gaze to him.

"I asked about your father," Castien said. "They haven't heard anything from Celes since the Solstice."

Ilyana looked down, keeping her face firm. "We'll figure out what happened for ourselves when we get there," Ilyana said, starting toward the dock. "Come on." In the distance, the chain started to slacken, falling beneath the surface of the water. "To Celes."

Castien sighed. *To Celes.*

CHAPTER NINE

INTERROGATION

Faelyn Titansworn strode down the dark stone hallway of Summerglass's dungeon, his headache reduced to a dull thrum. His concussion had been healed quickly thanks to the constant supply of Crystals he was drawing upon.

A set of guards led the way down the hall, with Faelyn, Eithor, and Reluraun in tow. General Falx insisted on attending the interrogation as well, for if Eithor's suspicions were correct, then this moment would finally provide some answers.

"You're certain this is going to work?" Reluraun whispered in Faelyn's ear.

Faelyn felt a spike of frustration. *He still doesn't trust Eithor.* Fine. This interrogation would hopefully change that. "I'm certain," Faelyn said. "This is the only way to confirm whether or not Hallan was involved in all of this."

Reluraun nodded, then fell silent.

"If Hallan still denies his involvement in the plot to kill your father, then I'm afraid that he may be speaking the truth," Eithor said. "And—as promised—I will leave this city if that proves to be true."

"You don't have to do that, Eithor," Faelyn said. "We—"

"I must stop you, Faelyn," Eithor said, holding up his hand and cutting him off. "If my predictions are incorrect, then you will have no use for me."

"But you're an Illusomancer," Faelyn said. "Even ignoring everything else, you are still a valuable asset for us."

"A Summoner's powers are only as useful as the Summoner behind them," Eithor said. "I have faith that my suspicions are correct. But if my instincts are wrong, then my counsel cannot be trusted."

Faelyn opened his mouth to speak but thought better of it. Eithor seemed set on leaving if he was proven wrong. A part of it made sense to him, for he understood that his credibility among the Council would be completely diminished if Hallan proved to have no involvement in the plan.

The lead guard stopped as they reached the end of the hall. They had arrived.

Faelyn recognized the small iron-barred window at the top of the door, allowing the smallest amount of light through to the cell beyond. The cell where the man who helped kill his father awaited.

The group needed to remain quiet, for Hallan would be able to hear them talking if they said anything now that they were close. This needed to be executed perfectly.

One of the guards unhooked the key from his belt and handed it to Eithor. He then stepped back, motioning for Eithor to advance.

Eithor stepped forward, signaling for the rest of them to stand up against the wall where Hallan wouldn't be able to see them from inside the cell.

Faelyn and the others obeyed; they wouldn't be able to see in the cell from here, but they could still listen. They watched as Eithor started drawing a glyph in the air with his finger. After completing the strange circular shape, he snapped his fingers.

Faelyn heard rushing footsteps and clanking armor. He whipped his head to the right, scanning for whoever approached.

Down the hall, he saw three Cyfali soldiers in green armor materializing out of turquoise frost, complete with the proper sound effects to make them seem completely real. The illusions rushed forward, their faces fixed in an aggressive frown.

Eithor traced another glyph in the air, this time forming what appeared to be a suit of green armor. With another snap of his fingers, the illusion came to life, and Eithor stepped into it.

In an instant, Eithor appeared to be a Cyfali soldier—rather than the man he was. Faelyn had to admit it looked rather convincing. He watched as Eithor waved his hands and walked around a bit, testing his own illusion. The illusion seemed to be attached to Eithor's body, making it seem as though Eithor was wearing Cyfali-green armor, rather than a Whisperer's robe.

Advancing toward the door, Eithor flipped down his illusory faceplate. The armor he "wore" looked fully formed—detailed, even. The forest-green coloration of the steel even seemed to shine in the torchlight, and the illusory armor plates shifted and turned with each of Eithor's movements, completely covering the Illusomancer so that—to the outside eye—he looked exactly like a Cyfali soldier.

The illusory soldiers arrived at the door, and at that moment Eithor slipped the key into the door and heaved it open. The soldiers stopped behind Eithor, swords drawn.

Faelyn observed the soldiers, trying to find a flaw in them. Indeed, their movements seemed a little too perfect, perhaps even predetermined. *That's because they are,* Faelyn realized. Eithor wasn't actively controlling the illusory soldiers—they were set to follow certain movement patterns.

Faelyn heard Hallan cry out as Eithor rushed in—still looking like a Cyfali soldier.

The illusory soldiers turned around as if standing watch, shifting slightly every few seconds.

"What's happening?" Hallan shouted. "Who are you?"

From where he was, Faelyn couldn't see inside the cell, but he heard Eithor respond.

"We were sent by the Council of Jaskye to rescue you," Eithor said. His voice was deeper, and he spoke with an impeccable Cyfali accent.

He could be very useful indeed, Faelyn thought to himself. *If Eithor can effectively impersonate anyone... think of what we could do with his abilities.*

"The Council?" Hallan asked. "Why would they—" Hallan cut off with a grunt, and there was a brief silence.

What was that? Faelyn started forward, but fell back as he heard Hallan speak once again.

"It's about time you saved me," Hallan growled, his voice coarse.

"What happened?" Eithor asked in his disguised voice. "Why did they put you here?"

"Because I helped kill the King, you blasted fool!" Hallan snapped. "The Council told me I would be given an escape route! What in Zephyr's Name took you so long?"

"You were acting on the Council's orders?" Eithor asked, ensuring that he confirmed Hallan's implications.

"Of course I was! What? You think I would endanger myself like that for no reason?" Hallan shouted, his voice rising. "Lord Jastira told me that Avenos needed to be killed; he gave me my orders, and I carried them out. I thought you said you were sent by the Council! Don't you already know all of this?"

Faelyn stepped forward. A cold, numbing rage rose in his chest. He passed through the illusory Cyfali soldiers, sending a flurry of turquoise frost through the hallway.

Eithor was right. The Cyfali had been behind this all along. Hallan was guilty.

"Faelyn!" Reluraun hissed, grabbing Faelyn's shoulder. "What are you doing?"

"We have what we need," Faelyn said, his voice cold. "Hallan admitted to being a part of the plot that killed my father—and with multiple witnesses. It's my duty as King to punish him for what he's done."

Eithor's head whipped toward Faelyn, seemingly caught off guard by Faelyn's premature approach. Eithor quickly pulled a hand away from Hallan's face and met Faelyn's gaze from behind the illusory faceplate. With a wave of his hand, the illusion dispersed. Another wave of his hand dismissed the Cyfali guards, causing them to dissolve into turquoise frost once again.

"Wait," Hallan said, rubbing his mouth.

Faelyn caught a strange green-blue light flicker across Hallan's face. It vanished in an instant.

"Wait, I don't understand," Hallan said, desperation seeping through his voice. He shied back against the wall. "What was all of that?"

"It was an illusion," Eithor said, twisting his hand.

"And you just gave us all the proof we need." Faelyn glowered, stepping into the cell.

"You don't understand," Hallan cried. "That wasn't m—"

"We know exactly what you did," Faelyn snapped. He raised his hand, brushing his golden hair out of his eyes. His hand lingered near his face. "I couldn't hurt you before," Faelyn said. "Not without knowing if you truly were guilty... But now? Now, I'm going to burn your entire *country* to the ground." Faelyn looked up, meeting Hallan's horrified gaze. "And I'm going to start with you."

The shame was gone. Fear and guilt no longer held him back. Hallan was responsible. *All* of Jaskye was responsible. Faelyn's father was dead, and up until this point he had just been burying himself in self-pity. But not anymore. Now was not the time for sorrow; it was time he started making things right.

This wasn't revenge—this was *justice*.

Hallan started screaming as Faelyn conjured a flame in his right hand, and then another in his left.

Eithor stepped back, a devilish smirk on his wrinkled face.

Faelyn advanced, strengthening the flames to a terrifying blaze, burning so brightly that he had to squint. But he didn't look at the fires. He stared directly at Hallan.

Hallan scrambled back against the wall, clawing at the stones as Faelyn finally reached him. But it was too late for Hallan, Faelyn was certain of that.

Faelyn closed his eyes, emboldening his flames to an other-worldly heat. And without a second thought, Faelyn lunged.

CHAPTER TEN

THE COUNCIL

Standing before the circular table of the Council's chambers, Faelyn felt cold. Massive pillars daunted the walls of the round chamber, and a large table of white marble sat before him. Nine chairs lay evenly spaced around the table, many of which were currently empty.

Faelyn's heart pounded in his chest, his pulse rising. He felt nothing as a nurse tended to his hands—which were still bloodied and bruised from yesterday's encounter with Hallan.

The nurse wrapped a fresh set of bandages around Faelyn's hands before hurrying out of the room.

Faelyn's headache was almost completely gone, thankfully. He was a little unsteady on his feet, and he was still sleeping rather poorly, but he was getting better. Faelyn tested the bandages on his knuckles. Pain spiked as a gash rubbed against the gauze the wrong way. He winced, but kept his face firm.

Worth it, Faelyn thought. An image of Hallan's charred, ruined flesh appeared in his mind. *Still worth it.* There had hardly been anything to bury after Faelyn was done with him. And honestly, it had felt good. A part of him had been wanting to do that all along, but once Hallan was confirmed to be a part of his father's assassination, Faelyn had finally been able to do it without feeling guilty.

Faelyn stepped up to the head of the circular table—a seat that was raised slightly above the others—and pulled back the large wooden chair. He sat down slowly. Something flickered in the back of his mind. A memory of his father.

This had been his chair, and now it was Faelyn's. Faelyn curled his hands into a fist despite the bandages. Cyfalion would pay. *They will pay.*

Reluraun sat to his right, in Elric's seat. To his left, Estmar, the current highest-ranking Whisperer in Arvendon, sat quietly. Beyond him sat Eithor. Faelyn had insisted that Eithor attend, for Faelyn intended to promote him to the role of Chief Advisor to the King, which would thus give him a spot on the Council.

"I suppose that we all have a lot to say, though none of us seem to be able to find the words to say it," General Falx said. There was an empty seat beside him—General Surge's.

"The Solstice wiped out several of my squadrons," General Derius—the leader of the Stormless Corps—said. "Some of which likely fell to one of my former soldiers."

"The Palace is being repaired as we speak, and the storm covers should hold against the Tempests well enough," Estmar said.

Luka's seat was empty as well.

"Now that we have confirmation of the Jaskyan Council's involvement in the attack, our course of action seems clear," Eithor said.

"We don't have many soldiers to spare for any sort of assault on Cyfalion," General Falx grunted. "Several of our troops are roaming Etherus looking for Avenos's assassins, and those who remain in the city have been tasked with rebuilding the Palace as quickly as possible to protect it from the storms."

"So we take a small force, just a few dozen men," Faelyn said. "And myself, of course."

"What are you planning to do?" General Derius asked. "With

such a small force, you cannot hope to stand against an entire capital."

"Leave that to me," Eithor interjected. "I have been formulating a plan, one that I think will allow us to do a great deal of damage with very little firepower."

"Is this truly the best way to respond?" Estmar asked. "The people of Arvendon are practically hysterical. Are you sure that sending their young King away like this is the correct course of action?"

"Cyfalion *killed* my father, Estmar," Faelyn growled. "I won't let them get away with that."

"That's not what I'm suggesting, I—" Estmar started.

"Then what are you suggesting?" Faelyn snapped, cutting him off. "Are you going to propose that we try to negotiate with them? Perhaps even discuss a treaty?"

Estmar closed his mouth, swallowing.

Faelyn felt the cold heat within him rise once again. "Cyfalion moved against us once already. Who's to say they aren't planning to do it again? They could already be organizing an invasion of Arvendon for all we know... We cannot afford to miss this opportunity to strike."

"*What* opportunity?" Estmar asked, planting his hands on the table. "We have no advantage."

"They still don't know that we are aware of their involvement in my father's assassination," Faelyn said. "They likely think that we are still blaming Celes; now is our time to make a move."

"They will have noticed Hallan's absence," General Derius said. "He was supposed to return to Cyfalion, what? Two days ago? Certainly they will know that something is amiss."

"All the more reason to move fast," Faelyn said, his pulse quickening. "We don't have a lot of time before they raise their defenses." He paused, reflexively looking behind his back. The door was closed, of course, but he wasn't looking at that. He had been looking for his father. For a moment he hesitated, wondering if this truly was the right course of action.

There was no one to protect him, no one to look over his shoulder and assure him that he was making the right decision.

"Faelyn's right," Eithor said. "The quicker this attack force leaves, the better."

Faelyn glanced at Reluraun, who looked like he was about to be sick. The Cloudwalker watched silently, saying nothing.

"There is another matter I would like to address," Faelyn said. "Eithor Vassellet has proven himself to be a valuable asset to both myself and the rest of the Council. When we were ready to release Hallan, Eithor insisted that he was guilty. As you all know, I have thus far been ruling without a Chief Advisor; I intend to change that. Mr. Vassellet has shown—without question—that he is the most qualified to rise to the position." Faelyn paused, curious to see if anyone would object. "As of now, Eithor will act as my Chief Advisor."

Silence followed his brief speech. Faelyn had been wanting to make good on his deal with Eithor ever since Hallan had admitted his crimes.

"Thank you, Your Grace," Eithor said, bowing his head.

Reluraun glanced at Eithor, opening his mouth. He closed it a moment later, thinking better of whatever he was about to say.

"I propose an assault on Cyfalion," Eithor said. "We would sail to Jaskye and lay anchor a few miles north of Cyfalion. The route is well mapped—with many sheltered bays along the way should a Storm Gale or Cyclone strike. I would need a handful of Scorchers along with a few crates of Incendiary... And portable catapults to launch the Incendiary, of course," Eithor added. "I have been tentatively making preparations for several days now, and I can be ready to depart for Cyfalion as early as tomorrow evening." He paused, looking to the other members of the Council. "Provided that the Council votes in favor of allowing this expedition, of course."

Faelyn looked from Eithor to Estmar, and then to the Generals, and finally to Reluraun.

"Your Majesty?" General Falx turned to him.

Faelyn inhaled, long and slow. He exhaled, and spoke, "War with Cyfalion is inevitable. If we can hit them hard before the fighting truly breaks out, that would give us a distinct advantage," Faelyn said. "They think that by killing my father they have crippled us. Let us show them that they are *wrong*."

Falx stood up, the scar across his face twitching as he smirked. "I vote in favor of the King," Falx said.

General Derius rose too. "I vote in favor of the King as well."

"I vote against," Estmar said, standing.

"So do I," Reluraun said, rising to his feet.

The only other present member, of course, was Eithor—now that he was Faelyn's Chief Advisor.

"I vote in favor of the King," Eithor said, his voice firm. He looked to Reluraun and Estmar, then smiled. "It's settled then: We leave tomorrow."

Faelyn nodded. "Tomorrow."

Faelyn had waited until the others had left before walking back to his chambers. Eithor had left first, going with Falx to select the Scorchers who would accompany them on their mission.

Derius and Estmar had left next, leaving Reluraun and Faelyn alone.

The Cloudwalker seemed distant—he had been ever since Faelyn had... *dealt* with Hallan yesterday. Reluraun looked up, meeting Faelyn's eyes. He seemed to be looking for something in Faelyn.

"Is there something you want to say?" Faelyn asked as he rubbed his bandaged knuckles.

Reluraun snorted. "I don't even recognize you anymore," Reluraun said, his voice low.

"My father was killed, Reluraun," Faelyn rumbled. "Would you expect me to be the same after something like that?"

"I wouldn't have expected you to murder a man with your bare hands," Reluraun said.

"Tell me: If Elric was killed and you had a moment alone with the man responsible, would you let him live?"

Reluraun hesitated.

"You can't tell me I was out of line. Hallan's confession would've led to a swift execution anyway," Faelyn said, waving dismissively. "I took the first steps toward justice, that's more than you can say."

"You brutally killed a man who—" Reluraun cut himself off. He swallowed, looking away.

"A man who what?" Faelyn locked his jaw. He felt the heat rising in his chest. "A man who what, Reluraun?"

"A man who might've not even been guilty," Reluraun blurted. His emerald eyes snapped back to Faelyn. "I'm sorry, but I still don't think Hallan did this."

"How could you say that?" Faelyn started. "He admitted to it! You heard it with your own ears!"

"How do we know that wasn't Eithor?" Reluraun asked, his voice rising. "You've seen how he can mimic others... How do we know he didn't trick us?"

"Why in Niventia's Light would he do that?" Faelyn said, dumbfounded. "What reason would he have to mislead us?"

"Because he's an *Illusomancer*, Faelyn," Reluraun said. "His powers revolve around misleading people! And we still don't even know where he came from!"

"I—" Faelyn stopped. That much was true; Faelyn didn't know where Eithor came from, nor how he got his Crystals, or powers for that matter.

"You didn't even think to ask, did you?" Reluraun snorted as if in disbelief. "All the trust you place in him, and you don't even know what his motivations are."

"Well, why didn't he betray us after my father's death?" Faelyn challenged. "The Palace was a mess for days... Why wouldn't he have used that opportunity to destroy us?"

Reluraun paused.

"All of this happened because I didn't listen to him," Faelyn said, growing quiet. "If I had listened when he warned me about the Solstice, then my father might still be alive." He looked up. "I won't make the mistake of dismissing Eithor's counsel again. He warned me that the city will fall under attack if we don't take action soon, and I intend to do whatever it takes to keep my home safe."

"Faelyn," Reluraun said, shaking his head. "Just... Just promise me that you know what you're doing."

"I promise," Faelyn said without hesitation.

Reluraun looked down, nodding. "There's just this *feeling* that I can't shake," Reluraun said. "I mean, my father said that he and Arthion had a lead in Celes. Is it possible that Celes had a hand in this too?"

"Maybe, but it's possible that your father was wrong, Rel."

Reluraun looked up again. "I suppose we'll know in a week or so —when he gets back from Celes."

"I suppose we will," Faelyn said. He turned toward the closed door. His guards would be waiting outside to escort him back to his rooms. "I'm sorry for being so hostile. With all that's been going on, I—"

"You don't have to explain yourself, Faelyn," Reluraun said. "I understand."

"You know, you could come with us," Faelyn said. "To Cyfalion, I mean."

"I want to be here when my father returns," Reluraun said. "Besides, I could help with the Palace repairs." Reluraun raised his hand, sending a soft swirl of air through the room.

Faelyn smiled softly. He honestly hoped that Elric would come back with *something*. More likely than not, he'll simply return with the assassins captive.

But I would like to get my hands on them, Faelyn thought, his mind shifting to the Stormless and the Dexteris. They would have to wait until after Cyfalion was dealt with, but Faelyn would find them. He would not rest until he killed everyone who had anything to do with his father's death. *Then, there will finally be true justice.*

CHAPTER ELEVEN
SAILS

Faelyn Titansworn stood aboard the ship, squinting through the evening light. The Wisps of the day were starting to fade, leaving only a few stragglers arcing and swimming across the landscape. Those that made it through the ward still lingered in the city, twisting and hissing through the streets.

Bells rang through the docks as ships loaded and departed. His own ship's bell rang after the last massive crate of supplies was loaded on the ship. Faelyn recognized the red paint on the large boxes. Those were filled with Incendiary—the flammable, explosive liquid that was used in small quantities to keep torches going. Eithor's plans had them launching Incendiary into Cyfalion using portable catapults, which would make the city much easier to set alight.

Finally, Faelyn thought. *When I first awoke following my father's death, I dreamt of burning the world. Now I finally get to do it.*

The crew followed shortly after the crates. It was a small group of eight Scorchers that Eithor had handpicked with Falx's help. Following them, of course, was Eithor himself.

Faelyn felt the rocking ship beneath him, savoring the strange thrill of the uneven ground. He could already feel the slight dampening of his emotions, not unlike what a Whisperer would be capable of. Though this numbness was brought on by rage, not Summoning. Estmar had offered to help Faelyn through his grief, but Faelyn had declined; his grief was what gave him the strength to do all of this. The Cyfali deserved to burn for what they had done, and now Faelyn could ensure that they would.

Eithor boarded last, followed by a heavyset man in a blacksmith's apron.

The man's clothing was stained with soot and coal.

Eithor had said that he was working on a new suit of armor for Faelyn to wear during the assault. He had made it exceptionally clear that he intended for Faelyn to survive the battle, and that would require more than just a little luck.

"Eithor?" Faelyn stepped forward, his legs still unsteady as the ship bobbed back and forth in the water.

"Yes, Your Grace?" Eithor bowed, stepping away from the armorer.

"Is that the armorer?" Faelyn asked, nodding toward the bulky man.

"Yes, that is Hubys," Eithor said. "He is putting the finishing touches on your armor. It's being constructed to resist great expulsions of heat, unlike what you're currently wearing." Eithor motioned to the white vest Faelyn wore. It was embroidered with gold, as was the white fabric of his pants. He wore it in honor of the Solstice, not because of what it meant to Niventia and the gods—but because of what it meant to *him*.

Cyfalion may have moved past that day, but Faelyn replayed it in his head every single night. He couldn't shake the memory no matter how hard he tried, and he knew that it would be with him until the end of his days.

The white clothing served as a reminder. It was a symbol, but most importantly, it was to ensure that Cyfalion did not forget what they had done. It was to ensure that they did not forget their terrible betrayal on a day of celebration, when Arvendon welcomed those from all corners of Auris into their walls.

Faelyn would ensure that the practice was put to an end. Niventia deserved no worship, for he now knew that she did not exist. When burying his father, a part of him had believed in her, *a part*. But now he knew that no god, no matter how benevolent or terrible, could ever have brought this upon him. His fate was the result of human cruelty, nothing more, nothing less.

"How are you feeling today, Your Grace?" Eithor said, looking Faelyn up and down. "The headaches are gone, I hope?"

"Yes," Faelyn said quietly. "And I'm feeling fine. Just focused."

"Ah." Eithor lowered his head. "I suppose I can understand that; we have a great task ahead of us. Cyfalion is a mighty city... It will not fall easily."

"It will," Faelyn rumbled. "The Cyfali have never come face to face with *pure* Titansworn rage. I can promise it won't be an encounter they soon forget."

Eithor stared off into the distance, where the sky was slowly dimming as the day grew long. "You know Lord Jastira will likely be there," Eithor said. "...The head of the Council of Jaskye."

"I know." Faelyn nodded. He hadn't told Eithor about his conversation with Reluraun, and he didn't plan to. Reluraun was wrong to assume that Eithor couldn't be trusted. The Illusomancer had done nothing but help Faelyn since the moment they first met. Faelyn's father might even still be alive if he had listened to Eithor from the start.

Yet he could not shake Reluraun's words. Of course, it would make sense that Reluraun favored Elric's instincts over Eithor's, but surely the only lead Elric had was on the assassins themselves—not those the assassins were hired by.

Faelyn closed his eyes, allowing the cold anger to slip in once again. Hallan had admitted to knowing about the plot, Faelyn had heard it with his own ears. There was nothing more to say on the matter.

He spun around as the boarding plank was withdrawn, and the small ship started going through the process of undocking. Faelyn felt stronger than he had in days; the Crystals had helped him heal from his injuries, and his grief had pushed him to finally take the right steps toward justice.

"I have a question, Eithor," Faelyn said.

"Ask away," Eithor said, glancing at him.

"Where did you find your Crystals?" Faelyn asked. "I mean, the Illusomancers have no Tempest, so they couldn't have accumulated anywhere."

Eithor fell silent. He stared off into the sea, watching as a dive-brisk leaped into the air, flipping before diving back into the water.

"And your powers," Faelyn continued. "When did you discover you had them? Or did you always have them?"

"I was born thinking I was Stormless," Eithor said, speaking slowly. "I lived my life without Summoning, until one day I came across a small group of people who were looking to change the world. I began helping them, for I was once a very prestigious scholar, and before long they uncovered a cache of Illusomancer Crystals that had survived the Vanishing." Eithor paused. "Imagine my surprise when I drew upon them for the first time..."

Faelyn looked at the elderly man, scanning his eyes.

"The cache was rather large, and I brought many Crystals with me when I came to Arvendon," Eithor continued. "I knew that I wanted to help you and your family from the start, for it had always been my dream to better this world, and I knew that if I could guide the most powerful family on Auris to make the right decisions, then I would be able to finally make some real changes.

"The quickest way to blend in among the nobility was to steal a Whisperer's robe and pretend to be one of them—they keep to themselves mostly anyway," Eithor continued. "Before long I started seeking out you, for it became clear that your father would never trust someone like me directly."

"And now we're here," Faelyn finished for him. He looked back to the dock, where the last members of the crew were boarding. "Who were they? The people who helped you find your Crystals, I mean."

Eithor fell silent once again. "They were powerful, *powerful* people. Stronger than any I have ever met," Eithor said. "Our goals aligned, and they welcomed me into their fold. Of course, once I discovered my abilities, they helped me cultivate my skills... They helped me train."

"And now?" Faelyn asked. "Where are they now?"

"The group fell apart, quite tragically actually," Eithor said, his voice growing distant. "Though I still keep in contact with their new leader; he continues to guide me in my decisions."

Hm, Faelyn thought. *Not the story I was expecting.* But now he had proof. Eithor's story was unremarkable, and Reluraun had been proven wrong once again. Eithor had no secrets, and no reason to betray Arvendon.

Moments later, the captain of the ship rang the bell again—a signal to depart.

Faelyn watched as the deckhands pulled up the anchor and untied the ropes keeping them with the dock. The rocking of the boat grew more intense now that they were floating by themselves.

The ship bobbed furiously for a few moments, unsettled by the initial departure. Shortly, the sails opened up, and Faelyn could feel the massive gusts of wind being caught by the large contraption. It propelled them forward, guided by the arcing of the sail that the captain controlled.

They were carried out to sea, slowly leaving Arvendon behind. Faelyn stared through the Wisps at the Palace once again, watching its bent form slowly grow smaller and smaller until it was too far shrouded in the Wisps to be discernible. The transparent white film of the ward greeted them after a few minutes. It rose overhead, diving into the ocean to protect the bay from the Tempests. Of course, the Tempests were not as bad out at sea. The concentrations of energy were considerably lower away from the land due to the absence of Summoners. Still, it was possible that their ship would have to pull into a sheltered bay to wait out a Cyclone or Storm Gale on the way to Cyfalion.

Faelyn climbed back to the upper deck, settling himself on the bow of the ship and leaning against the wooden rail.

Bells rang and ship hands shouted to one another, completing the final stages of separation. Faelyn eyed Arvendon in the distance, watching as it grew smaller and smaller. They were initially heading east so that they would be far enough from the shore to avoid being spotted, but then they would turn south. From there it would be an almost straight shot to Cyfalion.

Yet, even so, Faelyn could see Arvendon for quite some time. He remained there, watching as the marine wind blew across his golden hair.

Hours later, Arvendon faded to nothing more than a distant speck on the slanted bay.

Faelyn blinked a few times, his thoughts drifting to the very specific box below deck. He had carried it onto the ship himself, for he knew that he would want it in Cyfalion. Arvendon may be out of sight, but he still had something with him to keep it close. It was his city, and he would defend it until his last breath.

His father's murder would not go unpunished. Cyfalion had committed an act of war, and Faelyn fully intended to repay the favor —even with the Blood Sorcerers' return so close. Reluraun and Estmar doubted that this was the correct course of action, but Faelyn was confident.

The Cyfali needed to pay for what they'd done, and when he reached their shores he would bring the most swift and terrible storm of justice the world had ever seen. Burning Cyfalion wouldn't be enough.

Faelyn was going to kill Cyfalion's leader: Adresin Jastira.

CHAPTER TWELVE
CELES

The snow fell in the quiet morning. Waves battered the sides of the ship, rocking it ever so gently as it sailed into the harbor. Row after row of docks stretched out ahead, many of which were empty.

Castien Varic looked up, his eyes settling on Celes. The city sat on a peninsula, resting atop a set of cliffs overlooking the Salarin Sea. Celes bore a much different look than Arvendon. Where Arvendon was diverse and colorful, Celes was composed of only two colors: blue and gray.

Countless buildings—mostly in the shapes of rigid, separated squares—lined the cliff overhead, their stone bodies blending in with the dark cliffs. Almost every building's roof was a deep, cobalt-colored dome, giving the skyline of the city a pleasingly uniform look.

Snow continued falling as they passed through the ward, the transparent film in the air wavering as they entered. A sense of relief washed over him now that he was within another ward—for the Tempests were much weaker here.

Castien looked around, watching as Ilyana, Arthion, and Elric stood at the back of the ship, watching Sebol guide them toward the dock.

None of them had much sailing experience, so Castien was thankful that they had an experienced merchant seafarer guiding them. The journey had been quick, and largely uneventful. There had been a Cyclone on the second day, which forced them to pull into a sheltered, rocky inlet where they had lowered their sails and anchored for the day. Barring that, there had been no interruptions during their journey.

Castien's chest tightened as they drew closer to the docks. This place was going to be his new home? His breathing accelerated. Stepping back, Castien grabbed onto the railing of the ship, feeling the rhythmic flow of the waves beneath him. It seemed the prospect of never returning to Arvendon was finally hitting him, and it was hitting hard.

He could feel his mind darting to irrational thoughts. Trying to calm himself, Castien took a deep breath.

Elric spared him a glance but said nothing. He seemed content to let Castien suffer alone. And why shouldn't it be that way? Castien had brought this upon himself. This was all his fault. Things would never go back to normal, not just for him, but for *all* of Auris—thanks to what he had helped Ilyana do on the Solstice.

Of course, being met with the overwhelming view of Celes hadn't exactly helped those fears stay buried. The stone docks stood firmly ahead while the waves bobbed around them. The ship began turning and angling itself to dock—thanks to Sebol's work.

Castien looked beyond the docks, scouting out the landscape of Elos as he tried to distract himself. Snow covered the ground here, though Castien could imagine that the soil was still ruined and stony beneath, like in Etherus.

The Highlands stretched out in the distance, looming ominously, just barely within view. It was as if they were watching him, watching Celes. Castien shivered. Moments later he found his mind drifting toward the Starburner Crystal. This gave him some comfort, as it reminded him that he was likely not *completely* worthless.

The temperature had dropped quickly as they traveled north, and Castien was now left shivering in his torn vest and ripped pants.

The wooden ship creaked as it neared the docks, the short mast and small bow easily maneuvered by the others. They were now fully beneath one of the cliffs, making it impossible to see the rest of the city overhead.

Several workers and guards—each wearing a deep blue—filed out onto the docks to meet them.

Ilyana stepped down, stopping beside Castien.

He kept his gaze forward, focusing on syncing his heartbeat and his breathing. *Five beats in, six beats out, hold for three. Repeat.* He watched as the ship eased itself into place. The boat rattled as the anchor dropped. Ropes were tossed onto the ship, and Arthion and Elric tossed some back. The quick process of tying the ship down began, and before long the small merchant ship was fully secured.

"Don't worry," Ilyana said. "I'm royalty here, remember? I'll make sure you have a place to stay." She turned to him, offering a slight smile.

Castien felt his face quiver but did his best to keep his expression firm. He didn't respond.

Ilyana turned away, walking toward the dock on the right side of the ship.

"We haven't seen a ship in days, not since the news arrived from Arvendon," one of the guards said, extending a ramp and boarding the ship. "I'm surprised you even made it here at all."

Sebol rushed over to the side of the ship, tugging at his beard. "We made it just barely, good sir. We rushed out before Fairfrost could be locked down," Sebol lied.

The guard nodded to himself. He wore thick blue armor, with a fur coat bulging out from beneath. A sword lay sheathed at his side, and his silver helmet was rounded—with a curled indenture where the eyes were.

"Who are they?" the guard nodded to Castien and Ilyana. "They don't look like merchants."

"You'd think they'd recognize me—I used to spend a lot of time with the guards," Ilyana mumbled to Castien. Straightening her back and lifting her chin, she spoke again, "I am Princess Ilyana Nightingale, and I have returned to the city for the family conclave."

The guard paused. "Princess?" He quickly fell to one knee. "I sincerely apologize, we have been awaiting your return... My eyes simply neglected to remind me of who I was speaking to, please forgive me."

"You are forgiven." Ilyana nodded. "Please, tell me: Have my siblings arrived yet?"

The guard stepped back to his feet, looking to one of the dockworkers below.

"For the deliberation," Ilyana said. "As to who my father's crown should pass to."

The guard again looked to the dockworker for a moment. He turned back to Ilyana. "The King is alive, Princess," the guard said. "Forgive me for asking, but why would there be a deliberation now?"

Ilyana's eyes widened, her mouth opening slightly.

What? Castien started. *So King Nightingale is alive?*

Ilyana quickly composed herself, clearing her throat. "Forgive me for my mistake. Would you be so kind as to escort us to the Palace?"

"Certainly, Princess," the guard said, falling to one knee once again.

"And stop doing that," Ilyana said. "Please."

"Apologies, Princess," the guard said, hastily rising to his feet. He motioned for them to walk down the wide portable ramp leading down to the dock.

Ilyana went first.

Castien followed, feeling a little unsteady as he recovered from his earlier moment of anxiety. He turned around once he reached the bottom, seeing that Elric and Arthion had been stopped by the guard.

"They can come with us," Ilyana called. "They're allies."

The guard nodded, stepping aside, allowing Arthion and Elric to walk down the short plank to the dock as well.

Castien shivered as snow continued falling around them, landing in the freezing sea. Cold stone lay beneath his feet, covered in a slight layer of snow. Each of his footsteps came with a slight *crunch*, reminding him of his days in The Highlands.

"This way," the guard said, stepping onto the dock and leading them toward a small collection of buildings. There was a slight impression of a road starting just beyond those buildings... Though with the snow covering everything, Castien couldn't really see it.

These buildings were made of gray stone and topped with roofs of a deep blue—just like those in the city. Others might've found the architecture to be beautiful, but to Castien it was cold and unwelcoming.

His arm ached, the burn still feeling hot despite the freezing temperatures. How that was possible, Castien didn't really know, which made it all the more frustrating. A part of him wanted to wonder what the new King—Faelyn—was doing right now. He would likely still be searching for ways to track down Castien and Ilyana... If he wasn't busy trying to prepare for the Blood Sorcerer's return.

They approached the first building, which appeared to be a small warehouse with some shipping supplies. Castien could see through the large, open doors that several fires were going inside.

If only. Castien pushed the thought aside. He could stand a few more minutes out here in the cold if it meant getting answers more quickly. Ilyana's father was alive—that, he hadn't expected. The only logical explanation was that Ilyana's informant lied to her, but why?

Why would someone want to cause all of this? And how did they end up getting the Shadow-Swifts involved? *And how do the Blood Sorcerers relate to all of this?* Castien shook his head. Hopefully, this journey wasn't for nothing. If King Nightingale was still alive, then there was a very good chance that he didn't know any more about the situation than Castien did.

As Castien passed the second building—this one on the left—another thought struck him. The guards didn't seem to know that Ilyana was the one who killed King Avenos. Perhaps they knew that the assassin was an Elosian woman, but was it possible that Celes didn't know the killer's identity?

It seemed to be that way, though Castien supposed that Arvendon didn't know Ilyana's true identity anyway.

They started on what Castien now confirmed to be a snow-covered cobblestone road, which began inclining. Castien's feet felt sluggish, slowly reacclimating to walking on a surface that *wasn't* rocking. The walls of Celes became visible as they started turning to the right, heading up the hill and toward the entrance of the city. Their walls were not as tall as Arvendon's, nor as decorated.

The land leveled out as they reached the top of the hill a few moments later. Castien caught a glimpse of the other side of the peninsula and saw why Celes was said to be so defensible. Dozens of tall ships poked out from the other side of the cliffs to the north. *Celes's navy,* Castien thought. The city was vulnerable to attacks by sea, yet with a navy that size they could defend themselves.

The shorter, dark stone walls of Celes grew closer as they continued walking. Castien recentered his mind and his body, syncing his heart with his breathing and looking up to the guards standing atop the walls.

The guard leading them called up to those manning the gate, explaining that Princess Ilyana had returned, and soon the large wooden gates were being wheeled open by unseen pulleys. Castien looked to his side, where Arthion now walked beside him.

"I can't say I'm surprised," Arthion whispered. "I should've known there was another secret she was keeping from us."

"How could we be so foolish!" Elric cursed under his breath, walking on the other side of Arthion. "We've been helping a Celesian

Princess this whole time? Who knows what else she's been lying about!"

"We'll be fine," Castien said softly. "She told me just before you two found us. She hasn't been lying to me—and I don't think she plans to hurt us."

Elric cursed again. "You knew?" Elric narrowed his eyes, his hands slipping toward his daggers.

"What was I supposed to do? Tell you?" Castien started. "You never would've let us get this far if you knew." Castien paused, trying to pull back his anger. "Listen, I know you really don't give a shit about what happens to me anymore, but coming here was my only shot at surviving this whole thing. So don't try and tell me that I should've told you because we *both* know that if I had, I'd be in an Arvendi cell right now—if I'd even still be alive at all."

Elric closed his mouth, hesitantly releasing his daggers. "Cross me again and it'll be the last thing you ever do," Elric warned, turning his eyes forward. "You're on thin ice, *Stormless*," Elric spat.

That stung.

The gates were open entirely now, and their arrival had seemingly been announced.

Castien started forward at the direction of the guards, his mouth dropping open as he laid eyes on the inside of Celes for the first time. There appeared to be two major streets, each one heading off toward the sea, with a massive block of square buildings in the middle.

He looked around, watching as people poured out of the buildings to watch.

Ilyana kept her head up, trying to look powerful even as Castien was certain she was processing some very complicated emotions.

The blue, domed roofs of the buildings and houses began to seem a bit more impressive, for they were all decorated with carvings and inscriptions.

The snow-covered cobblestone streets were mostly uniform and solid, though the cold snow had clearly dug some holes in the road through its freezing and thawing. Castien turned forward, looking past the guards, letting his eyes follow the long road ahead. At the end, in the distance, lay a dark stone palace, bearing many tiers of short, blue-domed roofs.

The buildings on the left and right were mostly separate from one another, though there were only a few feet of space between them. Up close, the dark stone somehow seemed more elegant and dignified than Arvendon's random assortment of brick and mismatched stones. Castien grimaced still, for he missed those mismatched stones.

The left side of this street appeared to be lined with mostly shops and businesses, while the right seemed to be mostly homes and residences. None of the buildings were particularly tall, interestingly enough. Though this central road stretched on long enough that Castien had no doubt that the city had enough space.

He vaguely recalled reading when he was young that the buildings of Celes often opted to build *down,* rather than up. Cellars were incredibly common here, while they were almost nonexistent in all other cities of the world.

The walk went by quickly, for Castien was so wrapped up in his observation of the city and lost in the sound of the waves distantly crashing against the cliffs that he hardly even noticed the time passing. Within about ten minutes, they reached the Palace and finally saw some relief from the gathering crowds behind them.

The building was considerably shorter than Summerglass, and noticeably less extravagant. Although, truth be told, Castien was still impressed by it. The unique square architecture was interesting enough to outweigh his disappointment with the Palace's size.

They turned to the left, passing a few more gawking residents as they neared the main doors. The center of the Palace had a set of large stone doors with a deep blue lining, matching the blue-domed roofing.

"It's..." Arthion whispered. "It's beautiful," Arthion said, looking overhead as they neared the doors.

Elric grunted in disapproval.

Castien glanced sideways at the Cloudwalker. It seemed that he was far from impressed. Of course, he wouldn't be, given the fact that he had likely seen this city several times already. Castien looked ahead to where Ilyana walked with her head now bowed.

She did it for nothing, Castien thought. *She's realizing that she killed King Avenos without cause... She had been tricked.* Castien blinked. *Which means that none of this should've ever happened. I should still be in Arvendon. I should still be home.*

The massive stone doors were pulled open by guards, a loud clicking sound echoing through the air as the doors locked into their holding places. Castien turned around, the motion agitating his burnt arm. He winced, then turned back mid-motion. Castien's arm was still wrapped in the torn fragment of Ilyana's robe, and he had no doubts that the guards had noticed that.

The inside of the Palace was built of dark stone, just like the outside. Castien walked in, noticing the lack of obnoxious *clacking* as he stepped onto the floors. Celes was certainly not as wealthy as Arvendon, though there was a certain security to this Palace that he had never felt in Summerglass.

You're never going back there, Castien reminded himself. Besides, Summerglass wouldn't be much to see right now anyway, given the destruction that the Shadow-Swifts had caused.

"This way," one of the guards said, motioning for Castien and Ilyana to follow.

Elric and Arthion followed closely behind, still surveying their surroundings.

Castien started forward as another set of doors within the large square chamber opened. The room itself was largely undecorated, save for a few golden-framed paintings of past kings on the dark walls. Hallways spread out to the left and right, and from what Castien could tell, these went on for hundreds of feet. The doors that had opened were in front of them, and Castien soon realized that they must be entering the throne room.

Castien looked forward, taking a few small steps as the second set of doors finished opening.

The throne room was considerably fancier than the entry hall. While it paled in size compared to Arvendon's throne room, it was still a sight to see. The whole room was made of dark stone, but the ornaments of blue cloth and Crystal lighting fixtures gave it a bit of flair. Castien looked to the sides as he walked in, examining the ornate silver fastenings of the dark blue Dexteris Crystals. Overhead, a large circular chandelier hung just a little below the domed ceiling, shining down with dark blue light. Castien looked forward once again, finding himself briefly blinded by a large set of windows at the far end of the throne room.

I didn't realize that the Palace had been built so close to the cliff, Castien thought as he blinked a few times. The tall, skinny windows became clearer as his eyes adjusted, and he found himself staring out into the ocean far below. It was then that he turned his attention to the man seated in the center of the room, just in front of the many windows.

While Avenos had been somewhat on the larger side, King Nightingale was shockingly skinny for a monarch. The King's hair was short and dark. And his face was little more than a shadow against the bright light of the windows. Castien looked to the side, noticing that Ilyana and the others had dropped into a kneel. Castien did the same, doing his best to maintain his composure.

He blinked a few times as he stared at the blue carpet. He felt a strange sense of detachment. A part of him wondered if this was all a bad dream, and if he was really lying in his bed in Arvendon. *Bring yourself back,* Castien thought. Castien closed his eyes, then opened them again. He was here, and he needed to focus.

"You may rise," the King said.

Castien slowly rose to his feet, as did the others.

The King stood up, approaching slowly. Unseen Crystals clinked against each other within his armor, his face becoming visible against the glaring light as he grew closer.

Castien could see the resemblance between Ilyana and her father. The way his Elosian eyebrows curved... the slight tilt of his mouth... *Yes, this is Ilyana's father.* He had a short, pointed, well-kempt beard that looked more like a thick stubble than anything else. His eyes were the same powerful gray that Ilyana's were, bearing a sense of purpose that was almost intimidating.

He wore a pale blue, silver chestplate—one that didn't seem to be meant for casual wearing—with a long snowprowler-fur cloak draped over his back and shoulders.

Strange, Castien thought. *He appears to be dressed for a fight.* Castien raised his eyes to the King's crown. It was made of silver, and it was considerably bulkier than Avenos's crown from what Castien remembered. There were several blue gemstones placed in the crown, adding another level of elegance. A simple crown, but commanding nonetheless.

Reaching the group of four, the King stopped, surveying each of them.

It wasn't long before an uncomfortable silence settled over the group. Castien found himself trying to make sense of his surroundings once again, counting the guards and the lights to try and steady himself. *Twenty-four. Fourteen.*

He synced his breathing to his pulse, using the technique to calm himself once again.

The King's eyes finally settled on Ilyana. A moment passed before he wrapped her in a firm embrace.

Ilyana flinched, seeming shocked. Hesitantly, she lowered her arms against her father's back. "Is it really you?" Ilyana whispered, tears in her eyes.

"It is, Snowflake," the King said, pulling her tighter.

Snowflake? Castien thought. He smiled slightly. *Cute.*

"Niventia's Light," Ilyana breathed, closing her eyes.

Castien glanced at the others, gauging their reactions.

Elric looked annoyed, as was becoming usual. On the other hand, Arthion seemed to be smiling at the moment as well.

"How did you escape Arvendon?" the King asked, pulling back. "Following the assassination, I would assume no one was let out of the city."

"You know I have my ways," Ilyana laughed, wiping at her eyes.

"And tell me: Was it really one of our people who killed King Titansworn?" the King asked. "Were you at the Palace that night?"

Ilyana paused, swallowing. "Father..." Ilyana trailed off.

The King motioned for her to continue, his fur cloak flowing over his shoulders.

"I killed Avenos," Ilyana said, her voice grave. "I killed him on the night of the Solstice before escaping over the cliffs."

The King recoiled, his gray eyes wide. He stared at Ilyana, then looked at Castien, Elric, and Arthion. Turning back to Ilyana, he spoke, "Does Arvendon know?" the King asked. "Do they know that you were the assassin?"

"Yes," Ilyana whispered. "But so far as we know, they haven't made an attempt at retaliation yet."

The King breathed, shocked. "Snowflake," the King started. "Why?"

"Because Callum told me that you had been killed by an Arvendi assassin," Ilyana said, stepping forward. "I thought you were *dead*, father. Callum told me our best chance at making things right was for me to kill Avenos before news of your death reached the rest of Arvendon."

The King turned around, pacing back to his throne. "This is a disaster," the King said, fury finally shaking his voice. "What do you suppose I should do now? Arvendon's Summoners outnumber us three to one. They'll destroy us!"

"I know, I'm—" Ilyana started.

"*Don't!*" the King growled, his voice rising. "You've single-handedly doomed our city. Do you realize that?"

Ilyana said nothing, lowering her head.

"Centuries of peace, decades of working toward a strong, unbreakable peace treaty, and you throw it all away in a *single* night!" the King roared. He looked back to Ilyana, then scanned the rest of the group. "Izara's Shadow, we need to prepare the defenses."

"Father, I—" Ilyana started.

The King's hand flashed into the air, silencing her. His eyes were fixed on Castien—on his burned arm, which was still wrapped in a piece of Ilyana's cloak.

"*What* is that?" the King rumbled, pointing to Castien's arm.

Castien blinked, a surge of panic running through him. He looked at his arm, where the bloodied blue-gray fabric was still wrapped around his wound.

"Father, it's not like that. He was injured, and he needed something to protect the wound," Ilyana said quickly. "I promise, there's nothing more to it."

"Did he talk you into all of this?" the King growled. He approached Castien. "Did you tell my daughter to *murder* the King?" the King shouted.

Castien cringed, involuntarily shying back.

"He had nothing to do with it!" Ilyana roared, stepping between Castien and her father. "*Leave* him *alone*," Ilyana said, her words venomous.

The King retreated, then turned to Ilyana. "You should be ashamed of yourself."

Ilyana kept her head up this time, firmly standing in front of Castien.

"You've murdered our greatest ally, shattered tradition by giving a piece of your clothing to an *Arvendi*, and now you return to my city knowing that by doing so you're endangering us all?" The King's voice rose. "You have destroyed our future in one fell swoop. Is this what you wanted?"

Ilyana lowered her head but remained in front of Castien. "I'm sorry," she said, speaking slowly. "This is not what I wanted, I can promise you that. Just know that the only reason I did all of this was because I thought you were dead." Ilyana looked up, meeting her father's eyes.

The King advanced, Crystals clinking against each other somewhere in his armor. His face seemed fixed in a frown as he surveyed Arthion and Elric—who had remained silent for several moments now.

"State your names," the King spat. "And your purpose for being here."

"Arthion Aldrich, Your Majesty," Arthion said, dropping to one knee. "Whisperer of the late King Avenos Titansworn."

"Elric Knyvet," Elric said, though he didn't kneel. "Commander of Arvendon's Cloudwalker Regiment."

"We are here to uncover the truth behind our King's assassination," Arthion said. "Your daughter convinced us that there were greater forces at play, and thus we traveled with her to this city in hopes of discovering the truth."

The King grunted.

"They will need places to stay, Father," Ilyana said, her voice strengthening. "At least for a few weeks—until we can get this sorted out."

Eyeing Arthion and Elric, the King stepped toward Ilyana again. "You say that Callum told you I was dead?"

Ilyana nodded.

King Nightingale raised a curved eyebrow, looking almost exactly like Ilyana did when she made the same expression. "You swear it?"

"On my life," Ilyana said.

"Interesting," the King said, recovering his composure. "He has not yet returned from Arvendon—though he was supposed to two days ago. And he left Celes well before we were attacked. I don't see how he could've known about it before meeting with you."

"Wait," Ilyana started. "Attacked?"

"On the night of the Solstice." King Nightingale nodded. "A Shadow-Swift attacked the Palace, seemingly intending to kill *me*."

Ilyana glanced at Castien, then back to her father. "There were two Shadow-Swifts present in Arvendon on the Solstice," Ilyana breathed. "They attacked the Prince, and then fought one another."

"Three Shadow-Swifts on one night?" Elric turned to the King. "Are you certain there was one in Celes?"

"I wouldn't believe it had I not seen him with my own eyes," the King said. "But he was here."

"I have a question, if I may," Arthion said. "How did you survive the attack, Your Majesty? Shadow-Swifts are all but unstoppable. How did you manage to fight one off?"

"You are mistaken, Whisperer," King Nightingale said. "For it was Hykir and Likara who defended me from the Shadow-Swift."

"Who?" Ilyana asked.

Freyfallion names? Castien thought.

"The Blood Sorcerers," King Nightingale said. "The two of them have stationed themselves in the city."

"So it is true," Elric said softly. "Elos has fallen to the Blood Sorcerers."

"'Fallen' is not necessarily the right word," the King said. "The Blood Sorcerers entered the city several weeks ago—just as my emissaries say they entered yours—and warned me that a great threat was on the horizon. I allowed them to take up residence in an old tavern. In a later conversation, they claimed that they would need the help of our armies when the time came... I, of course, said that I would not surrender control of Celes's forces... But then there was the matter of the attack.

"During the Solstice's celebrations, a Shadow-Swift descended from the sky," the King continued. "Within moments, the Blood Sorcerers rushed to my defense. After a short bout with the Shadow-Swift, they managed to force him to retreat."

Gods, Castien thought. *They can even fight off a Shadow-Swift?*

"They returned to their tavern as soon as the threat was gone," King Nightingale said. "Whoever commands them has seemingly forbidden them from revealing their true plans, for they have hardly told me anything beyond what they need from our city."

"They want your armies... but for what?" Castien asked, speaking up for the first time.

"I am afraid I do not know," the King said, meeting his gaze. "But I can only surmise that the Shadow-Swifts are a part of the threat the Blood Sorcerers are warning us of."

"From what we understand, the Blood Sorcerers have sent members of their order to every capital on Auris," Ilyana said, her brow furrowed. "Would Shadow-Swifts really require such a large force to dispatch?"

"And why won't the Blood Sorcerers tell anyone anything about what they're planning?" Elric asked no one in particular. "They didn't even mention the Shadow-Swifts to King Titansworn, they just demanded control of the city."

The King stared at each of them, finally setting on Ilyana. "These are questions that I cannot answer," King Nightingale said. "But fortunately, I know of two in this city who might be able to help us."

CHAPTER THIRTEEN

THE CRYOSTALKER

Luka Delmorian stood in the frozen Frostfall, observing the city before him.

Four gates. Freyfall is positioned on a cliff overlooking the Northern Sea. Perhaps two miles across, one mile in depth. Walls surrounding the city, guard towers positioned every thirty feet. No easy points of entry besides the main gate. Luka completed his assessment and grumbled.

Freyfall was a large capital, one of the biggest on the continent. Luka had been here several times before, of course. Having traveled everywhere, save for Elan Taesi, there wasn't much that Luka hadn't seen. Elan Taesi was exclusively inhabited by reclusive Navesian monks who never accepted visitors, and thus Luka knew he wasn't missing much.

It had taken him longer than usual to cross The Highlands, but he had slowed his pace for the sake of trying to keep an eye out for the Blood Sorcerers. He had—shockingly—been unsuccessful. Yet, he was in Freyfall now.

It had been weeks since his last contact with the rest of the world. He hadn't spoken in quite a while, and why would he need to?

It was just him and his power... He was living life as it should be lived.

King Avenos would be wondering where he was by now, which was why his arrival in Freyfall had come at a good time. Luka had spent much of the journey climbing up the mountains, then sliding down them with the aid of his Summoning, though he admitted to taking his time with this.

The Blood Sorcerers were hiding somewhere in The Highlands, though there was far too much ground for Luka to cover alone. Besides, that wasn't his mission; he was supposed to investigate what they had done to Freyfall and then return to Arvendon before Velarus's legion arrived.

King Wickenhardt doesn't allow visitors, Luka remembered, his attention shifting to the task at hand. *I'll need to find a quiet way in...* Luka looked to the snow-covered road leading into the city. It was a busy highway, and he knew he wouldn't have to wait long before someone passed.

Moments later, a small caravan approached from the southwest. *A good opportunity to enter unnoticed,* Luka thought.

Luka lowered himself, drawing upon the Crystals hanging at his side and coating his feet in ice. A thrill *rushed* through his body as the glorious chill of Summoning burst through his veins. With a push, he began sliding down the mountain.

Relying on his flawless balance, Luka slid. He flew over the densely packed snow, speeding toward the caravan below.

Three wagons, twenty-four people, Luka counted quickly. *Many with their hoods up.*

The thrill slowly dispelled as he thawed his feet and slowed to a walk. Summoning was everything to him. It was a gift from the Six Gods that the Stormless would never understand. *What a terrible fate —to be Stormless,* Luka thought. *There is so much they do not know... So much they could never understand.*

Luka was perhaps one hundred feet behind the caravan now, and his silent approach had gone unnoticed. A quick diversion would allow him to slip into the back of the group with ease.

He slowed to a stop and reached down to the snow-covered ground. He readied the Crystals beneath his coat. With a *push*, he sent a powerful burst of ice burrowing underneath the caravan. Luka closed his eyes, guiding the underground mound of ice through the snow, toward the front of the group.

Once he was certain it was far enough in front of the group, he *pulled* on his power, commanding it to rise out of the ground.

Glancing ahead, Luka watched as a large ice spike shot out of the ground in a small explosion of snow.

People shouted in Utryan, running toward the front of the wagons, leaving Luka the perfect opportunity to pull up his hood and slip behind the back wagon. He walked closely enough to the wagon to be hidden from most who would be looking.

A few more people called out in Utryan as they passed the icicle, which Luka was quite proud of. No one would think much of it—Cryostalkers were among the most common Summoners in Freyfall, and they often liked to play tricks.

Many of the Utryans stayed up at the front, as they were only a few hundred feet away from the main gates by now.

Luka looked up as they approached. *Fourteen guards manning the gate, likely with dozens more just a level or two below.* Freyfall was a well-defended city, Luka would give it that.

"The Tower City," as it was called. The buildings were *massive*, and almost all of them were arranged as huge, sprawling keeps that housed dozens. There were nearly a hundred of these buildings in the city, and thus it was no wonder that Freyfall housed a disproportionately large percentage of Auris's population, though Suchara's population was still greater. Everything here was built of the same dark stone that made up the mountains of The Highlands, giving the massive city a rather ominous look.

The black walls of Freyfall were nearly the same size as Arvendon's, though Luka found them to be near worthless considering that any invaders would have the considerable advantage of high ground. Of course, Freyfall made up for what they lacked in geographical advantages by keeping their walls better defended than any other city on Auris.

Coming to a stop at the base of the stone gates, the caravan awaited entry. Snow fell on Luka's face as he watched the guards rush to the pulleys and levers. The snow felt warm on his dry, cracked skin.

The guards wore black, of course, and their armor was decorated with the same crest that was carved into the large stone doors: a greyfur. Luka's own armor was mostly covered with snow, and his brown cloak covered him well enough to conceal his identity; he could enter with no problems.

Luka looked upward, staring at the white dome that covered the city. *The ward.*

Freyfall had pushed their city as far as possible, placing buildings up against the edge of their ward. *Helionn's Sun,* Luka thought. *What has become of our world?*

Within a few moments, the gates had been pulled open and the caravan entered.

Luka entered slowly, feeling steady on the snow-covered ground as flakes of pure cold continued to fall from the sky. Frostfalls felt like *home* to him. Something about the cold, the snow, and the sheer frozen energy was just... calming.

As he passed through the ward, the flakes thinned. The cold grew less biting, and the winds grew softer. Luka quickly broke away from the group, staring out at the narrow streets ahead of him.

Freyfall hadn't changed much since his last visit, though it was a bit more crowded. Of course, the air today was considerably *less* cold than usual, so it made sense that there were more people out on the black stone streets.

A few guards patrolling the roads, nothing unusual, Luka noted, eyeing the black-armored soldiers weaving in and out of the crowds.

The city had long been dealing with the troubles of overcrowding. Luka was well-versed enough in history to know that Freyfall hadn't always been right up against the ward. Yet, due to Utryan customs, most people in the country ended up having more children than they had any right to, and as a result, one could only expect that their city soon became overpopulated.

Still, it was better off than Suchara, for people were not actively being forced out of the city to make room for others. Freyfall had access to the Northern Sea, which meant a good supply of snowfins were brought in almost daily to feed the city. On top of that, iceblooms from the Ice Fields in the North provided even more food. Yet, from what Luka had heard, the Ice Fields were becoming just as crowded as the city itself, despite the area not being protected by a ward. Of course, almost every day was a Frostfall this far north, so the wards were slightly less necessary for survival.

Massive keeps of black stone towered over him in all directions, some more than five or six stories tall. They were at least several hundred feet in width and length, with some surpassing even that.

The troops seem more active than usual, Luka noted, observing one of the keeps closest to the wall. Soldiers in black wheeled supplies and weapons in and out of the building with apparent haste. *Is there another conflict beginning in The Highlands?*

Luka turned his attention to the road ahead and began walking. He stepped out of the way of a merchant wheeling his goods, keeping his eyes fixed on the keep. Torches—fueled by Incendiary—glowed through the small slits of windows that dotted the keeps he passed.

Many of the rooms would be the homes of families, whereas others would serve as offices or even taverns. Freyfall had been organized in a fashion that promoted a close-knit community, though Luka could see plainly that it didn't appear to be working. Yet it was a fresh sight regardless. Luka couldn't believe that some people lived in Arvendon their entire lives without seeing any of Auris's other cities.

He passed by another large keep that served as a crossroads. The streets sprawled out in many directions beyond this central keep, with more massive buildings lining every inch of the road. Many people were walking, pushing various goods through the city.

Yes, the streets are crowded today, Luka thought. There were several covered areas around the buildings, with glowing torches and large barrels that were presumably waiting to be moved.

Luka passed by another set of buildings, making for the farthest part of the city—where the castle was nestled atop a cliff overlooking the Northern Sea. Thankfully, Freyfall was greater in length than it was in width, meaning that Luka wouldn't have to walk too far.

He passed by an exceptionally large building in what appeared to be the very center of the city. It was undoubtedly a cathedral, which made Luka start to wonder if it had been as extravagant on his last visit. Freyfall seemed to be trying to compete with Elan Taesi in their worship of Niventia.

Luka passed what he presumed to be the library—given the sheer *size* of the keep he was currently circumventing. Freyfall was famous for this building, though Luka had no interest in it. Anything important could be learned through experience, and he had *plenty* of that—so he had no need to waste his time between the covers of a book.

After several more blocks of walking, Luka grew closer to the castle.

Passing another keep, it finally came into view. The castle was actually shorter than most of the other buildings in the city. It made sense, given that the castle was built first and was left alone for the fear of placing too much weight on the cliff it sat on.

Luka paused for a moment, letting another Freyfallion citizen pass him as he stared out at the castle.

King Theurgi Wickenhardt's chambers would be on the western end. The King was... well, mad. Though even that term didn't do the King's deranged nature justice. Freyfall's royal family had long been known to inbreed, so it was to be expected that the practice would eventually catch up to them.

Avenos had always warned that Theurgi was more dangerous than Luka gave him credit for, but Luka did not fear him. Luka feared nothing, not even the Shadow-Swifts... *And not the Blood Sorcerers,* Luka thought with a snort.

The square rooftops of the castle were covered with snow, though the stone beneath was black. Within a few moments, Luka neared the small set of doors in the front of the massive building and paused before the quartet of guards.

Four guards, armed with cudgels. Breaking into the castle would be unwise. Better to reveal myself now, rather than forcing myself to fight my way in, Luka thought. Sneaking into the city with the caravan had saved him the trouble of being stopped at the gates. Besides, now that he was within the city, the guards here would assume that he was supposed to be here.

Luka bowed before the guards, then lowered his hood—revealing his Arvendi face. One of the guards would be fluent in the Eastern Tongue; Luka just had to wait for them to step forward.

"An Arvendi?" the guard asked, stepping forward. His puffy, bearded face bulged out from behind the black helmet—giving him a somewhat comical look. "Been a while since one of you has been let into the city."

"My name is Luka Delmorian," Luka said. "I have been granted entry to this city for the sole purpose of speaking with King Wickenhardt."

The guards exchanged a look, then muttered something in Utryan.

Luka sighed again. He had a strong dislike for men who spoke in another language in front of someone who they knew wasn't fluent. Though it was entirely possible that the other guards simply didn't speak the Eastern Tongue... Either way, it was annoying.

The guard turned back to Luka after a moment, a curious smile on his face. "Delmorian, you said?"

Luka nodded.

"You may enter," the guard said, stepping back to the door and using his key to unlock it. He pushed it open after a minute, then hesitated, motioning for Luka to enter. "King Wickenhardt is in the grand western chamber."

"I... know," Luka said, hesitating. *That was easier than I thought.* Luka advanced cautiously.

Something was off about this. Laying a hand on his sword, Luka continued forward. *Best to be on my guard.* He looked around the inside of the castle, feeling the horrible, suffocating warmth of the building crash into him. He weakened, thawing a bit of his power to keep himself cool. Luka relaxed as the ice returned to his veins, giving him that *rush.* It was not unreasonable. It was a Frostfall, and they were very common this far north. His Crystals would be refilled in no time.

The interior of the castle was largely bland and uninteresting. He was in the entry hall, which consisted mostly of dark furniture and bright torches. There were several massive banners bearing the imposing figure of a greyfur hanging on the black walls. A few slits of windows were present on the back end of the building, offering a view of the Northern Sea.

Luka turned to the left, passing a set of guards as he walked. *Four, again armed with cudgels.* He would be recognized here. The guards inside of the castle were rarely changed, and Luka found that his particular skin condition made him memorable.

Passing another set of guards—*five this time, led by a captain with a longsword*—Luka continued down the long hallway. Stone columns lined the corridor, along with countless rooms on either side of it. Luka knew that there wasn't much to be said about the government of Freyfall, for it was almost solely controlled by the King. Arvendon at least had the King's Council, and Luka knew Celes had the process of the royal family voting on their next leader. Freyfall seemed entirely based on tradition; the eldest son of the King would be the next ruler, and that was that.

Luka passed another set of closed doors defended by four armed guards dressed in all black. He strode past them, closing his eyes for a moment and feeling the glorious freezing sensation running through his bones.

By the time he refocused on the world around him, he was nearly at the King's chamber.

He paused before the large open doorway, which extended toward the west, rather than toward the sea. Theurgi had always made a point of keeping the King's chambers entirely on the interior of the castle, for fear of being attacked from the outside.

A quartet of guards stood outside the doors to the throne room.

One stepped forward, raising his hand. "Stop where you are," the guard commanded, speaking in the Eastern Tongue. "Your weapons and Crystals, please."

Luka paused. Something was certainly wrong here. His gut told him to keep his sword, but how would he get past the guards if he did? *I'll keep my Crystals,* Luka thought. He wore some on the outside of his coat, but the rest were safely hidden within.

"Of course," Luka said, unhooking his belt. He handed his sheathed sword to the guard, then proceeded to slide his Crystal ring off his belt as well. "Be careful with them," Luka said, handing the three ice-blue Crystals to the guard. He paused, feeling the *chill* within the jagged, glowing Crystals.

It called to him, but that would have to wait. He would retrieve his sword if necessary, and he had enough Crystals within his coat to get him through a fight if need be.

The lead guard nodded to one of his comrades, who promptly opened the set of double doors for Luka.

Pillars extended in all directions within the large throne room, making for many dark corners and crevices where hidden guards were undoubtedly stationed. Theurgi Wickenhardt was conversing with a man in dark robes as Luka stepped in. The King's gray beard was almost as scraggly and disheveled as his hair. He turned his dark eyes to Luka almost instantly, his conversation ceasing.

He waved the attendant off, shifting in his steel throne. The old man wore weathered black robes, watching with a predatory air as Luka strode through the dim chamber.

"Luka Delmorian," Theurgi boomed, his voice heavy and loud. His puffy Utryan face twisted into a strange smile. "I wouldn't have expected Arvendon to send someone so soon... Much less someone of your position."

"So, you know why I am here then?" Luka asked, stepping forward. He kept his footsteps quiet, slightly quieting the thaw of power into his veins so that he could focus.

"I would reckon that I do," Theurgi said, nodding. His voice was hollow. He seemed even more hostile today than usual.

Are the Blood Sorcerers turning the rest of Auris against us?

"So it's true that you've let the Blood Sorcerers take over your city?" Luka stopped a few dozen feet from the King's throne.

A group of six guards stood before the throne, many were likely Cryostalkers. Theurgi himself was a Whisperer, though he knew better than to try his tricks on Luka—he had already done that on their first meeting several years ago.

Theurgi's face twisted into a frown. He paused, looking to the guard with the most extravagant black armor—likely the commander. He said something in Utryan, sounding confused.

The guard said something back.

Another guard added something else.

Luka looked back and forth between the guards and the King, raising a cracked hand.

"Please," Luka said. "I know this to be true already, there is no use in denying it."

"I—" Theurgi started. He looked back to the guard and said something else.

The guard responded, seemingly starting another conversation.

"Stop hiding behind your language and tell me what is going on here!" Luka demanded. "King Avenos Titansworn has named me his top agent in foreign affairs, and I have the right to invoke his wrath if I must."

The King paused, once again holding up a wrinkled hand to silence the guard. He stared at Luka as if he were... searching. He looked back to the guard one final time, then turned his full attention to Luka.

"Well, this is truly a treat." King Wickenhardt grinned, showcasing his jagged teeth. "You left Arvendon before the Solstice, didn't you?"

"Well before," Luka said, advancing. "What does it matter?"

The King paused. A moment later, he started laughing wildly. "You don't even know, do you?"

Luka took another step forward, though he didn't dare get any nearer to the throne. "Know what?" Luka hissed. "What are you talking about?"

"Avenos is dead!" Theurgi boomed. He launched into a deafening laugh, throwing his head back and slapping his knee.

Luka froze. "*What?*"

"Someone finally took out the old bastard!" Theurgi cackled. "I knew it was only a matter of time, and now someone's finally done it!"

Luka stumbled back, stunned.

Theurgi merely continued laughing, the guards soon joining in as well. "Your King is dead," Theurgi hissed, his laughter suddenly ceasing. He leaned forward. "Dead."

"I—" Luka started. He suddenly went cold. His thawing quickened, his veins filling with an even stronger freeze. Luka lowered his eyes, running through the possibilities. It didn't take him long. "You're lying."

"I am not," Theurgi said. "Your King was killed by an assassin on the night of the Solstice. Cloudwalker messengers delivered the news a few days ago."

"But—" Luka breathed, his chest tightening. His muscles tensed, his pulse increasing. *Avenos? Dead?*

"We have aligned ourselves with another force—one that sees

you as an enemy." Theurgi leaned back. "I suppose that does make us 'enemies,' does it not?"

Luka stepped back. *The Blood Sorcerers.* Arvendon had not surrendered to their will, and so the rest of the world was turning on them at the Blood Sorcerers' command. It was the only viable explanation. Luka remembered that the soldiers had seemed strangely active today; Luka had seen dozens of them moving about around their keeps, which could only mean that they were...

"You're turning on us," Luka breathed. He turned his gaze back to Theurgi, sensing the cold heat of rage rising within him. "I saw the soldiers outside," Luka said, taking another step forward. "You're sending troops to Arvendon, aren't you?"

"The rest of the world is turning against your city," Theurgi said coldly. "Wouldn't want to be left out now, would we?"

"You—" Luka started, reaching for his sword. His hand met nothing but air. The guards on the other side of the door he had entered through still had his blade.

The commander reached for his weapon, as did the other soldiers in the room.

"Choose your actions very carefully, Cryostalker," Theurgi said, his voice low. "If you are not careful, this decision may be your last."

Luka remained still, feeling the *ice* in his blood. He could feel it pumping through his veins, cooling his muscles, freezing his mind... And it was *glorious.*

"If you let me go, I'm going to return to Arvendon and warn our armies of what's coming. You and I both know that," Luka said slowly.

Theurgi nodded, his dark eyes glowering.

Luka recognized the distant focus in Theurgi's eyes. "Izara curse you, Theurgi, leave my thoughts alone!" Luka shouted.

The look faded.

"I know you don't plan on letting me leave, regardless of what I say," Luka grunted.

"Ah," Theurgi cooed. "You are a quick one, Mr. Delmorian."

Theurgi leaned forward, his rough voice growing wicked. "You understand where I am coming from, then? I was simply planning to march on Arvendon with you in the city, but having you in *our* city—taking you out of the battle... The other nations will be indebted to us."

Luka began thawing more power from his Crystals. He watched carefully as the guards exchanged glances. *He must think I'm going to surrender...* And it was time Luka showed him that he could not be more wrong.

"Well then," Luka stepped forward, raising his hands. The air grew cold, ice crystalizing on his palms. "I suppose we should get started." Luka leaped into the air, shooting out a blast of ice, coating his immediate surroundings in frost.

The guards jumped forward, stepping between Luka and their King. Ice began coating their weapons, sharp frozen points appearing at the tip of each of their cudgels. *Cryostalkers indeed.*

Luka angled himself mid-air so that he would land directly on one of the guards. He crashed into the guard feet first, knocking him to the ground with a satisfying crunch. Luka then flipped back, landing in a half-squat. Ice flooded his veins. *Finally...*

He bolted for the doors, icing his feet and sliding with blinding speed. He crashed through the doors seconds later, sending the surprised guards on the other side flying against the walls.

Luka's sword clattered to the ground, as did his Crystals. One of the Crystals shattered as it dropped, releasing a puff of cold energy.

Luka grabbed his sword with one hand and his Crystals with the other, then turned down the hall.

Dozens of guards poured into the hallway ahead, racing toward Luka with their weapons drawn.

This was a trap, Luka thought. But he did not panic. *No...* He remained calm.

Luka spun around, barreling back into the throne room, this time with his sword.

Jumping from the ground once again, Luka crashed into the

closest guard, his sword angled forward. The soldier's chest was punctured effortlessly, Luka's iced blade sliding between his ribs with deadly precision.

Two guards advanced, shards of ice whistling through the air.

Luka ducked, reaching out and using his power to *pull* back one of the passing ice-daggers. He slid, icing his feet to move more quickly. Luka thrust his hand forward, forcing the shards to change direction. With a grunt, he commanded them to fly back toward the Cryostalker who Summoned them.

The soldier screamed, his reactions too slow to stop an ice shard from slicing through his shoulder.

Footsteps sounded behind him. The soldiers from the hall were finally entering the throne room.

Good, Luka thought. *Once they're all here I can slip past them and make a run for the main exit.*

Theurgi laughed again, watching from his throne with an almost giddy sense of excitement.

Luka inched closer to the door as the guards continued pouring in, dropping into a low slide and holding his bloodied sword sideways. He cut down another soldier, then stabbed the next.

The soldier wrenched away as he fell, tearing the blade from Luka's hands.

Luka cursed, ducking a cudgel as he held out both hands.

Frozen power poured into his palms, elongating and morphing into a sleek sword of ice. *Ice-blade.* Luka spun, his dry hands gripping the blade as he shoved it down the throat of another soldier.

The soldier coughed, spitting blood onto Luka's face.

Luka jumped, sending a cryokinetic push beneath him to boost himself. More power iced through his veins, filling him with the glorious rush. Luka spun, landing feet first into another group of soldiers who had filed in, showering them with razor-sharp ice shards as he fell.

Thawing more power, Luka reached out again. Another icicle

formed in his hand, shooting from his palm at his command and crashing into the armor of a guard.

The man shouted, falling back from the force of the blow.

Theurgi shouted something.

Luka smirked, feeling the rush again as he turned back to the ever-growing number of guards who poured in. He was beyond these men. Luka was beyond *everything*. His city needed him, and Luka was not going to let this cursed King keep him here.

Something slammed into him from the left, knocking him to the ground. Luka slid past the guards, crashing into a pillar with a painful *crunch*. Luka groaned but thawed a large burst of energy to numb the pain.

The rush came again, throwing him back to his feet to face his assailant.

A soldier wearing a mint-green band on his shoulder stood behind the charging guards. *Cloudwalker.*

Ducking another attack and icing his feet, Luka slid between the guards' flying cudgels. He heard screaming behind him, making sure to leave a trail of ice as he slid. The guards would be hitting each other, thanks to Luka's slicked floor.

The Cloudwalker raised his hands, throwing another gust at Luka. Luka growled, pushing through the slight inconvenience as if it were nothing. *Weaker than the last one...* Luka thought.

Then he saw why.

A blast of flame crashed into him from the side, then flared. His ice-blade melted instantly, as did the forming icicle in his hand. Luka slid to the ground, his dried skin sizzling at the air-fueled fire blast.

Luka twisted from the ground as the soldiers closed in, scanning for the Scorcher and the Cloudwalker. *More of Theurgi's Summoners are arriving.* But it was nothing he couldn't handle. This was child's play, and Luka... Luka was practically a *god*.

He pushed off the floor, landing on iced feet and sliding headfirst into the group surrounding him. Luka conjured several more ice spikes, feeling the rush in his veins once again.

Throwing out his hands, Luka let out a battle cry as over a dozen soldiers collapsed, felled by his shards. Luka continued, jumping once again as he charged the Scorcher.

He landed on something hard, then slid backward. With a start, Luka spun to face one of the original Cryostalkers—who had summoned a shield of ice around the Scorcher.

Luka spun back as the ice shattered, blasted to pieces by a fireball. The puffy-faced Utryans advanced, the Stormless guards forming up behind him. The Scorcher, Cloudwalker, and Cryostalker circled before him.

Grunting, Luka reached deep within himself, pulling up the very same power that had killed the nrekuma several weeks before. This wasn't going to be easy, but he *was* going to make it out of here alive.

The soldiers charged. A wave of fire flew toward him, a storm of ice riding beneath it, all pushed by a powerful Cloudwalker wind.

Luka *roared*, throwing his hands to the sky.

Ice exploded from the ground, shooting upward and impaling dozens of soldiers— knocking all three Summoners from their feet. Then, everything stopped. The room seemed to hold its breath as Luka brought his outstretched hands back to center, his palms still open.

He closed them.

The ice shattered, sending living and dead alike flying across the throne room, casting it into chaos. Luka grunted, feeling the toxic warmth of blood in several places on his body. His skin grew colder, plunging him into ecstasy and easing the pain. Permafrost was growing ever closer, and Luka yearned for it.

The cold grew more powerful, firing into his bones and muscles with a glorious ferocity as Luka sprinted for the doorway. The soldiers were still reorienting themselves, and Luka had ample opportunity to escape. It was almost like it had been too easy. Luka was a Cryostalker. No, not just any Cryostalker, he was *the* Cryostalker—the most powerful of his Sect on the continent. He was a special agent of Arvendon, and no one could stop him. Nothing would—

Just as Luka was growing near the doorway, someone entered.

Luka recognized the dark red, veined robe. *Blood Sorcerer.*

The Blood Sorcerer stared at Luka, intrigued. He raised his hands, orbs of blood conjuring in his open palms.

Luka growled, raising a hand and preparing a spear of ice.

His hand froze, stopping as if of its own volition. Red energy wrapped around his arm, forcing it downward. Seconds later, Luka froze entirely, unable to move.

He fell to the ground, his muscles locked.

"Impressive," the Blood Sorcerer mused.

Luka heard the footsteps as he approached, though he remained frozen—looking at the ground.

"I had heard stories of Arvendon's masterful Cryostalker—a warrior unlike any other," the Blood Sorcerer continued. "But I never would've expected *this.*"

Grunting, Luka tried to move. Whatever spell the Blood Sorcerer had cast continued to hold strong.

"Kill him!" Theurgi roared distantly. "He murdered my men! Kill him now!"

"No," the Blood Sorcerer snapped. "Take him to the dungeon and remove his Crystals. I'll deal with him *personally.*"

Luka's vision began to dim. A splitting headache came on as if out of nowhere, and within seconds Luka knew he was losing consciousness. *Arvendon will never know,* Luka's thoughts raced. *Freyfall is attacking, and they won't even know they're coming.*

"See you soon," the Blood Sorcerer whispered. And the whole world went black.

CHAPTER FOURTEEN

IGNITE

Faelyn Titansworn awoke to the sound of the waves crashing against the ship. He lay in the King's chambers of the small vessel, allowing his eyes to adjust to the morning light.

A sense of dread flooded his dazed mind, casting him into a state of general discomfort. This was normal, as he had spent the last five days angry and uncomfortable. The guilt set in soon enough, slipping into the pockets of his mind and slowly infecting each and every thought. Even as he turned over in bed, he accredited the movement to his failures. If he had listened to Eithor, then he wouldn't even be here right now. If he had protected his father, then he wouldn't have to do this.

Yet he hadn't done any of that. He *was* here right now, because he had taken the wrong turn at every junction over the last few weeks... And now, he had to make things right.

The peaceful rocking of the ship centered him. There was work to do today. After sailing for just under a week—counting the day that they spent docked in a sheltered inlet to avoid a Cyclone—the ship was finally nearing its destination.

It was time for Faelyn to get up.

Sunbirds cawed overhead, their passionate cries washing away the last of Faelyn's tiredness and bringing him to a state of lucidity. He rose from his creaky bed with little difficulty and slipped on a white-gold coat and matching pants before making for the door to the stairs. As always, he hooked a few Crystals onto his right hip just in case.

He wasn't sure when the ship would lay anchor, but he supposed it didn't really matter. The sailors who manned the ship had a certain sense of disorganization about them that Faelyn found to be a welcome change of pace from life in the Palace.

He opened the wooden door, striding up the rocking stairs as the ship swayed back and forth. The warm marine air greeted him as he stepped out onto the deck, appearing near the front starboard side. His cabin was the nicest on the ship, though it still only consisted of a small bedroom and washroom. The sun was beginning to rise, bringing with it the bright sunbeams and powerful heat of a Blazeday.

Faelyn soaked in the warmth, breathing it into his skin. A state of calm settled over him, filling his veins and blanketing his mind.

One of the deckhands stooped past him, making for the other end of the ship.

Faelyn stepped to the side, allowing him to pass without a word.

The deckhand wore dark brown clothing, though he had a red band wrapped around his right shoulder—marking him as one of the higher-ranking sailors. He reached a lever at the tail end of the small ship and shifted it to the side. The massive, thick white sail overhead turned ever so slightly, catching the wind at a different angle and pushing the ship closer to shore.

"What is he doing?" Faelyn asked another passing deckhand.

The young man stopped and bowed before answering. "We are getting close to our point of anchor, Your Majesty," the deckhand said. "Cyfalion is roughly four miles from here, and we have been directed to lay anchor near the approaching beach."

Faelyn looked south, seeing the tip of Cyfalion's massive clock tower in the distance. *Yes, we are getting close.* He glanced off toward the shore, where The Wastelands were becoming progressively greener with each passing hour. Storms were less intense in the South, for Blazedays, Wispwinds, Mistveils, and Slick-Days made up most of the Tempests—leaving very few Storm Gales, Frostfalls, and Cyclones.

The ghost trees slowly gave way to what were called "greenbranches," which were considerably taller, with many more twists and complex turns than central Auris's ghost trees. The greenbranches had a far denser coverage of the land as well, giving the South a very distinctive feel.

The entire landscape seemed to be covered by an assortment of shorter, green-leaved plants. Faelyn recalled learning about the flora of the South during his schooling when he was younger. He had forgotten much of it, but he did know that the plant coverage of Jaskye was far denser than that of the central and northern parts of Auris.

The greenbranches and plants covered the landscape to the extent that Faelyn could hardly see more than a few hundred feet into the jungles as they approached their docking point. *It will be easy to sneak up on Cyfalion,* Faelyn thought. This would be easier than he expected, for the wilderness of Jaskye seemed to provide more cover from both the Tempests and the Cyfali guards than Faelyn had anticipated.

The air had a strange moisture to it that confused Faelyn. It felt as if a Mistveil or Storm Gale had just ended, yet it felt like that *all* the time. It was strange, but he surmised that these conditions must be what allowed the strange plants of Jaskye to grow here.

As the ship neared the shore, the deep blue water became shallower, and Faelyn thought that he might even be able to see the bottom as he looked over the edge. He tilted his head back up, watching as the greenvines slowly came into view. *Greenvines, part of Cyfalion's crest.*

Faelyn had never been to Cyfalion, though he knew that the

buildings were said to be constructed mostly of a combination of greenbranch wood and stone. He also knew that the clock tower was considered one of the most impressive buildings on Auris. Turning back to the south, he observed the way that the *unbelievably* tall tower seemed to pierce the sky. Squinting, he could even make out the transparent arc of the ward just above it.

He turned back, leaning over the side of the ship and watching the beach grow nearer as he pondered a thought. No one—in all of Auris's history—had ever destroyed one of the wards. It was heresy in its highest form, and even now Faelyn knew it would be a step too far. Sure, destroying the ward would hurt Cyfalion *now*, but it would doom the entire city for the rest of time as well. And Faelyn... Well, Faelyn wasn't sure he wanted that in addition to the guilt he already felt. Yet, even still, he couldn't help but wonder what it might be like if one of Auris's five wards finally fell.

The wards were powered by Monoliths that had been built by the Rune-Writers, and they were positioned around what would later become the five major cities of Auris. Only those five wards were built, for only the Rune-Writers possessed the kind of power that could directly *ward* off the Tempests... And given that the Rune-Writers had died off in the Vanishing, Faelyn knew just as well as anyone else that no more Monoliths would ever be built.

A fun thought, Faelyn mused, thinking of the possibility of attacking Cyfalion's Monoliths. *But a foolish one.* Hearing footsteps to the side, Faelyn turned slightly to find himself facing Eithor.

"I know that this is your first time in Jaskye, and that you have never been to Cyfalion," Eithor said. "But trust me, Faelyn, this is the right course of action."

"I know it is," Faelyn said, keeping his eyes fixed on the shoreline.

"Then why the hesitation?" Eithor asked.

"Do not mistake my silence for apprehension, Eithor," Faelyn said, turning his gaze slightly.

Eithor nodded, his ice-blue eyes falling. His withered body

seemed stronger now than it had before... almost as if he had initially been acting weaker than he truly was. *Curious.*

That hot rage settled over Faelyn the longer he stood there. He needed to do this. This *was* the right decision. Eithor was right—just as he always was. *Then why am I questioning myself?* Faelyn shook his head, allowing himself to fall deeper into the hot anger. What he was planning wasn't wrong; it was justice.

"Are you comfortable with the plan?" Eithor asked after a moment.

"Wheel the catapults and Incendiary to the rise just northwest of Cyfalion, launch the Incendiary into the city once night falls tomorrow, and then burn as much of that blasted place as we can," Faelyn said, nodding. "Yeah, I'm comfortable with that."

"You need to be ready for a quick retreat," Eithor said. "We can't expect to hit the entire city and escape unharmed."

"I know," Faelyn said. "But that's where you come in."

Eithor fell silent, seemingly trying to process his words. "Your Grace?"

"You are an Illusomancer," Faelyn said, turning his head slightly. "You can create distractions for us, give us time to get the job done and get out, right?"

"Uh..." Eithor stuttered. "Certainly, Your Grace. A good addition to the plan."

Faelyn grunted, allowing his face to fall back into a frown.

Eithor stood beside him in silence for several moments, watching as the green jungles of Jaskye slowly grew closer. The rocking of the ship became less intense, and the sea grew shallower. It was not long before the deckhands were shouting to one another, lowering the sails and preparing to drop the anchor.

"Your armor is almost ready," Eithor said finally.

A loud *thunk* indicated that the anchor had been dropped and the landing boats were being readied.

Faelyn grumbled. He still wasn't entirely sure why he needed a new set of armor. Although he supposed that every time he had used his powers lately, a good amount of his clothing had burned off.

"I think that you will find it... satisfactory," Eithor said, the word dripping from his lips.

"How many Crystals does it hold?" Faelyn asked, instinctively reaching for the Crystals that hung on his right hip.

"More than you could ever possibly need." Eithor smiled. "The compartments are larger than anything Hubys has ever made."

Faelyn grunted, turning away and making for the opposite side of the ship where the landing boats were being hooked into ropes and lowered to the shallow sea.

"I want you with me," Faelyn said, walking away. He forced authority into his step, powering each footfall with an air of strength. "We will make for the shore and travel under the cover of the jungle toward the rise northwest of Cyfalion. Once night falls, we will attack."

"Of course, Your Grace." Eithor bowed and started after Faelyn.

Faelyn turned back to the jungle, feeling the scorching heat of the Blazeday on his back. If the others stayed out in the sun much longer, they would get sunburned. Faelyn, of course, didn't have to worry about that given that he was a Scorcher.

He couldn't help staring off into the wilderness—so different from The Wastelands back home. This land was foreign, even beautiful. But he was here on a mission to *destroy*. He meant to burn anything and everything his flames could reach. Over ten thousand people lived in the crowded city of Cyfalion, and Faelyn couldn't help but wonder how many of them would die in the assault.

Faelyn found himself eyeing the tip of the massive Cyfali clock tower—just visible over the rise to the south. *I doubt I can bring that down*, Faelyn thought. *But an intriguing thought nonetheless.*

"Come." Faelyn motioned. "We have no time to waste."

"As you wish." Eithor bowed again and slithered forward, approaching one of the boats as it was being loaded.

Faelyn started to follow him, scanning the deck as he saw Hubys carrying a large box with him. *That must be the armor.*

It was loaded onto one of the smaller shore boats.

Eithor had told him yesterday that it would be carried to the rise by the guards, for it was apparently too heavy to wear for long walks.

Faelyn's muscles would strengthen once he started tapping into his Summoning, so the armor's weight wouldn't matter during the assault, fortunately. But still, it would make their trip to the rise a little more inconvenient.

He strode forward, for it was time to board the boat and do what must be done. Yet, as he started walking toward it, a thought struck him. It was clear and crisp. It was a command, coming from the deepest parts of the building primordial rage within him.

He veered to the right, opening the door to the interior of the ship and disappearing down the stairs toward his cabin once again.

The morning light poured through the windows in the bow of the ship, illuminating the dull bed and reflecting off the small mirror in the washroom. Faelyn scanned the room, taking one final look at it.

When he returned, things would not be the same. When he returned, Arvendon would not be the only city suffering, and Avenos Titansworn would not be the only monarch who had fallen.

Faelyn reached his desk, his hand hovering over the object of his attention.

It shimmered in the morning light. It still disgusted him. Its image still haunted his dreams. Yet he knew that the time to wear it was coming. Over the course of the past few days, Faelyn had been growing more and more accustomed to the look of it. *Yes,* he would wear it soon.

Soon, he would become who he was meant to be.

Faelyn took a deep breath and grabbed his crown.

CHAPTER FIFTEEN

ANSWERS

Castien Varic watched as King Nightingale rapped on the tavern door. The building was smaller than Castien had imagined, though he hadn't been to any bars outside of Arvendon, so he wasn't really sure what to expect.

The tavern was built of the same dark Highland stone that the rest of the city was, and the roof was the same cobalt blue as all of the others in the city. Windows lined the outside of the building, though they were shuttered.

Within a few moments, they heard footsteps on the other side of the door. A slit opened at eye level, and a pair of dark brown eyes peered out at them.

"Yes?" the person—presumably a Blood Sorcerer—asked in a thick Utryan accent. His eyes scanned the group, then settled back on King Nightingale.

Castien looked back to where Elric, Arthion, and Ilyana stood a few feet behind. Beyond them was a small squadron of guards, for the King couldn't travel without protection, of course.

"Hykir, I need to speak with you," King Nightingale said. After Hykir's apparent hesitation, the King added, "I am still indebted to you for what you did on the Solstice. I can assure you that we mean you no harm. We just want to talk."

Hykir grunted, then Castien heard multiple locks clicking on the other side of the door. As he pulled open the door, Hykir frowned. He was plainly Utryan, as evidenced by his pale, puffy face and stout build. He wore a dark red robe that really didn't fit his form too well, as if it were hastily made.

"Thank you," the King said, stepping inside the small tavern. "With me are Elric, Arthion, and Castien... and, of course, my daughter Ilyana." King Nightingale motioned to the four of them, waving for them to enter.

The inside of the tavern was a bit underwhelming, as it had clearly been neglected by the Blood Sorcerers for a few weeks now. There were a few chairs and tables scattered about, likely untouched since the Blood Sorcerers arrived. Toward the back of the room lay the stone bar, which was complete with flagons and glasses hanging overhead from the low ceiling.

Castien had never really liked drinking, so he didn't go to Arvendon's taverns often. So while he didn't have much to compare it to, this bar seemed nice enough. Still, there were only a half dozen tables here, making this a smaller establishment than most.

Likely why they handed it over to the Blood Sorcerers, Castien thought.

"Allow me to gather Likara, she will want to be here too," Hykir said, walking toward the staircase built into the wall on the left. He disappeared up the wooden stairs, and Castien heard him speaking in Utryan somewhere above.

"Watch the door," King Nightingale ordered his guards. "Four on the outside, three in here with me."

The guards arranged themselves accordingly, and four of them walked out the door. Castien watched the soldiers clad in blue as they shut the door, ensuring that no one else could enter. There was likely a small crowd gathering outside, as Castien was certain that a meeting with the Blood Sorcerers wouldn't go unnoticed.

A few moments later, Hykir returned with an Utryan woman in tow. She wore the same style robe, which also didn't fit her very well. She had short black hair and black eyes to match, though there was a certain beauty to her Utryan face that Castien found intriguing.

"Please, sit," Hykir said. He pulled back a wooden chair at one of the tables and sat down, motioning for the others to do the same.

The others sat down, and Castien quickly followed suit, feeling uncomfortable. *Are we really about to have a meeting with Blood Sorcerers?* This was not how he thought this day would go.

"What brings you here today?" Likara asked in an equally thick accent. Her syllables sounded forced and inconsistent, which was common for an Utryan speaking the Eastern Tongue. She seemed to be more proficient in their language than Hykir, though.

"My daughter and her... *companions* recently arrived from Arvendon," the King said, speaking slowly so that they could understand. "We have some questions for you, if you wouldn't mind answering."

"We cannot answer," Hykir said. "Our Empress forbade us from sharing our plans."

Castien found the way he spoke to be interesting. He was very straightforward, likely because he wasn't completely fluent in the Eastern Tongue. Yet still, Castien appreciated the simple way he talked.

"I understand that," the King said. "But you must try to work with us. I have no doubts that you mean me no harm, for if you did, you would've let me die that night the Shadow-Swift attacked." King Nightingale paused. "But with all of the uncertainties right now, it would be greatly appreciated if you could shed some light on your intentions."

Hykir and Likara shared a look. Likara said something in Utryan, prompting Hykir to nod.

"Who are they?" Hykir asked, motioning to Castien, Elric, Arthion, and Ilyana.

"Allies of my daughter's," the King said.

"Certain?" Hykir raised a thick eyebrow.

"I am certain," Ilyana said, speaking up from her spot beside Castien. "They helped me escape Arvendon after King Titansworn's death; you can trust them."

"Hmph," Hykir grunted. He turned to Likara and spoke in Utryan.

She said something back, then turned to King Nightingale. "I am sorry, we cannot help you."

"Let's start with that," Elric said. He sat just behind and to the left of Castien, as he had pulled a chair from another table. "Why can't you share your plans?"

Hykir started to speak, but Likara cut him off. She said something to him, likely something about letting her do the talking since she could speak more smoothly.

"Our Empress has told us that our enemy has many spies," Likara said. "She says we cannot risk telling our plans to everyone."

"Your Empress... The Blood Empress, right?" Elric asked. "Who is she?"

"She gathered all of us," Likara said. "She pulled us from Freyfall and brought us to her fortress."

"Fortress?" Arthion asked. "Where? In The Highlands?"

"Yes." Likara nodded.

"How did she convince you to leave Freyfall?" Ilyana asked. "I mean, why did you go with her?"

Likara and Hykir shared another look. Turning her gaze to the guards at the door, Likara spoke: "Send your guards outside, then we can speak freely."

"My guards stay with me," the King said firmly.

"Then we cannot tell you anything," Likara said, her voice equally firm. "Our Empress has warned that anyone could be a Skin-Shaper or Illusomancer in disguise."

Ilyana turned to her father. "Are you certain that your guards are safe?"

"Positive," the King said. "This squadron has stayed by my side day and night from the start of this madness."

Likara looked to Hykir, then back to King Nightingale. "We were tempted with the Crystals of a Blood Sorcerer." Likara sighed. "Our Empress sent a distant relative of mine, Velarus Ravamoira, to recruit us."

"*Who* is your Empress?" Elric asked. "Where did she come from? What does she want?"

"I don't know," Likara said. "She has kept her true identity closely guarded. The only one of our superiors we know by name is Velarus, and that is only because we knew him before all of this started."

"So what? He just showed you a Blood Sorcerer Crystal and you decided to follow him to the ends of Auris?" Ilyana raised a curved eyebrow.

"It was... more than that," Likara said slowly. "We grew up thinking we were Stormless, just as Velarus did. But we were able to *draw* power from the Blood Sorcerer's Crystal." Likara paused. "That was why we went with him. Getting a glimpse of Summoning after spending our whole lives powerless... We couldn't resist."

Castien started. *So there are others like me,* he thought. "Where did the Crystals come from?" Castien asked. *If they can tell me where they found Blood Sorcerer Crystals, maybe I can find more Starburner Crystals.* Castien became aware of the shattered Crystal's weight in the pocket of his vest.

"In The Highlands," Likara said. "Our fortress is practically made of them."

Castien was pretty sure the entire table's jaws dropped collectively.

"I—" the King started. "An entire fortress made of lost Crystals?"

Hykir and Likara nodded. "We only stayed there briefly," Likara said. "To learn how to use our newfound abilities."

"This Crystal fortress," Castien said. "Where in The Highlands is it?"

"The Crystals are growing inside of a mountain, in one of the large cave systems of The Highlands," Likara said. "I'm sorry, we are forbidden from telling you the exact location."

"Well, you were also forbidden from telling us anything else, so why not tell us this too?" Elric said, running a hand through his auburn hair.

Likara stared at him, unamused.

"We... can come to an agreement on that later," King Nightingale said. "The Shadow-Swifts: They are a part of the threat you warned of, correct?"

"Yes." Likara nodded.

"And you said that you will need my forces to help fight them, right?" the King asked.

"Yes." Likara nodded again.

"If you are aiming to unite the continent against the Shadow-Swifts, then why was Velarus so hostile when he entered Arvendon?" Elric asked.

"And why did he claim that he would return with a legion of Blood Sorcerers?" Arthion added.

Likara seemed hesitant to answer this question. *Why?* Castien wondered.

"Arvendon is meant to be our Empress's new stronghold," Likara finally said. "She intends to lead our forces from Arvendon."

"Against what? Just the Shadow-Swifts?" Ilyana asked.

"The Shadow-Swifts and the forces they have been gathering," Likara said.

"What forces?" the King challenged. "The Shadow-Swifts have isolated themselves from the rest of Auris for *centuries*. What forces could they possibly be gathering?"

"Stormless," Hykir blurted, speaking up for the first time in several moments.

Castien blinked. *What?*

"The Shadow-Swifts are gathering the Stormless," Hykir said.

"Why in Izara's Shadow would the Shadow-Swifts want an army of Stormless?" Elric demanded.

"Because they aren't going to be Stormless anymore," Likara

said, her voice hard. "The Resurgence has been set in motion, and when the rest of Auris finds out... all hell will break loose."

"When the rest of Auris finds out what?" the King asked, leaning forward.

"That the Stormless aren't *really* Stormless!" Likara said. "They're Ancient Summoners who just haven't had access to their Crystals for almost a thousand years."

"The Ancient Summoners were wiped out in the Vanishing!" Elric challenged.

"No." Likara shook her head. "Their *powers* were wiped out, transformed into Crystals that are hidden inside the mountains of The Highlands." Likara paused. "The Crystals are still there—*that's* where our fortress is. Our Empress found the deposition point of the Blood Sorcerers' power, harnessed her own abilities, and began gathering other Blood Sorcerers while using the Crystal caves as a fortress."

"But..." Elric trailed off. "If the Stormless are really Summoners..." Elric turned to Castien, as did everyone else.

Castien felt his face heating up. His breathing accelerated, his thoughts racing. *Well,* Castien thought. *Now's as good a time as any.* He reached into his pocket, pulled out the fragment of the Starburner Crystal, and placed it on the table.

A stunned silence fell over the group. All eyes settled on Castien, yet no one dared speak.

Castien did his best not to squirm, but he knew he had done the right thing. They needed to know, and now they did. He had drawn power from a Starburner Crystal, and that was that.

"Well then," Likara said, breaking the silence. "You're a Starburner, aren't you? Our Empress has been looking for your kind."

CHAPTER SIXTEEN

THE SHAPE OF TRUTH

The library of Celes was everything that Castien had hoped it would be. Row after row of shelves lined each wall of the massive stone chamber. It was in the very center of the city, acting as the focal point for the layout of all of Celes.

Yesterday's conversation with the Blood Sorcerers had been eventful, to say the least. Castien finally had some answers as to why he had been able to draw power from the Starburner Crystal, and for that he was thankful.

Granted, he hadn't expected to learn that *all* of the Stormless were truly Ancient Summoners, but he couldn't concern himself with that right now; thinking about the widespread chaos that would undoubtedly arise when the rest of Auris found out that information gave Castien a headache. Besides, it wasn't like there was anything he could do about that, as he was still in disbelief himself.

But he could already feel his breathing growing shallow. He didn't need to lose himself in a spell of anxiety right now, he *couldn't*. There was important work to be done, and he needed his head clear. So, he completely ignored everything that he had learned yesterday. Centering his breathing, syncing it to his pulse, and clearing his mind proved to be an effective coping mechanism—just as it was an effective way to keep Whisperers from affecting his mind.

That was why I got put on that expedition in the first place, Castien thought, aligning his breathing with his pulse. *They thought the Blood Sorcerer was a powerful Whisperer in disguise, and they thought I would be able to resist his Whispers.* Castien took another deep breath. *Don't think about that, just stay in the present.*

After their meeting with the Blood Sorcerers yesterday, Ilyana had taken the liberty of catching her father up on what Castien, Elric, and Arthion's involvement in the situation was as well as what had happened on the expedition. Castien then allowed the doctors of the Palace to treat his arm and wrap it with a new bandage. By the time all of that was over, it was growing dark, and Castien found himself finally able to get some much-needed sleep.

Castien had slept in today—finding his room quite comfortable. The King had allowed them to stay in some of the vacant nobles' quarters of the Palace.

After a long rest—and a careful shave—he found Ilyana and made his way to the library... Bringing him to where he was now.

The librarians were mostly elderly gentlemen who were incredibly pale even by Elosian standards. Ilyana had done most of the talking and had directed the librarians to show Castien and Ilyana what books they had on Starburners.

"Well, given that not much has survived the Vanishing in terms of records and history books, I'm not surprised that we haven't found much," Ilyana said, sitting down. She laid the last book that the librarians had named on the table. Eyeing the thick, withered tome on the table, Ilyana sighed. "Listen, Cas, I'm really not one for reading... So I'm not sure if I'll be much help here."

"That's alright," Castien said. He half meant it.

"Where did you learn to read anyway? I haven't known too many Arvendi soldiers, but from what I could tell they typically aren't the brightest men," Ilyana said.

"I used to read a lot back at my parents' inn," Castien said, keeping his head down. "There wasn't much to do up there, so it became my primary way of passing the time I guess."

"Your parents run an inn?" Ilyana leaned forward.

Castien kept his gaze on the book, though his brain wasn't really processing the words at the moment. "They used to," Castien said. He flipped the page, skimming the passages for any mention of Starburners and Blood Sorcerers interacting; Likara had said that the Blood Empress was searching for Starburners after Castien's reveal, though she wasn't sure why.

Regardless, Castien's decision to show the empty Starburner Crystal had been a good one. As he and Ilyana sat there, Likara and Hykir were drawing up a map of how to reach the Blood Sorcerers' fortress.

Ilyana leaned back as if sensing that Castien wasn't going to say much on this matter. "How did you end up in the Stormless Corps, then?" Ilyana asked after a moment.

"It's a long story," Castien said simply. He flipped another page, skimming the old texts once again.

"I've got time," Ilyana said.

"Ilyana," Castien raised his head, his gaze firm. "I know that reading isn't your area, but I need you to understand that this information could be *vital* to understanding what is going on right now, okay? Forgive me if this is offensive to you, but I need you to be quiet for a while. If we can figure out why this Blood Empress wants Starburners so badly, maybe we can figure out what her goals are, or why she's fighting the Shadow-Swifts. Hykir and Likara may not know those things, but maybe something in this book can help us figure it out." Castien stared at her.

Ilyana blinked a few times, then glanced at the book in Castien's hands. "Alright then," Ilyana said casually, leaning back and propping her legs up on the wooden table. "Read on. I won't bother you."

"Thank you," Castien said, lowering his head.

Now that he was actually able to focus on the words, he could start reading once again—although this book didn't appear to be much help. Many of the words were smeared, and most of the pages were withered or chipped. This was surprising, given that the book itself wasn't actually that old. All of the true records from the ancient times had been written in the Ancient Tongue, and this book was merely a modern translation.

Granted, it had likely been written a few centuries ago, judging by the grammar and sentence structure. Languages changed quickly, which Castien had slowly come to realize. To think that there was more than just the Eastern Tongue... The Utryans spoke an entirely different language, as did the whole of Asari. Thankfully, both Suchara and Freyfall held many bilingual residents, for the Eastern Tongue was used on the entire Eastern Coast of Auris and had become a trading language of sorts.

Castien pinpointed the word *Starburner* on the page before him. He read the information carefully, trying to make sense of the old form of writing. It seemed to be a short passage about how Starburners were considered to be one of the less common Sects, at least from what historians could tell from the records of the time before the Vanishing. Revenants were rare as well, though the Rune-Writers seemed to hold the prize for being the fewest in number.

Is that why those three Sects tended to be leaders in ancient societies? Castien thought. It had been quite a while since he had thought about ancient history, but he vaguely recalled reading that Starburners, Revenants, and Rune-Writers often took up positions of leadership in ancient society. It likely had something to do with their abilities.

Starburners were more suited to long-range warfare and could contribute to battles from afar. This, naturally, made them perfect generals who could both give orders from a position of safety and fight at the same time.

Revenants, on the other hand, were known for Necromancy—the ability to reanimate the dead. This made Revenants crucial in fights. If one of their strongest warriors fell, they would be able to raise them once again. Revenants also seemed to have found a way to preserve their own lives. According to the book, a single Revenant once led a legion for over two centuries before his eventual demise.

Rune-Writers were always regarded as the most powerful, of course. Little was known about their powers, other than the fact that they seemed to be capable of *literally* anything. Ancient records spoke of Rune-Writers creating unbreakable locks, generating portals that allowed one to cross Auris instantly, and, of course, building the wards to protect humanity from the Tempests.

Naturally, there was a very good chance that this information was false, or at least twisted. Of course, this made studying the time before the Vanishing rather difficult. The only resources were translations of translations of records that were mostly either destroyed or in the form of veiled, confusing folk tales.

"I have to say, I'm a little surprised that I found you here," a familiar voice said, pulling Castien from his reading. He looked up, finding Arthion standing over the table, talking to Ilyana.

"I'm only here because of him." Ilyana nodded toward Castien.

"And why is he here?" Arthion asked, shifting his gloved hands as he readjusted the book he held.

Sound Waves and Crystal Shattering, Castien read the title. *Strange choice of reading material.* He met Arthion's eyes once again. "After yesterday—when Likara said that her Empress was searching for Starburners—I was hoping to find some answers as to why, seeing as Likara didn't know," Castien said.

"Well, I doubt you're going to find much," Arthion said. "You and I both know that the records from before the Vanishing are very limited. Besides, even the best scholars in the world haven't been able to confirm the specific abilities of each Ancient Sect."

"Yeah, I'm sort of figuring that out," Castien said. He looked back to the book Arthion held.

"I suppose we'll be meeting the Blood Empress soon enough anyway," Arthion said after a moment. "Just as soon as Likara and Hykir finish drawing up that map."

"We don't leave until Callum returns," Ilyana said firmly. "I need to find out why he lied to me that night before the Solstice."

Arthion frowned slightly. "Well, then let's hope he arrives here soon. The quicker we set off for the Blood Sorcerers' fortress, the better; then we'll all have the answers we've been looking for." He started off toward another table a few feet away—giving himself just a little more space to focus on his reading.

Castien looked off toward the distant stone walls of books. A candle sat on the table, and a set of presumably Incendiary torches hung on the pillars nearby, though no Crystals were hung in this room. Crystals were only used in lighting fixtures by wealthier cities, usually.

He reached into his pocket, producing the small fragment of the multicolored Starburner Crystal. The purple, gold, orange, and red of the Crystal was faded and frozen now, looking as dull as any old piece of rock. Yet Castien felt that he could still see the vibrant energy dancing within. *Pulling...*

"That was smart," Ilyana said. "Pulling out the Crystal and showing it to the Blood Sorcerers, I mean."

"Thanks," Castien said, his voice quiet.

"So you're a Starburner, I guess. How does it feel?" Ilyana asked, smiling a bit.

"I'm... not really sure what to make of it," Castien said. "I've always just thought of myself as a Stormless. Finding out that I'm something more is just... strange."

Ilyana watched him. "I suppose that makes sense," she said. "But it's something to be excited about, right? Finding out that you actually have powers?"

"Yeah, I guess," Castien said, closing his eyes. "Honestly, at this point, I just wish I had some more Crystals so I could know for sure."

"You still think you might not be a Starburner?" Ilyana asked.

"I don't know," Castien said, opening his eyes. "It just seems so weird... spending my whole life without Summoning and suddenly learning that I've been a part of one of the most powerful Sects all along? I can hardly wrap my mind around it."

"Yeah," Ilyana said, staring off.

Castien looked down. He found that it was better to simply avoid thinking about it. Without more Starburner Crystals, he wouldn't be able to do anything anyway, and maybe that was for the best. One part of being Stormless that he found he had unknowingly appreciated was the fact that no one really expected much from him. It was sort of nice, in a sense. When he did something good, people were pleasantly surprised, and when he didn't do anything well... that was sort of expected.

But now? Being a Starburner came with expectations, and frankly, Castien wasn't sure if he would be able to live up to those expectations. He wasn't like the heroes in the stories he had read as a child. They were all perfect; they were cool, confident, and collected... And Castien was just, well, he was just Castien.

He shook his head, feeling his pulse accelerate. *This is why I don't think about this stuff,* Castien thought. *All I do is get freaked out, and what good does that do?*

"Where is Elric?" Ilyana asked, breaking the silence. "I told the servants to inform him that we would be in the library, though he hasn't shown up. He's undoubtedly awake, so why hasn't he arrived yet?"

"Give the man some space," Arthion called from his table, overhearing. "Between the onset of Breezebone and the whole thing with... you know... you murdering his King and all, I'm sure that he's been in need of some alone time. Give him a bit, I'm sure he'll turn up soon."

Ilyana nodded. "Breakdown is never easy to deal with," Ilyana said, looking to Castien. "That's one thing you'll have to watch out for if we end up finding you more Starburner Crystals."

"Yeah," Castien said absently. He had to stop himself from thinking about Breakdown, for the prospect of Summoning actually *hurting* his body made him even less enthusiastic about the idea of not being Stormless.

Rapid footsteps sounded from behind them.

Castien turned around, squinting through the dim chamber to find a panting courier running through the maze of chairs and tables.

"A messenger," Ilyana said, rising.

They watched the young man as he straightened his blue coat, still red-faced from running.

"What news do you have?" Ilyana called out.

The messenger slipped by another table, finally arriving at theirs. He leaned against the table, nearly falling from exhaustion. His legs seemed to shake.

"Good heavens, boy, are you alright?" Arthion started, rising from his seat.

The messenger waved him off, taking another few gasps of air as he tried to catch his breath. "I—" the messenger started. "He—"

"Out with it!" Ilyana commanded, grabbing the boy by the shoulders.

The messenger looked up, meeting Ilyana's gaze. "Callum has returned."

Elric Knyvet stood in his room, staring out the tall, narrow window toward the Salarin Sea below. What had become of his life? He was a commander with no King and a man with no guidance.

Avenos had been more than just a King, he had been a *friend.* Now he was gone, and Elric stood in the same city as those responsible for his murder. Yet... he was expected to *not* kill them?

He still wasn't sure why he didn't just choke the life out of both of them the moment he discovered them on that beach. His arm ached, his lightened bones feeling brittle and frail in his skin. Elric grimaced, staring down the cliff again. He had never considered himself to be easy to manipulate, yet he had somehow been convinced by his King's killers that they might somehow *not* be the enemy, and that he needed to follow them to find out who the real enemy was. Yet, perhaps the most infuriating part was that they had been right.

Shadow-Swifts had aided in the assassination of Avenos, and one had attempted to kill King Nightingale as well. *Which means that this is all some elaborate plot of the Shadow-Swifts?* Elric shook his head. It seemed impossible. Shadow-Swifts rarely interacted with the rest of Auris, yet here they were... murdering kings left and right.

And the Blood Sorcerers... They had protected Nightingale? *Would they have protected Avenos?* Elric closed his eyes. He tried to quiet his mind, finding his inner peace just as the Whisperer had taught him during his treatment.

His eyes snapped open. He couldn't. He couldn't, he just *couldn't*. It was too much. Everything was too much. Avenos was dead. That in itself was too much, yet there was so much more.

Elric's ears perked up at the sound of footsteps. He listened as the light footfalls grew closer, and then stopped.

"Looking for answers in the sea?" a voice asked. Elric continued staring out the window as King Brennan Nightingale walked up beside him.

Brennan paused before another tall, narrow window, looking out into the water as well. He wore dark blue robes today, though Elric could only see them from the corner of his eye. Even now, Elric found himself reminded of Avenos. Something about Brennan—something about all kings—was just... different. They had an air of authority, and brought with them an indescribable sense of both safety and control.

"I used to do that as well," the King said, shifting his head to face Elric. "I hate to break it to you, Cloudwalker, but you won't find what you're looking for simply by staring out the window."

"I know that," Elric grunted. The sun was bright, and little blossoms of fire seemed to dance in the winds. A Blazeday—somewhat rare in the North. "I just needed some time to think."

"Unfortunately, in this particular situation, I've found that time doesn't help too much either," Brennan said, turning back to the window.

Elric looked to the side, glancing at his large, warm bed covered in furs. His coat sat neatly folded atop the blankets, his cap and goggles sitting next to it.

"Let me guess." Elric tilted his head. "You think that I should look for answers somewhere out in the real world, rather than searching my own mind?"

"In essence, yes," King Nightingale said. "Listen, Elric—was it? I know that this is a confounding situation for all of us. But trust me when I say that this is unlike *anything* I've ever seen before. If we truly want to make sense of this, we need to know what is going on."

"And how are we supposed to do that? March up to the Blood Empress in her fortress and demand answers? I'm sure she would love that." Elric's voice rose. "Or better yet, how about we head deeper into The Highlands and seek out the secret fortress of the Shadow-Swifts. Maybe they know something about all of this. Thank you *so much*, Your Majesty, I hadn't thought of those things before." Elric breathed heavily, allowing his words to settle. He blinked a few times. He had just said that to a King. *A King. Gods,* Elric thought. *What is happening to me?*

"You have to start somewhere," Brennan said, chuckling a bit. "I don't know where that 'somewhere' is, but I trust my daughter. If anyone is going to get to the bottom of this, it'll be her."

"With all due respect, Your Majesty, your daughter killed my King. I don't exactly trust her right now." Elric's eyes narrowed.

"And with all due respect to *you*, Commander, my daughter only did so because someone else told her that it was the only way to make things right," the King said firmly. "I know that you're in mourning, I know that you're upset, and I heard that you could've killed my daughter when you captured her," he continued. "Yet something told you to spare her, correct? Where is that 'something' now?"

Elric opened his mouth, searching for a response, but he had none. He slowly closed his mouth, raising his eyes to meet the King's gaze.

"Some part of you knows that there is more to this than meets the eye," the King said. "Something greater is at play here, you know that as well as I." Brennan stepped forward. "You may have lost your King, but I suggest you help us get to the bottom of this so that the rest of Auris doesn't suffer the same fate."

"I—" Elric took a step back.

"You are one of the most powerful Cloudwalkers on this continent," Brennan continued, his eyes alight. "And you are in a *very* rare position: You have the opportunity to help us discover what is truly at stake here. Be it Shadow-Swifts or Blood Sorcerers, I don't give a shit. We need to learn the truth. So I suggest that you stop brooding over the sea, and start *helping*," Brennan finished.

Elric took a step back, his heart beating faster.

The King's gray eyes stared into him with a burning intensity.

Elric blinked a few times, shaking off the shock of the King's sudden aggression. Brennan may have been kind, and he often seemed docile, but he was still a King. He had claws—even if they were hidden deep beneath the fur.

More footsteps sounded in the hallway, rapid footsteps. Within a few seconds, a young boy in a dark blue vest appeared in the doorway, red-faced and panting from exhaustion. It looked as if he had run here from all the way across the city.

"Your Majesty," the boy gasped in between breaths. "I have news."

Brennan stepped forward, his aggressiveness retreating behind the facade of calm once more. "Tell me," the King said softly, laying a hand on the boy's shoulder.

"Callum has returned," the boy said gravely.

Brennan's face fell.

Elric took a step forward. *Ilyana's contact.*

"Thank you," Brennan said quietly, sending the boy off.

The messenger disappeared, vanishing into the hallways once again. Brennan turned around slowly, meeting Elric's eyes again. "Come on." Brennan motioned to the door. "We're going to find Callum, and we're going to figure out why the hell he wanted Avenos dead. You want to know why your King was killed? Well, you might just be in luck."

Ilyana Nightingale tore through the streets of Celes. She didn't care that she was leaving Castien and Arthion behind. She also didn't care that she was practically knocking over everyone she passed.

Callum was back; the man who had single-handedly set in motion a series of events that was tearing the continent apart was back. Ilyana was going to find out who he was working for, and then she was going to kill him.

Never mind that he had grown up alongside Ilyana. Never mind that they had worked together for *years* now. He had betrayed them, and there was no turning back now.

Tapping more focus, Ilyana powered through the crowds, nearing the city gates within seconds. The world moved slower when she used her Crystals, though only slightly. Her peripheral vision took on a dark blue tint as she drew more focus. As she ran, people's reactions were slightly delayed, and the sunbeams of the Blazeday seemed sluggish.

When she ran, she was unstoppable. Callum may be quick for a Stormless, but she was the fastest woman in *all* of Celes. He wouldn't be able to escape her wrath even if he tried.

She continued sprinting through the streets, and she would not stop until she found Callum and made him pay. He had doomed Celes, and perhaps all of Auris. He had ordered the death of a King just as the Resurgence was beginning, and he had done so for no apparent reason.

Ilyana reached the large stone walls of the city's edge, sliding to a halt in the middle of the street. Everything slowly picked up speed, and within seconds the world around her was moving at a regular pace once again. The sunbeams danced a little faster, and the people moved a little more quickly, though Ilyana herself now felt slow and sluggish.

The crowd parted around her, some giving her dirty looks for her reckless behavior.

Ilyana didn't care. She scanned the crowd, looking to the side as the gates were slowly wheeled shut. *He's already inside the city.*

It took all of a minute for Ilyana to spot him, pushing against a pair of guards as they chained him. *Like he didn't see this coming...* Ilyana shook her head, then tapped focus and burst through the crowd.

The world slowed, Ilyana drawing even more focus as she approached him at a full-on sprint.

Callum whirled around as she crashed into him.

Ilyana gave herself a boost of focus, draining another Crystal and dragging Callum with blinding speed into an alley across the street. She threw Callum up against the wall and slid a blade from her boot to his neck in a matter of seconds.

Callum breathed heavily, pinned against the wall, his short black hair and sharp, curved Elosian features looking the same as they had that day before the Solstice.

"What in Izara's Shadow is the matter with you?" Callum hissed, pushing against Ilyana. The boy had always been thin and scrawny, so Ilyana was able to hold him down with ease.

She pushed harder, slamming his back into the stone wall once again.

He winced, closing his eyes.

Ilyana pressed the blade up closer to his neck—just close enough so that he could feel the cold steel on his throat. "Why?" Ilyana growled.

Callum's dark eyes widened.

Ilyana pressed the blade closer to his neck, nearly drawing a bit of blood.

"Are you insane?" Callum heaved, pushing Ilyana off him.

Ilyana stumbled back, keeping her blade raised.

"First, you tell me that you've found your own target and that you don't need my help anymore. Then, you tell me that I need to return to Celes immediately. Then, you kill *the King of Arvendon* and don't bother even giving me a heads up that the entire country is going to be on lockdown!" Callum shouted. "Do you have any idea how hard it was to get back here? The border was closed, and the guards were ordered to execute any escaping Elosians on sight. I had to go into The Highlands to circumvent the border, which took me an entire extra day, and hell, I'm lucky that I wasn't killed by a hungry snowprowler." Callum cursed. "And as soon as I get back here, I hear that you and your father have ordered my arrest!" Callum breathed heavily, rubbing his neck.

Ilyana stepped back. *What had he said?* She scanned Callum's dark eyes, looking for the slight quiver that was always present when he lied. It wasn't there. Ilyana looked away, then looked back, searching his face—now red with anger—once again.

"What are you talking about?" Ilyana asked, lowering the blade. "You were the one who told me to kill Avenos."

"Why in Izara's Shadow would I do that?" Callum shouted, his voice growing hoarse. "And why would you *listen* to me?"

"Because you told me that the Arvendi had killed my father!" Ilyana shouted.

Callum stepped back, his sharp face wrinkled in confusion. "What?" Callum breathed. "Wait, when even was this?"

"The night before the Solstice, when we had agreed to meet."

Callum frowned. "I wasn't even in Arvendon that night. I had left before dusk," Callum said, his voice lowering.

"Why would you leave before our arranged meeting?" Ilyana stepped forward, raising her blade once again.

"Because *you* found me earlier in the day and told me that you had everything taken care of, and that I needed to get out of the city immediately!" Callum hissed.

What is he talking about?

"Callum, I never contacted you before nightfall," Ilyana said. "I waited until darkness had set in, just as we had agreed."

"That's why I was a little surprised when you came to see me earlier," Callum said. "I even told you, 'We weren't supposed to meet until tonight.'"

"Callum." Ilyana sheathed the knife, then took him by the shoulders. "Listen to me. That wasn't me. Did you ever see my face?"

"I saw it with my own eyes, nearly as close as you and I are now," Callum said, his eyes burning. "I looked you in the eyes and asked who your target was, and you said—in a voice that I am one hundred percent certain was yours—'I can't tell you, but you need to leave.'"

"How—" Ilyana started. She looked into Callum's eyes once again, searching for that quiver. She found nothing. She lowered her gaze, closing her eyes. It was impossible. It was simply *impossible.*

"They're in there!" She heard Castien shout from outside the alleyway.

Ilyana stepped back, whirling to meet him as he dashed into the alley.

Arthion followed shortly after. Castien's blue eyes snapped to Ilyana, then to Callum, then back to Ilyana.

Arthion was panting, clearly exhausted from the run here. He laid a hand on the wall of the narrow alleyway, taking in big gulps of air to refill his lungs.

"What happened?" Castien asked, stepping forward. He ran a hand through his blond hair. "Is this him?" Castien nodded to Callum.

Callum locked eyes with Ilyana.

"Yes," Ilyana said softly. "But... I don't think he was the one who told me to kill Avenos." She stepped toward Castien.

Castien turned, his bandaged arm now slightly in front of him, held awkwardly out so that he avoided scraping it against anything.

Callum gave Ilyana a look when he realized what the bandage was made from. Ilyana cursed Callum mentally, though she didn't bother to explain that she hadn't meant it like *that*.

"What?" Castien asked, stepping forward.

Callum extended a soft hand. "Callum."

Castien took Callum's hand with his healed arm and shook it lightly. "If he didn't tell you to kill the King, then who did?" Castien asked.

Arthion stepped forward as well, seeming to have recovered his breath.

"I'm not sure," Ilyana said. She looked back to Callum, searching for any trace of a lie one final time. "I thought it was him, but now I'm not so sure."

Castien turned around, locking eyes with Arthion. The two whispered something to one another, then turned back to Ilyana.

"So what do we do now?" Castien asked.

Ilyana looked up. "We need to find my father."

King Nightingale's personal chambers were considerably smaller than Avenos's, at least from what Castien could tell. A few tables sat on the sides of the room, and there was a couch up against the window, but the small room was mostly open space. Castien stood near the corner, watching as the King paced in the center of the room.

Elric also stood in the center of the room, while Callum sat in a cushioned chair, facing them.

Arthion situated himself across from Castien, and Ilyana was positioned near the window, gazing out silently into the sea.

"So you weren't the one who told my daughter to kill Avenos?" the King asked, rubbing his black stubble of a beard.

"No, Your Majesty," Callum said, his voice firm.

King Nightingale raised his hand to his face once again, his brow furrowing in thought. The simple silver crown sitting atop his head glimmered in the bright sunlight shining through the large windows on the other side of the room.

"But Ilyana says that you were the one she spoke to," the King said slowly.

"Yes," Ilyana said from her spot in the corner of the room. She was looking out the window at the sea below, processing.

"And you, Callum, claim that Ilyana spoke to you earlier in the day?" the King asked.

"Yes," Callum said. "I saw her with my own two eyes."

"Hmmm," the King said, rubbing his beard again.

Castien watched Ilyana as she stood in the corner, looking out the window as if to find something that wasn't truly there.

"Well, someone has to be lying, then," Elric said.

All eyes turned to him.

"I'm just saying: It's not possible for someone to be in two places at once. Both of these individuals remember having a different conversation with one another, taking place at different times of the day. I'm simply pointing out that that appears to be impossible," Elric explained.

No one said anything.

Castien looked back to the King—who continued pacing.

"There was a code, was there not?" the King asked.

Ilyana turned back suddenly. "There was a code... And you knew it."

"Of course I knew it. You and I came up with it on our journey to Etherus, when you were first setting your plan to infiltrate Arvendon's court," Callum said.

"No, I mean that whomever it was I spoke to knew the passphrase," Ilyana said, rubbing her chin. "But you and I had agreed that we would not tell anyone, no matter what."

"And I didn't," Callum said.

"He's obviously lying!" Elric exclaimed, advancing toward Callum. "How could the person she talked to know the phrase if it wasn't you?"

"How could the person that I spoke to have known the..." Callum trailed off. "Oh no."

"What? What is it?" the King asked.

Elric stepped back, allowing King Nightingale to stand in front of Callum.

"I—" Callum started. He looked at Ilyana. "You never said your part of the passphrase."

"Then why did you let the person pretending to be me in?" Ilyana hissed.

"You practically knocked down the door!" Callum explained, throwing his hands up. "Besides, they *looked* like you! How was I supposed to know that the person who looked exactly like you, dressed exactly like you, and sounded exactly like you *wasn't you?*"

"So you just didn't think to ask for the second part of the phrase?" Elric asked, looking over.

"Why on Auris would I have asked at that point?" Callum exclaimed. "Whoever it was, they looked *exactly* like her. What reason would I have to question their identity?" Callum paused. "They didn't even ask me for any information," Callum said. "They just explained that they had found the target, and that they were going to take care of everything. I sort of assumed that because they knew about the whole situation, it had to be Ilyana."

"Apparently not," the King said, his brow furrowed. He looked off into the sea, pacing toward the window.

Castien watched curiously, trying to piece together what had happened.

"Let me get this straight," Elric said. "You heard a knock at your door or something, correct?"

Callum nodded.

"And then I assume you whispered your part of the passphrase through the door?" Elric continued.

"From the sea to the sky, yes," Callum said, repeating the passphrase.

"And then 'Ilyana' pushed open the door, and told you to leave Arvendon?" Elric asked.

Callum nodded.

"Yet then the real Ilyana met someone who looked and sounded and acted exactly like you later that night, after you had supposedly left," King Nightingale continued, picking up the narrative from Elric. "And this 'imposter' said his part of the passphrase, you answered, and he let you in."

"Right," Ilyana said from the window.

"Now when was this?" the King asked.

"After nightfall," Ilyana answered absently, still gazing out at the sea.

"And Callum claims that he was where?" Elric asked.

"I had just left the gates, and was starting up the Northern Highway," Callum said. "I can promise you that I wasn't in the city."

The King turned back to Ilyana. "Did Callum say or do anything that seemed out of the ordinary?"

"I—" Ilyana started. She looked down as if deep in thought. "He was maybe acting a little strange, and perhaps a bit more distraught than usual, but I had assumed that it was because he had been told that you were dead."

"In any case, you believed him," Elric said.

Ilyana nodded.

"And what happened after he told you that you must kill Avenos?" Elric asked.

"He told me that he had planted a large set of ropes and pulleys on the back side of the Palace, near the cliffs, for our escape. He also said something about a distraction, though he failed to tell me what it was," Ilyana said. "After I left Callum's apartment, I went all the way to Summerglass and found the ropes, and set them up over the course of the night before I finally returned home. Castien can verify that I returned when it was dark."

"I can," Castien said, nodding.

"And the distraction turned out to be a Shadow-Swift attack?" King Nightingale asked.

Ilyana nodded.

All eyes turned back to Callum, then to Ilyana.

"Once again, this is impossible," Elric said. "There's no way that both of them are telling the truth. Someone here has to be responsible for Avenos's death." Elric looked around.

Castien watched as Elric strode toward the window, staring out as the sunbeams danced around the glass outside, the warmth of the Blazeday bleeding through the glass.

"It was the Skin-Shaper," Ilyana said quietly.

"What?" Elric started, turning to where she stood in the corner.

"There was evidence of a Skin-Shaper in Arvendon, right?" Ilyana began. "And Callum and I both spoke with someone who *looked* exactly like the other person."

"So you're saying that a Skin-Shaper is behind all of this?" Arthion asked, speaking up for the first time.

"It's the most likely explanation," Ilyana said, stepping toward the center of the room. "This Skin-Shaper somehow knew what I looked like, transformed into me, and then met with Callum while impersonating me." Ilyana paused. "Then, after telling Callum to leave, the very same Skin-Shaper must've then assumed *Callum's* identity and proceeded to carry out the scheduled meeting with the real me later that night. Callum even told him the first part of the passphrase by accident," Ilyana added.

"So this Skin-Shaper... They are the one who wanted King Titansworn dead?" Castien asked, connecting the dots.

"It would seem that way," Ilyana said. "But they didn't want to do it themselves; they needed to pin the blame on someone else."

"And they did just that," Arthion finished. "And now we have no way of figuring out who this Skin-Shaper might be... Niventia knows we can't go back to Arvendon so long as you two are with us." Arthion nodded to Castien and Ilyana.

"And we have no way of warning King Faelyn that a Skin-Shaper might be in his court," Elric added, frowning.

All eyes turned to the King.

He sighed. "I wish I could offer more guidance on this matter," the King said. "But I wasn't there that night; whatever clues there may be, I wasn't there to notice them."

"I think that the obvious first step is to see if we can figure out who the Skin-Shaper is," Ilyana said. "Or at the very least, figure out what their motivations are."

"And figure out how in Calida's Claws they managed to get a Shadow-Swift on their side," Callum added.

"He's right," Elric said. "The Shadow-Swifts had to have been working with the Skin-Shaper. Why else would the Skin-Shaper have known about them ahead of time?"

"Is there any way to tell a Skin-Shaper apart from other Summoners?" Ilyana asked, looking around the room.

"Brands," Callum said. "I remember from the stories my mother used to tell me as a child—the ones that were meant to scare me out of talking to strangers. The story spoke of a man with a scar on his hand, as well as an old woman with the same scar, and finally a monster with—yet again—the same scar. As the story goes, all three of them were the same person: a Skin-Shaper."

"So what are you saying? We start checking people for brands?" Elric started. "That's just an old wives' tale anyway, we need something real to go off of."

"Well, it's all we have right now," Callum said, folding his arms.

"Why would Skin-Shapers even brand themselves anyway?" Elric threw up his hands. "That doesn't make any sense."

"Because they were *cursed,*" Callum said. He looked around. "By the Harbinger of the Rune-Writers."

Everyone stared at him blankly.

"Come on, no one ever heard the legends about the Rune-Writers' curses?" Callum snorted. "Seriously? Am I the only one who paid attention in my classes?"

A heavy silence fell over the room.

This is a mess, Castien thought. *Someone in Arvendon is a Skin-Shaper, and we don't even have a way of warning the city.* Between what the Blood Sorcerers had told them and the evidence of a Skin-Shaper in Summerglass, it was entirely possible that someone had been replaced. *But who?* Castien thought.

"It pains me to say it, but I don't think we can worry about this right now," Ilyana said, looking to her father. "The Blood Sorcerers will have the map ready for us before the day is out, and the sooner we cross The Highlands and get to their fortress, the sooner we'll have some *real* answers."

"She's right," the King said. "The Skin-Shaper is likely still in Arvendon, so there's nothing we can do. We need to keep our heads and stay focused."

"Velarus said he'd be returning to Arvendon in what? Three weeks now?" Elric said. "We need to figure out the truth as soon as possible. If Arvendon falls, this will all be for nothing."

"So what are you suggesting?" Arthion asked, turning to Elric.

"We leave for The Highlands tomorrow morning," Elric said. "We follow the map the Blood Sorcerers are making, find this 'Blood Empress,' and figure out why the hell this whole continent seems to be turning on itself."

No one protested.

"Right then." Elric nodded. "Tomorrow morning."

CHAPTER SEVENTEEN
THE FIRE KING

It was almost time.

They had been sneaking through the dense foliage of the Jaskyan jungles for hours now—wheeling the catapults and Incendiary with them. It would not be long before they reached the northwestern rise over Cyfalion.

The krellins clicked their shells together, the sound coupling with the wind and the clinking of Faelyn's Crystals to form a quiet symphony as the sun set. The group was walking on an incline now; their destination was near.

Their plan was simple: set up the miniature catapults, load them with Incendiary, cover the city with as much of the explosive liquid as possible, and then Faelyn would lead a small force of Scorchers to do as much damage as they could. Once they were satisfied, and Faelyn had killed Adresin Jastira, they would retreat.

Or will we even get out at all? Faelyn thought. He nearly stumbled over the greenvines and exposed roots below. Jastira would be in the clock tower, which even now Faelyn could see looming over the tree line. The clock tower was even bigger up close; it was easily one or two hundred feet tall, and its elaborate architecture impressed Faelyn even from a distance.

"We are getting close," Eithor said.

Faelyn turned, meeting the man's eyes as the steady creaking of the covered weapons wheeled over the vines. Faelyn looked to the side, watching as the box containing his armor was wheeled through the uneven landscape.

The Scorcher soldiers pushing it seemed less than content, but that was not his concern.

The carts further back were larger, perhaps the size of a person, and Faelyn could smell the vague torch-like scent on them. *Those contain Incendiary,* Faelyn thought.

There were six carts in all, several being wheeled by deckhands. There were eighteen Scorchers in their group, and each was one of Faelyn's highest-ranking guards. Faelyn himself far surpassed all of them, of course, but that was beside the point.

"You're certain Jastira will be in the clock tower?" Faelyn asked, stepping over another vine and ducking beneath a low-hanging greenbranch.

"Yes," Eithor said. "The clock tower is a temple to the God of Time: Zephyr. Jastira—being that he is the head of the Jaskyan Council—lives in the temple to give him an extra layer of divine protection." Eithor paused. "Or so they believe."

"How do you know all of this?" Faelyn asked. "Is this not your first time in Cyfalion as well?"

"Trust me." Eithor smirked. "My information is correct. Besides, have I ever misled you, Faelyn?"

"No," Faelyn mumbled.

Eithor nodded as they continued walking, ducking beneath another greenbranch. The landscape was densely covered with plants, even on the incline. All sorts of strange, leafy plants and twisting grasses blanketed the ground.

Faelyn felt his thoughts drifting toward doubt. *Focus,* he told himself. *Jastira ordered your father's death. This is your chance to make him pay.*

"The tower has several dozen levels," Eithor said. "Fighting Jastira inside of it will not play to your strengths."

"Your suggestion?" Faelyn asked.

"Draw him out," Eithor said. "Kill enough of his men, and I'm sure he'll join the fight. He's a powerful Cloudwalker, but nothing you can't handle... So long as you *don't* fight him inside the clock tower."

"Does it have any weaknesses?" Faelyn asked. "Any way to bring it down?"

"None that I know of—at least, not that you can exploit," Eithor said. "It would take the full force of a Storm Gale to knock it down, even a Cyclone might not do the trick."

"What's our point of entry?" one of the Scorchers asked from behind. Ayre, her name was.

"There's a gate on the western side of the city." Eithor stepped over another greenvine. "Burn through it and you'll have your way in. The flames will also be our signal to start launching Incendiary."

Fortunately, wards only affected the Tempests, meaning that the Incendiary jars would pass through the ward without resistance. All of Auris's wards were specifically created by the Rune-Writers to weaken the Tempests and the Tempests alone.

Faelyn was beginning to slip back into his thoughts when the group began to slow. The flora was starting to thin—the trees at least—and the rise was beginning to flatten. They were reaching the small outlook that Eithor had spotted from the ship.

We're here, Faelyn thought. He reached the top of the incline and slowly turned to face the city below.

Hundreds of red-roofed buildings stretched out below him. Massive greenbranches grew between them, painting a surreal tapestry of red and green far below. The ward stretched over the city, reflecting the light of the falling sun. The clock tower rose against the cloudy red-orange sky, its tanned stones shining in the evening hour.

Beyond the city, waves washed against the shore, giving the scene a measure of peace and tranquility. The city was *beautiful,* Faelyn couldn't help but admit it. It was unlike anything he had ever seen. The buildings were tall and pointed, and the way the colors all matched made the city seem even more... *perfect.*

It was stunning.

Faelyn centered himself, lowering his head. He stared at the white vest he wore, embroidered with gold. This garment was fashioned for the Solstice, in honor of Niventia... In honor of the night his father died.

Faelyn reached down to his side, where his crown hung from his waist. He held it in his hands, feeling its weight in his fingers. It was something that he had held several times before but never truly worn.

It was a burden that he always knew he would bear, but one that he had never fully comprehended. The crown came with a certain level of understanding, something that only the most enlightened individuals could process.

He hadn't understood that before, but he understood it now. Without hesitation, Faelyn raised the ornate, twisting golden crown to his head. He fastened it in place—using the hidden battle straps that Hubys had attached for him. The small fastens hid comfortably beneath his hair, obscuring them from view. Faelyn wanted to wear it for the battle; he wanted to make sure *every single person he killed* knew *exactly* who he was.

Five small catapults—likely new prototype models—were being set up behind Faelyn. Large nets hung beneath them, each one filled with ceramic jars of Incendiary. The *fiery* smell reached Faelyn's nostrils, sparking in him a rage that he hadn't felt since that night.

Faelyn raised a hand, igniting a small flame in his palm. The sight of such a fire brought back *every* emotion of the last few days. The despair and shock at seeing his father's blood-soaked corpse... the helpless rage as he fought the Shadow-Swift... the *blinding* fury with which he had attacked the Stormless assassin... and finally the insatiable hunger for revenge as he tore Hallan apart with his bare hands.

Everything came to a point, and Faelyn knew that every lingering doubt he had paled in the face of this cold, calculated rage. His life had been turned upside down. His entire *world* had been shattered, and now... now he could get his revenge. He could finally release the *mountains* of grief and anger that had been building for weeks.

Adresin Jastira had ordered his father's death, and Etenae Hallan had carried out the distraction that made the assassination possible. Faelyn had ensured that Hallan had paid for what he did... And now? Now, it was Jastira's turn.

After night had fallen, Faelyn adjusted his black cloak, pulling it tighter over his new armor. The yellow-brown walls of Cyfalion were accented with greenbranch wood, matching the architecture of the city within.

Faelyn could see the clock tower, even from beneath the trees. A temple for Zephyr... The place where the man who ordered his father's death currently rested.

Ayre walked beside him, her blonde hair hidden beneath her orange Scorcher helmet. She was the leader of the most powerful Scorcher division in Arvendon, so it was only natural that she would be part of their team here.

Their first step was blasting through the wall; from the clearing, they could see the silhouettes of a pair of guards standing just above the gate. The wall was perhaps twenty feet tall, though it paled in comparison to the size of the buildings it protected. Cyfalion had been built upward, rather than outward. In fact, the wall hadn't even really been visible from their outlook due to the greenbranches growing above it.

How many will we kill tonight? Faelyn found himself wondering.

They had lost dozens in the Shadow-Swift's attack on the Solstice, and the loss of his father had been even more devastating. True, the assassins weren't Cyfali, but they were working for Jastira. Cut off the head of the nrekuma and the body will die. This was not cruelty. This was justice. Besides, if Elric was tracking down the assassins themselves, then Faelyn would deal with them once they were imprisoned in Arvendon—the same way he had dealt with Hallan.

Something snapped in the distance, sounding almost like a branch breaking. Faelyn spun, searching for the source.

Eithor hunkered down a short distance away, apparently trying to make sure the sound didn't get him spotted.

Faelyn shook his head. Eithor was a wise strategist, but he wasn't exactly a soldier. Regardless, his illusions would give them the cover they needed to escape, so he was a necessary part of the plan.

Eithor turned a corner, disappearing behind the trees as he settled into his position. Adrenaline pumped through Faelyn's veins as his force neared the gate.

He hadn't done enough before. Eithor had tried to warn him of what was going to happen to the King, and Faelyn had thought that simply telling his father would be enough. But it wasn't. Faelyn could have done *so* much more, but he did not.

Now was his chance to change that. Now was his chance to hit Cyfalion *so hard* that they would be hurting as badly as he did.

Thoughts of Idris's ashen hands crossed Faelyn's mind. Breakdown was likely in his future. Faelyn doubted he would come out of this fight without losing some of his body to Ashwither—the Scorcher variant of Breakdown—but he didn't care. He wouldn't mind coming away from this fight with a scar or two. In fact, a part of him *wanted* a scar; he didn't want to forget this night.

The rage boiled within him, heating to an unstoppable blaze. Killing Hallan had been about more than just delivering justice. It had felt *good.* Faelyn hadn't wanted to admit it before, but now he did.

Faelyn had spent the last two weeks hiding from his true form. He had been running from what he truly was, but not anymore. He was a monster, and it was time to show the world just that.

"Stay back," Faelyn commanded. "Allow me to make our entrance." Faelyn stepped out from the edge of the jungle, setting foot on the dirt road toward the gate.

He took a step toward the wall, keeping his eyes locked on the pair of guards. His cloak brushed over his clothing, covering his armor. *Show them what you are.*

One of the guards called out as Faelyn grew closer to the yellow-brown wall and its wooden gate. The guard held up a torch in one hand, drawing his sword with the other.

The other guard raised a bow, drawing an arrow.

Faelyn lowered his head, raising one hand. He opened his palm, letting a slow fire burn through one of the openings in his silver armor. The armor had large holes around his hands to let fire through, and it trapped the rest of the heat in his body, redirecting it to his wrists.

The flame burned brightly, illuminating his black cloak and amber eyes from beneath the hood.

"Who are you?" one of the guards demanded.

"He's a Scorcher," the other guard said urgently.

The first guard stepped forward, raising his sword. "Show yourself!" the guard shouted.

Faelyn took a deep breath, and ripped off the cloak.

The silver armor—painted white and gold—glowed in the night. It was thick... thicker than any armor Faelyn had ever worn. Over a dozen Crystals lay in the massive chest plate, which had been painted to look like the vest Faelyn had worn the night of the Solstice.

The arms were massive, every inch of his muscles lined with Crystals. His legs were the same, the Crystals glowing from within the silver war machine. It was heavy, far too heavy for a regular man to lift. But with the power of the Scorcher Crystals so close... Faelyn's muscles were *invigorated.*

Even standing here, he felt the heat rising. Like a star in the night, he began to glow, letting his golden hair fall down the sides of his face. He could feel his crown—tightly fastened to the top of his head—beginning to heat up.

The guard gasped, stepping back.

Faelyn advanced, the heavy clanking of his armor sounding almost deafening to his ears. It was *finally* time.

"Who are you?" one of the guards shouted again.

Faelyn looked up through narrowed eyes, and he smiled. "I am King Faelyn Titansworn, and I am here to exact my revenge."

Faelyn roared, charging the walls. His rage exploded. The well of anger that had been building for weeks finally broke. Every missed opportunity, every mistake, every death had been leading to this.

And Faelyn was going to let it all out.

He screamed, launching himself from the ground with a pyrokinetic jump. He crashed onto the wall, throwing out his heavy arms and sending a massive blast of fire at the guards.

They were thrown back from the sheer force of the blast. Both guards fell to the ground, either unconscious or dead—Faelyn didn't care. He turned ahead, facing the city before him. The tower-like buildings spread out all before him, begging to be burned.

Faelyn's mind clouded. The heat of the battle seeped into his mind. It was over. It was too late for the people of the city. They wouldn't even have a chance to escape.

He threw out his hands, fire exploding from his outstretched palms. As if on cue, jars of Incendiary flew in overhead, crashing into the buildings beyond. Faelyn shouted, falling to the cobblestone streets and sending out a spiral of flame toward a massive square building to his left.

It ignited, the flames eating through the greenbranch wood with ease. He heard shouts from inside as the residents called to each other. Faelyn laughed, a wicked, horrible laugh. *Show them what you are.*

A jar shattered on the building, dousing it with Incendiary. Seconds later, the entire structure *erupted.* Fire exploded from the building, destroying every last fragment of it within seconds. Faelyn was thrown back by the blast, crashing through the crumbling walls of another burning building. But he didn't care.

He sent a burst of heat through his legs, launching himself out of the building and back into the streets. Soldiers began filing out into the roads, each donning their green armor.

Faelyn screamed, throwing out his hands. The heat rose through his lungs, then through his arms, and then out to his fingertips. The world seemed to hold its breath, and then... The fires surfaced.

Flames shot from his fingers, flying through the air with mind-bending speed and ripping apart the soldiers before him. Faelyn charged, feeling a burst of heat with each heavy pulse of his heart.

His father was gone. And these people were to blame.

Faelyn turned as another squadron of soldiers ran out from a building. He burned them with little more than a thought, feeling the heat numb his nerves. He then turned around, sending a blast of flame through the next building.

Incendiary crashed to the ground all around him, covering the roads. Faelyn reached out his hands, shooting flames in all directions. *Heat* crashed into him as the Incendiary exploded, vaporizing the soldiers and setting more buildings afire.

Screams rang out through the city as the people of Cyfalion realized what was happening. Faelyn spun around, finding armed soldiers filing out of the buildings that he had not yet touched.

Quick response, Faelyn thought. There were more soldiers ready to fight than he had expected. Faelyn spun, watching as a man floated into the air. *Cloudwalker.*

Another form appeared in the fiery night, dashing out into the streets in the blink of an eye. A dark blue essence trailed the figure. *Dexteris.*

Faelyn turned, charging at the Summoners first. He heard the soldiers running from behind, but he ignored them. Several of his Crystals had already burned out, but he had more than enough left.

He sent a massive fireball hurtling toward the Cloudwalker.

The Summoner spun out of the way. He dove toward Faelyn, a long, straight sword raised.

Faelyn shouted, slipping out of the way as the man swooped down, narrowly missing Faelyn.

In an instant, the Dexteris was upon him.

Faelyn felt the Dexteris's hands on his back. An instant later, the world *flipped*. His head crashed into the stones as he was thrown to the ground. The clank of his armor deafened him, and pain shot through his body.

He twisted, trying to rise to his feet.

The Dexteris was upon him again, swords raised.

Faelyn reached up, the world seeming to slow as the Dexteris swung the blade. Faelyn twisted his arm, using the hard metal armor to block the blade.

The blade clattered off Faelyn's forearm plate. Faelyn reached up with his other hand, grabbing onto the side of the sword and *pouring* heat into it.

The Dexteris screamed, the blade melting in his hands.

Faelyn jumped to his feet as the Cloudwalker narrowly missed another diving strike. Faelyn spun around, ducking just in time as the approaching wave of soldiers began to swing at him.

He leaped into the air, leaving behind a blast of flames.

The soldiers beneath him screamed in pain as their flesh burned.

Faelyn landed on the next group, holding out his hands and commanding his flames to form firm blades.

The conjured fire-blades materialized. Faelyn swung out, forcing them to length. They burned through the leather armor of the soldiers with ease. More screams filled his ears.

Faelyn dove to the side, dodging another Cloudwalker attack.

More Incendiary flew overhead, exploding when it landed on the flames a short distance away.

Something crashed into him from the side. He twisted in midair, finding himself being slammed into a wall by the Dexteris. Faelyn cried out, falling to the ground.

The Dexteris raised his hands to Faelyn's face, a blade flashing in the night. Faelyn twisted out of the way and slammed his fingers into the man's eyes. Seconds later, the man fell to the ground, smoke pouring out of his ruined face. *One Summoner down. One to go.*

A loud explosion sounded behind him. The other Arvendi Scorchers had finally broken through the wall.

Faelyn stood up and charged the nearest soldiers. He slid, igniting his legs as he kicked through one of the soldiers and burned the rest with an outward burst of flame.

The Cloudwalker crashed into him, pain screaming through Faelyn's side as a blade sliced his torso.

Faelyn reached up, roaring. He grabbed onto the Cloudwalker's armor and pulled the man down to the ground.

The Cloudwalker grunted, falling with a thud.

Faelyn dove after him, smashing an iron-clad fist into his face.

The man screamed, though he was instantly silenced as Faelyn burned through his skull.

Faelyn looked back up, scanning the streets. The other Scorchers of his team were fighting, and they weren't encountering much resistance.

They were burning through Cyfalion with ease. The damage to the city was already significant, for at least a dozen of the larger buildings had been completely incinerated. Faelyn grinned, realizing that he was covered in blood that was not his own. *Izara's Shadow, this feels good!*

The high of Summoning was greater than ever, and every blast of flame sent a surge of pleasure through his body. *This* was what he was meant to do. *This* was justice.

"SCORCHER!" someone roared from behind.

Faelyn spun to the massive clock tower. A man in a long green Cloudwalker coat stormed out. *Adresin Jastira.*

Four others followed him, each donning green Cloudwalker armor.

Jastira's dark skin shined in the flames as he lifted into the air. He screamed, launching toward Faelyn with the four other Cloudwalkers in tow.

Air *slammed* into Faelyn, flinging him backward like a blade of grass in a mighty Storm Gale. He cried out as he crashed into the building behind him, but the air did not stop.

The blast held strong, pushing him all the way through the building and out the other side. Faelyn felt his armor *crack* from the collision, and within seconds he was thrown against the city walls.

His head spun, throbbing from the impact. His muscles were stunned, and his armor damaged in several places. Adresin's blast had launched him over a hundred feet backward, and *through* a building at that.

Master Summoner, Faelyn thought. There had long been rumors about Jastira's abilities, and now Faelyn knew that all of them were true. This would not be an easy fight.

He slowly pushed himself to his feet as Jastira and his Cloudwalkers rose over the building before Faelyn. Feeling the heat pumping through his veins, Faelyn readied himself. His blood boiled as he prepared the first blast.

The five Cloudwalkers flew over the building and sped toward Faelyn.

With a pyrokinetic jump, Faelyn launched himself into the air—narrowly avoiding the blasts of wind they shot at him. Faelyn shot an arc of flame forward, sending it spinning toward the Cloudwalker on the right.

The Cloudwalker threw out her hand, pushing herself to the left and dodging the blast.

Faelyn growled, falling aimlessly back to the ground. He landed on his feet *hard* and found himself stumbling to recover his balance.

More air *smacked* into his body, tossing him against the inside of the city walls once again.

With a shout, Faelyn kicked off the wall and *threw* himself at the nearest Cloudwalker.

The man couldn't react quickly enough, and Faelyn was upon him in a mere second.

Faelyn screamed, grabbing onto the man's green helmet and melting his face. Faelyn fell to the ground, the Cloudwalker falling shortly after—dead.

"NO!" Jastira roared from above.

Sensing a blow, Faelyn sent a blast of flame to launch himself out of the way. Sure enough, Jastira's longsword flew into the ground where Faelyn had just been sitting—thrown by a telekinetic push.

Faelyn landed, sliding against the cobblestone road. The heat within him became hotter. Breakdown was drawing close, but he didn't care. Ashwither could dissolve his entire body for all he cared, but he *needed* to kill Jastira.

He shaped his flames into a sword, conjuring the weapon with nothing more than a thought and sprinting toward Jastira as the Cloudwalker went to recover his longblade.

Another Cloudwalker slammed into Faelyn from the side, grabbing onto him. The assailant carried Faelyn, dragging him through the cobblestone ground with painful efficiency.

Faelyn twisted, recovering his breath and grabbing onto the Cloudwalker's chest. Heat *sang* through him, coursing through his body, his lifeforce, his mind. In an instant, the Cloudwalker dropped, sending Faelyn clattering in his armor across the cobblestone streets.

Two down, three to go.

Faelyn groaned, his body aching. He rose to his feet, readying himself. With a glance, he saw that his fingertips were already gray and cracked. *Ashwither*. Faelyn thought. He turned his attention back to Jastira and the remaining two Cloudwalkers, all of the powerful heat within him growing even hotter.

The numbing warmth inside of him was becoming almost

unbearable. Pain swam through his torso, another Crystal burning out as Faelyn added more fuel to the cursed heat. He was running out of energy, and his body was starting to break down.

The first Cloudwalker hurled a dagger at Faelyn.

Faelyn sidestepped the dagger and readied a fireball. His body resisted as that heat rose. It felt like he was being seared out of his own bones. But Faelyn didn't stop, no... He pushed *harder*, overpowering the resistance and sending a fireball toward the speeding Cloudwalker.

It hit the Cloudwalker in the side of his chest, tipping him off balance and sending him crashing toward a building. He did not rise.

Jastira held back, sheathing his sword and weaving his hands together. He seemed to be preparing a spell of some sort.

I need to stop him, Faelyn thought. He was almost entirely focused on his own survival at this point, but he knew that much. If Jastira completed whatever spell he was beginning, Faelyn could easily be killed. *Where is Eithor's illusion?* Faelyn cursed. He could hear the Scorchers fighting a few streets over. But Faelyn needed to kill Jastira and make an escape *now*.

The remaining Cloudwalker dashed toward Faelyn with a long-blade extended.

Faelyn ducked, swiveling out of the way and sending a blast of heat to knock the Cloudwalker off balance.

It worked, and the Cloudwalker slammed into the wall of a nearby building. He groaned and stumbled to his feet just as a jar of Incendiary crashed into the building he leaned against. His eyes widened.

Faelyn sent a small fireball toward the building.

The building *exploded*, vaporizing the Cloudwalker and sending Faelyn flying back. His muscles were entirely spent now, and a quick prodding with his powers told him that he only had three Crystals left. However, in his current state, he wasn't even sure if he would have the strength to use them.

Jastira recovered himself after being thrown back by the explosion. He moved his hands through carefully practiced motions, resuming his spell.

Faelyn tried to jump to his feet, but failed. He was too exhausted to stand, his muscles *burned* everywhere. Even one more flame would send him over the edge. Faelyn laid there, raising a single hand.

He stared in horror, finding that his hand had almost entirely *disintegrated*. His fingers were gone, burned away and turned to ash. His palm was gray and ashen, and he could hardly move it at all. Ashwither was already doing permanent damage to his body.

But Jastira is still alive, Faelyn thought with a panic. *No.* He couldn't let this all be for nothing. Destroying the city was part of it, yes, but he was here to kill the man who had ordered his father's death... and Faelyn would not rest until he had done so.

And yet, he was just so *tired.* He slumped back against the ground, trying to keep his eyes open.

It was then that Jastira completed his spell.

Gale-force winds picked up all around Faelyn, and he soon found himself lifted into the air.

Faelyn's stomach lurched, his body levitating at Jastira's command. *No.* This was going to kill him. *This is going to kill me.*

Jastira roared, and sent Faelyn flying.

The world became a blur as Faelyn crashed through the city walls. Everything briefly went black as Faelyn slammed through several greenbranches, his head smacking into each one of them. He reached out to try and stop himself, but his ashen hands were no use.

Everything continued spinning. Faelyn vomited, struggling to remain conscious. He felt as if his head was going to fall off his body. It felt like his eyes were pulling themselves out, like his stomach was trying to crawl out his mouth. The heat in his bones did not dissipate, continuing to burn stronger and stronger until Faelyn could hardly feel anything else.

He tumbled through dirt and heard a *crack* as he collided with something hard.

Everything was dark and hazy. The world spun, blood lining the sides of his vision as Faelyn realized that he had likely broken something.

The black stone he leaned against was familiar. *The Monolith,* Faelyn thought, trying to clear his head. *One of the stones that powers the ward.* He groaned, reaching out and placing a hand on the Monolith, trying to reorient himself. He would not die here. *I will NOT die here!*

"WHY?" Jastira roared from afar.

Faelyn could hear rushing wind as Jastira flew toward Faelyn's spot against the Monolith. Jastira had pushed Faelyn all the way through the city wall and into the forest, up to the edge of the ward.

"WHY?" Jastira demanded, his feet colliding with the ground as he landed before Faelyn.

Twisting, Faelyn stared at the hundreds of Runic markings carved into the Monolith. He watched as the light film of the ward radiated eternally from the stone.

An idea struck him.

It was a foolish one, but it rooted itself in his mind nonetheless.

"You destroy a third of my city, kill all of my best soldiers, and for what?" Jastira started, advancing toward Faelyn.

Faelyn twisted, struggling to rise to his feet and pushing against the Monolith for support. He fell, his back giving out the second he put weight on it.

Faelyn spared Jastira a glance, finding that he was still roughly twenty feet away. *He won't kill me without an answer,* Faelyn thought.

"That crown..." Jastira breathed. "You're the new King of Arvendon, aren't you?"

Faelyn grunted. He reached within himself, drawing out his flames to form a brace around his spine. Crying out in pain, Faelyn locked the conjured brace into place and tried to stand once again. Every muscle in his body protested as he struggled to find his balance in this *unbearably* heavy armor. His strength was dwindling.

If he was going to do this, he would need to use everything he had left.

"You—" Jastira hesitated. "I don't understand. Why?"

Faelyn found his footing, preparing his powers. His eyes settled on the clock tower, now in the distance. "You ordered my father's death," Faelyn rasped, his throat dry from the ash.

"What?" Jastira started.

Faelyn closed his eyes, feeling an unbearable heat rising in his body. He opened his mouth, grabbing onto the heat and *strengthening* it. He pushed his hands against the Monolith, feeling the sheer *power* within the stone.

This was something no one on Auris had ever done, even in the darkest of wars. But Faelyn didn't care. He would have his revenge, and it seemed this was the only way to get it.

A bolt of lightning struck the clock tower, the *deafening* clap sounding throughout the jungle. Seconds later another strike followed, and then another, and then another.

The lightning, Faelyn realized. *It's not real... That is Eithor's distraction.*

It worked, for Jastira was now drifting away from Faelyn in a state of shock. By the time he turned back, he was too late.

The heat started to *burn.* Faelyn screamed, feeling his organs smolder as he grabbed hold of the growing fire. The world seemed to grow silent, the heat coming to a point.

Faelyn took a breath, and *poured* the divine flames into the Monolith.

Then, the Monolith exploded.

CHAPTER EIGHTEEN
ASHES

Ash swirled in the air, twisting and turning through the morning winds. It fell from the sky like rain, a quiet echo of destruction gently floating to the ground. White wisps swirled around, dancing in and out of the billowing smoke.

The sky was dim and gray. The air had a shadow of warmth, a lingering reminder of a long-gone heat. Ash continued to fall, coating his clothing and sprinkling down upon the doomed city.

The ward was barely visible, weakened to little more than a thin line in the air, rather than a firm barrier.

"I think I see him," someone said.

"He's still alive?" another voice asked.

"I don't know, but the boy is stronger than you'd think," the first person replied.

"He doesn't look conscious."

"He will be soon enough."

A face appeared over him, a pair of ice-blue eyes staring down at him.

He blinked a few times, trying to move. He could not.

"Your Grace... You've survived one hell of an explosion," Eithor Vassellet said, leaning back.

Faelyn Titansworn shifted his eyes, his lungs feeling hollow. Everything felt dry. It was as if every fluid in his body had been wiped out... leaving only this empty, ashen heat.

"What happened?" Faelyn croaked. His voice sounded impossibly distant. Even as he scanned the sky with his eyes, it felt as if he weren't really there. Something was wrong... Something was very wrong.

"I was hoping you might know," Eithor said. Stones creaked, and Eithor seemed to lean back. "I was creating my illusions from the rise just behind us when I saw you thrown against the Monolith." Eithor paused. "And then there was an impossibly bright light coming from right where I had last seen you... and then there was an explosion."

"I—" Faelyn whispered. "That was me."

"I figured as much," Eithor said.

Faelyn's limbs felt impossibly light yet so heavy that he could not lift them. *What is wrong with me?* He turned his head, hearing the clinking of Crystals against his ears.

"Wait," Faelyn whispered. He tilted his head a little more, catching sight of a dim yellow Crystal. "What is that?" Faelyn asked. His eyes focused on the small Crystal fragment. *Yellow?*

"Ah." Eithor looked over, raising a withered eyebrow. "There are several of these Crystal fragments scattered around where the Monolith once stood," Eithor said. "Wayfinder Crystals, judging by the color I believe."

"The Monolith..." Faelyn trailed off, coughing. He cleared his throat, squinting as another flake of ash landed on his face. "It's gone?" *Oh Gods...*

"You destroyed it in the explosion," Eithor said softly. He sighed. "Izara's Shadow, Faelyn. What were you thinking?"

"I—" Faelyn started, craning to see the now feeble ward overhead. "The city will be destroyed," Faelyn breathed. "I weakened the ward. All it will take is one Storm Gale and the whole city will be torn apart."

"Let us hope not," Eithor whispered. "Destroying a Monolith is the highest of war crimes, Faelyn, you know that. If the ward is still intact, even if only partially, then it is my hope that the rest of Auris will hesitate before turning on us."

"What have I done?" Faelyn slumped back. The ash continued falling overhead. His explosion had likely blasted the surrounding greenvines into oblivion, burning them to smithereens. The ash swirled, its gray and black flakes forming a beautiful tapestry in the sky. Wisps continued to dance around him, their hissing and whistling becoming apparent as Faelyn became more aware of his senses.

The useless Tempest was growing stronger, even here, where the ward was still partially intact. The Tempest was still weakened within the ward, but only slightly it seemed. The sun was rising behind the cover of the clouds as Faelyn once again failed to move his arms and legs.

"Faelyn," Eithor started again.

He kept his eyes forward.

"We did it," Eithor said. "I saw who I presume was Adresin Jastira standing near you when the explosion hit."

Reduced to smoke and ash, Faelyn thought. He had done it. Jastira was dead. So why did he still feel so numb? Why was the anger still there?

Faelyn took in another dry breath, groaning. His back was locked in place—likely badly bruised or broken. He had committed the highest of war crimes. Arvendon's allies would turn on him without hesitation now. He had doomed his city to destruction.

It was only fair, though. He had sentenced Cyfalion to a brutal annihilation at the hands of the Tempests, and it was only fitting that Arvendon would fall as well.

"What have I done?" Faelyn whispered, tears rising in his dry eyes. He still couldn't move.

"We need to leave," Eithor said. "I have raised an illusory mirror that should hide our presence, but we'll be found out if we linger much longer."

"Arvendon will fall," Faelyn rasped absently. "Arvendon will fall because of me."

Eithor turned away, "Ayre! Over here!" Eithor called, turning back to Faelyn. He rose to his feet. "We need to get him back to the ship," Eithor said to Ayre.

Faelyn felt a pair of strong hands on his shoulders.

More footsteps sounded, and two Arvendi Scorchers appeared at either side of him.

Faelyn tried to turn his head. A strike of pain shot through his neck, stopping him. He could only lie there, helpless. He was lifted into the air, carried by four people. His head tilted downward, and he finally was able to glimpse his body.

His feet had entirely melted away into ash, as had his hands. His arms and legs were a dark gray, cracked beyond recognition. His bare, exposed chest was as ashen as the sky, covered with small cracks and missing flakes.

It was as if his entire body were in the process of melting away. *Breakdown...* Faelyn dipped his head back, the lack of feeling in his severed nerves suddenly becoming all too real. He had survived. He had released enough power to burn through one of the Monoliths—which were previously thought to be indestructible. He had caused such a powerful explosion that there was not even a trace of Jastira left on this world. But Faelyn had survived. He had survived, and was now left with nothing but guilt and shame.

He closed his eyes, letting his head fall back into Ayre's arms. The slow beat of his carriers' footsteps rocked him off to sleep.

He had survived.

CHAPTER NINETEEN

CAPTURE

Thawing ice dripped from the ceiling of the cell. A cold wind blew beyond the barred windows on the opposite side of the room. His skin was hot. *Everything* was hot.

Luka Delmorian sat, slumped against the wall of his prison cell. What could he do? His Crystals had been taken from him, and a Scorcher guard was on the other side of the door in the corner of the room. Luka was able to catch a glance at this particular guard when he entered to check on Luka following a shift change. *A burly man, somewhere just above six feet tall, five Scorcher Crystals hanging at his waist, a cudgel in hand.*

Luka was trapped. Theurgi had captured him and was now marching on Arvendon. It wouldn't be more than a few more weeks before he arrived, and Luka couldn't even warn the people of his home.

He was alone, and for the first time in a very long time, he was powerless. Even now he felt the strange absence of his power. His blood was empty, his body was hot, and his skin seemed to grow drier. His hands had cracked slightly from the fight with the guards, but he was conditioned enough that it would take a much longer fight to cause further Breakdown.

He reached down, feeling along the hot stone of the cell. Of course, he was fairly certain that everything around him was actually rather cold; it was just warmer than he was accustomed to. His fingers closed around a pebble, which he promptly began tossing to himself. His reflexes were sharp when he had his Crystals—sharp enough that he would've been able to perfectly track the pebble as he threw it back and forth. Yet now he felt slow and sluggish. *A life without Crystals, what a terrible fate.*

He had formulated a simple escape plan, but it wasn't much. *Find a way to gain access to my Crystals without being noticed, kill the Scorcher, then fight my way out of the city and head southeast as quickly as possible,* Luka thought.

Luka was beneath the castle—of that he was certain. He'd been here for several days now. Amid the quiet, he could hear the waves crashing against the seawalls. Aside from watching the occasional krellin scurry by and waiting for his meals of rotten iceblooms, there was nothing to do. Thankfully, twice so far, he'd received a tear of a snowfin hide.

Luka had escaped worse prisons than this and had no doubts about his ability to break out of here when the timing was right. Once he did, he would have to make for Arvendon as quickly as possible.

Either way, he would survive. He always did. He always found a way to escape, and he always would. Yet everything was so hot in here that it was nearly impossible to think.

His body quivered and shook often, as if craving the cooling sensation of the Crystals. It was something that he had been lucky enough to avoid most of the time, but every once in a while—when his Crystals were empty for a little too long—he felt like this. It was almost as if his body had forgotten how to function without the power of the Crystals.

His mind drifted back to his original purpose in coming here. He had come to Freyfall to discover whether or not the Blood Sorcerers controlled the city... And given the presence of the one who knocked Luka unconscious, he was fairly certain that the Blood Sorcerers had secured Freyfall

Luka dropped the pebble, his side aching from whatever the Blood Sorcerer had done to him. *One of them probably orchestrated the assassination,* Luka thought. It would make sense. The Blood Sorcerers seemed to be twisting the world to their liking, bending every knee to their will.

Luka stopped himself, directing his thoughts to his former King. He should've felt something... more, as he did when he first learned the news. Yet he did not. Now he felt nothing more than a sort of distant, detached pity for Avenos.

The man had died—but it didn't *feel* like it. Avenos wasn't here anymore, but it still felt like he was simply somewhere else... just not here. Either way, the world would go on. Auris would keep living, and the people of Auris would keep fighting. If anything, his death only attested to the significance of the current conflict.

What was one death of a soldier compared to one death of a King? One meant nothing, while one meant *everything.* Or at least, one *should've* meant everything. Luka was more shocked than anything—shocked that his King was dead, yet that he felt hardly any sorrow.

Everything was just so hot. How could one think when every-thing was this hot?

His mind wasn't working properly. There was a pattern to all of this, and while the Blood Sorcerers seemed to be the answer, didn't Theurgi say there were Shadow-Swifts involved in Avenos's assassi-nation? *What part do they have in all of this?* Even if the Blood Sorcerers had aligned with the Shadow-Swifts, what was their goal? What was the point of all of it?

And who was behind it?

Luka's senses perked up.

He froze, feeling his pulse spike as the thrum of a Crystal entered the room. Seconds later, an ice-blue Cryostalker Crystal rolled across the ground just outside of the cell. His body began devouring it instantly, savagely feeding itself on the frozen power. Luka closed his eyes, feeling an icy calm wash over him, bringing clarity and reason to his scrambled thoughts. Everything was starting to make sense again. He was starting to feel again. Everything was—

"That's all you're getting, so make it last," a quiet voice said.

Luka paused, his eyes cracking open. *Wait... Why did they give me a Crystal?* Luka opened his eyes and looked around the dim room.

A robed figure stood in the doorway. The man walked in, his robes coming into focus in the dark torchlight. Luka squinted, making out the deep red threads of the clothing. He blinked a few times. *Red? Is this the Blood Sorcerer who incapacitated me?*

"When I received word of your arrival, I knew that I needed to speak with you... I also knew that putting you in a cell would be the only way to make you listen," the man said, taking another step closer to Luka's cell. "There is much that we have to discuss, yes, but more than anything, I simply wanted to know what makes the strongest Master Summoner of Arvendon... *tick*." He paused, turning his black eyes in Luka's direction. "Knyvet is impulsive, and hooked on the thrill of a fight. Surge is a cold-hearted killer, but loyal beyond reason. And the Nightingale Princess is mistrustful, even of herself." The man paused again, his voice low, yet curious. "Yet you... You, I was unable to analyze from afar. Each and every time I thought I had found a weakness, or a motive, I came up short."

Luka continued siphoning power, careful to keep the thawing slow.

"Yet the answer appears to have been right in front of my very eyes all along. For I see now that you wear your truth on your cold, cracked skin, Cryostalker."

Luka looked up, watching as the man paced back and forth just beyond his cell. He blinked a few times, his thoughts aligning again.

"You are *addicted* to the power of Summoning, aren't you?" The Blood Sorcerer stopped, spinning to face Luka. His robes flapped slightly, giving Luka a glimpse of the blood-red Crystals within. "You have grown so accustomed to traversing these lands with your Summoning and fighting your King's enemies that you have developed a dependence on your Crystals, haven't you?" The Blood Sorcerer took a step closer.

Luka looked up, meeting his dark gaze.

"And you are now so lost in their power that you don't even know how to function without them, correct?" The Blood Sorcerer's face twisted into a smile.

"What do you want?" Luka growled, his voice suddenly seeming very loud. His senses were heightened once again.

"I told you, I merely wanted to learn a little more about one of history's greatest Cryostalkers." The Blood Sorcerer leaned forward, bracing an arm against the bars of the cell. "You know, for someone trained so thoroughly in the art of politics, I would've expected you to have better manners." The Blood Sorcerer motioned to the now half-empty Crystal on the ground, clearing his throat.

"Thank you," Luka grumbled, sliding back against the cold stone wall. He heard a wave crash into the cliffs far below, the sound drifting through the window on the other side of the room.

The Blood Sorcerer started pacing again. "I can't say I blame you. I myself nearly went down a similar path when I first acquired the gift of Summoning a few months prior to this day."

"What do you mean?" Luka sat up. "You weren't always a Summoner?"

"Well, of course not," the Blood Sorcerer said, as if it were obvious.

What? If he wasn't a Summoner before, that would mean he was once a... Stormless.

"But as I was saying, the feeling of the blood in my veins, that *rush* of power... It's indescribable." The Blood Sorcerer turned to Luka once again.

Luka looked down, the implications slowly becoming apparent. "You used to be Stormless," Luka said, his eyes fixed on the ground. "Which means that you were powerless, and now you... Now you're a Summoner."

The Blood Sorcerer nodded.

"Except it doesn't work that way." Luka snapped his head up, staring at the Blood Sorcerer. "One is either born a Summoner, or one is born Stormless. There is no way to cross that boundary of birthright."

"There wasn't when we were young." The Blood Sorcerer winked. "Yet... things have changed."

Luka looked back down, savoring each drop of power that thawed into his veins.

"There is something else we must discuss," the Blood Sorcerer said slowly.

Luka's eyes snapped forward. "I don't suppose you're here to explain who you are?" He sat up, rising to his feet. His side ached, the wound seeming to worsen as Luka reached the end of the Crystal. "Or why you're conquering Auris, or why you're sending Freyfall's troops after Arvendon?"

The Blood Sorcerer sighed, stalking back toward Luka and pulling down his hood to reveal a perfectly shaven head. "You don't even recognize me, do you?"

Luka searched his memory, trying to place the familiar face. *The bald head... The dark eyes...*

"Velarus," Luka breathed. "You're the one who confronted King Avenos... The one we faced in The Highlands."

"Indeed," Velarus said. "And I came to Freyfall not to direct the city's forces toward Arvendon, but away from it."

"What?" Luka took a step forward. "Your Sect is responsible for all of this. Were you not the ones who pointed Freyfall toward Arvendon in the first place?"

"No, Luka." Velarus shook his head. "We wish to assume control of Arvendon ourselves. Yet Theurgi has been... *difficult* to control. And despite our influence over him, he commanded his troops to march on Arvendon as a way of finishing what was started in The Highland skirmishes." He paused. "I intend to return to the city with a force of Blood Sorcerers just behind Theurgi, hopefully limiting the damage his troops do and allowing my Sect to take the city for ourselves."

"The promise you made," Luka remembered. "You promised to return to Arvendon with an army of Blood Sorcerers in six weeks, and it's been over three."

"It has," Velarus said. "And the sooner we assume control of Arvendon, the sooner we can unite Auris against the Shadow-Swifts at long last."

"What?"

"The Shadow-Swifts had a hand in Avenos's death. What's more, I have reason to believe that *they* were the ones who encouraged Theurgi to send his forces toward Arvendon." Velarus paused. "Our control of this city is not so complete as it seems... The Shadow-Swifts have somehow gotten to Theurgi, despite our presence.

"The Shadow-Swifts were developing a plan to cause another Vanishing and take control of Auris," Velarus continued. "But something went wrong in their plan, and the result was what is starting to seem more and more like the Resurgence. Regardless of what they have done, this much is clear: They intend to conquer Auris, and they intend to do it *forcefully*."

"You're lying," Luka snorted.

"The evidence begs to differ."

"Then why did you threaten our King? If your only goal is to stop the Shadow-Swifts, then why would you force your way into all of Auris's capitals?" Luka challenged, stepping forward.

"Because we are not powerful enough to defeat the Shadow-Swifts on our own." Velarus fell silent. "Our Empress assured us that if we gathered the support of each nation and combined the forces of Auris into a united front, it would be enough to win. She said that the only way to unite the continent before the Shadow-Swifts executed their plan was to *forcefully* encourage Auris's cities to obey us, and she was right." Velarus paused. "Besides, given that we intend to lead the fight from Arvendon—and given Avenos's hostile disposition—we knew a forceful takeover of the city was the only option. We have the support of Celes and Freyfall... And if things go according to plan, Suchara and Cyfalion will soon follow."

"But..." Luka trailed off. "I don't understand."

"I don't expect you to," Velarus said, his voice hard. "But there is something you need to get through your frozen skull, Luka."

Luka met his eyes.

"I am not your enemy," Velarus said. "You have been fighting for the wrong side, and it would be in your best interest to change that."

Luka hesitated. "How do I know you're telling me the truth? Why should I trust you?"

"Freyfall plans to destroy Arvendon, which means that everyone you serve will be dead. Even if Arvendon still stands, we will take it for ourselves in the hopes of rallying what troops they have left against the Shadow-Swifts." Velarus's eyes hardened. "Theurgi intends to kill you before the week is out, so the way I see it, your options are to either listen to me or accept your fate," Velarus said.

"So, you want me to fight for you?" Luka snorted.

"Would you?" Velarus stepped forward. "Would you fight for me, if I asked you to? I have warned you of the threat the Shadow-Swifts pose. Were my words alone enough to sway you?"

Luka fell silent.

Velarus began pacing again. "This is precisely why we did not go about our conquest diplomatically. No one *believes us*, and even if they did, they wouldn't trust us."

"And who put your Sect in charge?" Luka asked, his voice rising.

"*We* did." Velarus advanced. "We knew of the threat months before the rest of the continent, so we had no choice but to step up and take the lead ourselves."

"And how did you know such things?"

"We—" Velarus paused. He blinked a few times, his face twitching. "Our Empress predicted it. She was the first to emerge with the power of a Blood Sorcerer, and everything she predicted has come to pass."

"And who is your Empress?" Luka asked, his voice low.

Velarus held his gaze, staring at him with black eyes. It was almost as if he were searching Luka's face for something.

"If you want to know who she is, then you can come meet her yourself," Velarus said after a moment. He turned away. "You can find us hidden inside a mountain in The Highlands." Velarus paused again. "Roughly twenty miles southeast of here, you will begin finding red markings on the stones; they were designed to lead new recruits to our fortress. Follow the markings and you should find the fortress. When you reach it, allow yourself to be captured and explain that you come on my behalf. *If* they believe you, they will tell you everything you need to know."

"I don't understand," Luka said. He slammed his hands against the bars, hot pain radiating through his cracked skin. "You speak in circles, yet you tell me each secret as if it were nothing... What do you want? What is it that you are trying to tell me?" His body shook from the exertion, his skin growing hot. He *needed* ice. He needed to Summon again. Without Summoning... he was weak.

"You want to know what I am trying to tell you?" Velarus hissed. "Try this: You have been inadvertently aiding the greatest threat that Auris has seen in centuries, and you need to stop." Velarus took a deep breath. "If you truly want to help this continent, then come find us. But if you want to lie here and rot until Theurgi kills you, then you can go ahead and do just that." Velarus turned away.

Luka stared. Memories of ice in his veins forced him to speak. "Wait," Luka croaked.

Velarus continued walking, nearing the door. He paused, his hand hovering over the handle. He reached into one of the pockets of his robes and produced something that shined in the dim torchlight.

"In a few days, most of Freyfall's soldiers will be completely out of the city," Velarus said quietly. "Your belongings and Crystals are in the second locked room on the left of the floor above us." Velarus turned to look at Luka once again, something softer in his hard eyes. "I know you are capable of change, Luka. I don't know if you believe what I have told you here today, and frankly, I don't really care. Yet trust me in this: Your help would benefit us greatly. I do not know what the Shadow-Swifts' next move is, and I do not know how to stop them. But if we do not try, then all of Auris will be left defenseless against whatever it is that they are ultimately planning."

Luka blinked a few times, trying to collect his thoughts through all this heat.

"We can help you, Luka," Velarus said, turning away. "But only if you help us." Velarus tossed something toward Luka, letting the object fall to the ground just in front of the bars of his cell.

Luka looked up, trying to see through the haze of torch heat. He reached out a raw hand to grab the object. His hand closed around the small object, and he pulled it through the bars. Luka opened his palm.

It was a key. *The key to the cell...* Luka looked up as the door swung shut.

Velarus was nowhere to be seen.

Luka was alone once again. He looked down once more, staring at the small silver key in his hands. Velarus had said that Theurgi planned to kill Luka, and Velarus had just handed Luka the key to escape.

What is going on? Everything he had said was impossible. The Shadow-Swifts had been dormant for centuries, and now Velarus was claiming that they were active once again? Not only that, but he theorized that they were planning to finish the Vanishing—whatever that meant.

This certainly made things more complicated. He could return to Arvendon as he had originally planned, or he could listen to Velarus and seek out the Blood Sorcerers. First, though, he needed to escape this prison. Velarus had given him the key, and though Luka was confident in his own ability to escape, Velarus had just made it much easier to get out of this cell.

The least Luka could do was ponder what he said. And maybe, when he was out, he would find that mountain in The Highlands. *Red markings...* It was a vague hint—one that was fairly unhelpful. Yet if Luka could find even one marking, then he would be able to follow the trail.

CHAPTER TWENTY

BLOOD & ICE

The Scorcher guard walked from the small stairwell outside Luka's cell to what Luka had deduced was a cramped room overhead. The steps on the stone above were quiet, but loud enough to hear if Luka listened carefully. They always followed a specific pattern, leading Luka to assume that the room had a direct path to the next chamber.

By looking out the window, Luka had put together that he was somewhere on the eastern side of the castle. While the Tempests raged, Luka could hear Crystals clinking only from straight ahead and to the left.

The Scorcher guard switched with another twice a day. Luka had determined that if he waited for the guards to switch, then waited a few *more* moments, he would give himself a nice window to escape. He needed to ensure that he had enough time to get out of the cell quietly and prepare for a confrontation with the guard.

The key seemed to burn through his hip where he had lodged it between his skin and the tight rope that he was forced to use as a belt. Thinking through the heat had been difficult, and it had taken him several days to put together all of the information that he needed for his escape.

Even now, just sitting here in the unbearable warmth of a cell that the guards had described as "cold," Luka could hardly think clearly. Escaping wouldn't be easy, despite the key. He would still have to fight his way past a Scorcher *without* his own Crystals if he hoped to escape with his life.

He knew his timing, and he knew his path of escape—to an extent. Velarus had told him that his supplies would be in the second room on the left on the floor above him. Getting in would be easy enough once he obtained the Scorcher's cudgel, and once he had his Crystals, he would have no trouble escaping the city.

Just the thought of the ice pouring into his veins sent him shivering with anticipation. Luka could hardly stand another minute in here with that obnoxious heat. Yet he had to wait. He needed to time this correctly, or it would all be for nothing.

Luka scanned the small area outside of the cell once more, looking at the small, pointed iron torch rest dangling half attached to the stone wall. There was a table with a small set of wooden chairs where the guards sometimes stopped in to watch him eat, most likely to make sure he wasn't holding on to any particularly hard iceblooms to try and pick the lock.

His plan was going to work. *It is going to work.*

He just had to wait.

Of course, waiting would give him time to think. And what else could he do other than *think*?

He mostly pondered what Velarus had said, though that often just frustrated him. Why would the Blood Sorcerers go about their conquest in such a way if they truly had good intentions? Were the monarchs and leaders of Auris really that closed minded that they would ignore a call to duty so grand as the prospect of the Resurgence?

And how could they explain the sudden appearance of the Shadow-

Swifts in Arvendon? Velarus said that the Shadow-Swifts had a hand in Avenos's assassination, yet that didn't make any sense. Why would the Shadow-Swifts want Avenos dead, especially when he was one of the few Kings who had not immediately yielded to the Blood Sorcerers?

If they truly were working against the Blood Sorcerers, then the Shadow-Swifts would've allied with Avenos, not had him killed, right? But then again, the Shadow-Swifts weren't the ones who had actually *murdered* Avenos—for Theurgi had said there was a designated assassin present. Of course, Theurgi could be lying too.

Zephyr's Watch! This is why I need to get out of here. With his only two sources of information being a Blood Sorcerer and a half insane King, Luka couldn't exactly figure out too much in terms of what was going on in the world.

Yet, from what little he could gather, he had determined that Velarus was likely lying—at least about some things. It would make sense if some of what he had said was true, for the best lies were always the ones that were wrapped in truth.

However, Luka was not about to give up an opportunity to find the fortress of the Blood Sorcerers. Velarus had practically given him a map to the location, and Luka might be the only non–Blood Sorcerer on Auris who possessed such knowledge. He resolved that he would find the hideout, meet this *Blood Empress* himself, and make his final judgment there.

Only after that would he return to Arvendon and rally what was left of their forces—if they even survived the attack—and ambush the Blood Sorcerers with the help of the Shadow-Swifts. Unless, of course, he decided that the Blood Sorcerers were telling the truth, in which case he would ally with them and do whatever was necessary to prevent the Shadow-Swifts from conquering Auris.

If Luka was being honest, he did *want* to believe Velarus. Yet the only issue he had with the man's logic was that the Shadow-Swifts had no reason to take over Auris and meddle with the Resurgence and the Vanishing. They were already considered to be above the law, and they wouldn't even have any use for the world if they were to take over. So why even bother conquering it?

There were still many pieces missing in this puzzle. And Luka could not put them together from the inside of this cell. With Avenos dead, he found himself feeling a bit more lost in terms of his morality. He had relied on the King to guide him down the correct path... Now that he didn't have that, how would he know if he was doing the right thing? It wasn't like he could just—

The door creaked, squealing on rusted hinges as the Scorcher pushed it open. The Scorcher walked in, taking a few steps into the small room, shot a glance at the torch, and looked down at Luka in his cage.

It always went like this. Each shift change, the Scorcher would come and check on Luka before relieving the other of his duties, just to ensure that Luka was behaving. Which meant that in a few minutes... *Yes.* The Scorcher turned around, snorting and shutting the door. It slammed shut, something heavy locking into place on the other side.

Luka closed his eyes, thinking through the heat and listening to the soft footfalls above him. After a few seconds, he was able to pick up the slight vibrations as the other Scorcher—now relieved of his duties—was returning to wherever he had come from.

A few minutes passed, and Luka was now certain that the Scorcher outside was alone. There was a table next to the door, and Luka knew that it would be hidden behind the door itself when the door opened.

Between the bar that Luka had heard slide into place several times, the door itself, the cell, the Scorchers, and the lack of Crystals, Luka had to hand it to Theurgi. He was expecting Luka to try to escape, and he had covered all possible openings. Yet he hadn't counted on Velarus offering Luka the key.

Of course, the key only removed one of the barriers to his escape, but Luka had no doubts about his ability to do the rest of the work.

Velarus clearly had high expectations, for he could've helped

Luka far more than he did. But... *This is a test,* Luka realized. *This is a test to see if I am truly as resourceful as the rumors claim, or if I am simply nothing without his Crystals.*

Luckily, Luka was about to prove that even Velarus had underestimated him.

Luka got to work quickly and produced the key from the small crease in his cracked skin. It burned on his skin, but he moved it to the lock and reached outside the bars, slipping it into the lock from the other side and pulling open the door as quietly as he could. It made no difference. The door squealed louder than Izara's Shadow.

Luka had prepared for this.

He leaped toward the wall, tearing the loose torch holder from the stone with a sudden throw of his weight. It gave with little resistance, sending him stumbling off balance.

The guard began moving outside, presumably removing the latch and checking what all the noise was.

Luka scrambled onto the wooden table, balancing himself, careful to avoid the old cups and plates.

The door swung open, and the guard rushed inside.

Luka held his breath, scanning the dark armor of the Scorcher's back as he peered into the cell. Luka held the iron sconce over his head and prepared for the Scorcher to turn.

Cursing, the Scorcher spun around, revealing the fist-sized opening in his helmet where his face was.

Luka dove on top of the man and plunged the sharp tip of the torch holder into the gap, feeling the *crack* of the Scorcher's skull as he pierced it.

The Scorcher opened his mouth to scream, but he was dead before the sound escaped his mouth.

Luka panted, heat running through his body as he sat over the warm corpse. He left the torch holder in the man's face, reaching for the steel cudgel at the man's waist instead. Luka lifted the heavy weapon, weighing it in his hands. It was different from what he was used to, but hopefully, he wouldn't have to fight anyone else until he found his weapons and Crystals.

It will have to do. He grabbed the ring of keys hanging from the Scorcher's waist and slowly rose to his feet, cudgel in hand, and made for the now open door leading into the stairwell beyond. There was, in fact, a bar hanging by the door frame, indicating that there had been one in place. *Good,* Luka thought. The more defenses there were to keep him in his cell, the more unexpected his escape would be.

The stairwell was shockingly small and cramped. There was hardly enough room for the stairs themselves, which hugged along the wall to the left as they rose sharply to the small door.

Luka started up them, arriving at the top step mere seconds later and reaching for the ring of keys. It took a few tries before he got the right one, but he had not yet been discovered. *Not yet.*

Pushing the door open, Luka examined the room that lay directly above his cell. He scanned the two doorways, thinking back to the direction that the guards had always walked. He took the left one and found himself stopping at the second door on the left.

Once again, the first key he tried was wrong. Luka looked up to the right, watching the short hallway for any signs of guards. Most of the soldiers would be out of the city, but that didn't mean that Theurgi's guards would leave, too.

He tried another, fumbling with the hot keys in his cold hands, trying to grasp the next one. It didn't work either. Luka cursed, looking down the hallway again.

Someone shouted something in Utryan from the room behind him. Luka jumped, his heart thundering out of his chest as he reached for the next key while searching for the source of the voice.

It had come from the room he was just in—likely from someone entering through the other hallway that Luka hadn't taken. Luka's fingers shook, the warm heat slowly overtaking them.

Footsteps sounded from his left. The guard had noticed the open door. It wouldn't be long before he found Luka. All Luka needed to do was find the right key, and he would be safe.

The footsteps grew closer, nearing the small hallway with each second until...

The lock clicked, the right key finally opening the door. Luka dashed inside just as the guard reached his hallway.

The guard cried out, once again saying something in Utryan.

But Luka merely smiled—as soon as he entered the small stone storage room, he could feel his Crystals.

He reached down to the chest, sensing the Crystals inside. Luka shivered, the euphoric cold searing his veins. Even through the walls of the container, he felt their power.

Ice surged through his veins, dribbling through the wood as Luka froze the lock. He kicked it off with ease, opening the chest and reestablishing his full connection to the Crystals.

Luka spun around just as the guard was entering, cudgel raised.

The guard shouted something again, jumping back slightly. His puffy face turned hostile, and his surprise quickly gave way to action.

Luka threw out his hands, thawing as much power as he dared. He laughed, feeling the *glorious* rush of ice in his blood. It coursed through his veins, pumping from his frozen heart down to his icy fingertips. It was perfect. It was *everything*... And it had been so long.

The man hollered, then swung his cudgel with a growl.

Luka watched it casually, then slipped into a low roll. He slid under the cudgel, grabbing the man's leg with one hand and latching onto his shoulder with the other.

Pulling the oldest Cryostalker trick known to Auris, Luka began to freeze the man's blood. It was a costly move for Luka. Blood-freezing expended a tremendous amount of energy, but as he felt the thawed power surging through his veins, Luka just couldn't help himself.

It was euphoric. It was a sense of power that was incomprehensible. After being away from it for so long, it was almost like he had forgotten what it felt like. But it was back now.

Luka threw the man to the ground, leaving him unconscious and only partially frozen. He would live, but he would be incapacitated for quite some time.

Luka quickly threw off his ragged shirt and shorts, putting on his dark leather armor and attaching his hood. He slipped his sword and sheath into place, adjusting his armor. Once it was in place, he was ready.

It felt heavier than he remembered. *Perhaps doing nothing for an entire week has weakened me,* he thought. He sprinted back to the small room and tore down the hallway to the left.

He had mapped out the castle in his head and knew that he had to be heading in the right direction. In his mind, he thanked Velarus for the helpful knowledge as he ran, though he was on the lookout for the guards more than anything else.

As he ran through the stone-floored castle, he found no one. It was almost as if the castle were empty. Luka followed the long hallway until he found a staircase. He took it upward.

Reaching the next floor—which Luka presumed by the increased decor was the main level—he found no one yet again.

A door opened to the right, and an unarmed servant in gray garments walked out carrying a tray. She screamed when she saw Luka, though he paid her no mind.

Where is everyone? Luka turned to the right and followed the main hallway toward the center of the Palace. Windows lined the wall to the left as Luka grew nearer to the entrance.

With still hardly a soul in sight, Luka found himself approaching the entry hall. There would be guards here; he was certain of that. Rounding the corner, Luka drew his katana.

Sure enough, eight guards stood in the large multi-pillared room. Luka cut down the first, spinning and surveying the others as he attacked.

The guards screamed.

Luka threw out his free hand, sending a spray of ice spikes into the air.

The spikes scratched a few of the guards, though the two in the back dodged them with an unnatural grace. The other guards charged, and Luka knocked them down with a few hits from the blunt handle of his sword. *You're welcome,* Luka thought, looking down as the Stormless men fell unconscious.

He felt so much power. So much control. The Crystals offered so much more than simple strength. They offered *domination.*

The two guards in the back exchanged glances, then raised their cudgels and charged. They moved with an unnerving speed, dark blue essences trailing them.

Dexterises. Luka ducked the first strike, icing his feet and sliding past the second in a quick move.

The second Dexteris cursed, then spun around as Luka unfroze his feet and slid to a stop.

It was going to require more than a quick swing to take Luka down.

Luka raised his free hand, twisting it into a point and Summoning a large swath of ice. He hurled the blast of cold energy at the first Dexteris, knocking him off his feet with a yelp.

The second Dexteris charged again, preparing his cudgel for a diagonal swing this time.

Luka slid to the right, arcing around the blade and grabbing onto the man's wrists as he moved. He iced the man's blood, stunning him. Luka pulled away, raising his sword in his right hand as the man dropped his cudgel, crying out.

Luka ended his life with a quick thrust to the chest. He kicked the man, pulling his blade out and wiping the sleek steel on his leather wrist guards. Luka raised his eyes to the first Dexteris, who was now rising to his feet wide eyed.

Luka raised his spare hand, preparing another ice spike when the man held up his hands, dropping his cudgel. Luka ceased and—with no small effort—silenced the rising ice within him. His veins cried out as the coldness dripped away.

"Please," the Dexteris pled in the Eastern Tongue. "Spare me."

His accent was thick... to the point that Luka could hardly under-stand him. But he considered his request. What was there to consider? This man had tried to kill Luka, true, but he was now on his knees begging for his life. Why would Luka kill him?

Luka approached him, sheathing his blade and laying both hands on the man's shoulders.

The man shivered at his cold touch, his puffy Utryan face quivering.

"I'm not going to hurt you, relax," Luka said. He paused, repeating himself and slowing his words so that the Dexteris could understand him. Luka scanned the man's eyes, searching for a sense of understanding.

"Thank..." the Dexteris fumbled with his words. "Thank you."

"Where are the guards?" Luka demanded.

The Dexteris turned his head slightly, his dark armor shifting.

Luka motioned to the unconscious guards on the ground—the Stormless ones. "Where?" Luka asked slowly, pointing at the guards once again, and then the hallway behind him.

The Dexteris's eyes widened, and he turned back to Luka. "With King," the man said quickly.

Luka waved the man off, who scurried gratefully into one of the hallways, muttering his thanks in his broken Eastern Tongue.

With the King? Luka looked around. *Where is Theurgi?* Luka stepped toward the stone doors of the castle and pushed them open slowly.

The cold air of the Frostfall was refreshing, yet Luka ignored it. He slid to a large stone near the castle and slipped behind it.

Strangely enough, there were *dozens* of guards pacing up and down the streets of Freyfall. *What is going on?*

Luka crept around the construction, icing his feet and sliding behind a massive crate further down the street. He watched as another squadron of puffy-faced, black-armored guards walked by, talking amongst themselves.

Weighing his options, Luka made a decision. He was exponentially faster than the guards when he iced his feet, and he would be too hard to hit with arrows if he caught them by surprise.

Sneaking around them would take too long, and by then his fight in the castle might be discovered. Though he did not regret letting the Dexteris live, he had no doubts that the man was alerting the other guards inside the castle.

Luka looked back, feeling the rising freeze in his blood. With a frozen glory, Luka made his final decision. He sprinted out from behind the crate and started down the long, winding streets of Freyfall.

The guards shouted, crying out and raising their weapons as Luka sprinted past them.

Luka iced his feet. The cold rushed through his bones, the ice coming to a point and wrapping around his feet like makeshift skates. With a sense of balance only acquired through doing this for many years, Luka slid with perfect stability.

He passed dozens of guards, each shouting and rushing after him. Yet they were no match for Luka. He slid by with blinding speed, partially thawing one foot to pivot and turn at the next fork.

The massive keeps of Freyfall rose above him, blurring by him as he slid. Luka felt his mind slipping into that basic state once again. He was losing himself in the cold... And he *loved* it.

He passed the grand library and continued toward the stone walls at the other end of the long street.

Someone shouted behind him, and a door opened. Luka ignored it all.

None of it mattered. The world was his for the taking. No one could catch him. He was free. The icy air dripped with frost and snow, filling his frozen lungs and sending waves of delight through his body.

He was *alive*. This was what it meant to live. This was everything.

Luka thawed one foot, pivoting, and slid again as he neared the wall.

The guards atop it cried out, drawing their bows and cudgels.

Luka reached down and sent a cryokinetic push through the ground, launching himself all the way over the wall.

Roaring with delight, Luka soared. He iced his feet again as he landed just beyond the wall, passing through the ward and sliding out into the wilderness once again.

He unfroze his feet after a few minutes and started up the incline that he had descended roughly a week before. *Gods, that feels like a long time ago.* Luka still moved quickly, feeling the slowly draining yet simultaneously replenishing power of his Crystals fluctuate.

Luka crested the top of the hill and turned around, taking one final look at Freyfall.

A shadowed silhouette hovered over the library.

Luka jumped slightly, his blood warming. The figure was floating, standing perfectly still on seemingly nothing. Luka stared after it, seeing the slight tendrils of darkness radiating from the man even from this distance.

Shadow-Swift.

Was Theurgi meeting with a Shadow-Swift? *Was Velarus right? Is that why Theurgi is sending his army to Arvendon?* But it... It didn't make any sense. Yet here Luka was, watching a Shadow-Swift hover over the library. He determined that if Theurgi wasn't in the castle, it was entirely possible that the mad King was in the library with the Shadow-Swift.

Luka turned away, starting down the hill. It then occurred to him that he hadn't seen the Blood Sorcerers during his escape. *Shadow-Swifts... But no Blood Sorcerers?*

He cursed and continued down the hill. Once again, Luka found himself without a source of reliable information. It would be *weeks* before he was able to truly learn anything. But right now, that didn't seem to matter.

He was free once again, but he needed to focus. His King was dead. His city was in danger, and there was seemingly a war brewing between the Shadow-Swifts and the Blood Sorcerers.

Luka needed answers... And he was going to find them.

PART II

The Shadow-Swift

CHAPTER TWENTY-ONE

WAYFINDER

en months ago...

Water slid over the sand, climbing up the sandy beach and gently colliding with his face. Waves crashed in the distance, the hypnotic rolling of the tides a steady drone on the cold shore.

Sand grated against his wet skin, stinging as it met the still healing cuts that marred his arms as he pushed himself to his knees. He grunted, falling face-first into the sand, his arms giving out. He groaned, another gentle wave rolling over his legs. He coughed, spitting out salty seawater as the wave crept into his nose, crawling over his face.

He sighed, shifting his legs, trying to gain some footing in the infernal sand. He felt something digging into his side—a piece of his armor. He cursed. It was cracked. It wasn't that he cared, for he hadn't even expected to be alive at this point, but it was an annoyance.

He twisted, pulling the shard of black metal from his chestplate, groaning as he did so. It hadn't broken the skin, fortunately, but it had come close. His legs felt as if they had been crushed—like their bones had been shattered into a thousand pieces and then slowly put back together, one piece at a time.

How the hell am I even alive? He thought, frowning.

Sand shifted to his right.

He stilled, rubbing his eyes and turning his gaze to the figure that he suddenly realized was standing over him. He closed his eyes as he rolled over, grunting once again. He assumed that he would be dead. Gone. Yet here he was, thrown back into a life of death and destruction once again.

"I don't suppose this is the Afterworld, is it?" Keries Nightbloom groaned.

"No, my friend," the figure said, his voice strangely smooth. "You are on the western coast of Auris, just west of Hirane. And you are very much alive."

Keries kept his eyes closed, reaching out for his Crystals. They were empty. He frowned. *They were full when I left Erydon...* he thought. *Curious.*

"How..." Keries started, his eyelids cracking open.

The figure that stood over him wore strange, white cloth garments wrapped in elaborate patterns that Keries could hardly follow with his eyes.

"How am I alive? How did you save me?" Keries asked.

The man laughed. "I did not save you, dear friend, you saved yourself." His gold-brown eyes sparkled, reflecting the steady flow of the waves over Keries's exhausted body. "Although it is very clear that you are in desperate need of our help."

Keries turned, suddenly becoming aware of the seven other figures with similar clothing standing behind the man.

The man extended his arm.

Keries stared at it warily, but took it.

"My name is Enzo," the man said, pulling Keries to his feet.

Keries grumbled, brushing the sand out of his beard and trying to stabilize himself. It felt as if he were standing for the first time in centuries. His bones ached, his muscles burned, his head hurt; but he was alive. "I'm Keries."

Enzo pulled down the wrappings covering his head, revealing a soft, smooth, strangely thin face. Keries noted the curved blade at his side, tilting his head. It wasn't a blade he recognized… And given that he had fought someone from nearly every corner of Auris, running into a sword he'd never seen was a rare occasion.

"I assume you are a Shadow-Swift?" Enzo asked, glancing at Keries's broken armor.

Keries looked down, a shadow coming over his eyes. He nodded slightly.

Enzo turned away, glancing at the seven other members of his group who stood silently, watching.

"Should I be thankful that you came across me?" Keries asked, his hand subtly drifting to his sword, which he now realized had been broken in half.

"Oh, we did not come here by mistake, Keries," Enzo said, turning back. "We were looking for you."

Keries frowned, once again glancing at his fractured blade. It was still sharp enough to kill. If anything, it would be easier from this distance, given that Enzo was so close and the blade was shorter.

"How could that be?" Keries asked, his gaze falling. "No one knew that I was planning to leave."

"Ah, yes, but that is irrelevant when you are one of our kind," Enzo said. He paced, almost seeming to glide with an ethereal grace that Keries had only seen in other Shadow-Swifts. But this man was not a Shadow-Swift, was he?

"And what exactly is 'your kind?'" Keries asked, raising an eyebrow.

Enzo paused, turning to the others of his group.

One nodded softly.

Enzo nodded back. The others lowered their masks and hoods— just as Enzo had done—and turned to Keries.

"We are Wayfinders," Enzo said, bowing his head.

Wayfinders? Keries wobbled a bit. Asteros and the others must've found a way into Epirac... *What has Asteros done?*

"Rest assured, my dear friend, our presence is not the result of your former order's actions, I assure you."

"But I—" Keries started. His head spun, the world seeming to tilt and turn with him as he fell once again, holding his head.

Enzo dashed to his side, slowing his fall.

Keries blinked, finding himself lying on the sand once again.

Enzo helped him sit up, holding him steady as he did so. "Easy," Enzo said, slowly pulling his gloved hands back. "Do not hasten yourself. Your body is still recovering from your plunge from the sky."

Keries shook his head, blinking again. He reached up with his hand, running it through his graying hair. "Your Sect is extinct," Keries said, narrowing his eyes.

Enzo looked away. "Auris *believes* that our Sect is extinct," Enzo agreed after a moment. He began to untie a section of his cloth robes, pulling back the white wrappings to reveal a row of pale yellow Crystals.

Yellow Crystals... Keries thought. He had never seen such a thing.

"Us Wayfinders were never wiped out during the Vanishing," Enzo said.

"But—" Keries started.

"How many Tempests are there, Keries?" Enzo asked softly.

Keries paused. "Seven: Blazedays, Storm-Gales, Cyclones, Slick-Days, Frostfalls, Mistveils, and Wispwinds... But the Wispwinds don't fuel the Crystals of any Sect."

"Ah," Enzo mused. "That is where you have been misled."

Keries's eyes widened. He looked back to the now closed pouch where the pale yellow Crystals were hidden. "The Wispwinds..."

"...Are the Tempest of the Wayfinders, yes," Enzo said. "It took centuries of deception to convince the world that one of the Tempests had nothing to do with Summoning when, in fact, it is the source of our power."

"Niventia's light..." Keries cursed, rubbing his forehead once again. "But what about accumulation? Why haven't Wayfinder Crystals been accumulating across Auris?"

"Attractors," Enzo said, smiling. "Ancient devices that attract the excess energy from the Wispwinds and deposit it in the form of Crystals wherever we place them."

"But... Where?" Keries asked. "Where are they hidden?"

"The attractors are buried around the Monoliths," Enzo said. "No one would dare dig near a Monolith, as most are too afraid of interfering with the wards the Monoliths power... But several times a year, members of my order sneak out under the cover of night and harvest the deposits," Enzo explained. "It is a simple system, one that has allowed us to remain undetected all these years."

Keries's head hurt. "What?" Keries rubbed his eyes again. "But all this time, you've just been hiding... where? To have stayed hidden for centuries..."

"Elan Taesi is our sanctuary," Enzo said. "We have kept our gates closed ever since the Vanishing, vowing only to leave when deemed absolutely necessary."

"Deemed necessary by whom?" Keries asked.

"By..." Enzo trailed off. "By me, I suppose. I lead the order. Though we base our actions on the Splinters we receive."

"The—" Keries started. "The Splinters?"

"Our visions," Enzo explained. "Divination, the ability to see the bits and pieces of our future, is the primary ability of our Sect, though it doesn't work as you might think. We don't simply *know* what is going to happen, but at random, spontaneous moments we suddenly are split between two worlds: One that is, and one that *will be*." Enzo motioned with his hands, mimicking the splitting of one line into two. "For a few seconds, we can see something in the future, at times something that is very far from the present day, and other times something that is only mere seconds away."

"And you found me because...?" Keries tilted his head.

"Three days ago, one of Tanyl's Splinters showed the eight of us on this beach, near that rock," Enzo said, pointing to a massive boulder just a few hundred feet off the shore.

One of the women behind Enzo nodded slightly. Her head was also shaved, and her face nearly as smooth as Enzo's.

"So, you saw yourselves on this beach and decided to come see what you were doing here?" Keries asked.

"We knew that there was something that would lead to us being on this beach, something important, so we came," Enzo said, gazing off into the fog.

It was only now that Keries realized it must be a Mistveil today. "You were led to the beach by yourselves, though," Keries said, rubbing his head and rising to his feet once again.

"In a way, yes," Enzo said, turning back to Keries. "Don't try to rationalize it in your head. We have tried for centuries to figure out what sort of science makes our abilities possible, but we have come up with virtually nothing."

Keries frowned, staring at the gentle waves. He shivered, a cool breeze blowing across the beach.

"Why am I important to you?" Keries asked. "I'm assuming that, if my presence attracted your kind, I must have some part to play in... whatever it is that you do."

"You are correct, it seems." Enzo nodded. "Several of our Splinters have shown troubling events taking place in The Highlands, courtesy of your fellow Shadow-Swifts."

"You're trying to stop them," Keries realized.

"I'm not sure what we're trying to do," Enzo said. "All we know is that they are tampering with Epirac, which makes them dangerous."

"You think you could stop them from triggering the Resurgence?" Keries asked.

Enzo lowered his head. "I fear we are already too late for that."

Keries gazed off, feeling the cold numbness return. *So they have done it... The Resurgence is here.* He glanced at the imprint in the sand by his feet. *A broken arm. A burning home. One final touch. A black Crystal. A fall from the sky.*

Lyseria.

"The Gods are not done with you yet, Keries," Enzo said, laying a hand on his shoulder. "Shadow-Swifts are not as easy to kill as you may think... So long as you have Crystals on your person, you are near invincible."

"You're saying that I healed myself?" Keries asked, touching his scratched skin and empty Crystals.

"Instinctually, yes." Enzo nodded, turning away. He started toward the rest of his group, who had been silently observing the entire exchange. "As you may've learned from the caverns your kind has been investigating, the Shadow-Swifts were not one of the original Sects of Auris," Enzo said. "Your kind is a diluted offshoot of the Revenants, given life only because the Revenants were able to stop the Vanishing before their energies were completely trapped. Your Tempest, Dyvnire, or 'The Silver Sun' as it is called in your tongue, was torn from the skies... But it was salvaged in the form of Lotius's Curse."

"What are you talking about?" Keries frowned again. "Lotius is the source of our power. Are you saying that it used to be something else?"

"Lotius used to be the golden moon," Enzo said, his voice firm. "The Harbinger of the Revenants redirected the remaining energy of the Revenants toward Lotius, giving it a gray reflection. *This* turned it into the source of the Shadow-Swifts' power, altering the chemistry of your abilities and your Crystals, diluting them."

"But then..." Keries trailed off. "Are you saying that I am a Revenant?"

"Every Shadow-Swift is a Revenant. Your Sect isn't natural, it is merely a reincarnation of the Revenants following the Vanishing," Enzo said softly. "Your former order is on the cusp of returning your Sect to its full power... and if that happens..."

"So, you are trying to stop them?" Keries asked once again.

Enzo paused, turning back to the others. "Yes, I suppose we are trying to stop them."

"How do you plan on defeating four Shadow-Swifts?" Keries asked. "I'm not even sure if I could take on one of them myself."

"With your help, and with these," Enzo said, patting the Crystal pouch in his robes. "I'd argue that if we play our hand correctly, we might just stand a chance."

Keries frowned, gazing off into the ocean once again. Mere hours ago, he had fallen from the sky thinking that he may not rise again... Yet now, he found himself thrown right back into the center of it all.

"Oh," Enzo said, turning back. He untied one of the Crystals from the inside of his robe. "You might want to get familiar with these," Enzo said, tossing him the yellow Crystal.

Keries caught it, examining it curiously. "I can't even use this," Keries said. "I'm a Shadow-Swift, not a Wayfinder."

Enzo smiled, turning. "Come along now, Keries, I fear that we have quite a lot to do, and very little time."

Keries paused.

Four of the Wayfinders pulled back their robes, revealing rows of Crystals that were a soft mint green. *Apparently, those ones aren't Wayfinders at all... but Cloudwalkers.* That would explain how the eight of them had gotten to him so quickly.

Gusts of wind began to wake around him, whistling alongside the quiet lap of the ocean. Keries stepped forward, slipping the pale yellow Crystal into his pocket.

Enzo extended his hand in preparation for the flight to... wherever it was that they were going.

Keries hesitated, then took it.

CHAPTER TWENTY-TWO
DEPARTURE

Castien Varic sat on the edge of the wall, legs hanging over the short drop. Wisps hissed and whistled below him, weaving in and out of themselves. The Tempest had settled over the land a few hours ago, and as the cloud-hidden sun had risen, the Wisps had only intensified.

The Highlands stretched out before him, the countless mountain peaks scraping the sky in all their gargantuan glory. Castien looked down, glancing at his bandaged arm. It still ached, though the pain had mostly subsided thanks to the cooling gels King Nightingale's servants had offered him. It was beginning to heal, slowly but surely. It hurt less and less with each day, and the blisters were beginning to scar over. Though he knew he should still avoid using it for at least a few weeks.

Of course, it was easier to think about his arm rather than think about what the Blood Sorcerers had revealed. All his life he had been insignificant, and powerless... *Stormless*. And now he was something more. *All* of the Stormless were something more.

And he hated it.

He didn't want to be anything more. Maybe once he had wanted to have power, but now? It seemed it was easier to stay in the hole he had dug for himself, rather than claw his way out of it. Of course it was easier to do that. It always would be.

Throwing aside all the glorified stigma around promotions and invitations to advance, Castien saw these things for what they truly were: a source of trouble. Every time he moved forward, he found himself thrust into a new situation—one that heightened his anxiety through the sheer *uncertainty* that it brought. Sure, some might say that it was a worthy trade, but Castien couldn't see how.

Wherever he was, he could never be satisfied... And when he finally got to where he was trying to be, all he could think about was where he had come from, and where he would go next.

Footfalls sounded behind him. They were soft yet calculated, carrying a sense of poise. Castien had always found that footsteps matched the person they belonged to, and Ilyana was no exception.

"We are leaving soon," Ilyana said, sitting beside Castien. She settled onto the dark stone ledge, watching as a guard passed behind them. "Your things are ready, right?"

"They are." Castien could feel Ilyana's eyes on him, piercing through his dirty blond hair and driving through his skull.

Ilyana sighed. "You worry a lot, don't you?"

Castien opened his mouth, turning slightly toward her. "Uh..." Castien tried to find his words. "Yeah, I guess."

Ilyana nodded. "Try not to," she said.

If only it were that easy. Castien grumbled. Yet there was something about the way she said it. Ever since Callum's return, Ilyana's confidence had rallied. Between learning that her father was alive and discovering that she wasn't the *only* one to blame for Avenos's death, it seemed she felt a little more sure of her own ability.

"Why was your father so upset that you gave me a part of your cloak?" Castien asked, breaking the silence.

Ilyana looked away, her face turning ever so slightly red.

Izara's Shadow... Castien thought. *Is she blushing?* That was a new look on her.

"Listen, don't think anything of it, Stormless," Ilyana said firmly. "I only did that because if I hadn't, your burn would've gotten an infection."

"Did what?" Castien asked, recoiling. "Why does it matter that I had part of your cloak? And don't call me 'Stormless' anymore, because I'm not, remember?"

Ilyana rolled her eyes, the blush fading. "Here in Celes, giving someone a tear of your clothing essentially means that you swear to fight for them," Ilyana said. "It's something like swearing loyalty to someone, I guess. But don't get any ideas; once again, I only did it because I *had* to," Ilyana snapped.

"Okay... whatever," Castien said, holding his hands up. "I was just curious."

Ilyana grumbled, rolling her eyes again.

Staring off at The Highlands once again, Castien felt his pulse accelerate. The Blood Sorcerers had given Elric the map to their fortress, and Castien and the others were set to depart soon. Leaving this city meant that he wouldn't be safe anymore. It meant that he would be closer to becoming a Summoner—which he still wasn't particularly excited about.

King Nightingale was currently debating with his advisors over whether they should tell the people of Celes what they had learned from the Blood Sorcerers. The knowledge that the Stormless weren't *actually* Stormless was a big deal, to say the least. Nightingale had argued that the knowledge wouldn't do anyone any good, at least not until the Stormless gained access to their Crystals.

Castien agreed, for the most part. If all of the Stormless found out that they had powers, but then were told that they didn't have any way of using them for the time being... that probably wouldn't be received well.

His pulse quickened further, his breathing growing shallow just from thinking about all of this. Castien quieted his mind, listening for his heartbeat. He smiled slightly as he found it, syncing his breathing. *Five beats in, six beats out. Hold for three. Repeat.*

His heart thumped quietly, bringing a certain peace to his soul. It was the eternal beat of life, and each person had their own. That had always been fascinating to Castien. From the lowly criminals to the royal Kings, each of them possessed their own rhythm.

He let the calming thrum of life wash over him, bringing his thoughts back from their dangerous sprawl. "You were right," Castien said softly. "About the whole thing with the Solstice... About there being something worth investigating here in Celes."

"You sound surprised," Ilyana snorted. "I'm not sure if you've noticed, but I'm often right about most things."

"You thought your father was dead," Castien shot back. He blinked. "Sorry."

"No, it's a fair point." Ilyana smiled. "I was wrong about that."

Castien looked forward once again. "I'm glad that we have a plan," Castien said.

"The map Hykir and Likara drew for us isn't as helpful as we would've hoped," Ilyana noted. "All they were able to tell us was that the Blood Sorcerers' fortress was hidden within one of The Highlands' mountains, somewhere in the central north of The Highlands." Ilyana paused. "They said we'll know we're close when we start seeing red markings on the rocks, though who knows how helpful that piece of information will end up being... It'll likely take us at least a few weeks to find it."

"Which means that we will be away from Arvendon when the Blood Sorcerers return," Castien said.

"Yeah." Ilyana nodded. "Although I'm not sure we'd be able to do very much in Arvendon anyway, considering how everyone there wants the two of us dead."

"Likara said the Blood Sorcerers won't attack us if we mention her name, but I'm still not sure if I believe that." Ilyana brushed back her hair. "I suppose that if many of the Blood Sorcerers are in Arvendon, then we will have fewer guards to worry about at the fortress if things go south."

"Yeah," Castien said absently. *Hopefully, it won't come to that.*

"Either way, we'll get some answers," Ilyana said. "For all of us."

He thought of the attempt on King Nightingale's life. *A Shadow-Swift tried to kill him,* Castien remembered. "This is all just so confusing," Castien said. "How can we be certain that we're on the right side of things?"

"I don't know," Ilyana said. "Likara and Hykir may've saved my father, but I'm still hesitant to believe everything they've said."

"Me too," Castien said, lowering his head. "Their Sect *is* still trying to conquer Auris, regardless of how they try to rationalize it."

"And oftentimes when one seeks domination, it isn't for a good cause... At least if history offers any indication."

"But should we really base our judgment off of the past?" Castien asked. "Just because something hasn't happened before, doesn't mean it can't happen now."

"But it does mean that it's unlikely," Ilyana said.

"Which is why we need to be cautious."

"Either way, the logical next step is finding the Blood Sorcerers and speaking to this 'Blood Empress.' She's the key to all of this." Ilyana stood up. "Now come on, we need to get moving."

Castien listened to the loud clash of wood against stone as the gate slammed shut behind them. He watched the guards shuffle back to their posts atop the wall, settling in as if the group had never even been there.

"Come on, Castien. We haven't even left the ward and you're already falling behind," Elric called back, frowning.

Castien followed Elric at the front, feeling comfortable in his new traveling clothes as he passed by a Wisp. King Nightingale had offered them all baths and fresh clothing—which they had gratefully accepted. Castien rubbed his clean-shaven face, smiling at the smoothness. His stubble would return within a day or two, of course, but he enjoyed the moment of comfort nonetheless.

They passed through the white film of the ward, and within seconds there were dozens more Wisps zipping around them.

"Likara told us that it was upwards of a week's walk to the fortress, which means we should probably all get comfortable with being in the snow," Elric said.

"And that also means that you should probably get ready to hunt down a few snowprowlers. I don't plan on starving anytime soon," Arthion added, chuckling.

"I'll sustain us for as long as I can," Elric said from the front of the group. "The Highlands are harsh, but we'll be able to go for long enough to find the fortress. Besides, my concern isn't food; it's the Shadow-Swifts."

"They have no reason to attack us," Arthion said.

"And they had no reason to attack Arvendon—or Ilyana's father." Elric grimaced. "We can't count on them to be neutral any longer. The world is changing."

"And we have to change with it," Ilyana said. "The Blood Sorcerers seem to be fighting the Shadow-Swifts. We may be able to use that to our advantage."

"How?" Arthion asked.

"In this group, we have two Master Summoners, a Whisperer, and a currently powerless Starburner," Ilyana said. "The four of us together can be a valuable force on either side of this conflict, and we need to be certain that both sides realize this."

Castien flinched. *Starburner.* Such a powerful word... Such a powerful burden. He stopped himself. It wasn't supposed to be a *burden*; he needed to try getting that through his head. Many would see it as a gift—one that he should use, should he happen to come across any Crystals. The ability to manipulate energy and light was not something to be taken for granted.

He felt the Crystal fragment in his pocket, tightening his fingers around it. His arm ached slightly, the burn still hurting a bit.

A Wisp passed through him, leaving a tingling sensation in his chest.

Castien laughed a little bit at the feeling.

"I was thinking," Ilyana said, falling back to Castien's side. "The Blood Sorcerers said that their Crystals were growing inside of a mountain—the mountain that their Sect is using as a fortress."

"Yeah, I remember." Castien nodded.

"So wouldn't it make sense that *your* Crystals could be growing inside of one of The Highlands' mountains as well?" Ilyana asked, brushing her hair out of her eyes.

Castien thought. "I suppose that would make sense," Castien said. "But there are hundreds of mountains in The Highlands. How could we possibly find out which one has Starburner Crystals inside?"

"True," Ilyana agreed. "But either way, finding your Crystals could significantly increase our chances of coming out of these mountains alive."

Castien frowned. She wasn't wrong; he just still didn't like the thought of having their survival rest on him. He felt like his humanity was on the brink of being taken away... When you become a Summoner, it doesn't matter who you are—all that matters is the power you possess. Castien shook his head. He knew Ilyana didn't mean it like that, but it still stirred his anxiety.

I'm a Summoner, like it or not, Castien thought. *The sooner I try and accept that, the better.*

CHAPTER TWENTY-THREE
LEGACY

The darkness awakened.

He felt the awareness return, that *attention*—the presence that had been absent for quite some time now. The quiet, inky black abyss and its occasional threads of gold had become familiar, even comforting. The soft thrum of dark energy was now pleasant, rather than discomfiting. But it was changing. His sojourn was ending. The sense of peace was fading, eclipsed once again by violet wings and a Silver Sun.

The cursed wings beat in the distance, carrying his adversary closer and closer with each passing second. The strange pressure on his mind returned. The shadows moved, resuming their silent dances. It wouldn't be long now...

Asteros. That was his name. Asteros opened his eyes, finding that they had never been closed. He looked around, slowly allowing his mind to adjust. His body was floating, yet he had been still for what felt like an eternity.

He had been asleep—dreaming, actually. Dreaming of a place where there was solid ground... a place with light, and warmth. Love.

But alas, it was only a dream. He was still in this wretched Void, drifting aimlessly through the unknown.

"I see you have awakened," the Emissary said, his wings slowing to a stop. He was somewhere in front of Asteros, the dark mists covering him.

"I see that you haven't yet discovered a less confounding place for us to meet," Asteros said. His voice felt distant, as if he had been removed from his body.

"Ten months later and your wits have still not abandoned you," the Emissary mused. "Your will is a strong one indeed."

Ten months? Asteros tried to blink, then remembered that he didn't need to. *Have I been here for so long?*

"Fear not, the time you have spent here has not been wasted," the Emissary said. "It was necessary, for even those with the strongest minds still possess ordinary bodies."

"What..." Asteros twisted, floating through the darkness. "What are you talking about?"

"You didn't think I kept you here for nothing, did you?" the Emissary asked. "Your body needed time to adjust, time to *evolve*."

"Evolve into what?"

"Mmmm," the Emissary hummed. "You will see, in time." The Emissary fell silent.

"Why did you wake me?" Asteros asked. He reached out, feeling the soft thrum of energy. It was still draining. The Resurgence had begun, but Asteros's power was still slowing it, and it seemed that he had unconsciously continued to resist the draining even through his slumber.

And Shalheira was dead. That was why he was here. That was when his life had turned upside down.

"There is something you must see," the Emissary said. "Your body has adjusted to the... *unusual* nature of this place, and your mind has finally come to terms with your imprisonment."

Asteros searched himself, seeking that quiet sense of comfort that he found in the darkness. It was there.

"How did you know?" Asteros asked. "How did you know that I have come to find comfort here?"

"Because I was once in your position," the Emissary said. "It wasn't long before the tilting darkness felt like home to me too."

"You—" Asteros started. "You were imprisoned here?"

"I still am," the Emissary said. "But my circumstances have changed considerably. I now find myself with much more control than most who set foot in the Void." The Emissary paused. "I know you have questions, Asteros, and it is time that I finally give you some answers."

The darkness shifted, and Asteros caught a glimpse of the winged figure hovering before him. Shadowy sands blew across his face, covering his eyes. Asteros felt movement beneath him, and then... ground.

The sands receded, and Asteros found himself standing in the center of a dark chamber. The roof was likely hundreds of feet above him, for it was so high that, in the darkness, Asteros could not even see it.

A torch ignited somewhere nearby, casting light on the colossal stone walls of the bare atrium.

The room appeared to be a chamber of the Ancient Stonemasters, though something was different. The walls were cracked, and the usual carvings were either faded or missing entirely. The room was rectangular, easily two hundred feet in width and one hundred feet in length.

"This chamber... It's larger than any I've come across," Asteros said, taking a step back.

The torch moved, carried by a gloved hand. The figure holding it faced away from Asteros, staring at the faded inscriptions on the chamber's massive black stone walls.

"Who is that?" Asteros asked, moving forward.

The Emissary did not respond.

Asteros took another few steps, approaching the figure. Asteros walked past the man's arm, peering beneath his thick black hood.

A familiar face stared blankly through him, a face that Asteros had not seen in years. It was wrinkled, and hard. The dark eyes beneath that hood focused, and the man frowned.

"*Haldir?*" Asteros breathed. He spun back to the shadows, where the Emissary lurked. "Why have you brought me to a vision of my former master?"

"Continue to observe," the Emissary said from somewhere above.

Asteros waved a hand in front of Haldir's face.

Haldir showed no reaction.

"He cannot see me," Asteros said. "I'm not truly here, am I?"

A few seconds passed, and Haldir took a step forward.

Asteros stumbled back, but Haldir merely stepped through him as if he were nothing. A slight turquoise frost shimmered, then lingered on Haldir as he continued forward. *That answers that question,* Asteros thought.

Haldir approached the wall, scanning the engraved symbols above him.

Asteros followed his gaze, finding a series of small square marks a few dozen feet up the wall of black rock. *Runes,* Asteros realized. There were protective Runes carved here, likely to keep invaders out. But these Runes were faded. Many of them were cracked or even completely broken.

Haldir's figure darkened, becoming slightly translucent as he phased part of himself into the Unbound. He lifted from the ground, carried by tendrils of umbrakinesis. Arms of darkness raised him to the collection of faded Runes, where Haldir promptly drew his sword.

"What is he doing?" Asteros asked, looking upward.

"Those Runes are not like the ones that you have encountered," the Emissary said, once again speaking from somewhere above. "These are even older, dating back to the first arrival of the Harbingers."

Asteros's breath caught. "The chamber is that ancient?"

"Indeed," the Emissary said. "Now, watch closely."

Asteros looked back as Haldir raised his Shadow-Sand blade to the wall. Asteros angled his head, observing.

Haldir partially phased the blade and began tapping it against one of the Runes. He tapped lightly, as if seeking some sort of reaction from the Rune.

The engraved square did not light.

Haldir pulled back, then drifted to the next rune. He raised his sword and prodded this one as well, only to get no reaction once again. He continued this process for several minutes, until he reached the sixth Rune. When he tapped the point of his sword against it, a small white light ignited within the square.

"About time..." Haldir muttered. He reached into a compartment of his armor and produced another tool, one that looked like a chisel of sorts. The chisel was made of Shadow-Sand as well, naturally. Haldir raised both the sword and the new tool, then Haldir almost completely phased his sword and *slammed* it into the rock wall.

Asteros jumped back, startled by the sudden motion. Seconds later he found himself approaching once again, watching with fascination as Haldir twisted the phased sword, lining it up with the slightly functional Rune.

Haldir lifted the chisel and started to chip away at the carving of the Rune.

The Rune seemed to resist a little, but whatever power it had left was so drained that it could not resist Haldir's efforts to remove it.

"Why are you showing me this?" Asteros asked, turning around.

"Before his passing, Haldir gifted you with a key that unlocks Rune-Doors, correct?" the Emissary asked.

Asteros didn't respond.

"Didn't you ever wonder *how* he created such a thing?" the Emissary continued. "Your former master was far more resourceful than you believed him to be. He was seeking knowledge that he knew would be locked behind Rune-Doors, so, naturally, he searched for a way to open them."

"And he discovered that faded Runes could be removed from their writing place..." Asteros continued.

"And forged into a key," the Emissary finished. "A key full of nearly drained Runes—Runes that would pull energy from functional Runes when close enough to do so."

"Runes are capable of siphoning energy from one another... and Haldir discovered this?" Asteros asked.

"After many years of experimenting, yes."

"And using this knowledge, he gathered drained Runes, then forged them into a small device that was capable of stealing energy from Rune-Locks, thus disabling them?" Asteros questioned.

"The energy that was drained would then dissipate, as the faded Runes aren't capable of holding energy for long anymore," the Emissary added. "It was a genius invention, even by Kataurielan standards."

That word, Asteros thought. *Hadn't he said it before?* "But..." Asteros started. "What knowledge was he seeking? What was he looking for that required such a device?"

"That, Asteros, is what I am about to show you..." the Emissary said. "You may think you know a great deal about your former master, but he hid far more than you could possibly imagine. So settle in, my friend, for you still have *much* to learn."

CHAPTER TWENTY-FOUR
RETURN

Faelyn Titansworn sat by his cabin's window, watching as Arvendon slowly grew closer. It had settled on the horizon at first, a distant horror in his mind. But then it had drawn closer, slowly, inevitably, crawling to its full size.

There was no escaping this moment. Faelyn didn't even really care anymore. He was numb. It was a feeling that he had been craving for weeks now. None of it mattered anymore, everything was set in stone. Cyfalion's ward was weakened, and the city was doomed. Their forces were likely rallying for a counterattack on Arvendon. And the blood would be on Faelyn's hands.

It was a thought that brought Faelyn no remorse. Harrowing as it was, Faelyn didn't care. *History will understand,* he thought. A boy who lost everything... Responsible for losing a little more. Why shouldn't he just let it happen? All Arvendon had ever done for him was provide a source of stress and fear for him and his family. Why even bother with it?

The crashing of the waves changed, slowing. They were approaching the dock. Divebrisks dove around the outside of the ship, flashing their fins. A flock of blazecrest passed by overhead, their flaming wings illuminating the morning sky even further, battling against the heavy fog of the Mistveil as it settled over the city.

They passed through the ward, and the blazecrest turned back. Animals didn't like the inside of the wards—not as much as they liked the outside, at least.

Faelyn turned back, his eyes settling on the cracked silhouette of Summerglass Palace. It was looking better than it had when he left, with much of the Palace having been rebuilt over the last few weeks.

Hauling in the white stone from The Highland's mines would have been a difficult task, but a few of the warehouses in the waterfront district of Arvendon were filled with it, just in case the Palace needed repairs.

Like a ship sailing on calm seas, Faelyn thought. Arvendon worked so harmoniously, so *perfectly*. It was fascinating... And it was disgusting.

The ship lurched to a halt as they reached the dock. A set of footsteps heralded the approaching deckhands. Faelyn stayed staring out the window, watching as the sailors and traders milled around the docks despite the descending mists.

Seconds later, he felt a strong set of hands on the back of his chair.

The deckhands began pushing him on his hastily built device, which rattled horribly as it rolled.

He passed by his uncomfortable bed, and then his dresser, and finally came to the foot of the stairs. He reached up, using his bandaged nubs-for-hands to hold his crown in place. The golden coating had worn off in places, leaving the crown with patches of silver, especially around the twisted points.

The deckhands grunted, lifting his chair from the bottom and starting the tedious process of carrying him up the stairs. Faelyn brushed his white-gold vest with his free bandaged nub, waiting impatiently as the chair tilted and turned.

After several minutes, he reached the top. Staring at his legs—

where the ankles cut off a few inches too soon—Faelyn couldn't even feel sorry for himself. He looked to the side, catching sight of Eithor and Ayre.

They watched him with solemn eyes, not daring to say a word.

A wooden ramp hooked onto the edge of the deck, locking into place for Faelyn's departure. The deckhands pushed him forward, grunting with exhaustion after carrying him up the stairs.

He was lifted a short distance again and placed atop the ramp cautiously. It had several bumps to act as stops, though Faelyn didn't mind. If anything, it slowed his descent enough for the gathering crowd to get a good look at him.

A collective gasp ushered through those who observed his return. He didn't blame them. Seeing their King leave with a promise of vengeance and return with neither hands nor feet... It couldn't exactly be a very inspiring sight. Though that was exactly what Faelyn wanted. He could have returned in secret, surrounded by guards to block the views of others, but he did not. He wanted them to see what had happened to their leader... Their most powerful Summoner... Their King.

It was the only way to fully deliver the solemn message of defeat that he was hoping to convey: Arvendon was doomed—and he was okay with that.

The journey back to the Palace was long, to say the least. Faelyn didn't mind. Nearly everyone in the city had gotten a good look at him on his way back. It was likely to be all anyone talked about for the rest of the week.

The doors of Summerglass Palace creaked open, pushed by the guards who spared pitying glances at Faelyn. The entry hall looked smaller than usual, and the Incendiary lamps smelled of death. This place was a graveyard of his memories, reminding him of all that he had tried to forget on his short trip.

Being back here now... It would've been too much, had he been able to bring himself to care. A few nobles whispered among themselves as Faelyn passed. He made a point of continuing to stare forward blankly. *Why acknowledge them?*

He turned to the left, where they soon approached the first of many sets of stairs. There was a collection of eight assistants by his side now, each of whom would aid in carrying their King to his rooms. Faelyn had yet to move into the King's chambers and was still living out of his old rooms.

It took all of a minute for General Falx to approach him from behind.

"I see your trip to Cyfalion was unsuccessful?" Falx raised an eyebrow, his scarred face twisting with disgust.

Faelyn said nothing and continued staring at the wall in front of him.

They started ascending the stairs, four guards carrying Faelyn at a time.

He moved to clutch the sides of his chair, only for his nubs to rub along the wooden wheels. He sighed, leaning back again, surrendering himself to whatever rocking and tilting would come about as a result of the carrying.

"The Palace is being effectively and quickly rebuilt," Falx grunted. His vermillion armor clinked against itself as he climbed the stairs alongside Faelyn. "We have repaired the physical damage for the most part, though I fear that the psychological toll that this has taken on our nobles and citizens will take much longer to quell. I would recommend that you deliver a personal speech to ease their fears."

Faelyn said nothing, keeping his face hollow. He didn't care anymore. What was the point in telling him all of this if he didn't care? What was he going to do about any of this?

"Izara's Shadow, Faelyn, has your mind been broken as well?" Falx cursed after a moment.

"If only," Faelyn snorted, turning his head slightly. The chair tilted to the left, and Faelyn lurched to the side. It stabilized after a second, leaving him helplessly uncomfortable while his assistants labored beneath him. "Unfortunately, the dreams of insanity are only far-fetched wishes of mine, not realities."

"What happened in Cyfalion?" Falx asked, his voice hard. "I heard from the first Scorchers to arrive at the Palace, but I want to hear it from you."

"What do you think happened?" Faelyn turned his head back to the front, staring at the arriving wall. The stairs reached a turn, and his chair was set down. Another set of guards who had been following approached, switching out with those who had been carrying him to allow them to replenish their strength as they carried him through the next flight.

"You destroyed a Monolith," Falx said gravely. "The highest of all war crimes."

The guards grunted, lifting him up another flight before switching out again.

Faelyn had gotten used to being pushed around. "It was the only way to make Cyfalion pay," Faelyn said. "Burning a few buildings... That would've accomplished nothing. Buildings can be reconstructed. But killing Adresin Jastira and destroying a Monolith in one fell swoop... How could I resist?"

"Calida's Claws, you really have gone mad," Falx swore. "Do you realize what you've done? Cyfalion's remaining forces will already be on their way here to do the same to us. Suchara is their greatest ally, I can only assume they will be marching on us as well."

"Let them destroy our Monoliths," Faelyn said absently. "Arvendon is doomed either way."

"We need to prepare the city," Falx said firmly. "I can organize the ranks and arrange for extra defenses to be constructed. We have lost many Summoners since this whole ordeal began, and some—

like General Surge—are still out of the city. But if we play our cards right we can—"

"No," Faelyn said.

"What?" Falx started.

"No," Faelyn repeated. "When the Cyfali and the Sucharans arrive, we will allow them to take the city through whatever means they wish to do so. Fighting them will only delay our inevitable fall." Faelyn paused. "I have broken an unspoken law of Auris, and now the entire city must pay the price."

"Faelyn, you cannot simply surrender our—"

"You will refer to me as 'Your Majesty,'" Faelyn snapped, his voice cold. "And if I see you making preparations for war, then you will be removed from your position."

"But the Council will—"

"I don't give a shit what the Council says." Faelyn turned back to the stairs ahead. "You cannot hold a meeting without the King present, and I have no intention of calling an assembly any time soon." Faelyn paused. "Every city has its rise and fall, and now... now it is time for Arvendon to fall."

Faelyn sat in his rooms, staring at the miniature copy of The Duel: the ancient mural of the Gods. He had always been fascinated with the painting, though now he had a new understanding of it—a desire to see it reincarnated.

The Silver Sun drew his eye more than anything, pulling his attention to the back of the painting. He held the small copy in his nubs, struggling to get a good grip on it.

Three Gods on each side, bringing destruction to the lands at either of their backs. This very painting was one of the reasons he had commanded Falx to stand down. When two great powers fought one another, destruction was inevitable. There was no point in resisting.

Faelyn set the painting down, his eyes lingering on the dark silhouette of Izara—Goddess of Death. He wondered if she was treating his father well. He supposed the only way to find out was to join the two of them himself. It would all happen in due time. When the Cyfali attacked, Faelyn would be executed by either his own men or the invaders. His death was on the horizon.

A knock at the door brought him from his sorrows.

He turned, his makeshift wooden wheelchair rattling as he shifted. He could hardly move it on his own because, well, he didn't have hands. The servants had promised to construct him a more stable, less rickety version, but Faelyn wasn't even sure he deserved the luxury.

"It's Eithor, Your Majesty," a voice called from the other side of the doorway.

"Come in," Faelyn said, his voice empty. He sat there, staring at the ground as Eithor opened the door.

Faelyn could hear the guards shifting nervously as they let Eithor pass. They were still uncomfortable with the Illusomancer.

"It's painful to see you like this," Eithor said. He shook his head and sighed. "Perhaps if you had stopped before targeting the Monolith..."

"It doesn't matter," Faelyn said. "Arvendon's fall was meant to happen, and all that we have done is expedite it. No empire, no matter how grand and powerful, ever lasts. The lucky ones may make it a few thousand years, but nothing is permanent. Everything falls, everything dies. To deny such facts is to be in denial of life itself."

Faelyn could feel the Illusomancer's ice-blue eyes on him. Faelyn knew that the others pitied him. He knew that they felt sorry for the way things had turned out. He knew that they were simply placing their sorrowful emotions onto his image in an attempt to avoid facing their own problems. It was a shameful practice, but one that he suffered with grace, nonetheless.

"I did not come here without reason," Eithor said. He reached into his robes, producing a fragmented yellow Crystal.

The Wayfinder Crystals that were near the Monolith site, Faelyn thought. He hardly remembered those first moments after he woke up. In fact, he hardly remembered the week-long journey home from Cyfalion, as he had spent much of it asleep. Everything was simply a blur lately.

"These Wayfinder Crystals..." Eithor started. "They indicate a far more shocking truth than I first suspected."

Faelyn tilted his head.

"The Resurgence is beginning, yes, but I fear that the Wayfinders returned long before all of this began," Eithor said. "Hiding their Crystals under the Monoliths was a wise way of keeping their presence a secret. I'd even wager that our own Monoliths have Wayfinder Crystals around them."

"Why does it matter?" Faelyn shook his head. "Who cares if they're back?"

"The Wispwinds," Eithor said. "I was thinking... and I can only surmise that the Wispwinds are not useless after all, and that they are the Tempest of the Wayfinders."

Faelyn raised an eyebrow. *That is an interesting thought.*

"Which begs the question: In what other ways have the Wayfinders tricked us?" Eithor said. "If they were able to convince the world that one of the Tempests was worthless, *and* ensure humanity that they were extinct... who knows what else they could've done?"

"A fair point," Faelyn said. "But what are we supposed to do about it?"

"That I do not know," Eithor said. "But perhaps they have a part to play in all of this. Between the Blood Sorcerers and your father's assassination, I wouldn't be surprised if the Wayfinders were behind it all."

"You think so?" Faelyn met Eithor's eyes.

"I don't know," Eithor admitted. "But either way, we need to be *very* careful moving forward. For all we know, our future may already be set in stone."

My thoughts exactly. Faelyn closed his eyes. *We're all going to die.*

CHAPTER TWENTY-FIVE

THE INN

Castien Varic pushed through the knee-deep snow, pulling his thick coat around himself. He breathed out, then breathed in. He synced his respiration to his heartbeat and felt the warmth pulsing in and out of his veins. *Warmth, warmth, heat...* Castien opened his eyes—his manifestation of heat failing miserably.

He tightened his masked hood and looked out through the eyeholes. The Frostfall raged around them, blanketing everything in even more snow. The mountain they were presently ascending was steep and littered with boulders.

Elric led, his Cloudwalker coat stained with wet spots and snow.

Ilyana was behind him, wearing her traveling cloak, along with Arthion, who was still wearing a large gray robe.

"How much further?" Arthion called out through the violent Frostfall.

Snow fell heavily, dominating Castien's vision. He shuddered as he placed his hands on the edge of the next boulder, pulling himself further up the steep slope.

"Not far," Elric shouted back.

Castien could barely hear them over the howling wind. The mountains stretched in all directions, endlessly. His world was all mountains now. Truly, in his mind everything was just mountains. Everything else seemed to fade away in The Highlands, and it was just mountain, after mountain, after mountain... after mountain...

They were over a week into their search and the map had already proven to be useless. Every mountain looked the same, and they had no way of knowing where in The Highlands they were. Not to mention that they were yet to even see any of the vague landmarks Likara had mentioned.

Stones with red painted on them—that was all she had said. *Superbly helpful.* Castien grumbled.

"Wait," Castien said, his mind slowly coming out of the numb, thoughtless traveling state that it had been in. "How far to what?"

"Our next stop," Elric yelled.

The mountain was growing steeper—almost to the point where climbing without a handhold was difficult. Castien could not see the peak through the thick snowfall, though judging by how far they had climbed, they were likely getting toward the top.

Arthion—to his credit—had turned out to be in far better shape than any of them had expected. He hadn't complained once about all the climbing, and even given his lack of physical strength, he somehow was able to keep a solid pace that sometimes even surpassed Elric's. Of course, Elric was choosing not to fly so that the rest of the group could keep up, so it wasn't *quite* that impressive to say that Arthion was outpacing him.

If anything, Castien was the slowest among them. Ilyana—being a Dexteris—had taken the whole journey with ease. Castien hadn't really been bothered with the distance or the climbs, but the *cold?* Six Divines above... The cold was unbearable. He had never been so cold in his life.

The air itself seemed to pierce through Castien's bones, biting his skin and freezing his blood. Just when he thought it couldn't get any worse, the wind started blowing. And when *that* seemed like it couldn't get any worse, the snow started falling again—or night fell; both were equally terrible.

Yet he persevered. At first, the cold had felt nice on his burn, but the novelty had worn off quickly. Now he was trudging through the snow for the eighth day in a row, trying to think about anywhere but here.

Elric seemed to slow up ahead, signaling that they were nearing their next stop. It was likely a cave of some sort—as many of their previous stops for the night had been. Elric spent each morning scouting out shelters from the skies, then rejoined the group and led them accordingly.

Castien looked up to the dim, barely noticeable glow of the sun behind the thick clouds. Today had gone by fast, and the realization that nightfall was approaching gave Castien a bit of a smile despite the cold that night would bring. Of course, other than the glorious relief of sleep, there wasn't much to be excited about. The shelters were usually just caves that had naturally formed in the mountains. Sure, they provided relief from the wind, but not much else.

Castien rounded the rise, pushing through the snow to get a clear look at the next cave—only to learn that this wasn't a cave—or not a normal one, at least. Castien squinted through the thick Frostfall, trying to figure out what he was staring at.

It was an inn.

It was built into a cave for cover, with a small garden of iceblooms just before it—which was protected by an outreaching cleft of rock. The inn looked just like the one he had grown up in. *Could it be...?*

No. *We couldn't have come that far.* Castien blinked a few times, looking around. The world suddenly felt very distant. There was no chance they had gone that far southwest. It was impossible.

There were dozens of inns in The Highlands—which most people didn't realize. Running one of them offered the epitome of what one would call "the simple life," as there really was nothing to do other than grow iceblooms, hunt snowprowlers and greyfurs, and tend to the occasional traveler.

But this inn couldn't be his. This had to be a different one. It couldn't be that one. It wasn't.

Castien could tell already, even just from the way that the outer walls had been built, that it *was* in fact different, thankfully. He could never go back. He had left for a reason.

"Well, let's go in!" Arthion snapped. "I'm freezing my bones off out here. What are we waiting for?" The Whisperer shook his head, muttering something as he marched through the snow toward the thick wooden door. It had been built into the stone wall that covered the mouth of the cave.

Castien followed, his senses slowly detaching as memories of home returned to him. His feet felt heavy, and even the cold became a distant whisper in his mind. There was little to be said of his thoughts at the moment. Even as he walked, his mind was trapped in a loop.

He wasn't thinking about anything. There was nothing else... And his body was seemingly moving of its own accord. Castien was cowering away in the folds of his mind, hiding from the past and letting his semi-conscious body face the future.

Watching from a distance, the footfalls and steady shifts of his body became comfortable. He walked toward the wooden door, watching as Arthion pulled it open with a heave. Arthion stumbled inside, allowing the warm light to shine through the doorway.

Elric held open the door, keeping it still as Ilyana entered.

Castien neared, but stopped a few feet short. He froze right before the door, standing at the entrance.

Elric sighed, reached forward with strong, gloved hands, and pulled him inside.

Castien stumbled, feeling his senses slip away from him. For once, his breathing didn't increase; it *slowed.* His heart began to slow as well, seeming to drown in its own blood. The world seemed to be getting further and further away. His mind was sliding toward a comfortable shadow, letting it take him further and further and further until—

Castien awoke.

The room was warm. His bed was softer than he remembered. Somehow, his soldier's cot had gained fur blankets over the course of his slumber. His eyes peeled open, revealing the small, cramped stone room. A curtain had been drawn across the narrow doorway to give him the illusion of privacy. A small chandelier of candles hung low over his bed, almost close enough to touch.

No. He was back. He was *here* again. He was... *He was...* No.

It was... different.

A small wooden cabinet to his right told him so. The little night table hinted at such differences as well. He was not there. He was somewhere else. He was somewhere safe.

And his head hurt. He rubbed it, feeling the bandage over his forehead. He looked over at his left arm, feeling the cold wrapping over the burn. It came back to him quickly, the rest of the world and his memories melting in with surprisingly little resistance.

He was safe.

He was in The Highlands with Elric, Arthion, and Ilyana. He was searching for the Blood Sorcerers' fortress, which was somewhere in these mountains. He was safe.

Castien swung his legs over the edge of the bed, planting them on the cold stone floor. He felt a rush to his head, almost blinding him briefly. It passed quickly as he adjusted to being upright. His boots lay beside the bed; someone had taken them off for him. His coat was mostly free of snow as well. Whoever had brought him to this bed had taken good care of him.

Castien barely remembered entering the inn, though he couldn't recall much else. He discerned that he had fainted and resolved to rise from his bed and apologize to the others for making a scene. He slipped the thick leather boots on his feet and opened the curtain.

There was a large hearth in the center of the common room. It was surrounded by chairs, and beyond that lay a collection of long tables and benches.

Elric sat at one of the chairs, a large mug of presumably mead in his hand.

Ilyana and Arthion sat near him, also watching the hearth.

It was Ilyana who noticed him first.

"Well, it looks like he's alive," she said, raising her mug and smiling.

Arthion grinned as well, but carried no drink in his hand.

"Indeed, it does," Elric said, turning around. "Are you alright? You took quite the fall there."

"He's standing; he seems to be fine," Ilyana said.

Elric waved her aside, then turned back to Castien.

"I'm fine," Castien said, his voice coming out a little harsher than he meant it to. "Thank you," he added.

"Ah, the sleeper awakes," a voice said from somewhere to the left.

Castien spun, looking past the stone supports of the room and finding a large, bearded man sitting behind a wooden table.

"I'm glad you're doing alright, lad." The man had an Utryan accent and a puffy Utryan face, though his Eastern Tongue was good.

We must be getting pretty far into The Central Highlands, Castien thought. "Sorry about that," Castien said, approaching the small table the man sat behind.

"It's quite alright," the man said, extending a hand as he set his book down. "Yomec."

Castien took his hand, memorizing the man's name and shaking his hand softly. Castien's head felt a little heavy, though he stayed on his feet.

"I own the inn—as you probably assumed."

"I did, yes," Castien said uncomfortably. He looked around, trying to shake the feeling of familiarity from the area. He couldn't.

It was just too much like... *Like...*

He closed his eyes, feeling that *pressure* on his head again. It was coming back. His anxiety rose, pounding through his heart and into his blood. He opened his eyes, seeing only the same stone walls that he had grown up in. *It's like I'm right back where I started.* He opened his eyes.

There. In the back right corner, there was a door. Castien barely acknowledged whatever the man—Yomec—said next. He didn't care. He was *back* in this... This...

Castien pushed off the table, his legs wobbling as he stumbled toward the door. The world seemed to be closing in on him. He passed more curtains, and more rooms, and more chairs, and felt the cave itself collapsing over him. Everything was falling apart... He hadn't thought about that place in *years*. And now, his carefully constructed walls were being torn apart, brought down by the simple similarity of two inns in The Highlands. Everything that had been happening for the last month had distracted him from the memories, but now they were back just as suddenly as they had disappeared.

And Castien couldn't take it.

He made for the door. He had to get *out*—and he would.

Castien stumbled through the door, walking out into the darkness beyond. It was night, but he didn't care. It didn't matter. Nothing mattered. All that mattered was that he needed to get *out* of that damned inn.

The cold snow froze its way through his traveling clothes, burning into his bones and icing his veins. He didn't care. The snow was still falling lightly in the cold night, pushing Castien toward the continued rise to his left.

Wrapping around the cave of the inn, Castien climbed the slight slope. His lungs began to burn as it steadily grew steeper. It wasn't long before his muscles ached too. Everything was numb. There was no rhyme or reason to his movements, nothing felt real, but the steady beat of his heart gave him all of the justification he needed.

It was rapid. It was intense. He needed to settle it.

Bitterly piercing his skin even further, the cold began to truly dig itself into his body. Castien ignored it, pushing through the night-time freeze and continuing up the slope.

He reached out, grabbing hold of a boulder and pulling himself up a particularly steep section of rock. It was just like the night he had left. It was eerily similar. He was trudging through the cold snow, without a plan, without any sort of idea where he was going.

Castien's feet moved of their own accord, plowing through the thick snow with each passing step. He wouldn't stop. He couldn't stop. It was almost like he was—

Castien's foot caught a stone, bringing him to a grinding halt and putting him face down in the snow. He breathed heavily, his muscles burning with fear. Not even bothering to rise, Castien simply lay there. Maybe he could just lie here for a really long while, and when he was ready, he would move on—perhaps even go back to the inn.

But he couldn't face that now. He wasn't sure if he would ever be able to, but the thought of it was nice, nonetheless. Perhaps in a few days, he would be able to try again, or maybe he would simply wait until the group left and rejoin them afterward.

He wasn't sure how long he lay there before he felt the soft vibrations in the snow.

Castien twisted, sensing the footfalls with a strange awareness. The night around him was quiet—remarkably quiet. The Highlands had always bore a certain degree of peace that nowhere else on Auris held.

Nothing but the soft, silent snow, and the slow rise of the sister moons overhead. The world always seemed slower when it snowed —Castien wasn't sure why that was. It simply felt as if all of Auris had been placed under a Whisperer's calming curse, and the whole world was simply in a slow state of steadiness so long as the soft white flakes fell from the sky.

The footfalls sounded again.

Castien squirmed, twisting to see who had the *nerve* to follow him all this way after such a short time. He blinked, rubbing the snow from his face.

Someone approached him from behind.

Elric Knyvet sat down beside him, taking a long, deep breath and brushing the snow from his coat.

"You probably shouldn't be out here," Elric said. "There are snowprowlers. Wouldn't want you getting eaten now, would we?"

"Yeah," Castien said, composing himself. "I'm sorry for running off, I just—" Castien trailed off. He didn't need to talk about this right now. For all he knew, Elric was still debating whether or not he should kill Castien for helping assassinate Avenos.

"Castien," Elric said, taking off his hat and running a hand through his auburn hair. "I know that a lot has happened over the last few weeks, and as I'm sure you gathered, I was very angry at you and Ilyana for what you did to King Titansworn."

Castien remained silent, lowering his head.

"But after what we learned in Celes... I realize that this is all far more complicated than I thought," Elric said. "I know that I said I would get you an appointment with a Whisperer to start working through your anxiety, and I want to say now that I'm sorry I didn't follow through on that.

"Now, I know that I'm no Whisperer, but I'd be happy to listen if you're willing to talk about why that inn keeps either making you pass out or run away," Elric continued. "You don't have to, and I understand if you don't want to talk to me, but I'm saying now that I'm sorry for how the last few weeks have been." Elric paused. "Losing King Titansworn... It's been difficult. But I know now that the only way to honor his memory is to bring the true mastermind behind his murder to justice. You and Ilyana were merely the instruments this person used to do their dirty work. The two of you are not my true enemies."

Castien felt a warmth in the back of his eyes. Hearing Elric apologize... It helped. It was strange, as Castien should be the one apologizing for what he helped Ilyana do to Avenos, but still... It was nice. Elric had been a nice support to have, someone who understood Castien's anxiety. And Castien had missed that.

"Would you like to talk about why the inn sets you off?" Elric asked.

Castien took a deep breath, then looked out at the falling snow and barren mountainscape once again. *Five beats in, six beats out. Hold for three. Repeat.* The jagged peaks of The Highlands stretched out endlessly around him. Lone trees swayed in the distance below, painting their eerie shadows on the land beneath them. Stars shined overhead, lighting the way for travelers far below. Folds of the enigmatic, blue-green waves of light floated in the sky above, weaving between the stars.

Castien hadn't seen the lights in months. They were even more beautiful than he had remembered, despite the stains of anguish that painted those skies in his mind.

Elric turned and started to rise. "I understand," Elric said, taking his silence as an answer. "We need to be getting back, Castien." Elric stood up.

"It was my parents," Castien said softly, closing his eyes. He let the words flow out of him, releasing his inhibitions and speaking without thinking.

Elric sat back down, settling into the snow next to him.

Castien heard the soft rustle of his jacket as he buttoned it up, reminding Castien that he was still out in the freezing cold—but he could stand it for the time being. "They ran an inn in The Eastern Highlands, where I was raised," Castien said. His mind faded, leaving behind a place that was void of all thought. He spoke slowly, doing what he could to keep his voice steady.

Castien continued. "My father was a Whisperer, and my mother was Stormless. My parents were kind to me, and they were kind to each other." He took a deep breath. "They wouldn't let me go far, but it was a nice way to live. I knew I didn't want to run the inn for my whole life, but it was nice nonetheless." Castien paused. "Then I started to grow older, and I presented no evidence of being a Whisperer. Given that my father was one, I should've been one as well, but I wasn't. For some reason, I had no powers. My father tried to use his Whispering on me in an effort to awaken my powers—which made my mother unhappy... She even spent several months teaching me a breathing technique to resist Whisperers, as a result." Castien sighed. "Then something happened... A letter meant for my mother came in the mail one day, and it was intercepted by my father.

"It was a letter from someone who claimed to be *my* biological father—a Stormless man—and it was seemingly a response to another letter my mother had sent." Castien paused. "My father read it, accused my mother of having an affair... an affair that led to *my* birth. And suddenly it all made sense: I wasn't a Whisperer because the man who I thought was my father *wasn't really* my dad." Castien swallowed. "That alone proved that I wasn't my father's son, at least in my dad's eyes... My family fell apart within days. My mother abandoned me a few weeks later, leaving without a word. And my father? He grew to hate me. And I was left with him. I was alone with a father who hated me because I wasn't even really his son." Castien looked down. "I left three days later, traveling to Arvendon on foot. I joined the Stormless Corps as soon as I reached the city, and that was that," Castien whispered. "I left my old life behind, and being in this inn... It just brings all of the memories back."

Elric was silent for several minutes. "Your mother never sent for you?" he finally asked.

"Even if she tried to, she would have no way of knowing where I am," Castien said. "I don't even know if she's still alive."

"And your father?" Elric asked.

"He still runs the inn, so far as I know," Castien said softly. "But I'm not sure anymore."

Elric stayed silent for several moments, then turned to Castien.

Castien kept his gaze forward, feeling a soft hand on his shoulder.

"I can see how being in the inn would bring back those memories," Elric said. "And those are *heavy* memories to carry, Castien. I see now where much of your anxiety comes from."

Castien shrugged.

"I can help you, if you'd like—just as I tried to when we were on that first expedition," Elric said.

Castien looked back to the mountainscape again, letting the reassurance wash over his troubled mind. It kind of felt good to tell someone about his past. It still hurt, yes, but it somehow made him feel better to finally let it all out.

"Why do you want to help me?" Castien asked.

"Because I see myself in you," Elric said softly. "I suffered from anxiety as well, but I found my way out. I want to help you do the same."

"But—"

"These things... They aren't just in your head. They are *real*. These feelings are real and they are *terrifying*," Elric said. "But I fought my way out of it. I know the techniques, and I can teach you. But you have to promise me one thing."

Castien turned away, lowering his eyes. "What is it?"

"I need you to promise that you are going to try," Elric said. "I know it may seem hopeless, I know it may seem impossible, but it's not. I can give you a boost, but this is not something that will go away simply with kind words and a little bit of cognitive training. Without a personal drive to *heal*, I cannot help you," Elric said, his voice falling off. "So I ask you now, will you promise that you will at the very least try to improve? Because trust me when I say that I know how it feels, and that living that way isn't living... It's just existing."

Castien took a long, deep breath. He felt the air slip into his lungs, filling them to their limits. He felt his heartbeat rise in his chest, the blood flowing through his arms and legs—all throughout his body. He would do it. He knew that he needed to face these feelings, sooner or later. And the longer he waited, the stronger they would become.

Castien opened his mouth, and whispered, "I promise."

CHAPTER TWENTY-SIX

THE KEY

Asteros Silverglade closed his eyes, taking a deep breath. The sensation of breathing was one thing that still felt foreign to him in this strange place. He wasn't even sure if he *needed* to breathe here, but it seemed unnatural not to. Yet the continuous echo of his respiration on unseen walls was still discomforting.

There was still a *pressure* in his head, making it harder to think.

The black sands shifted, rustling in the phantom winds of the Void. The scene was changing once again. Somewhere overhead, the Emissary used whatever strange powers he possessed to prepare what was next.

"Are these memories?" Asteros asked through the shifting sands.

"In a sense," the Emissary said.

"But these aren't your memories, are they?" Asteros asked. He reached into the twisting black sandstorm around him. The sands parted around his hand, curiously avoiding his touch.

"No. The memories that I am showing you belong to Haldir," the Emissary said, his eerily hypnotic voice washing over Asteros's mind.

"The scene I showed you several months ago—the original Vanishing—was the memory of another."

"Endon's?" Asteros guessed. "The Harbinger of the Revenants?"

The Emissary hummed in confirmation.

"How do you have access to these memories?" Asteros further questioned. "If you can see all of this, then what do you need me for?"

"All of your questions will be answered in due time, Asteros," the Emissary rumbled. "Now come, the next memory is ready."

Asteros looked forward, watching as the spinning sands receded into darkness, leaving him standing in a small stone room.

Nearly one half of the room was taken up by a pit of coals and fire —a forge of some sort, judging by the setup. Various tools were laid about, indicating that whoever had been here last was not yet finished with their creation.

Haldir stepped into the room, slipping through a narrow door in the back corner behind Asteros. Haldir looked even older without his armor on; between his wrinkled face and long, almost white hair, it was clear that this memory took place toward the end of Haldir's unusually long life.

Asteros watched as Haldir resumed his work at the forge. "Where are we?" Asteros asked, looking around the walls of black rock.

"We are in Erydon," the Emissary said from above. "In a hidden room obscured by a false wall at the back of Haldir's rooms."

"*What?*" Asteros breathed. "There is a secret room in Erydon?"

"Not anymore," the Emissary said. "Haldir destroyed this place shortly before his death."

"But..." Asteros looked around. "Why? This place could've been valuable to us."

"This was his secret workspace," the Emissary said. "When he knew that his death was approaching, he chose to erase his work... And so, he used his umbrakinesis to loosen the rocks overhead and cause a cave-in."

Asteros fell silent, watching as Haldir lifted a small, Shadow-Sand ball using a pair of tongs.

Haldir stepped forward and plunged the ball into the fire. He held it there for quite some time, then removed it from the forge. Haldir then turned to another table, where several small chunks of rock lay carefully arranged. He used another pair of tongs to pick up one of the rock pieces, allowing Asteros to get a better look at it.

Just as Asteros had suspected, there was a faded Rune on the front of the rock.

Haldir turned back, sticking the Rune into the fire as well. He heated it for nearly a minute before taking both the ball and the Rune over to an anvil in the corner of the small room. He closed his eyes for a moment, as if focusing on something.

A few seconds later, a pair of umbrakinetic arms grew from his side, reaching out to hold the tongs in place. Haldir reached down and picked up a hammer. He lined the Rune up to a specific spot on the ball and began hammering the heated pieces together.

"This is how he forged the key?" Asteros asked over the rhythmic *clank* of the hammer.

"After several months of research and experimentation, yes," the Emissary said.

"And yet my question still stands: What did he need it for?" Asteros stepped forward, waving a hand through Haldir. Just as before, Haldir's form dissolved into a sort of turquoise frost wherever Asteros touched, only to reform as soon as Asteros removed his hand.

"One moment," the Emissary sighed.

A wave of that same blue-green frost washed across the scene, pushed by black sand across Asteros's vision. Within seconds the room had changed: The fire was dying down, and the tools had been returned to an orderly arrangement on one of the tables.

Asteros turned around, searching for Haldir.

Voices sounded on the other side of the doorway, familiar voices.

He started toward the corner of the room, then slipped through the narrow exit. Coming out to Haldir's former chambers, Asteros paused.

Two figures were standing at a table in the center of the room, seemingly reading over a map of some sort.

Haldir was facing toward Asteros, but the other person... Asteros narrowed his eyes in confusion. He recognized that black ponytail anywhere.

Asteros advanced, rounding the small wooden table to find Lucien Shade standing opposite Haldir, now facing Asteros.

"What is *he* doing here?" Asteros growled. "You mean to tell me that Haldir kept his work a secret from me, but not Lucien?"

"Indeed," the Emissary answered.

"This must've been only a few months before Haldir's death," Asteros said, aware that he was mostly speaking to himself. "Lucien looks roughly the same age as he does now." Asteros paused. "Why was this kept a secret from me?"

The Emissary hummed in confirmation. "Patience, my dear friend, there is still much that you have not seen."

"What are they looking at?" Asteros stepped forward. He scanned the map on the table. It showed The Highlands, though it had a considerable number of marks on it.

Several mountains throughout The Central Highlands were marked with an "X." Several more were circled, and a few simply had a slash drawn through them.

"Kondos, Lirim, Faras, Sundrak..." Asteros read. "If they're looking for the chambers that I found, then they're looking in the wrong places," Asteros said, continuing to scan the circled mountains.

"They weren't looking for the safehouses that you discovered," the Emissary said. "They were looking for something else."

"Then what?" Asteros asked. "Beyond the Stonemaster hideouts, there aren't any more secret locations that we would have any way of knowing about."

"Haldir stumbled upon a door several decades before this

moment—the door to the chamber that you saw him in a short time ago," the Emissary continued. "The Runes had faded, so the lock was no longer functional... But upon realizing that there were many more chambers like that one, Haldir began looking for a way to get inside those that had working locks."

"I think that we advance to Faras next," Lucien said, speaking from within the memory.

"Lirim is closer to Herul," Haldir said, naming another mountain. "If we are basing our investigations off of proximity, it would be most logical to try Lirim next."

"We have been *trying* proximity," Lucien sighed. "Why not try somewhere further away? Perhaps that is where we have been wrong."

"The others have had valuable information," Haldir countered.

"Information that has always led us back to this table," Lucien said. "We've found several outposts, but none of what we've been searching for."

Haldir bit his tongue, his hard eyes scanning the map once again. "Fine," Haldir said. "We leave tonight. Let's hope this door isn't so difficult to find as the last one."

Lucien nodded. "Thank you." Lucien bowed. "Your consideration is appreciated."

"You've proven yourself to be wiser than most," Haldir said, his voice low. "Your counsel has been insightful."

Asteros watched curiously as Lucien walked away, slipping out of the room. "Lucien has never spoken to me with such respect," Asteros said.

The Emissary laughed. "That's because he doesn't respect you."

"I still don't understand," Asteros said. "What were they looking for?"

"Underground testing chambers," the Emissary said. "Dating back to the time of the Harbingers—my time."

"But..." Asteros started. "Why?"

"Because, dear Asteros, there is something that those of my time were researching, something that has been lost to the ages," the Emissary said. "It was the wish of your former master to recover this forgotten process."

"What sort of process?" Asteros asked.

The Emissary seemed to shift his attention to Asteros. "You still do not trust me," the Emissary said.

"Of course not, why would I?" Asteros frowned.

"Then why do you listen to my stories?" the Emissary hummed.

"I have little choice, it seems." Asteros folded his arms. "Yet you speak of things that interest me, and thus I am choosing to listen."

"You wish to know the knowledge I possess, yet you still fight against the Resurging energies," the Emissary mused. "Strange..."

Asteros looked back, feeling the subtle drain of his near-endless power as he slowed the Resurgence. "I will hold my position until you give me reason to surrender it," Asteros said. "What you have shown me thus far has been intriguing, but it gives me no reason to abandon my stance."

The Emissary seemed to think. "A wise answer." The Emissary paused. "Though I must warn you, what comes next is a bit more... *excitable*. Are you sure you're prepared?"

Asteros lowered his gaze, then closed his eyes. *Whatever gets me back to Auris sooner.* "Show me."

CHAPTER TWENTY-SEVEN

REUNION

Castien Varic continued through the Frostfall, feeling the light snow fall on his shoulders.

Elric walked beside him, explaining the various techniques that he had either developed himself or been taught by his Whisperer. He spoke from behind the scarf that covered his face, but Castien could still hear him decently well.

The slight depression surrounding them was more of a small gully than anything else, Castien supposed. They knew that they were in the general area of the Blood Sorcerers' fortress, but they still had no idea how they were actually going to find it. All they could see out here was mountain, after mountain, after mountain.

Castien nodded, suddenly aware of his breathing. He synced it with his heartbeat and continued walking. "How did you do it?" Castien asked, breaking the silence. "How did you stop these anxiety attacks?"

Elric turned to him. "It takes a lot of time to get to where I am today," Elric said. "It is unfortunate, but it is true. Although you have the power to reach this position—everyone does—it takes a little practice."

"Alright, so tell me what I need to practice," Castien prodded.

Elric laughed. "Well, for starters, I think that it may help if you understand what is happening to you first. I know you're eager to learn how to fight it, but learning about the nature of what is happening within your body can be just as beneficial as the techniques to combat it."

"I'm terribly sorry, I couldn't help but overhear you," Arthion said, drifting from the front of the group toward the back.

Ilyana stayed at the helm, guiding them through the midday Frostfall.

They were taking turns at the front of the group, where they were tasked with being on the lookout for any stones with red painted on them.

"If you are talking about what happened at the inn a few days ago, I remember that," Arthion said, joining in on their conversation. "As a Whisperer, I know more than most about the nature of the human mind, though I didn't receive as much training for dealing with personal issues as others of my station. Perhaps I can offer my advice in addition to Commander Knyvet's?"

"That would be appreciated. Thank you, Arthion," Elric said, his goggles twisting slightly to reveal a smile in the eyes beneath.

Castien looked to the Whisperer, finding himself with a sudden appreciation for the man. Arthion had put aside his distrust for Castien and Ilyana for the sake of uncovering the truth, and now he was even helping Castien overcome his struggles. Not many men of his position would be strong enough, nor wise enough, to recognize that some things are greater than simple duties and loyalty.

Castien looked up to the surrounding mountaintops, gazing at their peaks with a sense of awe and curiosity. They towered over him. Snow fell over their sides in drifts, pushed by the strong winds of the peaks.

A shadow seemed to appear at the top of the mountain.

Castien squinted. Atop the ridge nearest to him, there had been a slight silhouette. It seemed like nothing more than a boulder, but Castien was all but certain that it hadn't been there before.

Shadow-Swift? Castien thought with a start. There were no other inhabitants of the mountains—none that were human at least. A Shadow-Swift meant certain death. Their only chance of surviving would be to simply hope that they were ignored.

Castien looked back to the ridge above. The shadow was gone. Perhaps it had been nothing. *It has been a long trip, after all,* Castien thought. Besides, it was far enough away that the whole thing could've simply been a trick of the light.

"The most important thing in those situations is to find out what exactly is triggering that reaction in your body," Elric said, continuing in the middle of a conversation.

Tarathiel's Stones! Castien cursed himself; he hadn't been paying the slightest bit of attention. "What reaction?" Castien asked, trying to play it off casually.

"The activation of your body's panicked, defensive mindset," Elric said.

Castien tilted his head slightly, taking a second to process what he had missed. Now that he thought about it, it made sense. The way he felt when he was in that inn was nearly exactly the same way he felt any time he was in a fight... Only, there was no fight at all. *Curious.*

"Obviously, your most recent event in the inn was caused by the environment, but others can be caused by something someone says —or does—or even just a random thought of yours," Elric continued. "The point being, trying to completely isolate yourself from all possible sources of this feeling is both impossible and pointless."

"What do you suggest I do instead?" Castien asked, trying to bring his mind back to the conversation.

"The first step in handling these situations is being able to recognize when they are beginning," Elric said.

"Meaning?" Castien turned his head to face Elric and Arthion.

"It is important to recognize the early signs of one of these events and teach your body to tell you that something may be happening," Elric said. "For example, I could always tell that one was beginning because my heart rate would increase. My breathing would follow shortly after, and then everything else would come crashing into my mind all at once."

"Whisperers can aid in slowing this process. Powerful ones can even prevent the distress in your mind altogether," Arthion added. "But keep in mind that the more dependent on one's power you become, the harder the fall will be when you are inevitably cut off from it."

"Once you recognize the signs of an event, you need to start telling your mind what to do. It may sound strange, but it's easier than it sounds," Elric continued. "The Whisperer I trained with always told me to give myself a few minutes to forcibly calm down my thoughts, and focus on slowing my breathing. Once I was able to do that, I started to find a way to distract myself from what was happening," Elric said. "I would list things that made my environment safe, or reasons that it would be alright to have an event, but overall, I would simply try to find a task to occupy myself with— sometimes it can be something as simple as having a conversation with someone."

"And then..." Castien said.

"That's it," Elric said. He laughed. "That's it, Castien. I know it seems like I've told you nothing at all, but that's all it takes to overcome these—that, and a little practice, I suppose."

"That's..." Castien started. "That's it? But it seems so simple," Castien said, trailing off.

"And that's because it is," Elric said, his voice warm. "I know that it will be hard to remember these things the first few times you experience an event after learning them, but I promise that I will be there to remind you. I know that look in your eyes when I see it, and if I ever spot it again, I'll do everything I can to guide you out of it."

"The truth is Elric's strategy is one that I've never heard of,"

Arthion said. "It's very kind of him to share it with you. Elric has truly shown himself to be worthy of my honest respect."

"Arvendon has plenty of good men on their side... Luka and Surge are far more dedicated to the crown than I." Elric said. "That one, though." Elric nodded to Ilyana up ahead. "I don't know if I can say the same about her."

"There's more to her than you'd think," Castien said. He blinked a few times, not realizing that he had spoken. *Did I just defend her?*

The others fell silent. Castien felt a slight warmth within, despite the falling snow and the bitter cold. It was strange—the way he felt about Ilyana. He had gone from disliking her to trusting her to hating her... to slowly trusting her again.

Movement caught his eye to the left. Castien tilted his head, spotting a distant shadow moving atop the nearest ridge.

The others noticed it too. Arthion and Elric both stopped in their tracks.

"Ilyana!" Elric called out.

"What is it?" Ilyana grumbled, approaching through the thick snow. "I think that I might actually be on the trail of—"

Elric pointed.

Ilyana paused, following his gloved finger.

Castien watched as the silhouette stood up. *That's definitely a human,* Castien thought with a start. His pulse quickened, his muscles tensing, not with anxiety, but in preparation for a fight. If there was someone spying on them in The Highlands...

The figure moved... toward them.

"Get ready!" Elric shouted. His daggers slipped from their sheaths into his hands, called by unseen winds.

Ilyana drew her butterfly-blades from their spots on her back, and Castien readied his crossbow. The damned device was annoyingly clunky, and even holding it up with his bandaged arm while trying to load the bolt seemed to take an eternity.

Castien's heart thundered. He stole a glance upward, catching the distant figure leap off the ridge. It slid down the mountain, approaching them with blinding speed. *Shadow-Swift? Or a Dexteris?* Either way, Castien needed to be ready.

His gloved fingers were numb from the cold. He hastily fumbled with the metal bar, pulling it up and over the holder toward the back. The wires tensed, holding strength in them once again as the bolt quivered Castien's unsteady hand. He struggled to load it into place. *No!* He couldn't load it, not under this pressure.

Castien looked back to the figure, finding him sliding on feet that looked slick. *Cryostalker.* Castien raised the crossbow, waiting for Elric's word as the figure continued approaching.

Elric's figure tensed, then loosened slightly.

"Wait. Hold your fire!" Elric shouted, lowering his daggers.

"Are you mad?" Ilyana hissed.

"No..." Elric said, pulling down his scarf to reveal his rosy face and a firm smile. "I recognize that armor. That's not just any Cryostalker... That's Luka."

Castien lowered his still unloaded crossbow, watching as the Cryostalker slid closer and closer. He squinted through the Frostfall, realizing with awe that the man was sending out a thin sheet of ice through his feet in a constant stream, keeping him moving at an impressive speed.

The Cryostalker lowered his hood, sliding with a beautiful sense of grace as he neared the group. The leather armor was exactly as Castien had remembered it, along with the bald head and pale, cracked skin.

"I couldn't believe my eyes when I saw it," Luka said, hopping from his stream of ice and landing in a soft stop roughly twenty feet away from them. "You can imagine my surprise when I was searching The Highlands, and I saw an Elosian woman, a Cloud-walker, a Whisperer, and a Stormless traveling together. I knew that such a strange group could only be comprised of you four."

"Luka..." Elric started. He took a few steps forward, as did Luka. "It's good to see you again, my friend." They embraced.

"It's good to see you too," Luka said, pulling back. "What are you doing out here?"

"We received a clue as to the location of the Blood Sorcerers' fortress, and we are now attempting to locate it and learn the true goal behind their conquest," Arthion answered.

Luka stepped back, bringing a gloved hand to his cracked, ghostly white chin. "I am here for the same reason."

"What do you mean?" Ilyana asked, advancing.

"It's good to see you again too, Ilyana." Luka rolled his eyes. "But I too was given a clue to help me locate the fortress, and I know that finding the fortress is the only way I'll ever get to the bottom of all this."

"Weren't you heading to Freyfall?" Castien asked, shuddering against the cold.

"I *went* to Freyfall, and I learned some things that are rather important to our cause," Luka said, his voice turning grave. "One of which is right behind the mountain back there." Luka pointed behind him.

"What?" Elric asked. "Is that where the Blood Sorcerers' fortress is?"

"I wish it was, my friend," Luka said. "But unfortunately, on the other side of that mountain, there is a large gully where Freyfall's army is currently marching."

"I—" Elric stuttered. "That would mean they're going southeast, which would mean that they are—"

"Heading for Arvendon, yes," Luka finished. "And, as you may've guessed, they're not going into the city as allies."

A heavy silence fell over the group. Castien felt his pulse quicken. Arvendon... His home was being marched on at this very moment. The city would be able to defend against Freyfall, but if they had no warning that they were coming...

Freyfall was powerful, but not nearly as powerful as Arvendon—or even Suchara, for that matter. After the skirmishes in The Highlands over the past few years, Castien's faith in his people was strong. But fighting in one's own city was very different from fighting in the mountains. Their city was defensible, yes, but preventing any of Arvendon's people from falling was impossible.

"I take it you've heard about Avenos's assassination as well?" Luka asked.

Castien shot a look at Ilyana, who stared forward.

"We did," Elric said. "We were in the city when it happened, but between the two Shadow-Swifts and the chaos that they caused, we were unable to save the King."

"And you thought that it would be wise to leave the city after it had just lost its King?" Luka questioned, his demeanor changing.

"It was necessary," Elric said calmly. "Trust me, Luka, we didn't want to leave, but we had no choice."

Castien blinked a few times, feeling his pulse settle. *Elric isn't telling him about our involvement?*

"Interesting." Luka looked around, then upward. He scanned the sky, finding the faint imprint of the sun beyond the clouds. "There's something I need to tell you about first."

"Which is?" Elric prodded.

"Something that I learned in Freyfall—about the Blood Sorcerers," Luka said, meeting their eyes. "I'm... I'm not so sure that they are our enemies."

"We have reached the same conclusion," Elric said. "But we are still uncertain of their motives."

"So you know about the Resurgence then? And the Shadow-Swifts?" Luka asked.

"To some extent," Elric said. "What have you been told?"

"That the Shadow-Swifts are the ones responsible for the Resurgence," Luka said. "And that they orchestrated Avenos's death."

"We put together as much," Elric said. "But we don't know if what we've been told is true."

"I know." Luka nodded. "But the Blood Sorcerers believe that the Shadow-Swifts have something else planned, and that it's only a matter of time before they put their plan into action."

"But what more could they possibly want?" Ilyana asked.

No one answered.

Castien looked to Ilyana, then to Elric. It seemed that what Likara had told them wasn't entirely false.

"Either way, our first step is finding the Blood Sorcerers' fortress," Luka said after a moment.

"Agreed," Elric said. "We were told to look for rocks with red markings on them, though we have yet to find any."

"Figures," Luka muttered. "The few that I've found were over that rise back there," Luka said, pointing behind himself. "They seem to be pointing me in the direction of the fortress—though I diverged from the path when I saw the four of you."

"How did you find the markings so quickly? How long have you been out here?" Ilyana asked.

"I've been searching for several days, and you forget that I can move much faster than most." Luka paused. "Though so you can you, I suppose."

Castien snickered.

"Well then, what are we waiting for?" Arthion started. "Show us the way, Luka. We'll follow you."

"I fear that it may still be quite some time until we find the fortress, but I will show you the clues that I've found so far. This way," Luka said, motioning north.

Makes sense, Castien thought. *The markings would need to be spread across a wide enough area to make it easy for prospective Blood Sorcerers to find, but how specific can simple markings be?* Castien started walking, feeling the bitter cold bite his skin once again. He tightened his hood, content to hide behind it now that the conversation was over.

They needed to hurry. Time was not a luxury that they had. If they wanted any chance of uncovering what was happening with the Resurgence, and if they even *hoped* to try and help Arvendon before Freyfall attacked...

Niventia's Light, Castien thought. *We need to move fast.*

CHAPTER TWENTY-EIGHT

ORDERS

It was several days before the knock that Faelyn Titansworn had been expecting finally sounded. It was a time of deep focus for Faelyn, though it had begun in despair and numbness.

Idris had been working with Faelyn on a new method to aid him in his paralysis, but Faelyn needed a break.

And now, sitting facing the wall of his bedroom, listening as one of his servants read a storybook aloud to him, Faelyn heard the knock on the door. He dismissed the elderly servant, knowing that this visit was coming.

The servant slipped out through the servant's exit, disappearing into the shadows, leaving Faelyn alone in his chambers.

"Come in," Faelyn said. The handle turned, and the door creaked open. Faelyn kept his new chair facing the wall, away from the door—not that he could've turned it himself, anyway.

He heard footsteps, soft ones.

Faelyn turned slightly, feeling his golden hair shift. He caught sight of his friend closing the door behind himself.

This was likely regarding Faelyn's order that no one was to make preparations for war in anticipation of the Cyfali attack. They were going to be defeated anyway; they might as well surrender and hope some of them were spared.

Falx had been most resistant, but he had no choice... Though Faelyn suspected that the old general was still trying to find ways to prepare for the Cyfali assault.

This was a natural part of history. People gained power, and people lost it. People lived, and people died. Faelyn had tried to deny all that had happened—he had tried to deny that it was *his* fault—but it was no use.

Running from destiny only tired one's legs. There was no point fleeing your fate, for it would find you no matter how far you went, or how well you hid.

Faelyn heard more footsteps, and felt a pair of hands grab onto his wheelchair. The chair turned slowly, granting him a full view of the room.

Reluraun stepped out from behind him, pulled out a chair from the table in the corner, and sat down.

Faelyn met those emerald eyes, watching curiously to see what Reluraun would do next. The Cloudwalker was strong willed, but he had a tendency to hesitate.

"Aren't you going to say anything?" Faelyn asked. "I've been waiting for you to come visit, and now that you're here... You're just staring at me."

Reluraun surveyed Faelyn's disabled state, looking him up and down twice. "Why did you do it?" Reluraun asked softly. "Why did you do all of this?"

"It was war," Faelyn said. "There are no rules in war."

"And yet you have broken one," Reluraun said. He shook his head. "Destroying a Monolith... Izara's Shadow, what were you thinking?"

"Cyfalion hurt me," Faelyn said. "They destroyed my family, and therefore attempted to destroy Arvendon. I was simply returning the favor."

"Jastira is dead," Reluraun said. "The city has already suffered extensive damage from the Tempests since you weakened the ward."

Faelyn said nothing.

"Hundreds have lost their homes," Reluraun said. "The walls have nearly fallen entirely, and the city has been irreparably damaged."

Faelyn remained silent.

"Helionn's Sun, Faelyn! You've lost your hands and feet, have you lost your mind as well?" Reluraun's voice rose. "Can you not see what you've done?"

"I did what I felt was right," Faelyn said. His voice was calm and distant. It was almost as if he were an entirely new person. He wasn't sure who he was when he had left for Cyfalion, or even when he had awoken from the battle. All he knew was that he was someone else now. *Someone... different.*

Reluraun snorted. "You were blinded by your own rage, weren't you? You didn't even stop to consider it, did you?"

"You don't know what it's like," Faelyn said softly.

"*Don't* try that with me," Reluraun snapped. "My father has been gone for *weeks*. Damnit, you think I'm not upset too? The difference is I'm not about to doom an entire city simply out of spite."

"Is that why you think I did it? Out of spite?" Faelyn shook his head. "I did it for the sake of justice."

"And what is all of this, then?" Reluraun asked. "Why are you ordering Falx to stand down and surrender the city? If destroying Cyfalion was 'justice,' then what would you call the surrender of Arvendon?"

"Justice as well."

Reluraun scoffed in disbelief. "You're insane."

"I'm doing what's best for our city," Faelyn said. "Cyfalion will march on us with the intention of destroying Arvendon. By surrendering, we give ourselves a chance of surviving."

"You realize they'll execute you, right?" Reluraun raised his voice again.

"Would that be such a bad thing?" Faelyn tilted his head. "I have no *hands,* and no *feet,* Reluraun. Death would be a relief."

"For you, maybe. But for the rest of us?" Reluraun shook his head, looking away. "Why bring everyone else down with you?"

"We're all going to die anyway. Why does it matter if I expedite that process?" Faelyn asked. "No, that is no crime in my mind."

"I'm going to prepare the city," Reluraun said. "We cannot simply roll over and die."

"You will obey my orders and prepare only for a surrender," Faelyn said firmly. "I am your King; you will do as I say."

"And if I don't?" Reluraun challenged. "We all feel the same. You are the only one who wishes to surrender."

"It does not matter," Faelyn said. "I am a Titansworn, and my word is law."

"What of the Council?" Reluraun started. "They will overrule you."

"The Council was only meant to advise me," Faelyn said. "It is my right as King to do as I please; the Council can only call a meeting with my blessing, and without an assembly, no rulings can be made."

"Faelyn," Reluraun said, his eyes hard. "You—"

"You will refer to me as King Titansworn or Your Majesty— whichever you prefer," Faelyn said, cutting him off. "But you will *not* call me by my first name."

Reluraun snorted, running a hand through his auburn hair. "I can't believe you." Reluraun turned away, making for the door.

"Guards," Faelyn called calmly.

The door opened seconds later. One of the guards—clad in orange Scorcher armor—entered.

"Assign two men to watch over young Reluraun here," Faelyn said. "I want him monitored twenty-four hours a day. Ensure that he makes no effort to contradict my plans to surrender."

Reluraun's jaw dropped. He spun to Faelyn, eyes alight. "You cannot be serious." Reluraun cursed.

Faelyn held his gaze. "Guards, you have my orders. See to it that my wishes are fulfilled." Faelyn paused. "And escort Mr. Knyvet to his rooms, please. I would like him to remain there for the rest of the day."

"Yes, Your Majesty," the guard said. He took Reluraun by the wrist, guiding him out of the room.

"You're going to get us all killed, Faelyn," Reluraun said as he was pulled toward the door. "Our blood will be on your hands."

Faelyn nodded slightly.

Reluraun was pulled out of the room. The door shut behind him, leaving Faelyn alone to ponder his words. *Our blood will be on your hands.*

He didn't care.

CHAPTER TWENTY-NINE

THE DUNES OF DESPAIR

Soft gray sand rose and fell through the vast desert. The sweet Blazeday winds blew grains of it into the air, casting the sand toward the sky, only for it to fall once again. The barren wastes lacked any life, save for the occasional krellin.

It was a fascinating scene to any who had come from somewhere else, and Elias Surge was experiencing it while sliding over the dunes at a frightening speed.

The Dunesail had proven to be much quicker than walking, and for that, Surge was thankful. However, he had to admit that he was more than a little afraid of falling out.

A silly fear, of course—as were all fears. Yet it was a fear that he had nonetheless, and a fear that kept him a comfortable distance away from the wooden railings at all times.

Saevi Embrore, on the other hand, was perched on the bow of the vehicle, breathing in the hot desert air with an indecipherable excitement. She stood on the slightly raised front of the wooden deck, holding onto the railing with one hand.

She laughed, whooping and crying out whenever they crested a particularly large dune.

Surge shook his head. It was an interesting experience—riding on a Dunesail. Yet he certainly had no desire to stick his head out the front and shout with pleasure. He would have ridden a Storm Gale all the way to Suchara if it weren't for Saevi, but they had agreed that they would stick together after separating from the expedition crew several weeks ago.

The small two-person crew of the Dunesail kept busy with the workings of the vehicle. Both were from Goldenleaf, where Surge and Saevi had boarded the vehicle. Both were also originally from Asari.

The taller of the two, Tariq, ran across the small deck—barely more than twelve feet across—to the other side. He grabbed onto one of the levers sticking out from the deck and pulled it back as they reached the bottom of another dune.

The other deckhand, Izaat, scrambled across the rear deck. He quickly reached the mast of the Dunesail and began cranking the attached lever.

Surge looked to the front of the vehicle, watching as the landship slowly turned upward to ascend the next dune. The dune was easily sixty feet tall, thanks to the violent winds that led to the wide, clumped dispersal of sand throughout the Dunes of Despair.

Looking up, Surge caught a glimpse of the inside of the large, tunneled sail at the top of the ship's mast. He spotted the Scorcher and Cloudwalker Crystals within.

Tariq had explained how the vehicle worked before they had departed from Goldenleaf, saying that it used cracked Scorcher and Cloudwalker Crystals to generate heat and air—the combination of which in a focused wind tunnel led to propulsion.

The sleek, curved bottom of the vehicle slid with ease across the sand. More flaps protruded from the sides of the vehicle—more sails to help lessen the weight of the ship. With the continued cranking of the lever, Izaat was tightening a clamp around the cracked Crystals inside of the sail, which caused them to release more energy.

The Dunesail began to climb the mountain of sand, propelled by the wind and heat produced in the focused tunnel. The vehicle picked up speed, sliding further and further up the dune until they reached the top. Yet this time the view was different. Instead of endless waves of gray-sanded dunes, before them lay a mass of a yellow-brown coloring, with speckles of green tossed all around it. The mass itself resembled a *colossal* castle, one that was several hundred feet in length, width, and even height.

The capital city of Suchara was now within view.

The Dunesail turned downward, and the cranking stopped. Izaat and Tariq released their levers and let the sleek bottom of the ship do its job. The vehicle started sliding down the hill, wings on the side still extended to ensure it didn't get too heavy and start sinking into the sand.

It moved slowly at first, but soon began to pick up speed as it sailed down the back side of the dune. As if on cue, Saevi climbed up on the mast of the small ship and began whooping with excitement once again.

Despite himself, Surge smiled. He held onto the mast separating the middeck from the rear, keeping him far from the edges. Yet, as he felt the wind in his face, he began to understand why some were jealous of the Cloudwalkers. It was an indescribable feeling, one that Surge had only experienced on the bow of a fast ship at sea... and it was wonderful, and terrifying.

Sure enough, the Dunesail reached the bottom of the dune, and Tariq and Izaat began to crank their levers once again to raise it over the next one.

Saevi turned around, walking the roughly ten feet between where Surge stood and the front of the ship.

"Did you see that?" Saevi asked, her amber eyes still alight with pleasure.

"You acting like a child? Yes, I did. It was hard to miss." Surge snorted.

"Not that," Saevi snickered. "I meant Suchara."

"That was hard to miss as well," Surge said, his voice low and gravelly. "We should reach it in a few hours, no?"

"I would expect so," Saevi said.

They had originally planned to circumvent the Dunes of Despair until they reached the shortest point of crossing, and then continue on foot. Yet that would have taken many weeks, if not months. By some grace of the Six Divines, when they had arrived in Goldenleaf to resupply, they had discovered a small set of vehicles called Dunesails. Tariq had said that they had been invented in Suchara a few years back, though they were now kept on all edges of the desert to make crossing the dunes easier and faster.

"We will be there several weeks ahead of when we expected to arrive, and given that we don't exactly have a lot of time, I think that we need to get to work right away," Saevi said. "I know Suchara well, and unfortunately, the Thalas are not exactly the most welcoming of outsiders."

"That means they should reject the Blood Sorcerers as well," Surge said.

"I suppose," Saevi said, shrugging. "I assume we're a little ahead of the Blood Sorcerer that was sent to Suchara, though I wouldn't be surprised if they ended up taking a Dunesail as well. Either way, we need to hurry."

"Right," Surge said.

They crested another dune and began to slide downward. Surge caught another glimpse of Suchara in the distance. He smiled grimly. The world itself seemed to be within the grasp of the Blood Sorcerers, and though Surge and Saevi had been disconnected from any source of information for several weeks now, he knew that their mission remained relevant regardless. An alliance with Suchara was of vital importance, and that was exactly what Surge was going to establish.

The Dunesail slid to a stop, coming to a steady halt as Tariq and Izaat deployed the landing rakes.

Surge stood beside Saevi, watching the grand capital of the south rise over them. The city itself was essentially one giant fortress. The walls rose high over the interior, where there were buildings with dozens of floors shoved up against one another. The incredibly narrow streets within looked as if they were all inclining toward the Royal Palace on the western end of the city—at least from what Surge had seen from atop the nearest dune.

Hundreds of gigantic, yellowing tan buildings rose over the city walls in a chaotic cluster that looked like one big lump of windows and walls. Some of the buildings were probably a hundred feet tall, for Surge could see the roof of one of the large keeps seeming to scratch the top of the ward.

That must be the Palace, Surge thought. He looked further down, following the long, trailing height of the castle down to where he lost it among the other rising structures. It was unlike anything Surge had ever seen.

Several half-destroyed sandstone homes were scattered throughout the outskirts of the city.

"Why are there homes beyond the ward?" Surge asked, looking forward. The subtle white glow of the ward was visible a few hundred feet ahead—the tan walls of Suchara barely within them.

Saevi fell silent, staring at the scattered rubble of the sandstone homes. Sucharans walked around near them, sweltering beneath the brutal heat of the Blazeday. Many wore sand cloaks, which covered them from the sun and blowing dunes alike. The sand here was still gray, though Surge could see even from here that the sands were almost golden inside the ward.

"The city is full," Saevi said quietly.

The large sandstone walls of the city were easily twenty feet tall, with Sucharan guards donning yellow and black cloth-covered armor. Even from here, Surge could recognize the curved Sucharan blades and golden masks the guards bore.

Surge thanked the pilots of the Dunesail, handing them a bag of coins as he had promised, and stepped down from the vehicle.

Saevi followed, landing quietly beside him on the gray sands.

He pulled his gray cloth cover tighter over his vermillion armor to further cover it. The cloak was small, of course, for Surge could never find garments large enough to cover himself unless he had them specially crafted for him.

Saevi had changed clothing entirely and now wore a sleek black and gold outfit that somehow resembled both armor and a dress at the same time. It was a Sucharan design—one that she had purchased in Goldenleaf to help "blend in," though if Surge was being honest, he suspected that she just liked the way it looked.

The Scorcher took the first steps, guiding them through the jumbled ruins of homes that were once standing. Saevi stopped, allowing a robed woman pushing a large cart of sandworms and desertspines to pass. Surge caught a glimpse of her tan skin—similar to Saevi's.

Saevi was born in Suchara after all, it seemed. This wasn't necessarily a given, for there were many of different races in Arvendon who had been born in the city and never left.

Surge continued scanning the broken buildings around him, watching as the poor families and children huddled beneath what little cover was left, seeking refuge from the sun of the Blazeday. Sunbeams drifted around them, riding the sandy winds and brightening the already blinding desertscape.

"Many families have been forced out of the city, and because the highest amounts of sandworms and desertspines are near the wards, they chose to stay here and try to survive," Saevi explained, her voice low.

"Why doesn't the city just let them in?" Surge asked, keeping his eyes on the suffering families.

"You don't understand." Saevi shook her head. She said nothing more and continued weaving through the rubble.

Surge stepped over a particularly large chunk of shattered stone.

He looked to the side, his eye catching the corner of his greatsword. It was not-so-covertly concealed beneath his cloak, making an obvious protrusion in the cloth. He had brought it out of necessity. Suchara was famously unwelcoming of foreigners. Yet, as Surge walked over the ruptured settlements of exiled citizens, he began to understand why.

The powerful Blazeday sun beat down on Surge's back, beads of sweat forming on his forehead. The rest of his body was already sweating, of course, and Surge couldn't exactly say that he was comfortable at the moment.

With the walls seeming to grow taller and taller, Surge knew that he was nearing the entrance. A large set of sandstone stairs led up to the gate. They were crumbling in several places. Even the pathway leading up to the wall was beyond the ward.

Just as they reached the front of the gate, they passed through the transparent white film. Almost instantly, the air grew comfortably cooler. The sunbeams thinned, many of them bouncing off the ward.

Surge grimaced, staring up at the guards craning down to look at him from the top of the wall. Surge eyed the sigil of a curved blade on the guard's chest.

The guard said something in Sucharan.

Surge blinked a few times at the jumble of vowels and sharp consonants. He took a deep breath. *This is why I don't like going to the West.*

"I don't speak Sucharan. Do you have anyone among you who speaks the Eastern Tongue?" Surge asked, speaking loudly so that he could be understood. "We—"

Saevi cut him off, talking back to the guard in what sounded like flawless Sucharan. She spoke quickly, with smooth enunciation and a quick pace. It seemed Surge's hypothesis that she had been born in Suchara was correct.

Saevi waited as the guard responded.

She said something back, then he did the same. The conversation continued for several minutes, then ended with the guard saying something that seemed mean spirited and turning away.

"What happened?" Surge asked.

"The city is closed," Saevi grumbled. She squinted, staying within the ward and looking out at the desertscape.

"Did you bother to mention that we have vital information for the Queen?" Surge asked, stepping forward.

"I did," Saevi said. "They said that they were absolutely forbidden to grant anyone without the proper papers into the city." Saevi stood there for a moment, staring at the wafting sands over the gray dunes in the distance. She started walking down the steps.

"So what, you're just going to give up?" Surge raised his hands. "We travel all the way across the continent and you're just going to go home?"

"Oh shut up," Saevi grumbled, shaking her head. She took a sharp left turn at the bottom of the steps and started walking along the base of the wall, just beyond the ward. "I'm not giving up." Saevi continued to follow the wall.

Surge started after her, squinting as he exited the ward and reentered the pounding heat of the desert. "Where are we going?" he asked, his voice rough. His feet sunk into the gray and tan sand as he walked, making his steps *infuriatingly* slow. Each time he stepped he seemed to slide back slightly, making it nearly impossible to move with efficiency. Yet Saevi somehow maintained a brisk pace despite all of this, and strode through the sand as if it were solid ground.

"We're going around the city," Saevi said, walking quickly.

Surge broke into a slight run, his disgusting sweat-soaked armor sliding against his skin as he jogged. "What for?" he asked, trying to catch up. He picked up the pace. "Saevi!" Surge shouted, grabbing her by the shoulder.

"We can't get into the city through the main gates, alright?" Saevi said quickly, clearly annoyed. "So I'm leading us around the city so that we can enter from the western side."

"How would we be able to get into the western gate if we can't get into this one?" Surge growled.

"We aren't going in a *gate*," Saevi said, her amber eyes narrowing. "We're getting in through an alternate way. But first, we need to get there." Saevi rolled her eyes. "So stop complaining and get comfortable, because it'll be over a mile until we reach the Oasis."

The Oasis turned out to be much larger than Surge had expected. After walking through the sand for what felt like hours, Saevi and Surge had turned the corner and reached the western side of the city. The wall still stood even taller here—several hundred feet taller, as this side of the city backed up to the Palace—meaning that they couldn't simply walk in, leaving Surge wondering what Saevi was planning.

Large, skinny trees that fanned out with bright green leaves at the top dotted the Oasis—palm trees, they were called. Surge had never seen such a thing, though the way they swayed in the desert breeze was strangely relaxing to him. A large pool of water lay on the back side of the city, rising right up against the wall. Surge assumed that this was the Oasis for which the small area was named.

The Oasis was within the ward. Very few buildings dotted the land here—for the area was mostly underwater—save for what appeared to be some sort of water-pumping facilities. These were stationed on small sand mounds that protruded as islands in the middle of the light blue lake, with various pipes running to and from the structures. A large set of pipes also ran directly from the Oasis to the city walls, disappearing inside and presumably delivering water to all of Suchara. Surge watched as the water flowed, pushed by mechanical pumps, flowing toward and away from the city in a rhythmic pattern. He had never thought about how Suchara was able to acquire enough water to support their population, but this explained it.

The sand here was a yellowish gold as well, adding to the lush feel of the area. This, in addition to the prickly green plants and palms that dotted the shores of the lake, made for quite a pleasant scene.

Saevi paused, then took a few steps toward the eastern shore—which was right up against the city walls. From here Surge could still hear the bustle of the city above. Saevi knelt, staring into the bright blue water.

"What is it?" Surge asked, rubbing his brow. He had been sweating profusely, of course, which one would think he would be used to by now—he was not.

"I'm trying to figure out if my plan would work," Saevi said, lowering a hand into the water. She cupped it, and let it pour out as she raised it back up. "You know this is the water source for all of Suchara?"

"I assumed as much," Surge said, folding his arms. "The city must be a mess to run. Between the climate and the population, I can't imagine the kinds of decisions the Queen must make."

"Queens," Saevi corrected.

Surge turned to her. "What?"

"Suchara has two queens: Siraye and Sariah Thala," Saevi explained, keeping her eyes fixed on the water.

Surge raised an eyebrow, keeping his arms folded. *Why on Auris would a place have two monarchs?*

"If they disagree, the tie is broken by whoever is next in line for the dual-throne," Saevi said, as if reading his thoughts.

"The royal family," Surge said. "They're Voltarians, right?"

Saevi nodded. Surge grimaced. Other Voltarians always made him uncomfortable—save for General Falx, of course. Surge preferred it when he was the only one with control over lightning and electricity, and the thought of having to share that power... It unsettled him.

"I think this might actually be possible," Saevi said after a moment, staring at the water.

Surge walked up behind her, standing over her as she watched the water. "What are you watching for?"

"I'm watching the currents and seeing if I can trace how far it is from here to wherever the water is deposited beneath the city," Saevi said. "And judging by the occasional bubbles, I'd guess that it's not very far at all."

"Wait, how do you know that the water is deposited beneath the city?" Surge asked, folding his arms once again.

Saevi didn't answer, but instead kept watching the water. Her head started to nod slightly, as if she were counting something. "Let's go," Saevi said, looking around. "I think this will work." She continued scanning the surrounding area.

A few guards dotted areas around the pumphouses, but other than that it was entirely void of people. Surge watched the guards for a moment—who didn't even seem to be paying any attention to Surge and Saevi.

"What are you doing?" Surge grumbled.

Saevi had begun unhooking her armor plates, leaving only the light black and gold cloth that had been wrapped around it. She laid out her Sunspear, the orange and silver intertwining metals wrapping around themselves. "I'm making it easier to swim," Saevi said. "Swimming that far with all that armor would be impossible."

"We're *swimming*?" Surge started. "And wait, you're just going to leave your weapon here?"

Saevi leaned over and picked up the Sunspear. She clipped it onto her back once again and rolled her eyes at him.

Surge grumbled. He could've gone to Suchara with anyone, and he had ended up going with her. He was realizing now how insufferable this woman truly was.

"I'd suggest you lose that armor," Saevi said, turning toward the water. "Otherwise, it'll become your coffin."

"Wha—" Surge began.

Saevi dove into the water, cutting him off.

Surge took a deep breath, grunting at the infuriating woman. She was just so... *Ugh.* He started to unhook his armor, the heavy red pieces dropping to the sand with soft thuds. Surge did have to admit that he felt much lighter without it. He had gotten used to traveling in a full suit of armor a long time ago, and—thanks to the enhanced strength his Crystals loaned him—he was able to do so without much difficulty.

Yet it still felt strange. Thankfully, he was able to keep his bright white Crystals attached to the belt he wore as a part of his black underclothes. He kept the gray cloak on as well and made sure to refasten his greatsword to his back.

After a few moments, Surge was ready to get into the water. The pounding heat was unbearable at this point anyway. He started toward the shore and jumped in the warm, clear water without hesitation.

Panic flooded him. Water was not exactly the most familiar environment to him, and it had been several years since he had tried to swim. Yet his training soon took over. Before long, he was breathing and pushing with his legs rhythmically.

He opened his eyes slowly, water stinging them as he spotted Saevi ahead, still under the water. He swam after her, noticing that the Oasis was rather shallow. She was clearly waiting for him, for he caught up to her in a matter of seconds.

Looking around, he realized that the large barrier to his left was actually a wall. He looked to Saevi, who began rising for a breath of air. Surge's lungs started to ache, and he did the same.

Breaking through the surface of the water, Surge reached up with one hand and pushed back his black hair. He touched his beard as well before turning to where Saevi treaded water next to him. She glanced to the side, making sure that the pumphouse guards hadn't noticed, then turned back to Surge.

"There's a pipe below us. We're going to swim inside, alright?" Saevi said between breaths. "The current should propel us forward.

Before long, we'll be at the deposit. That will get us inside the city, though I'm not sure where."

Surge nodded, taking the time to catch his breath rather than waste this time talking.

Saevi took a few more gulps of air, and then dipped back under the surface.

Surge followed, his eyes stinging as he opened them under the water once again.

Saevi started to swim near the large opening in the lower part of the wall. As she grew closer, she started moving faster. Surge followed her and felt himself pulled toward the massive metal pipe as well. She disappeared inside, sliding into the metal infrastructure and swimming with an almost blinding speed thanks to the current. Surge grumbled, then threw out his arms and legs, propelling himself forward.

The pipe approached quickly, and before he knew it, the sun-soaked bright blue waterscape was replaced with the dark, suffocating metal around him. His lungs were already beginning to ache, so he started swimming faster. The current was taking him further, pushing him down the long straightaway through the tunnel. At various intervals, a large pumping device was stationed along the edge of the pipe, pushing the water deeper into the city.

Surge's lungs truly began to burn now. He felt his pulse quickening, and his eyes beginning to dart. He would be alright. *Everything will be fine. It's just water.* Yet he *hated* water.

His lungs screamed, and he found himself exhaling in the water. Bubbles slipped from his mouth. The tunnel seemed to darken. There was a mass in front of him—presumably Saevi.

For the first time in quite a while, Surge started to panic. The feeling flooded his veins like the water in his lungs. He wasn't going to make it. Saevi had been wrong. There was far too great a distance between the deposit and the Oasis. Everything was... Everything was...

Light appeared above him as he passed another pump. Slender

hands pulled him upward. He kicked and found himself being pulled out of the water.

Pushing himself up, Surge took in a breath. He slumped out of the water and lay down on the cold stone floor of... wherever he was.

His lungs quivered and spasmed. He coughed, feeling the wetness of his insides as he tried to breathe. He coughed again, his lungs burning as his body refused to take air in.

Finally, with one final cough, he spat out a large gulp of water. His lungs opened, welcoming in the sweet, damp air of this place. He rolled over to his side, feeling exhausted. His side was cramping, and his legs were exhausted.

He noticed a figure standing over him.

Surge looked to the side, finding Saevi standing with her hands on her hips.

He quickly turned over, involuntarily coughing one more time as he rose to his feet. He folded his arms, ignoring what had just happened.

Saevi rolled her eyes and turned around.

The room they were in was, in fact, a large deposit. There was the massive pool of water to their left where they had just come from—it made up most of the room. Water was continuously flowing in from one side, and disappearing into a set of vertical pipes on the far side of the room, only to be replaced with a new wave from the pipes.

"Well," Saevi said, brushing her soaking wet black hair out of her eyes. "We made it—though for a moment it seemed you thought you wouldn't."

Surge grumbled.

Saevi turned away, facing the tan sandstone staircase built into the sandstone walls.

Everything looks so bland here, Surge thought. Though he supposed that Suchara didn't exactly have much access to the traditional building materials of the east.

"Where to now?" Surge asked. He grunted again as he brushed the slick water from his muscled arms.

"These stairs should take us to the lower part of the city," Saevi said. "Keep your hood up and try to stay unnoticed, alright?" Saevi flipped up her black hood, though it was still soaking wet. Surge did the same with his gray cloak. The cool dampness of the cloth was a welcome change from the oppressive heat of the desert Blazeday.

The stairs were only a few stories tall, and though Surge's heavy, water-soaked body struggled to get up them, he was grateful to be returned to land.

Before long, Saevi had reached a large iron door in the shockingly tall building. They had wound around a set of pipes several times as they entered the stairwell, and now they were at the top. The rhythmic pumping of the water was the only sound.

Saevi grunted, pushing open the heavy iron door and letting in the overpowering sounds of the city.

An assault of odors and sights overwhelmed Surge the second he stepped out into the brightness.

The Blazeday was still shining brightly, nearly blinding him. They stood in a small, multi-tiered alleyway. Each and every surface around them was made of that same yellow-tan sandstone. Surge's nostrils were flooded with the smell of unwashed bodies and human waste. He coughed a few times, pulling his cloak over his nose to block the smell.

The alleyway was barely ten feet wide, though there were *way* too many people crammed in. Each wore a multicolored cloak of some sort, making the whole scene a massive jumble of color.

Surge looked to the left, then to the right.

Hundreds of people stretched out in the narrow, stair-filled alleyway on either side. Carts and stands lay at periodic intervals. Laundry hung from lines overhead, strung between two tall blocks of buildings making up the alleyway. The buildings themselves were dozens of feet tall, and filled with dark, open-air windows.

People shouted in Sucharan, the cacophony of harsh voices grinding against Surge's ears. Surge looked to the side, covering his ears while trying to keep the cloth over his nose.

"Now do you see why the Queens are forced to kick people out of the city?" Saevi shouted over the roar of the crowd.

Surge's eyes widened, the horrific odors already making their way into his nostrils once again.

Saevi started down the small set of steps and led Surge into the mass of people. Countless buildings towered over him in all directions, forming an impossibly complex series of convoluted alleyways with no true streets. From here, the whole city seemed to be on a sharp slope, leading upward toward the massive keep to the west. Steps filled each alley, and Surge saw one group of people trip and fall down, creating a cascade of falls and injuries.

More shouting accompanied the falls, and somehow that worsened the stench. Saevi led them down the alley, then turned onto another even *more* crowded alleyway. Someone bumped into Surge and shouted at him in Sucharan.

Saevi turned back, muttering something in the language and pushing the man away with a sharp shove.

"Where are we going?" Surge shouted over the chaos.

"Sandstorm Keep," Saevi hissed over her shoulder. "We're going to meet with the Queens."

Surge shook his head as he barely dodged a huge cart of rotten sandworms. The smell poisoned his nose once again, making him feel nauseous. He turned ahead to realize that he had fallen behind Saevi. He stumbled over the little steps, trying to find a way to catch up to her. More shouting surrounded him. More buildings stretched overhead. More people swarmed the streets. From what he could tell, the entire city was like this. Surge took a deep breath—which was a mistake—and started walking again.

This city was a disaster, but that didn't matter. They were on a mission, and they could not forget that. They needed to warn the Queens of what was coming. If they didn't, all of Auris could fall under the control of the Blood Sorcerers.

Surge had entered this city seeking an alliance, and one way or another, he was going to leave with one.

CHAPTER THIRTY

FUSION

Asteros Silverglade's feet collided with the ground, causing the pressure in his head to spike. He looked to his left and right, orienting himself in the next memory that the Emissary was constructing.

The black sands were receding, leaving a trail of turquoise frost in their wake. Illusory snow fell violently, pelting the narrow, jagged walls of this place.

No, not walls, Asteros realized. *Mountains.* He was standing in a deep ravine, set right between two of The Highlands' mountains. Crooked, uneven slabs of snow-covered black rocks surrounded the small ravine, leaving hardly enough space for Asteros to stand.

Just ahead, two figures in black trudged through the snow, pushing through the raging Frostfall. They were making their way toward an almost hidden crevice at the bottom of one of the ravine's steep declines.

"Is that the entrance they're looking for?" Asteros asked. His voice sounded quiet against the howling wind of the Frostfall.

"It is," the Emissary said from above. "As I said, the chambers were underground."

"So they were," Asteros said. He looked up, staring at the massive mountain face of what he presumed was Faras. "How long did it take them to find this?" Asteros asked, turning around. The ravine was extremely well hidden, for it was surrounded on all sides by steep slopes.

"Several hours," the Emissary said. "The heavy Frostfall slowed their progress considerably, but they found it regardless."

Asteros advanced, catching up to Haldir and Lucien. They were nearly to the crevice, and thus on the precipice of discovering whatever secrets awaited within the testing chamber.

"This must be it," Haldir said, his low voice barely reaching Asteros's ears.

"I would hope so," Lucien snorted. "We've been looking for hours."

Haldir shrugged off the comment and pushed onward. Moments later, he reached the gap in the rocks. He examined it, looking down into the opening with narrowed eyes. The crevice was no more than a few feet in length, and it was barely large enough for a person to fit.

Lucien stopped by Haldir's side and reached forward. He shot a pulse of umbrakinesis through the gap, closing his eyes as he did so.

Asteros reached out with his abilities instinctually, searching for Lucien's pulse of energy. Though, as he expected, there was nothing there.

So this truly is all an illusion, Asteros thought to himself. *Fascinating...*

"It opens up down there," Lucien said, opening his eyes. "The drop is only a few feet, and there doesn't appear to be anything living down there."

"If this is what we presume it to be, nothing will have been down there for almost two thousand years," Haldir muttered.

"We're making history, old friend." Lucien smiled.

"That we are," Haldir agreed. He patted Lucien on the back, and jumped into the crevice.

Lucien followed a few seconds later, landing with a thump.

With his enhanced eyes, Asteros was able to see Lucien dust himself off once he stood up. Asteros took a deep breath, and jumped down. Given that this entire place was an illusion, the landing was much softer than expected, though the terrain *did* still change, indicating that whatever illusion the Emissary was controlling did include some physical components.

Perhaps he truly does have some control over the Void, Asteros thought. His enhanced eyes fully adjusted to the darkness, and he soon located Haldir and Lucien standing before a narrow stone door.

The door was perhaps seven feet tall and two feet wide, and it was fairly unremarkable—unlike the other doors that Asteros had seen. There were a few Runes clearly etched into it, and there were some carvings around these to amplify the Runes.

"Let's hope this works," Lucien said.

"It will," Haldir said softly. He reached forward, slipping off his Shadow-Sand gauntlet. With a pause, Haldir lightly touched the central square Rune.

The Rune pulsed. Within seconds, it began to glow a soft white, indicating that it was still active. The lines carved around it soon lit as well, followed by the other four Runes that were etched on the front of the door.

Haldir inhaled, then exhaled. He reached into his chestplate compartment and produced the newly forged key.

The key looked much the same as it did when Haldir passed it on to Asteros. Of course, that change of possession was likely only a few months from this memory.

"Wait." Asteros paused. "If Lucien was with Haldir for all of this, then why did he act surprised when I told him about the key?"

"He assumed it was destroyed by the cave-in Haldir caused," the Emissary said from above. "Though, of course, he could hardly access those memories by that point because... Well, you'll see."

Infuriatingly cryptic, Asteros thought as he turned back to Haldir. *Though when has he ever answered something clearly?* Asteros watched as Haldir raised the key.

Haldir released it, allowing the key to hover in place. It approached the Runes almost eagerly and began to pull on the energy held within. Small white tendrils of light stretched out from the Runes, moving toward the key.

Within seconds the energy was feeding into the key, draining from the Runes. It seemed that the key worked even more efficiently immediately after it was forged. *Curious,* Asteros thought.

Not even a moment later, the Runes were all but drained. The heavy door no longer glowed. The key, meanwhile, was shining with the light of a small star. It dropped into Haldir's open hand.

"After you," Haldir said, motioning forward.

"I think not." Lucien bowed. "Without your work, we would never have found this place; you lead the way."

"Always a gentleman..." Haldir shook his head, his wrinkled face twitching into a smile. Haldir braced his shoulder against the door and planted his feet. With an enhanced heave, the door started to move.

The stone door ground against the stone floor, producing a horrible screech as Haldir continued pushing. He grunted, taking small steps forward. Darkness rumbled, becoming visible around his shoulder as he pushed.

With one final throw of his weight, Haldir pushed open the door, allowing it to grind to a halt on unseen hinges. Haldir held out the still glowing key—using it as a torch—and started into the darkness.

The passage declined almost immediately, the flat stones turning into stairs not more than a few feet inside the door. The key continued to glow, providing some much-needed light in the dark passage. Even with Asteros's enhanced eyes, he was having trouble seeing down here.

Haldir started down the stairs, following the slight curve of the tunnel with caution.

Lucien followed shortly after, careful to ensure that the door didn't shut behind him.

Taking a few steps forward, Asteros entered the narrow passage just behind Lucien. He scanned the smooth walls of the hallway, noting the way that the stones were carved. This place was obviously meant to be kept secret, indicated by the sheer *narrowness* of the walls. Asteros could hardly fit between the sides of the corridor without turning slightly.

Fortunately, the stairs soon came to a landing, where the walls diverged and opened up into a larger room.

Asteros looked around, examining the walls. Weapon racks were fixed to the sides of the room, with a few decaying spears and swords remaining from whenever this cavern had been in use.

"This was where the guards were stationed," the Emissary said from above. He spoke with an unnerving softness. "No guards were ever positioned outside of the door, for that would give away the location of this chamber," the Emissary added.

Rooms broke off to the left and right, likely more chambers meant for the guards. Asteros watched as Haldir and Lucien peeked into one, finding a collection of beds and a long-abandoned firepit.

"This was before the Ancient Sects had been Vanished," Asteros said distantly. "What was it like back then? To have twice as many Summoners... It must have been overwhelming."

"It was all we knew," the Emissary said. "Of course, the ordinary Summoners were never our primary concern at the time."

Asteros thought for a moment, allowing his dark eyes to scan the rest of the room once again. "The Harbingers?" Asteros asked.

"Indeed," the Emissary said. "They may be nothing more than legends to those from your time," the Emissary said. "But to us... they were *Gods*." The Emissary trailed off. "Even one Harbinger could single-handedly turn the tide of a battle."

"It must've been a nightmare to lead an army," Asteros said, shaking his head. "Just knowing that at any moment, a Harbinger might suddenly wipe out your entire legion..."

"It was... a harrowing experience to say the least," the Emissary said. "My unit lasted longer than most." The Emissary seemed to pause. "One can only run from the Harbingers for so long, though."

Asteros hesitated. "You were a commander?"

The Emissary did not respond.

"If you were that strong, then how did—" Asteros started.

"Direct your attention to the scene," the Emissary said firmly. "This is a matter for another time."

Asteros looked over.

Haldir and Lucien were moving toward the end of the room, which led to another staircase leading even further down.

"What reason do you have for keeping these secrets from me?" Asteros asked, starting to follow Lucien and Haldir.

The Emissary remained silent once again.

Of course, Asteros grumbled. He followed Lucien and Haldir down the staircase, where they came to another landing. This one was smaller than the first, though it seemed that more rooms spread off from the central landing here.

"These must've been the bedrooms for the researchers," Haldir said from within the illusion. "If I'm correct, the next room will be what we're looking for."

"Why would they have kept the testing chambers at the bottom of the tunnels?" Lucien asked, raising an eyebrow.

Haldir lifted the key, shining its stark white light into the corridor at the other end of the room. "These experiments would have required great focus to conduct," Haldir said, his voice hard. "Putting them at the end of the fortress would've ensured that no one interrupted them."

Lucien grunted, then stepped forward. He seemed to be looking at some of the supplies that this chamber's inhabitants had left behind—a few cooking utensils and a couple of torn blankets.

"Come," Haldir instructed. He started toward the hallway at the end of the room, finding yet another staircase. This one turned slightly, leading Haldir, Lucien, and Asteros down at an angle. It was also considerably longer than the others, for it seemed like it was several minutes before Haldir finally reached what appeared to be a large stone door.

"This must be it," Haldir said. He lowered his eyes to the large handle, then examined the ancient hinges.

"The locks are on this side..." Lucien observed.

"The people of this time would've been more concerned about keeping their subjects *in*, rather than keeping others out." Haldir reached forward, removing the iron bar before the door. Seconds later, Haldir pushed open the door itself. He led the way inside, ignoring the screech of the ancient hinges and stepping into the room within. The key in Haldir's hand cast the entire chamber beyond in an eerie white light.

Lucien followed, and finally, Asteros did as well.

The chamber's ceiling was low, and the room was littered with iron tables, bolted to the ground. There were some sort of straps or restraints hanging off of them. Next to each table was a stand holding a strange assortment of ancient tools. The room itself was not terribly large, perhaps a few hundred square feet at most.

The spaces between the tables were minimal, making the room feel rather cramped. Yet, toward the other end of the room, the floor was open. Here, there were several contraptions that looked entirely foreign to Asteros. Some were large, while others looked to be no more than a few inches in size.

Asteros stopped by one of the tables, staring at the dried blood on the straps. The jagged metal tools were bloodied as well. There were Crystals on the stands, though they were all drained, of course.

"This place," Asteros started. "What *happened* here?"

Black sands rustled overhead. A plume of black smoke fell from the ceiling, settling on the floor right beside Asteros. Given that Lucien and Haldir didn't react, it didn't seem to be a part of the memory.

The black smoke swirled, twisting and turning into a humanoid shape. Finally, it receded... And there, in that chamber deep within Faras, Asteros laid eyes on the Emissary's true form for the first time.

The Emissary was shorter than Asteros would've expected. And much to his surprise, he looked entirely ordinary. The Emissary's hair was a deep black, much like Asteros's. His eyes, however, were a bright brown-gold. His face was beginning to wrinkle with age, though his features were still softened with a strange youthfulness. He wore a black cloak that covered his entire body, curiously hiding his figure.

"It's nice to finally... *see* you," Asteros said, stepping back.

"I felt it was deserved," the Emissary said. His hypnotic voice seemed to match his figure rather well. "If we are going to be working together, you were going to have to see me eventually."

"Working together?" Asteros tilted his head. "What do you mean?"

"Asteros," the Emissary said, clasping his hands together. "There is something to be found in this chamber, something that your friends only scratch the surface of." The Emissary began pacing. "Haldir possessed ancient journals, passed down from Shadow-Swift to Shadow-Swift, that hinted at the scientific advancements of the Ancient Times. Those, of course, were eventually destroyed by none other than Haldir himself—as I will later show you." The Emissary paused. "Haldir was searching for a way to revive the advancements of my time, though he lacked the proper knowledge to do so... You and I, however, *have* that knowledge."

Asteros took a step forward.

The Emissary raised his hands, and the entire room began to shine with a turquoise frost. He smirked, then snapped his fingers. The room began to transform, sent back through time, and returned to what Asteros presumed to be its original state.

The turquoise frost sparkled as it washed over the room. Crystal light fixtures materialized overhead, newly refilled in the memory. As the resplendent, electric-white Voltarian Crystals shined, the transformation slowly took place in the rest of the room.

The damaged walls were restored to the smooth, uniform stone that they had once been. The tables were cleaned of their rust, and the ancient tools seemed to grow even sharper. Finally, the people materialized, coming into shape from the blue-green light.

Many of them wore unfamiliar black overcoats, likely after a style that had long since been forgotten. Others wore dark armor—guards, Asteros figured—and on the tables lay a few unfortunate souls dressed only in plain woven trousers.

Asteros quickly picked out the ones in the dark coats to be the... *scientists?* Asteros thought. *Is that what they are?* They were scattered throughout the chamber, though there was a large gathering of them around a table on the opposite side. Asteros stepped forward, lowering his eyes to the young man on the table closest to him.

The man's head was shaven, and his eyes were closed. His arm had dozens of fresh stitches along a deep cut. There was some sort of small lump under his skin, right where the incision had been made.

Asteros squinted, trying to place what the unnatural lump might've been. It looked almost as if there was an *object* that had been surgically implanted in the man's skin. The object's jagged form was noticeable, even through the skin.

Asteros shivered, a chill running down his spine. He considered himself to have a strong stomach, but this... This was unlike anything he had ever seen.

Asteros advanced to the next table, slipping through one of the... *doctors? Who exactly are the ones in the overcoats?* Asteros thought. He stopped, staring at the next man. This one was unconscious as well. His arms had seemingly been left alone, though one of his legs was still bleeding from a small incision. Once again, there was a jagged mass just under his skin. The cut was made just above his knee and was still partially open.

Asteros stepped back, watching as a doctor arrived at the table and began tending to the man.

The doctor reached over to the table and picked up a suture. He started to sew the man's leg shut, seeming to pick up where he had left off. He said something to another doctor a few tables over in a language that Asteros did not understand.

"What is that?" Asteros asked, pointing to the object under the man's skin.

"The basis of our experiments," the Emissary said, approaching Asteros from behind. His cloak dragged behind him, lightly whispering against the dark stones of the chamber.

Asteros looked to another table, where an unmoving man was strapped in place. The skin of his face had turned an ashen gray, and his mouth hung open at an odd angle.

Dead, Asteros realized. *But from what?* Asteros advanced, getting a closer look. There were multiple stitched incisions all across his body, and around each one, the man's skin had turned that same ashen gray.

Asteros averted his eyes from the increasingly unsettling sights around him. "Haldir wanted to bring this back?" Asteros asked. "Why would he..." Asteros paused. "You were here for all of this, weren't you?" Asteros turned back to the Emissary. "This isn't someone else's memory... This is *yours,* isn't it?"

"To some extent," the Emissary said softly. "This scene combines my memories with those of others." He laid a hand on the table closest to him, his hand passing through it with a flurry of turquoise frost.

"But..." Asteros started. "Where are you? In this memory, I mean."

The Emissary turned toward the gathering of doctors at the other end of the room. "Why don't you go take a look?" The Emissary motioned toward them.

Asteros followed his gaze, laying eyes on the gathering of people once again. They had positioned themselves around a table, but Asteros wasn't able to see who was on it from here. He started forward, weaving between tables and pushing through illusory doctors. Asteros started to scan the faces of the men he passed, finding that none of them were the Emissary.

"I still don't—" Asteros stopped as he reached the gathering.

There, on the table, lay the unconscious figure of the Emissary. Several doctors worked on him. One of them was standing behind the Emissary's head, holding out his hands. A strange red light emanated from his palms, falling over the Emissary's illusory body.

A Blood Sorcerer, Asteros realized. *Positioned there to stop him from bleeding?* Asteros lowered his eyes to the Emissary's body, then froze.

The doctors had made several large incisions, one in each of the Emissary's arms, and one in each of his legs... And in each one of the incisions, there was a *Crystal*.

Asteros watched with shock as one of the doctors adjusted the small, turquoise Illusomancer Crystal inside of the Emissary's arm. It glowed brightly, illuminating the open flesh around it. The bleeding, of course, was still being halted by the Blood Sorcerer.

"*Izara's Shadow!*" Asteros cursed. "What are they doing to you?" Asteros spun around to face the Emissary's true form.

The Emissary stood silently, watching with distant eyes as the doctors continued to work on his former body. "They were making history," the Emissary said. He turned to Asteros. "They were giving me the powers of an Illusomancer."

"But..." Asteros started. He closed his eyes, rubbing his head. "Isn't that how you've been showing me these memories? Through illusions?" Asteros looked back to the Emissary's body on the table. "This was before the Vanishing. There were no Stormless during your time, so why would you need to be *given* powers? Weren't you already an Illusomancer?"

The Emissary laughed slightly. "Oh, Asteros." The Emissary started to pull back his cloak, revealing deep, jagged scars down the center of his arm—matching the location of the incisions that had been made in the memory-Emissary on the table. The scars glowed slightly, as did the skin around them.

The Crystals are still there, Asteros realized. He turned back to the table, watching as the Blood Sorcerer moved his hands in careful motions. The memory-Emissary's arms began to glow, and the Crystals started to sink deeper into the open cuts.

Asteros felt a slight tingling at the back of his mind. It was that same pressure that he had felt ever since he arrived in the Void. He turned back to the Emissary.

"Asteros," the Emissary said. "I was not born an Illusomancer."

The pressure in Asteros's head intensified.

I was born a Whisperer, a voice said into Asteros's mind.

Asteros stumbled back, his mouth hanging open. He stared at the Emissary in disbelief.

"How did... How did you—" Asteros stuttered.

"The forces I was aligned with were trying to discover a way to expand the powers of a Summoner... to give one person the power of *two* Sects," the Emissary said.

Asteros found himself unable to breathe. It made sense now— how the Emissary had created these illusions, and how he was somehow accessing the memories of others, even how he was putting pressure on Asteros's thoughts.

"*How?*" Asteros rasped.

"It took decades to perfect," the Emissary said. "There were rules to the procedure that we had not yet learned." The Emissary paused. "We did not know that in order for the subject to survive, they needed to have traces of the second Sect in their bloodline; and, given that the Harbingers had only recently arrived, not many of us came from parents of two different Sects."

Asteros stepped back, slowly recovering himself.

"My father was a Whisperer, but my mother was an Illuso-mancer," the Emissary said. "When I was selected for the experiment, I was given a choice of which Sect's powers I would like to add to my abilities. To honor my mother, I chose to undergo the proce-dure to become an Illusomancer, and to gain those abilities in addi-tion to what I already possessed.

"The procedure itself is very complicated," the Emissary contin-ued. "One must first acquaint themselves with the energy that they wish to have implanted—sometimes for many months—and then they must ensure that their body isn't harmed by the presence of another Sect's power. If the body doesn't reject it, then the surgeons can proceed... After much experimentation, our researchers found the location of certain nodes on the human body where the Summoning energies are converted into power, and it was there that the new Crystals had to be implanted.

"With the help of a Blood Sorcerer—both to stop the bleeding and to force the new Sect's power into the subject's bloodstream—the procedure can be done successfully," the Emissary continued. "Hybridization, they called it." The Emissary trailed off. "And I was the first one to ever survive the surgery."

"So you..." Asteros could hardly breathe. "You're a—"

"A Hybrid, yes." The Emissary nodded.

"And Haldir... Haldir wanted to revive this procedure," Asteros realized. "He wanted to find a way to gain more power." Asteros paused. "But did he?"

The Emissary shook his head. "Even if he had truly attempted it, he would've failed."

"I just don't understand," Asteros said, shaking his head. "How was any of this even possible? And why does no one in my time know about this?"

"Our adversaries never discovered how to replicate the process for themselves," the Emissary said. "Upon our defeat, we destroyed every record of it, thus ensuring that no one would be able to recreate the process." The Emissary paused. "Fortunately, you and I will soon be freed, and thus the procedure may return at last."

Asteros closed his eyes, taking a deep breath. It seemed impossible. Everything he had ever known *made* this impossible. And yet, it was possible—the Emissary was living proof.

"Why show me this? Just to flaunt your power?" Asteros asked, his voice hard. "You said that we will be working together. What does this have to do with any sort of alliance between us?"

"Asteros." The Emissary laughed. "I did not show you this without purpose. I showed you this because Auris's next Hybrid..." The Emissary smirked. "...will be *you*."

CHAPTER THIRTY-ONE
AN ALLIANCE

It took three days for Sandstorm Keep to send a response. Elias Surge pulled the cloak tighter over his face, keeping to the corner of the room that he and Saevi had been staying in. The inn wasn't exactly luxurious, and their room was hardly big enough for the two of them to stand. It had been an absolutely miserable three days, even by Surge's standards. Yet here they were, sitting in the hot, muggy room as Saevi peeled open the parchment.

She scanned the yellowing paper quickly, pausing only once to wipe sweat from her brow.

Surge watched impatiently, folding his arms and grumbling as the annoying woman took her time reading the message. Luckily, he and Saevi had barely talked over the last few days. Both of them were in such poor spirits thanks to the disgusting conditions of the city that neither was in the mood for conversation.

Yet the time for diplomacy and dialogue was now. If Surge's prediction was correct, then they would be summoned to meet with the two Queens, Sariah and Siraye Thala, before the day was out. Though, given the look of confusion on Saevi's face as her amber eyes reached the bottom of the paper, Surge began to suspect that that was not the case.

"What does it say?" Surge huffed.

"It says…" Saevi trailed off. "It says, 'In light of current events, we think that a meeting with two of Arvendon's leading representatives would be of the utmost importance.'"

"What in Tarathiel's Stones does that mean?" Surge grumbled. "Current events?"

"I don't know," Saevi said, shaking her head. She turned around, staring at the tan sandstone walls of the small room. The wooden bed creaked as she leaned forward. Saevi tossed the letter onto the bed.

Surge leaned back against the wall, the floorboards beneath him creaking as well. *Gods…* How did anyone live in a place like this? It seemed like every building was on the brink of falling apart.

Surge blinked a few times, feeling the sweat-soaked cloak he wore with an annoying level of awareness. He had purchased black Sucharan garments out of necessity—for he didn't want to walk around in his underclothes all day. The shirt and pants were simple enough, and their dark color made them rather unremarkable.

He could hear the sharp shouting of Sucharan citizens beyond the closed window on the left side of the room. Somehow, it was once again a Blazeday in Suchara—Saevi said that most days it was.

It was concerning for Surge. He enjoyed a routine Storm Gale just so that he could count on the quick means of transport. Without a Storm Gale, he would have no way of returning to Arvendon in any reasonable amount of time. Yet Arvendon was fine—it had to be. Everything was fine, except for this city, of course.

"We're wasting our time." Surge stood up. "We need to meet with them as soon as possible. We're going to warn them about the Blood Sorcerers, and we are going to forge an alliance with them."

"And how do you suppose we'll do that?" Saevi asked, raising an eyebrow.

"By telling them the truth." Surge started for the rickety wooden door, reaching out and grabbing his steel greatsword as he passed its place on the wall. Surge reached for the door with his other hand, swinging the massive weapon over his shoulder.

He hadn't had a bath in weeks, not that it mattered. This city was disgusting, and he needed to get this over with so that he could return home as soon as possible. He grunted, pulling open the light wooden door and starting into the cramped, rickety hallway beyond.

"Elias, wait," Saevi called.

Surge paused—out of reflex.

"I know you're impatient, but it's worth trying to figure out what's going on."

"What do you mean?" Surge grumbled.

"Think about it," Saevi said. "The innkeeper was hesitant to give us a room—and this is the fifth one that we tried. The Queens want to meet with us because of some recent event, and we have been cut off from any source of news for several weeks now."

"Wouldn't you have heard something about it on the streets by now?" Surge grunted, turning around. Everything seemed dim despite the blinding heat.

"Not if the people of Suchara weren't discussing it," Saevi said. "I've spent enough time in the Keep to know that the Queens do what they can to keep any and all news of other cities off of the streets. They do not like their people getting involved in foreign affairs."

Surge took a step forward. "Why did you not mention that you grew up here? To anyone in Arvendon, I mean."

"I—" Saevi trailed off. "It's not something that I like to talk about, but that's irrelevant. The point is, if they know something that we don't, it will be difficult for us to stay in control of the situation. How are we supposed to forge an alliance if we don't even know the state of the continent?"

"Alliances are merely a mutual illusion of trust," Surge said. "If you want someone to *truly* obey and understand you, then you need to make sure that your demands are heard, and met."

"So, you're going to threaten them if they don't listen to us?"

"I would rather not, but if it comes to that, then I would have no trouble doing so." Surge paused. "Arvendon has a long history of building alliances through *force*. You underestimate the influence a few subtle threats can have."

"And you underestimate the value of learning what may've happened in Arvendon during these last few weeks," Saevi countered. "You do realize that our home could've been attacked while we were away? Celes could've gotten wind of the Blood Sorcerers' threat and chosen to attack us while we're weak, or maybe the Blood Sorcerers themselves decided to return early."

Surge fell silent. Arvendon would be fine. Avenos was a good leader—a great leader—and he was one of the most powerful Scorchers Surge had ever seen. It would've taken a literal *Shadow-Swift* to truly bring harm upon the city, and no one from the mysterious Sect had left The Highlands for centuries.

"Please," Saevi said, advancing. "Give me two days, and then I will have gathered enough information to properly prepare for this meeting. Please, Surge. Let me try."

Surge stared her down, keeping a firm sense of indifference in his eyes. He paused for a moment, his thoughts moving slowly.

"Fine," Surge mumbled, stalking back into the room.

"Thank you." Saevi nodded. "I'll leave right now. You're welcome to come with me, if you want."

"No," Surge grumbled. "I can't stand another moment out in those vile streets. Come back when you're done, and you'd better have information for me."

"I will," Saevi said, turning away. "Stay here, I'll be back in a few hours with what knowledge I can find."

Surge fell silent, watching as she stepped out the door and closed it quietly. Surge sat for several minutes, counting as the seconds ticked by. He had been lying, of course. Why would he wait two days for Saevi to search for information when she might not even come up with anything? Every second they wasted trying to piece together what happened in Arvendon was a loss. All they had to do was meet the Queens, and the truth would come out.

That logic was exactly what led Surge to his decision. He was going to storm the Keep, and he was going to talk to the Queens. But he was going to do so peacefully.

It had been long enough. Saevi would be far enough away by now. Avenos needed this alliance, Surge could feel it. His city—his *country*—needed this, and he was going to do everything in his power to help his people.

Surge opened the door and walked into the creaky hallway. He started down the rickety wooden stairs, dragging a hand along the sandstone wall as he did so. He soon found himself on the first floor of the inn. Several Sucharans turned to look at him, their dull eyes pausing on him only momentarily. He continued past the jumble of wooden chairs and tables without a word, barely sparing a glance at the cloaked man working the bar. Surge neared the door and grimaced at the sound of the chaos beyond. The smell even seeped through the walls, offending his nostrils.

Surge took a deep breath, and opened the door.

The walk to Sandstorm Keep had been somewhat long, and between the heat of the Blazeday, the overpowering odors, and the deafening crowds of people, it had been *very* unpleasant.

Surge didn't exactly know where he was going. He simply followed whichever street led upward. The Keep was the largest building in Suchara, though with the way the city had been built, all of Suchara was just one colossal building, in a technical sense. The Keep was toward the top of the ward, and the base of it sat atop the rest of the city. Surge was sure that it extended several hundred feet downward, though the most impressive part of the mostly square architecture was the sheer height of the building before him.

Surge took a few steps forward, the crowds thinning as he neared the front of the Keep. Four guards were standing before a large, likely locked wooden door that seemed to lead into the Keep. The guards were all dressed in black and gold armor. Curved blades hung at their sides, accompanied by round shields that they held in their free hands.

One of them turned to Surge as he neared the large wooden doors. Apparently, he had crossed whatever line was considered the barrier between the city and the Keep.

The guard shouted something in Sucharan. It seemed to be fairly threatening. Of course, everyone in the city seemed malnourished, so the guard's frame was thin and frail, which made him considerably less intimidating. One of the other guards, the largest of the group—though still small in comparison to Surge—reached for his curved blade.

"I'm sorry, I don't speak Sucharan," Surge said loudly. "I only speak the Eastern Tongue."

The guards looked at each other. Their eyes settled on the guard furthest to Surge's right, causing the man to shake his head.

"I speak the Eastern Tongue." The guard stepped forward, his accent thick. He emphasized the wrong parts of the words, making it clear that he *barely* spoke Surge's language. But it should be enough.

"Good." Surge stepped forward, causing the other guards to flinch toward their weapons. Surge eyed the black and gold shields, as well as the blades. They would be easy to defeat, but he was certain that there were dozens more guards inside the Keep—not to mention Summoners.

"I come with a missive from the Queens." Surge held up the letter, though he could not read it.

The guard took it, scanning it quickly. "I—" the guard stuttered, trying to form the sentences in Surge's language. "You're Arvendi General, aren't you? Elias Surge."

"I am." Surge nodded. "I am using this letter now. Please grant me an audience with the Queens."

"You…" the guard blinked a few times. He nodded and turned around. "Follow me," the guard said, his words sharp.

Surge glared at the other guards, who stared back with daggers in their eyes.

The guard reached down to his waist and produced a small key. He said something in Sucharan to the other guards. The other guards approached the large wooden doors.

Surge stood behind them, noticing the four small keyholes in the center of the twin doors.

The guards stuck their keys into the respective places and turned all at once.

The door clicked open, and the large wooden slabs that had been covering it slowly pulled back. Surge watched in surprise as the doors were opened by some sort of mechanical device activated by the keys. He took a step forward, staying close behind the guard who was leading him inside.

The huge sandstone palace had an entryway that nearly rivaled Summerglass's in its grandeur. It extended upward several stories, with balconies of tan sandstone at each level above. Massive pillars of the yellowing stone stood in all directions, upholding the curved ceiling far above. A large Crystal chandelier hung in the center of the room, bearing Scorcher Crystals that cast the whole room in a bright orange light.

Red leather furniture lined the walls, as well as the large indenture in the center of the room. It was a lowered platform, bearing mostly sofas and tables likely for social gatherings. Hallways extended to the right and left, though they were short in comparison to those in Summerglass.

The guard led Surge to the right, taking him past several paintings that seemed to depict Sucharan royalty. Each figure wore elaborate black and gold armor in their portraits, and the large golden necklaces they wore marked them as monarchs. The portraits came in pairs, as did Suchara's leaders.

Surge knew very little about their government, though he knew that the Thala family had ruled for generations. Saevi had explained that each bore two children, and the two eldest were chosen to be the seats of government for their near-lifelong terms. As one grew older, one from the next generation replaced them, allowing the monarchs to retire before their deaths. It was a curious system, though Saevi had said that it had worked rather well. Though, now that Surge had seen Suchara for himself, he saw it as a recipe for disaster. Why else would the city be struggling so dramatically?

The guard led him to a circular stairwell at the end of the right hallway and started ascending with him. Every once in a while, they would pass a guard or servant, and the guard leading him would have to explain Surge's situation.

Before long, they reached the top of the long, spiraling sandstone stairs, and Surge found himself at the end of another short hallway. The guard led him back toward the center of the Keep, guiding him toward a room on the far side of the building. A large set of wooden doors, and a small set of stairs leading up to it, clearly marked this as the throne room.

Curious, Surge thought. Putting the throne room on the top floor of the Keep seemed foolish, as it made it more likely that any powerful Summoner invaders would simply attack the bottom and bring down the throne room on top of everything else.

Yet, as the guard finished his explanation to the throne room guards, Surge began to see why the Queens had positioned their throne room in such a way. Even as the doors had just begun opening, Surge found himself blinded by the bright Blazeday sun.

The throne room was wide and tall. Massive windows made up the entirety of the back wall, allowing the sunlight to flood into the room. The only breaks in the large panes of glass were the two sandstone pillars that were positioned a few feet apart in the very center of the back wall.

Surge reached the top of the short staircase, setting foot on the sandstone and iron floor. He lowered his eyes to the base of the pillars, finding two shadowed thrones in their wake. Someone else stood in the throne room, talking in Sucharan.

The figure turned, his face still unreadable in the blinding sun as Surge's eyes struggled to adjust.

A female voice said something in Sucharan, and the man grumbled.

Surge looked down, scanning the sandstone and iron floor, realizing that he was standing on what appeared to be a large circular design. *It's a sundial,* Surge realized. It didn't appear to be functional, as light only came in from one side of the room. But the elaborate circular design made for a nice decoration nonetheless.

The elaborate pillars and torches that lined the room were dwarfed by the sheer *brightness* of the Blazeday sun pouring through the windows. Yet, the dozens of guards standing along the edges of the room—that Surge was only just now able to see as his eyes adjusted to the light—didn't seem the least bit bothered.

The Sucharan man brushed past Surge, muttering something in Sucharan that Surge presumed to be a curse. He ignored the man, and continued forward across the massive sundial, nearing the center of the large metal circle.

"I presume you received our message," a female voice called from the shadow of the right throne.

Surge squinted, coming to a stop roughly twenty feet before the thrones. Both were still in the dark shadow of the columns of sandstone directly behind them, creating an ominous sense of mystery around them. *Carefully built,* Surge thought to himself. Such an effect was curiously dismaying, though Surge was simply so impressed by the simple trick of light that he couldn't be bothered by it.

"It seems that he did, though he came without his partner," the other woman said from the throne on the left.

"Unsurprising," the first Queen snorted. "Look at how he squints beneath Helionn's brilliance... This man is so foolish that the Sun God's judgment is already made apparent."

"Perhaps that's what makes him so intriguing, wouldn't you

say?" The second Queen seemed to lean forward, as evidenced by the slight protrusion in the shadow.

Surge's eyes finally adjusted, allowing him to lay eyes on the sister Queens as they sat on their simple yet luxurious thrones. The chairs were made of solid gold and iron.

"His skin is pale, and pink," the first said after a moment. "Though not so much as others of his city."

"You speak the Eastern Tongue almost flawlessly," Surge said, stepping forward. He entered the shadow of one of the pillars, allowing him to get a better look at the Queens.

Both had long black hair, one wearing it parted to the right, and the other to the left. Their skin was a deep tan, accented by their dark eyes. Their dresses mirrored each other as well. The one on the right wore an elaborate, curving, black dress covered with gold embroidery, whereas the one on the left wore a gold dress with black lining.

"We were taught from a young age to speak your language," the one on the left said. "Our parents always said that it was *much* easier to discuss politics with your enemies and allies alike if you spoke their language with them... And Helionn knows that no one in the East will bother learning our language." The Queen shook her head, her voice firm. She was younger than Surge had expected. Both looked to be in their mid-thirties.

"And they have proven themselves to be correct," the one on the right said. "And in situations like this—when we have an *unwelcome* guest in our city—it is especially helpful to be able to ask them for ourselves what *exactly* possessed them to sneak through our walls."

"Let us not waste this gentleman's time," the one on the right said. "I am Sariah Thala, and while I would have you introduce yourself, I can already infer who you are, Elias Surge."

"It is very bold of you to enter our city without permission, given what has recently occurred," the other one, who must be Siraye, said. "Not many would be brave enough to do so, especially considering our relationship with Cyfalion."

"I—" Surge started. He blinked a few times, his thoughts growing heavy. "Cyfalion?"

"The attack," Siraye growled. "Don't assume us to be fools. Someone of your position would surely know about such plans months before they were put into action."

"What are you talking about?" Surge took a step forward, a single strand of lightning arcing across his fingers.

"Sister," Sariah said, holding up a gloved hand. "He may not know." She leaned forward, staring at Surge with inquisitive eyes. "Where did you come from, General?" Sariah asked, beckoning Surge forward.

"We came from The Highlands," Surge said. "We have been cut off from all communications for several weeks now, and didn't stop in Goldenleaf for more than an hour, not long enough to pick up any information."

"We? And where is the one you were spotted with? It would seem that you two have parted ways." Siraye leaned forward as well, her eyes sparking.

Surge blinked a few times.

He eyed the woman's waist, spotting the subtle glow of white Crystals.

"I—" Surge started. He needed to know what happened in Cyfalion. Saevi could wait. "Tell me what happened in Cyfalion,"

"You truly don't know, do you?" Siraye laughed again. "Helionn's Sun, that's quite the twist."

"*Tell me*," Surge growled. "I was named by King Avenos Titansworn as the leader of Arvendon's Summoner Legions. Such a position entitles me to know any news of my city's actions."

"Well then." Siraye smirked. "This is *interesting*." Siraye broke into another wicked cackle. "I suppose you don't understand why we are hesitant to honor your position, hmmm?"

"Elias!" someone shouted from behind him.

Surge spun, watching as the large doors opened once again.

Saevi Embrore sprinted up the steps, entering the room in a flurry of flying cloaks and footsteps.

"Saevi?" Surge stepped back, his pulse quickening.

"Elias," Saevi panted. "There's something wrong. There's been a mistake. In Arvendon...the King... Cyfalion," Saevi breathed, trying to catch her breath.

"Saevi." Surge's voice rose. "What happened?"

"Your King is dead!" Siraye cackled.

Surge's heart stopped. His eyes fell, his muscles growing firm. He turned, very slowly.

Siraye continued laughing. Sariah lowered her gaze.

Surge went numb, feeling the cold heat of rage in the back of his mind, accompanied by the unmistakable pit in his stomach. *Dead?*

"I tried to tell you to—" Saevi started, rising.

Surge turned around, his eyes wild. "Dead?" Surge shouted.

Saevi stumbled back.

Lightning rumbled in Surge's blood, blinding him. It rose, coursing through his veins, pumping through his heart and surfacing at his hands. Electricity crackled at his fingertips, sparking across his fingers. Fires and wind picked up around the room as the Summoner guards readied themselves.

More lightning appeared around Sariah and Siraye. The Voltarian Queens stood up. Sariah gave Surge a warning glance.

"The new King Faelyn Titansworn recently led an attack against Cyfalion, claiming that Jaskye is responsible for Avenos's death," Sariah said.

Surge stumbled. "Cyfalion?"

"He destroyed one of Cyfalion's Monoliths in the attack, weakening the city's ward," Siraye said gravely, a bolt of lightning arcing across her body. "He has violated the most ancient of our continent's agreements."

No. Surge turned to her, his eyes hard. His mind shut down, leaving a dark rage in its wake. He had no control over himself. His King... Faelyn... A Monolith destroyed?

"Adresin Jastira was killed, and the city he leaves behind is now subject to a more dangerous form of the Tempests, thanks to *your* new King," Sariah said.

"What?" Surge breathed, his muscles heavy. "That's impossible." *Faelyn wouldn't do that.*

"We have a very strong alliance with Cyfalion and the Jastira family, and we have sworn our loyalty to them in times of war," Sariah continued. "They are preparing to launch a counterattack against Arvendon, and we intend to assist them. Our troops are set to leave tomorrow. We know about the Blood Sorcerers' return, and we know that you likely came here seeking an alliance, but we cannot grant your request. We will not kill you, but I *must insist* that you leave as soon as possible. For someone with your loyalty, I know you would want to be standing with your home as it falls."

Surge fell to his knees. Everything... Everything had fallen apart in a matter of seconds.

It had only been a few weeks, yet the home that he had left would soon be in ruins. His King was dead. The new King had violated the oldest agreement on Auris, dooming Arvendon. Surge needed to return home. Sariah was right. Arvendon didn't stand a chance—not against two armies—but Surge wanted to be there for the final stand. He was a soldier, and he had vowed that if his city ever fell, he would fall with it.

"A Storm Gale is on the horizon—according to our prophets," Sariah said. "In a few days, when it arrives, you should use it to return to Arvendon. Until then, try to stay out of our way. I'm sorry we couldn't help you, Surge... But this is beyond any of us." Sariah lowered her head. "Saevi, take him back to your inn, and keep him there until the Storm Gale."

"Yes, Your Majesty." Saevi bowed, then stood and wrapped her arms around Surge, pulling him to his feet.

"Saevi," Sariah called. "I'm sorry that things ended the way they did... But it's good to see you again."

"It's good to see you too." Saevi turned away, and pulled Surge as he half-walked toward the door.

Surge moved absently, his feet rising and falling on their own. Arvendon was doomed. The city was in danger, and there was a good chance that young Faelyn didn't even know the extent of the threat that they faced.

But regardless of what was coming to his home, Surge would do *everything* in his power to defend it.

CHAPTER THIRTY-TWO

STALLING

"The key to recovering from the events is simply giving yourself the ability to," Elric said. "While that may seem strange and confusing, I'm going to help explain it to you."

Castien Varic nodded, continuing in the deep, rocky snow, following behind Arthion and Luka. Ilyana walked alongside Castien, carefully avoiding walking next to Elric.

Elric's lessons had been helpful—*I think,* Castien noted. Technically speaking, he hadn't put them into practice since learning them, but arming himself with the knowledge to fight his anxiety gave him a certain sense of control that he had lacked before.

Following the red markings on the rocks, however, had *not* been helpful. They had been walking for the better part of a week now, following a marker only to lose the trail and have to circle back. Oftentimes they struggled to re-find the marking they had seen last, further delaying their search.

The process had been infuriatingly slow. Castien was well aware that they were losing time, but what could they do? They needed to find the Blood Sorcerers, and Castien knew that they were *so close*. It would be foolish to give up now.

"I've noticed that I never feel right until I sleep again," Castien said, bringing his mind back to the conversation.

"Which is completely normal." Elric nodded. "I know that seems inconvenient, but if sleeping *is* actually possible, then that isn't exactly your worst option."

"What is my worst option?" Castien frowned.

"Your worst option would be to sulk in your own misery and anxiety," Elric said. "I know that when I put it like that, it seems obvious, but all of us have done it before. I can't figure out why our mind tries to do such things, but... Maybe it's just Niventia's way of making sure everything provides a challenge to learn from."

"Yeah, I guess," Castien said.

Ilyana glanced at him from the side, then looked forward.

He tried to piece together what the look meant. She was a strange woman, to say the least. But she was admirably strong. She had handled her father's supposed death as well as the guilt of killing Avenos with relative ease.

Or is that just how she presents herself? Castien wondered. That was the more likely explanation. That, or she simply never felt guilty about killing Avenos to begin with.

"...Other than that, using a distraction is most definitely your best bet," Elric finished.

Castien blinked. He hadn't been paying attention. "Sorry," he said, a little embarrassed. "Could you say that last bit again?"

Castien could feel Elric's emerald eyes piercing through the goggles, staring into Castien's soul. Elric shook his head, sighing, but he repeated himself anyway.

"I was saying that if sleeping wasn't an option, then the best way to recover is to distract yourself with your favorite activities," Elric said, settling his voice. "For me, it was always sparring with a friend or practicing my Cloudwalking. Both are very... therapeutic for me."

"Got it," Castien said. He paused, looking ahead through the light Frostfall to find Luka stopped before an unusually shaped boulder.

"What is it?" Elric called out, approaching.

Luka dropped down to his knees, looking at a small red marking toward the bottom of the rock. He appeared to be softly reading something to Arthion, who started looking upward toward where the sun was hidden behind the thin clouds.

"It looks like we're close," Luka said a little louder as Castien and the others approached. "'Continue northwest until reaching the black boulder,'" Luka said, reading from the back of the small, rounded rock.

Castien took a few steps over, catching a glimpse of the blood-red paint that had been marked toward the bottom of the boulder.

"Wait," Arthion said, looking to what was apparently the northwest, then back to Luka. "Northwest leads us *down* that slope, not up," Arthion said.

"Then that's where we're going," Luka said, rising from behind the boulder. They had been walking between two rises, with the path doubling back and following one of the mountains further upward to the west.

"But wouldn't the entrance to the Blood Sorcerers' hideout be somewhere near the peaks so that it's harder for invaders to access?" Arthion asked.

"Trust me when I say that the simple location in The Highlands is repellent enough for most attackers. If anything, it would make more sense for the entrance to be on ground level. That way the Blood Sorcerers can more easily come and go," Luka said.

Arthion frowned beneath his gray hood. "So we've been looking in the wrong place all along," Arthion whispered.

"Hmmm?" Luka asked, stepping forward.

Castien was standing right beside Arthion, and realized that he was probably the only one who could hear him. Arthion was right. They had been looking for the entrance higher up in the mountains

—expecting it to be near the peaks—but they had been wrong, it seemed.

"I'll scout ahead," Elric said. He stepped forward, nearing the steep ridge that led downward. Another mountain rose in the distance, barely visible through the falling snow.

Elric dashed off the ridge, leaping into the air and blasting forward. The Master Summoner slid through the air as if the winds themselves pulled him forward. He slid downward, continuing toward the mountain with frightening speed. He skimmed against the distant snowbanks, then disappeared into the mix of boulders and snow-covered rocks beneath.

Castien waited with the others, staring at the mountain in the distance. It was little more than a few miles away, and it seemed to be to the northwest.

Luka folded his arms, watching the ground curiously as he waited for Elric to reappear.

Arthion shuffled impatiently.

Castien knew that Elric would be back within a few minutes. The Cloudwalker was powerful enough that he could cover ground ten times faster than any of them. Though Castien knew that it was not without a cost. Elric had worsened his Breezebone by using his Cloudwalking to scout out their next marker.

A few minutes later, a figure appeared in the air, rising from the maze of rocks and snow below, settling in the winds directly across from the group. He launched forward, then veered to a halt, sliding into the snow beside them. Elric rose to his feet, brushing the snow from his thick coat.

"Well?" Arthion asked, stepping toward the Cloudwalker.

Elric walked forward, passing between Luka, Castien, and Ilyana. He stopped at the front of the group, looking over the steep, rocky ridge that led down to the maze below. He raised a hand and pointed toward the mountain.

"That's it," Elric said. The mountain was just like any other— jagged, vaguely round, covered with thick, stony rocks and ridges, topped with snow, and, of course, hundreds of feet tall. It looked just like any other mountain on the outside, yes, but Elric had just confirmed that it was far from ordinary.

Ilyana took a few steps forward, settling next to Castien "We found it," Ilyana breathed. The snow fell quietly, making the silence feel a thousand times louder. After so long in the mountains, wandering aimlessly, the prospect of actually finding the fortress seemed impossible. Yet here they were... staring at it.

Within were dozens, if not *hundreds*, of Blood Sorcerers. Fighting anything more than two would even give Elric trouble. When their group was ambushed in The Highlands on their original expedition, they had only been spared thanks to the mercy of the Blood Sorcerers.

The Blood Sorcerers would have an even greater advantage this time. They were in a strange position. *As are we,* Castien realized. He did not know which side of history he would end up on, but he knew that what was going to happen next would change the course of Auris.

Whether or not they chose to side with the Blood Sorcerers, this decision could drastically affect the future of the continent. Castien felt as if he held the power of fate in his own two hands, and here, standing with this group of Summoners—all of whom had fought their way to this very spot—Castien knew that whatever happened next, it would be big.

Luka took a step forward and started descending the slope.

Castien Varic planted his feet firmly in the snow, reaching the bottom of the slope after what had felt like an eternity. The boulders rose above him, the snow now up to his knees. Castien could feel the biting cold. He could feel the tireless exhaustion in his bones... He could feel *everything*.

Arthion followed close behind Elric, followed by Luka, who was directly ahead of Castien.

Ilyana was in the back, keeping watch for any stray creatures.

They were getting close, *very* close.

A part of him started to get excited. His mind started to race, his heart rate increasing. It wasn't like the times when his pulse overwhelmed him. No... This was adrenaline. This was knowing that he was on the verge of uncovering the truth behind the events of the last few weeks.

Everything that had turned his world on its head... It all came back to the Blood Sorcerers.

Within minutes, they turned a corner, rounding one particularly black boulder that was a little below Castien's position.

Elric stopped first, followed by Arthion, then the rest of the group.

Castien paused, his muscles jittery with anticipation. The boulder stood before them, seemingly covered in a strange paint that rendered it black as night. Snow covered the top, hiding the slightly darkened color from above. It was a small marker, but it was a marker nonetheless.

Luka approached the boulder, walking around it in search of the paintings. Most of it appeared to be unmarked. Part of the boulder was slightly raised, making for a small space where one could write on the underside. Luka noticed the area and got down on his knees, peering under the boulder. Castien approached, catching sight of the red paint, which appeared to be a... *drawing.*

It was a vague depiction of rocks, with a red arrow pointing into a small gap in them. Castien made note of the pattern. *A large rock to the right, three smaller ones to the left, one triangular one below it.*

Castien paced back toward the rest of the group, scanning the face of the mountain before him. At first, he looked upward, trying to spot the entrance somewhere along the middle-lower part of the massive peak, but he had no luck.

Then he looked further upward, trying to see if it was near the peak after all. Once again, he couldn't seem to locate the right set of rocks. He was scanning too quickly; he had likely missed it.

"Castien," Luka said, reaching back and tapping him.

Castien looked down, pulled from his search.

Luka pointed, his finger extending forward, level with the ground.

Castien followed his arm, all the way to the point of his hand. There, at the base of the mountain, not more than fifty feet away, was the *exact* pattern from the drawing. Sure enough, between the telltale rocks, lay a small opening.

It looked like no more than a small indenture, but it was *so* much more. It was their key to the future. Luka took a step forward, as did Elric. Castien followed, Ilyana at his side.

A hand grabbed his shoulder.

Castien whirled, the hand sliding against his still healing arm. Castien yelped, startled.

Arthion stood behind him, his hand extended.

"Arthion." Castien cursed. "You scared me."

"My apologies," Arthion said. "But I think we should all wait."

"What?" Luka spun. "We finally found the Blood Sorcerers, and you just want us to *wait?*"

"Doesn't this all just seem a little too easy?" Arthion asked, pacing. "I mean, why would they leave those markings on the rock like that? They could be luring us into an ambush."

"They could be," Elric said, stepping back toward them. "But they aren't."

"Only people whom the Blood Sorcerers have *specifically* chosen to induct into their Sect would be capable of finding those markings, let alone following them. Why would anyone be looking for these markings if they didn't know about the Blood Sorcerers?" Luka challenged.

"I don't know," Arthion said. "It just doesn't seem right."

"Arthion," Castien said, taking a step toward the Whisperer. "Calm down."

"I—" Arthion started. His eyes seemed to be searching for something. "I can listen to their thoughts," Arthion said. "If I can get close enough, I should be able to use my Whispering to pick up on the Blood Sorcerers' thoughts, even from out here."

"But..." Elric started in protest. "What if they detect you? We can't give ourselves away."

"Trust me," Arthion said. He started backing up toward another boulder. "If they have anything waiting for us in there, I'll be able to pick up on it. This could save our lives."

"Where are you going?" Castien asked.

"I need to be far enough away from the four of you to ensure that I hear the Blood Sorcerers' thoughts—not yours." Arthion turned slightly, approaching a particularly large boulder. "I know you may not see the value in this, but if there's an ambush waiting for us, then this way we'll know about it."

"Wait, Arthion!" Elric advanced.

"I'm sorry for delaying us," Arthion said. "But I need to make sure this is safe... for all of us." Arthion turned a corner and vanished without a trace.

Elric and Luka exchanged a glance, as did Castien and Ilyana.

"Well, we can't go in without him," Castien said.

"Am I the only one who thinks that was *really* strange?" Ilyana started. "I mean, what the hell? Where did any of that come from?"

"Let him go," Luka said, stepping back. "He has reason to be worried. Perhaps his Whispering may finally prove to be useful; he's never had a chance to use it until now," Luka added. "He just wants to help—and make sure we're not going to get killed the second we go inside. We'll set up camp over there—there seems to be a small cave past the boulders. If he's not back soon, we'll go face the Blood Sorcerers without him."

Castien sat quietly beneath the cover of the small cave. The Blood Sorcerers' passage was so simple, so plain, yet it seemed to stare back as Castien watched it. Something about it was menacing in a way that Castien couldn't explain.

Somehow, the fact that the answers to all of his questions lay on the other side of that opening had become progressively more unnerving—rather than calming. He had put off the thoughts of being a Starburner for as long as he could.

He had ignored his true self for far too long now. Being a Summoner would change things. It would change *everything*. When he was young, he had dreamed of someday being special... being that one person who somehow defied all laws of physics and Summoning and gained powers despite being Stormless... And he had thought about what he might do with such powers.

He had envisioned himself storming castles, demanding justice for the Stormless, demanding that the Summoners right their wrongs. Yet he realized now, standing on the other side of it all, that there was a reason no Summoner ever thought to do such things.

Summoners had much greater problems than the annoyances that were the Stormless—who were unable to form any sort of effective resistance anyway. For a Summoner to start concerning themselves with the Stormless would simply be a waste of time.

Yet, the Stormless wanted to fight. They wanted to *help*, and so the Summoners let them. The Summoners of the world had all forged an unspoken agreement to keep their Stormless armies separate from the Summoner legions and let them fight on their own.

It was almost like parents watching their children play from a distance. Nothing was ever serious, and no one ever really got hurt. If things started to escalate, one of the parents would simply step in and remind everyone that it was all just a game.

But it wasn't a game. Lives were lost year after year in these pointless Stormless skirmishes—all so that the Stormless would be so distracted fighting each other that they wouldn't bother to turn against their Summoner masters. Not that it even mattered, for one

Master Summoner could kill an entire squadron of soldiers with nothing more than a thought.

The idea disgusted Castien. It was a horrifying and unnerving realization that he was a Summoner, not a triumph. His life would never be the same, and though he had always thought that what he was doing mattered, now when he screwed up, there were real consequences.

It was no wonder that the Summoners had simply ignored the Stormless. Why would they bother with those who were so far beneath them? Why would the Stormless matter to them?

Though now, staring at the opening in the rock, Castien couldn't help but feel sick to his stomach. His arm burned with a phantom fire. *Will this burn even scar?* Castien found himself wondering.

Summoners could use Crystals to heal themselves. No injury was permanent to them. Sometimes, even death seemed like a far-fetched myth to Summoners. Stormless could die with a simple club to the head, while Summoners could carry out large-scale duels and battles before even beginning to tire.

But it didn't matter anymore. It was too late. Castien's fate was set for him, and whether it had been written by Niventia, Izara, or some other cursed God, it didn't matter. Castien couldn't ignore who he was... *what* he was.

The truth will always find you, no matter how hard you try to hide.

"Where is he?" Elric asked, pacing impatiently.

"Give him more time," Luka said. "We're all a little overwhelmed, maybe he just needed some time to decompress... And like I said, his Whispering could provide some useful information."

"He's been gone for *hours*," Elric grumbled, turning to Luka. "How much longer are we going to wait?"

"It's nearly nightfall," Luka said, raising his ice-blue eyes to the darkening sky. "If he isn't back by tomorrow morning, we'll enter the fortress."

"Tomorrow?" Elric cursed.

"We are in no hurry," Ilyana said. "The only reason we would try to get this over and done with would be to return to Arvendon—which is futile at this point."

"Why do you say that?" Luka asked, turning to the Dexteris.

"Because by the time we get there, there won't be an Arvendon to return to," Ilyana said.

"What are you talking about?" Elric challenged.

"You heard Luka: Freyfall is marching on Arvendon," Ilyana said. "Celes's relationship with your people is strained at best, and the rest of the world..." Ilyana snorted. "They're simply waiting for a reason to destroy your home."

Castien flinched. Her tone was harsh, harsher than he had ever heard it before.

She looked back to the ground.

Elric continued pacing, the fury in his steps evident. "If that damn Whisperer isn't back by sunrise, I'm going to drag him here myself," Elric muttered.

"And how do you plan to find him?" Luka asked. "All you know is that he went around a corner and disappeared. There's no telling where he is now."

"Which is precisely why I should go look for him," Elric said. "He could very well be lost, and he would have no way of getting back to us."

"*Or* he could be listening to the Blood Sorcerers and gaining vital information, like he said he was going to," Luka said. "Listen, we're waiting for Arthion. He'll come back when he's confirmed that this isn't a trap."

"It doesn't matter anyway," Ilyana said. "Just relax, if he's not back by tomorrow morning, we'll figure something out—we've already established that."

"Ilyana's right," Luka said, turning to the Celesian. He smiled slightly.

Castien raised an eyebrow, watching the exchange curiously.

"Fine," Elric said, though he did not stop pacing.

Castien turned back to the opening across the clearing. From here, it looked like little more than a jumble of rocks amid the mountain. They would enter soon, and when they did...

If Castien *did* find more answers inside—and Crystals—then... When he emerged from this mountain, he would no longer be Stormless. He would be a Starburner.

CHAPTER THIRTY-THREE
UNITY

Asteros Silverglade stepped back. "Me?" He gaped. "The next Hybrid is going to be *me*?"

"You are among the most powerful Summoners on Auris, Asteros," the Emissary said. "But none of us can reach our full potential without a little... *help*."

"Why?" Asteros retreated further. "Why me?" Asteros looked around, watching as the Emissary's memory continued to play out. "Why not Lucien?" Asteros asked. "You already have him."

"Lucien lacks the will to be a leader," the Emissary said. "He fell to our influence too quickly." The Emissary paused. "Why do you deflect your responsibility? The opportunity before you is one that very few are offered. Why try to turn it down?"

"I—" Asteros started. He lowered his head. "With all due respect, I'm not entirely confident in your abilities as a surgeon."

"Which is why I am not going to do this alone," the Emissary said. "Help will arrive, soon enough."

Asteros turned back to the scene. "What do you even want me for?" Asteros asked. "Why are you doing all of this?"

"You will learn in due time," the Emissary assured him. "You assume our intents to be malicious—they are not. But you are not yet ready to learn the full truth."

Asteros grumbled. *What on Auris does that mean? Why does he say I'm not ready? Why show me all of this?* He centered himself. It was no use arguing with the Emissary. Asteros was in his domain, under his control. He had no choice but to play along with the Emissary's games.

"What did Haldir and Lucien discover?" Asteros asked. "You said that Haldir failed to replicate the procedure, but surely he didn't leave here empty handed."

"They found a record," the Emissary said. He walked over to one of the empty tables beside his illusory self. On it, there was a strangely thick book. The Emissary opened it, revealing thin slabs of stone, rather than pages, on the inside. "The Tempests were feared even in my time," the Emissary said. "As such, many records were made using stone, not paper."

"And Haldir found one?" Asteros asked, advancing.

"He did," the Emissary said. "The record he discovered detailed my life after the procedure... Mostly for the purpose of tracking my health and any ailments that might've resulted from the surgery." The Emissary closed the book. "The journal was continued even after our defeat. Thus, the location of my prison was noted as well, leading Haldir—"

"To Epirac," Asteros finished. He shook his head. "They went to Epirac, didn't they?"

"Guided by the journal they discovered, yes." The Emissary nodded.

"But how did they get in?" Asteros asked. "We needed the help of the scholars, for we didn't have Starburner blood."

"Ah, but Haldir did," the Emissary mused. He strode over to the far wall, where a collection of filled syringes lay. "You see, those of my time thought that blood transfusions would ease the process— and they were right, to some extent—so they gathered samples of blood from each Sect.

"The blood had dried and crumbled over time, but even its essence was enough to open Epirac's lock," the Emissary said. He turned back. "Haldir and Lucien entered Epirac several years before you eventually followed."

"But Lucien was with us when we entered," Asteros said. "He was with us the entire time, helping us uncover the location of a place that he had already discovered..." Asteros trailed off. "Why?"

"Why don't you take a look?" The Emissary smirked, waving a hand.

Black sand and turquoise frost washed across the room. The walls reshaped, transforming into the curved chamber that Asteros knew all too well. Epirac's walls rose around him, and Crystal veins materialized in the stone below. Within seconds, Asteros was standing in a different version of the very room he was trapped in.

The Devourer's Stone stood in the center of the room. Its darkness was almost overpowering; even its Runes did not glow.

Haldir's figure materialized to Asteros's right, and Lucien's to his left. The pair stepped forward in silence, examining the Stone with caution.

"What do you think it is?" Lucien asked, narrowing his Elosian eyes.

"A tomb, perhaps?" Haldir suggested. "The final resting place of the first Hybrid?"

"Why the Runes, then?" Lucien raised an eyebrow. "What's the point of protecting a corpse?"

"The Revenants were likely still thriving at the time of this stone's creation," Haldir said. "I would imagine that defending corpses was a rather common practice."

"Hm," Lucien grunted. He stepped forward, careful not to touch the glowing vein of red light beneath him. "And what do you suppose *these* are?" Lucien asked, motioning to the seven veins that shot out from the Stone.

"I'm not sure," Haldir said, kneeling. He reached forward, dragging his hand across one. "They don't seem to be dangerous."

"And the Stone itself?" Lucien asked.

"It's been here for thousands of years," Haldir said, rising to his feet. "I would be surprised if it was still capable of harming us."

"Are you certain?" Lucien asked. "Faras's Runes were still active."

"And even those were not dangerous to touch." Haldir smiled. "There is nothing to fear, my friend."

Lucien turned back to the Stone, his sharp features twisting into a frown. "Something about it feels... *wrong*."

"Fear is not in our blood, Lucien," Haldir said. "This stone is what we have been searching for. If we can discover how the first Hybrid was created, we could replicate the process for ourselves."

"And you're certain that he is in there?" Lucien advanced.

"If he's not, then I'm afraid we may never find him," Haldir said. "This is our only chance. So draw your blade, Lucien. Let us get to work on dissecting this... unusually large rock." Haldir drew his Shadow-Sand sword, phasing it partially.

Lucien followed suit and stepped forward.

"I'll start on this side, you start opposite me," Haldir said, positioning himself just beside the Stone.

Lucien sighed, drawing the longer of his two blades. He cautiously approached the Devourer's Stone and settled into place.

"On my count: One, two," Haldir said, raising his sword. "Three!"

Haldir and Lucien slammed their swords into the Stone simultaneously.

White light flashed, blinding Asteros.

Lucien and Haldir were thrown back, slamming into the curved wall behind them.

Lucien crashed to the floor first, his sword clattering across the ground. He twisted, groaning. His body shook for several seconds, then ceased.

After a moment, Lucien moved again, rubbing his head. "What..." Lucien started. "What happened? Where am I?"

Haldir groaned, pushing himself to his feet. "Gods above," Haldir muttered. "I suppose you were right, Lucien." Haldir turned, finding that Lucien was still lying on his back. "Lucien?" Haldir rose to his feet, shaking slightly. He dusted himself off and walked over to Lucien, offering his hand to help him to his feet.

"What's going on?" Lucien asked, rubbing his head again. He took Haldir's hand and stumbled upright. Lucien turned to the Stone. "What is that?"

"Lucien," Haldir started. "Now is not the time for jokes."

"I didn't say it was," Lucien snapped.

"Then why—" Haldir stopped, taking a deep breath. "You are being serious?"

"Haldir, what are we doing here?" Lucien growled, stepping forward. "Where have you taken me?"

Haldir opened his mouth, then hesitated. He brought a hand to his head, as if in pain. "Do..." Haldir started. "Do you hear that?" Haldir asked, his eyes cracking open. "That... voice?"

"I..." Lucien started. "What is it saying?"

Haldir focused, narrowing his eyes. "Violet wings," Haldir said. "Flashes of white... None of this makes any sense."

"And a Silver Sun," Lucien said softly. He lowered his head, and the scene froze.

Asteros stepped back, stunned.

"The moment they touched that stone, I gained access to each of their memories," the Emissary said, floating down to Asteros's side. "That is how I can see these moments. Their memories became mine, and thus, I became able to recreate them for you." The Emissary turned to Asteros. "By touching the Stone, the Whispering was able to take effect as well... granting me the ability to influence their thoughts."

"Your Whispering?" Asteros asked.

"Lucien's is one of the weakest minds I have encountered," the Emissary said, ignoring the question. "Within seconds, I was able to mask many of his memories, allowing me to take much greater control of his thoughts than what would usually be possible." The Emissary paused. "Haldir, on the other hand, was stronger than most. I was able to influence his mind, but only slightly at first."

"So Lucien..." Asteros breathed.

"He has been under my control for several years now," the Emissary said, nodding. "Even now, he still hears my whispers, just as you did before you returned to this stone."

"Violet wings and a Silver Sun," Asteros said softly. "Flashes of white..." Asteros met the Emissary's eyes. "That was all you, right?"

The Emissary didn't answer; he simply smiled.

"You gain control over anyone who touches the Stone?" Asteros asked, breaking the silence.

"Not complete control," the Emissary said. "But, in essence, yes."

"How?" Asteros asked. "How is the Stone that powerful?"

"Asteros, you need only look at the sheer *number* of Runes on the Stone to answer that question," the Emissary said. "When it became known that our leader would retreat to the Void, a few of us were encased in stones like this. The stones were created by some of the most powerful Rune-Writers of our time—even the Harbinger herself—to ensure that our mistress would not be without allies when she returned.

"Never had this level of Runic power been imbued into singular objects... They took months to create," the Emissary continued. "The Runes established a direct connection with the Void, not only taking us there, but allowing us to make use of its *advantages*.

"We soon learned that our Whispering was amplified in this Realm," the Emissary continued. "And such a clear connection gave us more control than we thought." The Emissary paused. "By touching the Stone, one is instantaneously transported to the Void, causing a complete lapse in consciousness and control. Thus, that brief moment allows our Whispering to take root in one's mind, enabling our influence to persist even after one has left the Stone."

Our? Asteros opened his mouth, but the Emissary cut him off.

"The other stones were built so that only one guided by our

mistress could release those within," the Emissary said. "But this one is... different. Ours is a more lasting prison."

"How many of you are there?" Asteros questioned.

"There are two others: the Sleepwalker and the Interloper," the Emissary said. "They are Hybrids, like myself, waiting to be freed so that we may finally claim victory over our adversaries." The Emissary fell silent. "So that we may finally free both Auris and Katauriel."

Asteros's head swam with questions. *Multiple Hybrids? Freeing Katauriel—the Realm of the Gods?* Asteros closed his eyes.

"Asteros," the Emissary said, interrupting his thoughts. "I can see that you are lost... For there is still one *vital* detail that I have not told you: Haldir did not die simply of old age." The Emissary paused. "We are almost there my friend; you will have your answers soon... I think it is high time you see how your former master met his demise." The Emissary smiled, and the scene began to change for what Asteros hoped was the last time.

CHAPTER THIRTY-FOUR

TRUE AUTHORITY

Asteros Silverglade straightened as the scene settled. He found himself in Haldir's secret room once again, though the forge was dark this time. A small Voltarian Crystal sat on one of the tables, illuminating Haldir's haunted figure.

Haldir was hunched over the table, writing something. His face was unshaven, and his eyes were darker than Izara's Shadow. He was writing in a journal, moving the quill pen with an urgent desperation.

Asteros peered over his shoulder and began reading.

Four days have passed since my encounter with the Stone. The voice continues to whisper into my thoughts. I can hear it even now... Telling me to surrender to it. Telling me to fall into the shadows.

Perhaps more alarmingly, Lucien seems completely unbothered. He hardly remembers the event, and I fear that with each passing day, his mind is being reshaped. I have told him to be strong; I have told him to fight the whispers, but I fear that he has already surrendered.

I do not blame him—I could not, knowing that I am the reason he encountered that Stone. My every thought is plagued with its touch. My words come out wrong, and my body feels overcome with a sickness for which there is no cure. With each moment that ticks by, resistance becomes more difficult. My mind tires, and my body begins to fail me.

In my search for the secrets of the past, I have inadvertently accelerated the return of an ancient evil. The whispers speak of greatness... of the future that they can promise me. They speak of a world without Tempests, a united Realm with one true leader.

But I see through the fog. I can hear the venom laced within these sweet whispers. The darkness seeks revenge. This evil had been defeated time and time again, and so it retreated, hiding in the Void where it could watch from afar, waiting until the moment was right. That moment is now.

The Resurgence will soon be upon us—the reversal of the failed Vanishing. I can only surmise that the Vanishing was this evil's first attempt at vengeance, but that it somehow went awry, further delaying this creature's return. I fear that this being will not fail again. With two Shadow-Swifts on its side... It may already be too late.

Haldir looked up, his eyes desperate. He looked to the left, and then to the right. Haldir wrote something else, then hurried out of the small secret room.

Asteros looked down, reading again.

Unless... Unless there is something that can be done.

Haldir returned, carrying an armful of books. He left again, returning moments later with another armful of journals. He stopped, his dark eyes wild with desperation. After a moment, he tore out a blank page from one of his journals and started writing.

When he was finished, he exited the room. He paced his main unhidden chambers before finally setting the paper down on his desk. He signed it, then set his pen down one final time. Haldir sighed, hanging his head in defeat.

The Rune-Key was sitting on the desk as well, the dark stone glimmering in the Crystal light. Haldir slid it over, placing it beside the paper. He stepped back, seeming to ensure that everything was as it should be.

Asteros advanced and began reading the letter on the desk. He recognized it immediately.

Asteros,

Where to begin, old friend? There is so much to speak of, and yet I have so little time remaining. I fear that my death is mere moments away, and thus, it is time for me to leave Erydon forever.

You will become the new leader of this clan. The Shadow-Swifts will obey you, and you alone. I know what you must be thinking, but allow me to put your fears to rest: You will say that you are not ready, you will say that it should be someone else... But, Asteros, trust me in this choice. Only under your leadership will this clan survive.

My hand tires even now. There is more I wish to say, but... my control is waning. I can only hope that you will not suffer the same fate as me.

May the Afterworld reunite us,

Haldir

Asteros looked up, his eyes feeling weak. His knees quivered; his muscles tingled. This was the note that Haldir had left. Asteros recalled reading it for the first time, likely only a few hours from the moment he was seeing.

Lucien had claimed that Haldir left. He said that he spotted Haldir sneaking out shortly before Asteros discovered the letter when looking for Haldir.

"But—" Asteros started, his voice quiet. "Why? I don't understand."

The Emissary materialized beside Asteros. "You will, Asteros." The Emissary turned to Haldir. "The performance is not over just yet."

Asteros followed his gaze, watching as Haldir entered the secret room and then sealed the false wall from within. Asteros ran forward, passing through the wall in a flurry of turquoise frost, his mouth quivering.

Haldir stood in the center of the small room, surrounded by piles of his journals—his research. The forge did not glow in the darkness. Haldir knelt, lowering his head.

"There is nothing to be done," Haldir said, his voice shaking. "I cannot beat you, but I will not surrender." Haldir looked up, tears in his dark eyes. "You will not have me. You've already taken Lucien, but you won't take me." Haldir raised his hands, his fingers glowing with umbrakinetic energy.

The darkness intensified, and the energy rumbled. Soon, Haldir's entire body was covered in dark energy, barely contained by his elderly figure. Haldir took a deep breath, and *released.*

Dark energy exploded through the room, crashing into the ceiling, causing it to collapse. Haldir was crushed by a falling stone. His work was buried within seconds, as was his corpse.

The room was gone an instant later, reduced to nothing more than rubble behind a false wall.

Asteros fell to his knees, a tear sliding down his cheek. Haldir... *This* was how he died?

"He destroyed both himself and his work to prevent us from using him," the Emissary said in the darkness. "It was his choice, not ours."

"You *monster!*" Asteros screamed. He jumped to his feet and lunged at the Emissary.

The Emissary vanished into a cloud of turquoise frost. "You cannot kill me, Asteros," the Emissary said, his voice now coming from somewhere above.

"You did this!" Asteros shouted. "You did *all* of this! Haldir died because of you." Asteros trailed off, shaking. "And you had Lucien lead me to Herqen, didn't you? You erased his memories, and made us find out everything for ourselves... Just to lead us to... to... *you.*" Asteros closed his eyes, swiping at his tears.

He felt hot; his mind raced. This was wrong. *Everything* the Emissary had done was so *wrong.* Even now, Asteros himself had been lured back to the Stone by the Emissary, and now he was trapped.

And Shalheira... She never would've died if the Emissary hadn't done all of this.

"We had to test you," the Emissary said. "Your bloodline was mixed, and your ambition was strong." The Emissary paused. "From the moment we first spotted you in Haldir's memories, we knew you would be *perfect.*" The Emissary's voice began to move. "But we had to make sure you were up to the task... We needed to test your ability to lead, your ability to discover, to explore, to fight..."

"What do you want from me?" Asteros demanded. His voice was raw, weak with useless rage.

"I want you to be my mistress's next champion," the Emissary said after a moment.

"Izara's Shadow!" Asteros cursed. "Enough with the riddles! Who is your mistress?" Asteros demanded.

The Emissary laughed. "An amusing choice of words..." The Emissary paused. "Tell me, Asteros, do you believe in Gods?"

"No," Asteros growled.

"Well then, Asteros, you may want to reconsider," the Emissary seemed to smile. "For the one you will be serving is Queen Izara, Goddess of Death, and Harbinger of the Whisperers."

Asteros Silverglade sat atop the darkened ledge several hours later, watching Lucien's illusory form. The Emissary was not showing Asteros a memory, but instead a current view of what Lucien was doing.

The Emissary had given Asteros some time alone following his reveal, allowing Asteros a moment to gather his thoughts. The Gods were not deities—they were simply Harbingers. But they were real nonetheless, and they were behind *all* of this.

Lucien was standing at the bottom of a large gully in the mountains. Several dozen people stood before him, awaiting orders. They were dressed in thick fur coats, and many of them seemed uneasy. Asteros supposed he would be a bit anxious too if he had been forced into the mountains by a Shadow-Swift.

"Who are the others?" Asteros asked, glancing to the side.

The Emissary was standing a few feet away, leaning against a shadowy wall. "Stonemasters," the Emissary said softly. "Though Lucien hasn't given them their Crystals yet."

"Stonemasters..." Asteros said, feeling the ancient word on his tongue. The Emissary had insisted that Izara was a hero—not the villain Asteros imagined her to be. Yet, he had given no evidence to support his claim. "Why has Lucien been gathering Stonemasters?" Asteros asked. "Or, I suppose, why has Izara been forcing him to do so?"

"Izara doesn't control Lucien," the Emissary said. "At least not anymore. She helped me infiltrate his mind, but he has since been largely under my control... Though his motivations have mostly aligned with ours by now, I suppose." The Emissary paused. "The Stonemasters are needed to construct our fortress," the Emissary said, answering his question.

His motivations? Why would Lucien willingly fight for Izara? Asteros had very little understanding of what, exactly, Izara's motivations were. The Emissary had divulged so much, and yet that final piece of the puzzle was still missing. *What does she want?*

"What good would a fortress do all the way up here?" Asteros asked after a moment, looking around at the snowy gully.

"This place is known as the Crystal Vale," the Emissary said. "Do you recall where the Ancient Energies were sent after being taken from the skies during the Vanishing?"

"They were deposited inside different mountains of The High-lands," Asteros said. "Right?"

"Indeed, they were," the Emissary said. "And five of those moun-tains are right here, in this vale." The Emissary pointed to a moun-tain on the opposite side of the clearing. "Illusomancer," the Emissary said. He pointed to the right. "Stonemaster, Rune-Writer, Skin-Shaper, and Starburner," the Emissary said, his finger slowly moving from mountain to mountain. "The Blood Sorcerers were displaced further than the others, for their energy was absorbed first—and the Revenants wished to make it harder for their greatest adversaries to recover their power."

"And the Revenants themselves?" Asteros asked.

"Their Crystals are within Epirac," the Emissary said. "It will not take much to release their energy, as the power that you used as a Shadow-Swift is still in the air. In fact, you and I will be the ones to release the Tempest of the Revenants—when the time is right."

"Bold of you to assume that I will help you," Asteros snorted.

"You will," the Emissary said.

"Izara will force me?"

"No," the Emissary said softly. "You will do it of your own accord, rest assured."

He turned his eyes back to Lucien. Asteros was continuing to delay the Resurgence using what little control he still had, though he wasn't even sure what good his efforts were doing. The Resurgence had begun either way; there was nothing to be done about that.

"Shattering enough Crystals would bring about the return of the Ancient Tempests," the Emissary said. "If sufficient energy is freed from those Crystals and returned to the atmosphere, the Tempests of old will descend once again."

"And how do you plan on shattering all of those Crystals?" Asteros asked. "By hand?"

"We don't intend to at all," the Emissary said. "We will mine them instead... After the Stonemasters construct a proper fortress, they will aid Lucien in excavating the Crystals from the mountains...

As you know, in this world, those who hold the Crystals hold the *power*."

"I still don't understand," Asteros said. "Why even trigger the Resurgence if you were originally trying to cause the Vanishing?"

The Emissary sighed. "Izara's prison is very unique in nature. There must be a large transfer of energy between the Void and Auris in order for the barrier between our worlds to weaken... And so, we devised a plan to remove the Tempests and funnel them through the Void in what we called the Vanishing," the Emissary said. "But the spell was not completed—Endon, the Harbinger of the Revenants, stopped it—and so our initial plan failed.

"Izara's bounds were then tightened, making it more difficult for her to escape," the Emissary continued. "Centuries later, we turned to a Resurgence... The Resurgence you triggered in Epirac? It channeled enough energy through the Void to allow Izara to escape."

Asteros's heart sank. "She's *already* escaped?"

"With the help of another, yes," the Emissary said softly.

Asteros grumbled. Of course there was someone else. There was always someone else involved. Izara seemed to have more allies than he would've anticipated. She was a Goddess, he supposed, but a nearly forgotten one. Much of what the Emissary spoke of was happening in the Realm of the Gods, he reminded himself. Beliefs could be very different there, for all he knew.

"But our work is far from finished, Asteros," the Emissary spoke. "The Resurgence granted Izara a window to escape, but it will require *another* transfer for you and me to return to Auris."

"*What?*"

"When you harnessed Endon's power and fused yourself to the Devourer's Stone, you inadvertently trapped yourself in the Void," the Emissary explained. "*You* are the final piece of Izara's plan, and while she recovers her strength in Katauriel, you and I are left here to prepare ourselves."

He was trapped after all, then. The Emissary was not the only thing keeping him here. *There is always something else.* "If she was trapped for so long, why did no one kill her?" Asteros asked, the thought striking him. "And why was she still able to use her abilities as a Whisperer, even from the Void?"

"She could not be killed," the Emissary said absently. "Her Whispering was too strong; anytime Niventia and her forces would rally enough troops to capture her, Izara would infiltrate the minds of Niventia's soldiers... Which is why Niventia ultimately decided to lay a trap for her, one that would imprison her in the Void." The Emissary paused. "And she wasn't able to use her influence until recently... After her bounds were tightened following the Vanishing, she was powerless—until someone unchained her, that is."

The unnamed ally again, Asteros thought. *What role do they have in this?*

Asteros looked back, watching as Lucien began handing out light brown Crystals to the formerly Stormless workers. "Why not gather Rune-Writers as well? Would they not be valuable to the construction of a fortress?"

"There are none left," the Emissary said.

Asteros started. He turned to the Emissary. "What?"

"Almost all of them were killed in the war of my time," the Emissary said. "A few survived to the time of the Vanishing... But once they lost their powers, they were hunted by the Shadow-Swifts."

"Why?" Asteros asked, his mind seeming to slow.

"Those Shadow-Swifts had—until recently—been Revenants, and after most of their power was taken by the Rune-powered Devourer's Stone, they deemed the Rune-Writers a threat to their existence," the Emissary said. "And so the Shadow-Swifts killed them... every last one of them."

Asteros pondered this for a moment. *So one Sect truly is extinct... But what left is there to do? What goal could Izara possibly have?* "What does she want?" Asteros asked, finally voicing the question. "Izara, I mean. Why go to all this trouble? And why did Haldir resist her will so adamantly?" Asteros paused. "What does she plan to do now that she has returned?"

"She wishes for free will, the freedom to control her own actions," the Emissary replied. "She wishes it for all of us, actually, not just herself. And as for Haldir, I assume he simply misunderstood our intentions."

Asteros blinked. That was not the answer he expected. Cliché though it was, Asteros had assumed Izara wanted to simply *destroy* Auris, or something of the sort.

"You mean to say none of us have free will?" Asteros asked.

"Not so long as Wayfinders walk among us."

"What do you mean?"

"You are aware of the Wayfinders' abilities, correct?" the Emissary asked.

"Divination: the ability to see the future. What of it?"

"The futures that Wayfinders see are absolute... Meaning that whatever they see *will* undoubtedly come to pass." The Emissary's voice grew hard. "Indirectly, this confirms that everything we do is already set in stone—long before we do it."

Asteros stepped back. The words washed over his mind like waves on a sandy beach. *Then...* Predestination was real? And Izara wished to put an end to it?

"So all of this, everything that we've done, you mean to say we had no choice in it?" Asteros asked slowly.

"That is what Izara believes." The Emissary nodded. "And, given the evidence, it seems very likely that she is correct; though our actions within the Void are slightly different."

"What do you mean?"

"From what we understand, the force that allows the Wayfinders to peer into the future is *rooted* in the Void," the Emissary said. "You may recall that it matters not when you enter the Void, but *where*. You likely saw golden threads weaving through the darkness before I began showing you these visions—those are Wayfinder visions... punching temporary holes in the Void to peer forward in time."

"But..." Asteros trailed off, trying to wrap his mind around the idea. *Is it possible that these people aren't who I think them to be?* Asteros was certain that Izara and the Emissary were the epitome of evil. *Could it be that they're not?*

"Wait," Asteros said. "Wouldn't that mean that you can use the Void to manipulate time for yourselves too?"

"We are... working on a way to do so," the Emissary said, shaking his head. "Whatever forces power this place are far beyond our comprehension. I doubt we will ever come to completely understand them."

"But the Wayfinders make use of them nonetheless," Asteros said as he turned forward again. "So that is why Izara was defeated, then? The Wayfinders manipulated the future?" He began connecting the dots in his mind. "And that is why Auris remembers Izara as a villain?"

"That is what she suspects," the Emissary said. "Though she seems to believe that her Whispering shrouds us from the Wayfinders' view, thus explaining why we have managed to survive all this time."

"Meaning that there is a way to free ourselves," Asteros said slowly. "There is a way to reclaim our own wills... And everything that's happened in the past... None of that was my fault, was it?"

"If you wish to look at it that way."

"Shalheira's death." Asteros inhaled. "That was predetermined? And the fracturing of my clan, that as well?"

"If our mistress is correct." The Emissary nodded.

Asteros looked forward, suddenly feeling lighter. He wasn't to blame. All that he had done was destined to happen. Shalheira's death wasn't his fault. Which meant... *The Wayfinders took her from me,* Asteros realized with a start. *They are responsible for all of this.*

"The Wayfinders of Auris are currently assembling a force— likely in an attempt to protect Zephyr, their Harbinger," the Emissary said. "Izara plans to remove him as soon as you and I have freed ourselves."

Asteros looked to the Emissary. "Then why on Auris are we still here? You said there needs to be another transfer of energy. Why not initiate it now?"

"Because Izara has not yet prepared the Shift," the Emissary said. "You recall I mentioned that we were devising ways to make use of the Void's unusual properties?"

"That's what we're waiting for," Asteros realized. "She is planning another Vanishing?"

"Not exactly." The Emissary shook his head. "Something far greater."

Asteros closed his eyes. The sheer volume of information that he had just been given was staggering enough, but the idea that his actions were predetermined? That answered so many of his questions. He knew, somehow, that he wasn't responsible for his actions leading up to his imprisonment. *I couldn't have been.* It was something else guiding him—no, *forcing* him down this path.

"You say her fight is for free will," Asteros said, meeting the Emissary's ancient gaze. "I believed her motives to be sinister in nature, not... noble." Asteros lowered his head. "I admit, Emissary, I have been terribly mistaken all this time.

"The threat you face is one that I was not even aware of, but now..." Asteros continued. "Now I understand what you are fighting for, what you stand for; why you have done all of this."

The Emissary smiled. "You see, Asteros, our intentions are not so malicious as you once believed."

"No," Asteros admitted.

"Lucien is raising an army to counter that of the Wayfinders," the Emissary said. "He will give us the time we need."

"For Izara to prepare," Asteros finished.

"We have preparations of our own to make as well," the Emissary said softly. "The procedure we intend for you is not a simple one. You must be ready."

Asteros met his gaze once again. He had been searching for a purpose for his entire life. Fighting to win free will for all of humanity? Asteros supposed that he *did* feel different here in the Void. *Could*

I be feeling the power to choose? Is that why he had felt so strange… Because in the Void, the Wayfinders couldn't reach him?

If the Emissary was telling the truth, then all of humanity was under one Sect's control, and no one even *knew*. Asteros had once been searching for control himself, not so long ago. Yet now he was seeking something different. A dark fire ignited within him, filling him with a greater sense of purpose than ever before. This was a higher calling. He was no longer fighting simply for himself; he was fighting for *all* of Auris.

Each and every path he pursued had led to a dead end; he knew this one would not. He wanted a purpose, and he had finally found one.

Asteros smiled. "You say you wish to free humanity?"

The Emissary nodded.

"When do we start?"

CHAPTER THIRTY-FIVE

THUNDER AND FLAME

Elias Surge sat silently in the dark room.

Saevi shuffled around behind him, gathering her things. It was late at night—or early in the morning, depending on how one looked at it. The Storm Gale would arrive soon, and with it Surge's pathway home.

It had taken a great deal of focus to pull his mind from the recent tragedies and prepare himself for Stormriding. Incredibly dangerous, and *very* difficult to do correctly, Stormriding was arguably the most useful ability of the Voltarians. It was a feat that he had accomplished before, but only a few times.

Stormriding was a gift that surpassed all abilities of even the other Sects. It allowed one to fly with a speed that even a Cloudwalker could not match. And it seemed that getting back to Arvendon quickly was of the utmost importance.

Avenos was dead, and Faelyn had already plunged the kingdom into war. And now it fell to Surge to pick up the pieces and put the kingdom back together.

"It's always difficult for me to leave this city," Saevi said, breaking the heavy silence. "It was difficult even when I was exiled."

Surge said nothing, turning to where his greatsword lay against the wall. It shimmered in the reflection of the sister moons Lotius and Oria. It had gone unused for several weeks now. Surge wanted nothing more than to use it to save Arvendon from the path that Faelyn had put it on.

"You know, it wouldn't kill you to take somewhat of an interest in my past," Saevi said, turning around.

"And why would I do that?" Surge grunted.

"I don't know, maybe there's something worth learning about me." Saevi shrugged. "I guess you'll never know."

"Guess not."

Saevi fell silent, the slight shuffling of her feet halting. They both knew that it would take her several weeks to get back to Arvendon, whereas it would only take Surge a few hours.

"I was born in Suchara," Saevi said after a moment. "But I'm sure you've already figured that out." Saevi fell silent again.

Surge leaned forward, resting his elbows on his knees as he sat on the rickety old bed.

"I was fairly respected in this city, given my Summoning powers. I even befriended Queen Sariah before she ascended to the throne."

"Hmph," Surge grunted.

Saevi sighed.

He angled his head toward her. Despite himself, he found that he was waiting to hear what she had to say next.

"We had a falling out," Saevi said after a moment. "Suchara's overpopulation issue was becoming too great for the royal family to handle, and they resorted to quite literally exiling poorer citizens from the city at random so that there was enough room within the ward for those who were allowed to stay."

"That clearly didn't work out too well for them."

"I knew it wouldn't," Saevi agreed. "I told Sariah that exiling innocent citizens was not the correct way to solve our problem... that we were sending people to their deaths. But she disagreed with me." Saevi paused. "She told me that the exiled would be able to survive, and I said they wouldn't—due to the lack of food and the severity of the Tempests."

Surge raised an eyebrow, feeling the pale light of Lotius shine on his scarred face. Auris was truly a mess. Perhaps a war wasn't such a terrible thing after all... The West of Auris was struggling with over-population more and more as the days passed.

"So she exiled *me*, claiming that if I didn't agree with her policies, then I had no place in her city," Saevi said, her voice low. "I went to Arvendon with a caravan of merchants, and proved myself as a soldier within a few months. Not three years later, I found myself as one of the most trusted non-native Scorchers in Avenos's army—I think that's why he chose me for the expedition."

Surge winced at the name. Avenos couldn't be gone. *He can't be.* Surge had only been gone for a few weeks, and in that damningly short amount of time, everything had fallen apart.

"Do you think Arvendon will truly fall?" Surge asked, closing his eyes.

"Do you want the truth? Or do you want me to say something that will make you feel better?" Saevi asked.

Surge grunted.

"Alright..." Saevi started. "With two armies on the offensive against Arvendon, I would say that we don't exactly have very good odds. Not to mention that many of our Summoners have likely already perished in whatever events led up to Avenos's assassination and the attack on Cyfalion."

Surge nodded. She was right. Many of their Summoners had likely already fallen. Arvendon had held the position of dominance that it did due to its high concentration of Summoners, but now that it likely didn't have that... It truly didn't stand a chance.

He turned toward the window, staring out at the pale gray moonlight of Lotius. Oria shined next to it, partially shrouded by the Storm Gale clouds that were rolling in. Surge stared, letting his mind go blank as he tried to escape the cruel truth of what was now his existence.

A shadow moved across the sky.

Surge blinked. It was gone.

It reappeared, sliding across the starry night into the shadow of Sandstorm Keep. Surge leaned forward as the figure vanished into the massive structure.

"What is it?" Saevi asked.

Surge stood up, nearing the small window. He laid his sweaty hands on the sandstone frame and watched the Keep.

"Surge," Saevi said.

A bright red flare soared into the night, a strange whistle screaming through the air with it. Surge watched as the red spark of flame arced toward the stars, then back to the ground, the loud screaming whistle accompanying it all throughout.

Saevi cursed, threw her pack over her back, and sprinted for the door.

"What was that?" Surge spun.

"An alarm," Saevi said, retying the Crystal pouch at her waist. "It came straight from the Keep—which means that the Royal Palace is under attack." Saevi leaned down, grabbing her Sunspear and making for the door.

"Where are you going?" Surge growled, grabbing his greatsword and Crystals before starting after her.

"The Keep," Saevi called over her shoulder as she began running.

"Why?"

"Because," Saevi spun around, screeching to a halt.

Surge stopped.

Saevi blinked a few times, her eyes darting back and forth. "Because, regardless of what happened between us and them, the Queens may be in danger, and we may be able to save them..." She started, her demeanor changing. "Besides, if we save the Queens from an attack, then we may have a chance at forging this alliance after all." Saevi turned away and dashed down the stairs.

Surge followed, the heavy clanking of the greatsword on his back a familiar sound. He still wore the dull, sweat-soaked cloak to blend in, though he knew there would be no mistaking who he was.

Saevi ripped open the door to the inn and sprinted out into the still crowded streets of the night.

Surge stuck close to her, the muscles in his legs alive with the thrill of adrenaline as he passed row after row of slowly waking homeless citizens.

A few minutes later, Surge and Saevi reached the front of the Keep. The guards were nowhere to be found, and the door was slightly cracked. Surge and Saevi exchanged a glance. Surge looked up, hearing shouting and the clash of steel far above.

"Surge," Saevi started, taking a few steps toward him. "Did you see anything through the window at the inn?" Saevi stared at him, her eyes hard. "If we're about to go in there, then we need to know what we're up against."

"I saw a shadow move across the sky," Surge said. "We need to be ready for anything."

Saevi's eyes grew distant. She turned toward the shouting above.

A shadow in the sky was an extraordinarily bad sign.

Saevi turned, pushing open the large wooden doors and dashing into the huge atrium and veering right. Surge followed closely, keeping his breathing steady and rhythmic. The shouting was coming from upstairs—so that was where they headed.

They reached the stairs quickly, twisting past a few stray servants who were fleeing the upper levels.

Saevi cursed them as cowards, but pushed past them without a second thought.

Surge grumbled, hearing his Crystals clink against each other at his waist. They were awake, begging to be unleashed. Fighting at the top of such a massive building was risky, but it was a risk that Surge was willing to take. If he and Saevi were right about what was happening here... then they would need to throw everything they had at this assailant if they wanted to stand any chance of survival.

Passing another landing, Surge continued pounding up the

stairs, his legs and lungs burning. It didn't matter. Another landing came and went, leaving only one left up above. Surge pushed onward. Now was no time to slow down.

Saevi grunted in exertion. They neared the top of the large spiral staircase and Saevi stretched out her hands.

Her black and gold dress sparkled with newfound light as fire materialized in her palms. The *whoosh* of the wind and the spark of the flames ignited her fury, bringing the Scorcher's power of Summoning to life.

Surge itched to do the same with his lightning, but he resisted. *When the time is right.*

They reached the hallway.

Dozens of corpses littered the landing, dark red blood splattered amongst them all. Fallen swords lay beside the bodies. Shattered armor still clung to the torsos of those it had failed to protect.

This was not a fight. This was a *massacre.*

Surge cursed, pushing past Saevi. They neared the throne room within seconds, throwing the doors open and ignoring the fallen guards at the base of the stairs.

Surge screeched to a halt. It was too late.

A dark figure stood in the center of the throne room, holding a gasping and choking figure by the throat.

Saevi shouted.

The man reached forward with a black blade, his midnight armor making him nearly invisible in the darkness.

Surge opened his mouth, but no sound came out.

The man impaled the screaming figure, her golden dress now soaked in blood.

Surge let out a breath. He knew this woman from the second her golden crown crashed to the ground, rolling to a stop in the pool of blood at the killer's feet.

Siraye Thala's lifeless corpse was hurled through the air, crashing through the massive glass windows on the opposite side of the room. Her body disappeared, falling away into the night.

Saevi screamed, throwing her hands forward. Dozens of fireballs launched into the air, whistling toward the Shadow-Swift.

Surge held out a hand to stop Saevi, but it didn't matter.

The figure tensed, then vanished into thin air. The fireballs soared past where he once stood, crashing into the shattered window that Siraye's corpse had been thrown through.

Saevi gasped, freezing.

The man reappeared in a swirl of darkness, confirming Surge's worst fears.

The Shadow-Swift smirked, his Elosian features twisting around his pointed black beard. Long, pony-tailed black hair cascaded down his shoulder. He held a short sword in his right hand. He raised a much longer sword in his left, shifting into an offensive stance.

It was too late. They didn't stand a chance. No one fought a Shadow-Swift and survived, Summoners and Stormless alike.

Saevi charged, flames burning through the darkness.

The Shadow-Swift ducked, sliding across the iron dais toward Saevi.

Surge called out, his voice dying in his throat.

The Shadow-Swift reached out, howling with laughter as he swung his swords.

Saevi cried out, leaping back with a blast of flame.

The Shadow-Swift cackled, one of the blades slicing the surface of Saevi's arm as she jumped back.

Saevi twisted, screaming at the wound. It was shallow, but it would hurt nonetheless.

The Shadow-Swift dropped his blades, opening his hands. Dark energy formed in his palms as he prepared his attack.

Saevi's eyes widened.

The Shadow-Swift thrust his hands forward, sending a wave of darkness toward the Scorcher.

The shadowy energy crashed into Saevi, throwing her against the wall, *hard.* She slumped to the ground, unmoving.

Surge turned to the Shadow-Swift, a cold rage coming over him.

"You're the Voltarian," the Shadow-Swift mused, picking up his blades. "Oh, this is going to be *good*!" The Shadow-Swift bared his teeth. His dark eyes drank in the bloodshed, nearly seeming to glow in the night.

A soft wind blew through the shattered windows, lifting the hood of Surge's cloak. Surge took a deep breath, and stepped forward.

He drew his greatsword, tearing off the dull cloak with his other hand.

Sariah's body was nowhere to be found, and the Shadow-Swift was still here, which meant that she might still be alive.

There was still a chance.

Surge drew upon the power within him. Lightning arced across his body, thunder booming through the chamber. His hands electrified, his greatsword now glowing with energy.

"I've always wondered what it's like to fight a Shadow-Swift," Surge said softly.

The Shadow-Swift grinned, howling with laughter once again. Then, he charged.

Surge planted his feet, stamping his right foot and sending a pulse of lightning through his sword.

The Shadow-Swift slid across the floor, blades extended.

Surge prepared, then with all of his might, he *swung* his massive greatsword over his head, directly into the charging Shadow-Swift.

The Shadow-Swift vanished in a whirl of darkness, disappearing without a trace just as he had when fighting Saevi.

Surge cursed. He knew what came next. With a grunt, Surge threw his free hand toward the ground, sending a strong pulse of lightning into the floor.

The iron dais electrified, and Surge shot into the air from the force of the blow.

Just as he rose above the floor, the Shadow-Swift appeared below him—blades pointed exactly where Surge had been standing not a second before.

The Shadow-Swift leaped back, a bolt of lightning arcing into his armor.

Surge landed feet first in the center of the electrified dais, his body alive with lightning. He reached forward, directing his greatsword toward the Shadow-Swift and sending a *massive* blast of lightning through it. His muscles sang, filling with the thrill of the fight.

Thunder cracked, the deafening explosion sounding through the room in an instant. Surge's ears rang. Stone crumbled, the pillar behind the Shadow-Swift collapsing as the lightning crashed into it.

The Shadow-Swift was nowhere to be found.

Surge cursed, then blasted himself into the air again.

Just as he had predicted, the Shadow-Swift reappeared with his blades extended right where Surge had been standing a second before.

Surge twisted in midair, willing the lightning toward his feet. He sent out a blast, pushing off the crumbling wall and soaring toward the Shadow-Swift with blinding speed.

The Shadow-Swift turned with the speed of a Dexteris, parrying the strike with ease. The monster met Surge's eyes, then laughed. The Shadow-Swift vanished, disappearing for a quarter of a second before reappearing next to Surge.

Surge felt the unmistakable, piercing stab of a blade in his lower abdomen. He grunted, turning and preparing a blast. Pleasure flooded his veins, pouring through his muscles and running down his arms.

He let out a roar, forcing his electricity into a point. His body shook with anticipation for the briefest of moments, and then Surge *let it out.*

Thunder cracked once again.

Blinding lightning arced. But this time, it hit the Shadow-Swift *square* in the chest.

The Shadow-Swift flew backward, crashing into the wall with a crash.

Surge sprang to his feet, clutching his side as blood poured from his stomach. The wound wasn't too deep, and the blade had avoided any vital organs. Surge would survive—if the Shadow-Swift didn't finish him off.

The Shadow-Swift rolled to his feet. His black armor was cracked —nearly shattered—but the man himself appeared to be completely unharmed. The Shadow-Swift smiled, his Elosian features curving into a wicked grin.

That blast should've vaporized him. A lightning strike that powerful would've obliterated even a Master Summoner, and yet this Shadow-Swift was still alive. The strike had barely even broken his armor.

He was invincible.

Surge slid into a defensive stance once again, his side aching. It was too late to give up. If this was how he died, then so be it, but he was not going down without a fight. He held his free hand to the wound and began cauterizing it to stop the bleeding.

"Siraye!" someone screamed.

Surge's eyes shot to the doorway.

The Shadow-Swift spun.

Sariah Thala stood in the entrance to the room, a hand raised to her gaping mouth as she took in Surge, the Shadow-Swift, and the bloody scene around them. By the time she realized what was happening, it was too late.

A midnight blade flew across the room, thrown by the Shadow-Swift.

A puny spark of lightning arced from her fingers as she tried to defend herself, but the Shadow-Swift's blade was through her heart before she could react.

Surge breathed, pushing through the pain of his electric cauterization. He forced his eyes open, watching as the Shadow-Swift appeared before Sariah, throwing her corpse from his blade.

Her body rolled to a stop at Surge's feet, dark blood marring the fallen Queen's beautiful face.

The Shadow-Swift turned to Surge once again, growling.

Surge sealed the wound with a grunt, preparing for the next attack.

He charged.

Surge prepared a defensive blast.

But the assassin slipped past him, launching into the air and all but disappearing in a flurry of darkness. He shot through the shattered window, disappearing into the night without a trace.

Surge turned, staring off into the slowly brightening morning sky. The Shadow-Swift seemed to have fled. His targets were eliminated—there was no reason for him to stay and risk losing to Surge.

Thunder rumbled, lightning striking beyond the windows on the other side of the long hallway outside the throne room. The Storm Gale was beginning.

Spinning, Surge surveyed the half-destroyed throne room, Sariah's corpse, and finally Saevi's figure. He stared at her for a moment, watching the slight rise and fall of her chest.

He leaned down, raising an electrified hand to the cut on her arm. After a few seconds, he had cauterized the wound.

The blast of darkness would have likely broken a few bones, but she would live. Aggravating as she was, she had become a valuable ally, and a good friend. She would be forced to remain in Suchara to heal, meaning that her return to Arvendon would be delayed even further—that is, if she still wanted to return to Etherus's capital.

Despite himself, Surge hoped that he would see her again.

Blinking, Surge looked around once again. There was no trace of the Shadow-Swift, and every man who had tried to fight him was dead by now. *Except me.*

The sky darkened further as the Storm Gale set in. Within moments, the soft patter of rain began. It was time to leave.

There was nothing more he could do here. Suchara was lost, and its armies were marching toward Arvendon at this very moment. Surge had no choice.

He limped over to the shattered window, sheathing his sword

and preparing his thunder. Lightning illuminated the sky overhead, calling him. The rain began, washing the blood from Surge's chest.

Surge took one final look at the ruined throne room, then turned to the sky above. He readied a blast and launched himself into the air. He caught the thundering clouds with ease, altering the direction of the natural lightning to propel him east, toward Arvendon.

With strike after strike, Surge launched further and further east. His Crystals began draining, but that didn't stop him. It was time to go home.

CHAPTER THIRTY-SIX
THE EMERALD CRYSTAL

"That's it," Elric Knyvet said, standing up. "We've waited long enough."

"Elric," Luka warned. "It's been over a day. At this point, we should be more concerned for Arthion's safety than for our sense of haste."

"Well, fine then," Elric grunted. "I'll just go looking for Arthion." He glanced over at the rest of the group, where Castien and Ilyana lay quietly as the sun set yet again. They had waited longer than they planned to. Arthion had been gone for almost a day and a half now, and Elric had run out of patience.

Waiting like this... It was not who he was, not anymore. He needed to do something. He clenched his fists, then released them. The Blood Sorcerers were so close, yet that blazing idiot Whisperer thought it would be a good idea to run off and try to eavesdrop right when they found the fortress!

For all they knew, Arthion had been either ambushed by the Blood Sorcerers or mauled to death by a snowprowler. Either way, he was holding the group up.

Elric stopped himself. It wasn't that he didn't care about

Arthion... The man had been a good friend to Castien, and he had offered some good insight over the last few weeks. Elric closed his eyes, seething. It was just...

Elric had always been taught that if he wanted something, he should *go get it.* Though with Arthion missing, they couldn't enter the fortress—at least according to Luka's logic.

He knew that the delay was hurting Castien too, whether the boy admitted it or not.

Yet even still, Elric smiled softly at the young man. Elric watched Castien's slightly freckled face twist into a smile as he caught Elric's eyes. His short, dirty blond hair and bright blue eyes bore that tell-tale look of repressed anxiety. He still had some work to do, yes, but Elric would get him there.

First and foremost, however, Elric needed to find Arthion.

Elric was running low on Crystals once again, for it had been quite some time since the last Cyclone. He would have enough to find Arthion and even fight off a few snowprowlers or Blood Sorcerers if he had to, but if he got into an elongated conflict, he would be out of luck.

Elric started off into the snow, which was now falling slow and quiet. Night was setting in quickly, though there was still enough light to see by.

"Good luck," Luka muttered as Elric walked away from their collection of boulders.

Elric looked to the left and played Arthion's motions back in his head.

The Whisperer had turned left, then vanished around the boulder to the right of that path. Elric knew where to start.

Drawing breeze from his Crystals, Elric prepared the force of air beneath his feet. Within seconds, a solid platform of air was beneath him. He extended his hand upward, pushing himself toward the sky.

He snapped on his goggles with his other hand, preparing for the flight ahead. When he was roughly thirty feet above the ground—

and around ten feet above the tallest of the boulders—Elric extended his other hand.

He drew more breeze from his Crystals and shoved himself forward with a gust of wind. It always took a strong push to get himself going, but once he was moving, it became easier.

Elric lurched forward, pushed by the invisible hand of air. The rush of Summoning greeted him once again, filling his body with pleasure. He flew *far* too fast at first, shooting himself almost a hundred feet forward in little more than a few seconds.

"Calida's Claws!" Elric cursed, altering the winds to slow his movements. As he went on, there were fewer boulders beneath him; they opened up into a makeshift path that led further northward, as if wrapping around the mountain.

It was narrow, and met with a sharp incline up other slopes to the south and to the west. Elric looked north, scanning the thick crevices and small clearings beneath the overhanging boulders and ridges.

Still no sign of Arthion. Any footprints would've been covered by a new layer of snow by now, but that didn't matter. Elric would find a way to discover Arthion's location, whether he found his trail or not.

The snow fell peacefully, making the whole world seem very quiet in that moment. Elric looked up, watching as the sister moons Lotius and Oria began to rise.

Stars were beginning to dot the sky, painting a tapestry as they mixed with the blue and green waves of light that wavered in the air far above. They were thin, and rare this early in the night, but the lights would become more visible as the evening went on.

Elric turned back to the ground below. It was beautiful, yes, but he needed to focus.

Arthion had likely never been to The Highlands before. Which would mean that he would still be distracted by the northern sky. True, they had been here for several weeks, but something about experiencing the scene when one was alone was simply... indescribable.

And snowprowlers were nocturnal. Elric had seen and hunted a few on this journey, but none of the group members had been actively attacked by one. Elric looked around, a sudden urgency filling his mind as the likelihood of such an attack finally hit him.

His heart started pumping faster, forcing him to draw more breeze from his Crystals. Elric's battle instincts switched on like a Voltarian-Crystal light fixture.

Arthion was in danger. The Whisperer may be inexperienced in combat, true, but he was no fool. Whether he was nervous about the Blood Sorcerers or not, he would've returned by now—that much was certain.

Elric lurched forward, instinctually drawing a strong burst of breeze from his Crystals. The rush filled his body, the rising excitement of a fight coursing through his veins. Elric lived for these moments.

Winds ripped at his strapped-on hat, his goggles, and his thick coat, but Elric let them. He thrived on these winds. The winds were his; the *sky* was his. Elric was practically a god, and no one could stop him.

Something caught his eye below.

Elric swirled to a stop, lurching to a sudden halt at his mental command and dropping from the sky. He reached out a hand, slowing himself with a strong gust of breeze as he fell. Seconds later, Elric lowered himself to the ground.

He brushed the snow from his jacket, whirling to locate whatever it was that he had spotted from the sky.

There was a slight trail of dark snow leading past his feet. Elric cursed, stepping back as he noticed the small trail.

Not darkness, he realized. *Blood*. Elric leaned down, staring at the thin, stained line in the snow. Yes... The red tint was visible even in the moonlight. It was blood... And blood meant that Arthion had been injured.

Injured by... Elric's eyes followed the trail to the right, where it twisted around the corner and off into the maze of boulders.

He turned back to the left, searching for whatever he had spotted from the air. The blood grew thicker, the trail growing darker and more prominent as Elric's eyes slowly followed it back toward the Blood Sorcerers' mountain.

"What the..." Elric started.

A mass lay in the blood-stained snow a few dozen feet away.

Elric stepped forward, following alongside the thickening trail of blood. Something was different about the mass. It was too... animalistic to be Arthion, but it was too *pointed* to be the corpse of a snowprowler.

The sister moons returned from their hiding place behind the clouds, shining their bright lights on the world below. Elric neared the mass, noticing the bloody trail in the snow thickening even more as he grew closer.

Dark red blood seemed to cover the corpse, and Elric slowly began to realize that he was not staring at flesh; he was staring at *bone*. Elric cursed again, careful not to step in the blood as he neared the creature. He approached it, drawing a mint-green Cloudwalker Crystal from his vest for a brighter light source. He was now nearly close enough to touch the mass, and he finally got a good look at it.

"Arthion..." Elric whispered. "Surely..." Elric looked back to the trail of blood, then the direction he had come from. "This can't be your work."

The mass was indeed a corpse, and it was not human. It was in fact the corpse of a snowprowler, though somehow *only* the bones remained. Yet... some were missing. Two of the snowprowler's legs were entirely gone.

Elric cursed, the putrid smell of the body finally piercing through his coat's mask. The carcass was bright white in places—as if the bone had been picked clean—though most of it was still covered in dark blood. Whoever had killed it was likely bleeding too. Why else would there be a trail?

He pinched his nose with one hand, extending the Crystal with his other to give himself more light. Suddenly, the silent night did not feel so peaceful. An eerie sense of quiet settled over him.

The thrill of Summoning vanished without a trace, leaving a feeling of unease that Elric had not known for years. Whatever had done this... It had torn the creature's skin and flesh from its body, leaving nothing but a few bones behind. The closer Elric looked, the more he noticed. Massive chunks of its ribcage were missing, as well as bits of the two remaining legs.

This was not the work of Arthion, or even the Blood Sorcerers—it couldn't be. This was the work of something far more sinister.

Elric stood up, backing away from the carcass. He looked back and to the right, where he had come from. He then looked to the left, where the trail of blood continued through the snow.

What sort of monster waits between the cracks of these boulders? He couldn't follow the blood. He should get the others, and they would investigate together.

But Arthion was out here—alone with this creature—and every second Elric wasted was a second he couldn't afford.

No. Elric could not wait. Returning to this spot with the others would take far too long. There was nothing the others could do anyway, not against a creature like this. Izara's Shadow, Elric wasn't even sure if he could do anything.

He hadn't turned around when he found the Blood Sorcerers' cave in the southeast Highlands all those weeks ago. Elric did not wait. Elric did not hesitate. Elric was a Cloudwalker—one of the most powerful on Auris.

He was the best there was, and if there was ever a Summoner who did not let fear control him, it was Elric. Years of being dominated by anxiety and hesitation haunted his past, yet now that he was past it, he vowed to never again let fear dictate his actions.

Elric would continue forward. Arthion needed his help. There may be a creature far more dangerous than anything Elric had ever encountered on the path ahead, but Elric would go anyway. Elric

Knyvet was not afraid… Not anymore. He took a firm step forward, shoving his anxiety down to a place where it couldn't reach him. He buried it, drowning it.

The blood went around the corner, and so did Elric. Guided by the moonlight and the Crystal he held, Elric traced the trail of blood around the corner, and through the maze of boulders.

Elric sidestepped a stone, following the trail of blood through the turns of the rocks. The crunch of his feet on snow was the only sound in the quiet night. The moons were now rising higher into the sky, shining their strange lights on the snowscape below.

He paused, coming to a stop as he reached another fork in the boulders. *Am I making a mistake?* There was certainly a line between courage and stupidity. *Have I crossed that line?*

A rising pool of dread and unease in his stomach silenced the thoughts immediately. It was a familiar feeling, of course. It was a feeling that he had felt *so* many times, and a feeling that he had hoped to never feel again.

It was the feeling of helplessness. It was the feeling of being stuck waiting… watching while your world fell apart.

Pushing the thought aside, Elric continued. The crunch of snow beneath his feet felt louder now. He ignored it.

The trail of blood was thinning, now reduced to a steady trickle across the snow. It pooled a little to the right here, as if the wounded creature had stopped for a moment. It then continued further ahead.

Elric frowned, squinting through the lightly falling snow. Following the trickle of blood, Elric sensed a clearing up ahead. Through the large boulders on either side, he could see the slight glow of moonlight around the next corner. Sure enough, the boulders opened up to reveal a small clearing—much like the one where the others were camped.

Elric frowned again, approaching what appeared to be another pool of blood. He leaned down, examining the width and depth of the pool. It wasn't overly large, but it was deep enough that it had been quite some time since the creature was here.

He turned forward, seeing that the trail had stopped. He turned to the right, not seeing it continue on that way either. Elric looked around, confused. The small, stained puddle of snow seemed to be the last of the trail.

Elric caught a glimpse of darkness to the left—in the snow. He turned, approaching the strange, discolored portion with caution. Sure enough, another small collection of blood drops lay in the stark white snow.

It's bleeding less, Elric thought. He looked to the right, seeing if it continued through the boulders. But after a few seconds of squinting and looking, he couldn't find any traces of it.

He turned back, facing toward the sharp incline of another mountain. *Where could it have gone? It was here... Then it started to bleed less, and then it went that way.* Elric rubbed his chin.

There was a dark patch of snow along the incline. Elric squinted at it. He slipped the Crystal that he had been holding back into his coat. Raising a hand, he called upon his Summoning again. A force pushed beneath him, propelling him upward and toward the dark patch.

Narrowing his eyes, Elric scanned the snowy patches mixed into the sharply rising rocks. A collection of blood droplets lay on the snow, just large enough to see from a short distance away.

Cursing, Elric looked further up the mountain. *Was the creature flying?* It was either that, or the creature was frighteningly good at climbing.

Elric drew more breeze, pushing himself upward against the rising winds. He spotted another patch of darkness in the snow and continued onwards. The wind rushed around him as he picked up speed. The process became quick and easy, and Elric was now certain that the creature was flying.

It had turned off from its ascent and started going sideways toward another mountain to the south. It later turned back west.

The drops of blood were becoming sparser, but Elric followed their trail with little trouble. There were a few times when he had to double back and retrace his steps, but before long he was at what he was *certain* was the final ascent. This mountain was easily a few miles away from the Blood Sorcerers' fortress, and judging by the way that the creature had flown straight up this mountain, Elric was fairly positive that this was its destination.

Elric slowed to a stop near the top of the mountain, feeling the cold bite of the wind on his face. The trail of blood had stopped entirely now. Its final traces were on a patch of snow beneath what appeared to be a small indenture in the rocks. Elric tilted his head.

Pushing his hand forward, he lurched toward the opening. Seconds later, he extended his other palm. He veered to a stop just in front of the gap. It was small—no bigger than a few people in width —but it was more than big enough for most living things to fit through, except for maybe a nrekuma.

Silencing his Crystals, Elric dropped the last few feet to the slope. He opened the secure pouch within his coat, seeing that one Crystal remained. Getting back to the group would be cutting it close, but this was more important. Arthion was still missing, and Elric was beginning to suspect that Arthion had been attacked by whatever killed the snowprowler. Elric doubted that the Whisperer could've walked this far through the rocky slopes of The Highlands, but Elric might at least be able to discover *what* had attacked Arthion.

Elric took the final Crystal from his pouch and held it out. He stepped into the crack.

Darkness greeted him, staved off only by the dim, mint-green glow of his Crystal. The walls of the cavern were narrow, and the slight dripping of water coupled with the sudden presence of thick, stuffy air confirmed that this cavern went deep.

Awfully intelligent for a savage beast, Elric thought. He had never heard of a creature like this being able to find such a small home so far away from its hunting grounds. In fact, he was fairly certain that humans were snowprowlers' only predator in The Highlands. The snowprowler was an apex predator, just like the nrekuma.

It occurred to him now, finally, that something was very *wrong* about all of this. Something was strange about the carcass; something was strange about the way that the creature had walked, then seemingly flown. Something was *wrong*.

But it was too late to think about that now. Standing in the narrow, thick-aired cavern, Elric knew that there was no turning back. The only way to go was forward.

Squatting down, Elric sensed the descent of the rocks he walked on. He cautiously took a few steps forward, using his free hand to hold on to the rocky wall and keep his balance.

How old is this place? Elric thought, the dread rising once again. This time, Elric did not push the fear down. In a place like this... with a creature that was capable of both flying and killing an apex predator... Elric knew that he should be afraid.

But he was a predator too. Elric was one of the most powerful Summoners in the world, and whatever waited within the jagged walls of this cavern, he could kill it. Elric continued through the small cave, steadying himself as the walls angled to the left, then back to the right—yet ever downward.

Time became relative, and Elric began to wonder if this cavern was truly just a random cave. Yet something was *wrong*. Something was different. The dread burned stronger as Elric started to think these things. It was almost as if the feeling were telling him that he was wrong... Telling him that letting his guard down was the last thing he should do right now.

The air grew colder. Elric froze, feeling the distant echoes of wind. He took a deep breath, feeling the dread spread to his arms. It spread to the rest of his body, shaking his steps. His body began to tremble with fear.

He was nearing the end of this cavern—where there was some kind of other entrance. He could feel it. The cold air steadily grew ever more frozen, and the distant whispers of wind became louder.

A breeze whistled through the cavern, echoing off the jagged rocks of the small passage. Elric froze. He was close.

Something brightened ahead, signifying an opening of some

sort. Elric listened, hearing nothing more than the soft whistling of the midnight winds. Whatever cavern he was approaching, it appeared to be empty.

Elric took a few steps forward, then noticed a turn in the passageway. He had reached a corner, and with a few steps downward and to the right, he would presumably arrive at the source of the wind.

Another breeze echoed, icing his bones. The dread grew almost unbearable, begging him to turn and run. But Elric did not listen. He had spent half of his life listening to that dread, but not anymore. He would not waste another second making that same mistake, despite how *wrong* this whole place felt.

Certain that there was nothing on the other end of this corner, Elric took a step forward.

A deep, emerald glow became apparent. It was the light source ahead, near the opening. At first it seemed indistinguishable from Elric's Crystal, but as he grew closer, he realized that it was something far more sinister. Elric turned the corner, drawing his dagger to the palm of his free hand.

He nearly dropped it in shock.

Around the corner was an almost fully formed room, and it was filled with *drawings*. Drawings, books, and papers of all kinds. There was a large opening in the rock on the opposite side of the room, forming what looked like the mouth of a cave. Yet it appeared to be directly in the middle of a cliff face, for beyond the opening there was only a sharp drop of several hundred feet.

Elric gripped the dagger even tighter, feeling his knuckles go white. His heart thundered in his chest, his eyes shifting to the makeshift stone table in the corner, where countless bones and chunks of flesh lay casually scattered about.

But that wasn't the worst of it... *No...* That was far from the worst of it.

All around the room, giving light to the darkness, were *emerald-green* Crystals. Not mint-green, like Cloudwalker Crystals... No. These were not Cloudwalker Crystals. These were the Crystals of a *Skin-Shaper*.

It all clicked. The creature that had killed the snowprowler—and likely Arthion as well—was a *Skin-Shaper*. The missing flesh and bones, the sudden formation of wings... It all made sense... Elric had just stumbled into the lair of a Skin-Shaper.

The horrific smell of rotting flesh assaulted his nose as he stepped forward, the frozen breeze icing his dread-filled bones. Everything was wrong about this place. The Crystals... The drawings... The books... *What is going on?*

Elric suddenly sensed a light. A light—coming from behind him. Elric scanned the room, catching glimpses of the sketches: a barbed tail, a set of massive wings, a pair of claws... Yet the most prominent of them all was a collection of incredibly detailed bodies of what appeared to be the lungs and throat. *What?*

Elric turned completely, realizing that there was another opening in the room—this one leading deeper into the mountain. But it was not a passage. It was a cliff.

He stepped forward, closer to the bright emerald Crystals. Elric leaned back, staring out into the vast cavern below. It was filled with Skin-Shaper Crystals... Crystals that appeared to be growing out of the mountain itself.

Accumulation? Elric gasped, stepping back. A Crystal mountain like the Blood Sorcerers talked about?

This was groundbreaking. Elric didn't care about finding the creature anymore. He didn't care about Arthion—he was probably dead anyway. All that mattered was getting back to the group. They needed to know about this. All he had to do was go out through the opening, fly back north, and—

A sound came from beyond the mouth of the cavern. Elric spun, hearing something beating against the wind outside. It grew closer.

Elric dove back to the corridor he had entered through, acting on his instincts.

A *whoosh* entered the room seconds later, then stopped. Footsteps sounded on the hard stone. *That was the beating of wings*, Elric realized.

The Skin-Shaper had returned.

Something else sounded in the small room: A sudden rush of wind, followed by an almost otherworldly sound that Elric could only describe as a *shift*. Elric quietly dropped to his knees and leaned forward ever so slightly—staying within the cover of the passage.

A humanoid figure stood in the center of the room, darkness radiating from him—cascading from his midnight armor like water from ancient falls. *A Shadow-Swift?* Elric nearly cried out. *A Shadow-Swift* and *a Skin-Shaper?*

The other figure stood behind the Shadow-Swift, his hazy form highlighted by the large, curved wings that protruded from his silhouette. Elric could hardly even make out the shapes of the two men, but he didn't risk looking further. He slid back against the wall, listening.

"You took too long," a voice said. It sounded further away—likely the Skin-Shaper's.

"I needed to be careful," the Shadow-Swift replied, his voice strangely smooth. He spoke with an eerie calmness, one that possessed an otherworldly sense of conviction.

"And did you do it?"

"I did," the Shadow-Swift said. "The subjects have been taken captive, and we will break them before the month is out."

"I hope the wait was worth it," the Skin-Shaper spat.

"It was," the Shadow-Swift growled. "Thanks to me, we may have a way to reverse Breakdown. I apologize for the delay... But do not forget who is in charge here, Soran."

"And do not forget that *I* am the only reason we know where the Blood Sorcerers are now. I told you the Arvendi would find them."

The Shadow-Swift fell silent.

Elric tilted his head. *What is going on?*

"We don't have time to bicker," the Shadow-Swift said after a moment. "Your companions will be wondering where you are. You've been gone for what, almost two days now?"

"They trust Arthion," Soran said. "They haven't seen the brand—they won't suspect a thing."

Elric's heart dropped. He clamped a hand over his mouth, his eyes bulging, his heart pounding. The dread finally became unbearable, nearly pushing Elric to collapse. Arthion wasn't killed by the Skin-Shaper. Arthion *was* the Skin-Shaper.

All along, Arthion had been working against them. Elric put it together in a matter of seconds.

It was Arthion who orchestrated Avenos's death. It was Arthion who tricked Ilyana and Callum... It was Arthion who had sent Arvendon spiraling into chaos.

"Either way, they will be expecting your return," the Shadow-Swift said. "Be prepared for a fight inside—I have removed a few, but there are still dozens of Blood Sorcerers within that mountain."

"Well then, I suppose I found *it* just in time..." Soran—Arthion —said.

Elric could feel the Shadow-Swift's energy rising.

"Found what?" the Shadow-Swift growled softly.

"The perfect pitch, Lucien," Soran said. "I found it, along with a number of ways to enhance my body and boost the sound."

"What?" the Shadow-Swift—Lucien—breathed.

Elric's muscles tensed, his limbs tingling.

"Once I get deep enough into the fortress, all it will take is a few seconds to attune to the tone and alter my body... Then the Blood Sorcerers will be left powerless." Soran laughed, his voice dark.

"And so will you," Lucien said quietly.

"Ah, but I will have already transformed." Soran paused. "Besides, the Cryostalker and Dexteris will be powerful enough without their Crystals... I doubt the Blood Sorcerers have any *true* combat experience."

A heavy silence settled over the pair. Elric's mind raced. *Arthion betrayed us.* No. Arthion was never on their side to begin with.

Arthion had been lying all along... And now Arthion had found a way to destroy the Blood Sorcerers.

But the Shadow-Swifts were the ones behind all of this—according to Luka. Arthion was working with them, which meant that...

Izara's Shadow. Elric needed to get back to the others. He needed to warn them before Arthion returned. He had to tell them that the Blood Sorcerers were not their enemies. Arthion would destroy them —and he would use Luka, Ilyana, and Castien to do it.

Suddenly, it all made sense. The Shadow-Swifts were so few in number, and so secretive in nature, that they were enacting their plan almost entirely through the manipulation of others. Avenos's assassination... The destruction of the Blood Sorcerers... The Shadow-Swifts were behind everything, and it seemed as if every single Summoner on Auris was playing the part of their pawns—and no one knew.

Yet he couldn't leave. Between the Shadow-Swift and the Skin-Shaper, Elric had no chance of escaping without one of them noticing. Even if he could find his way through the dark corridor, they would most definitely hear him.

"Show me," Lucien said, breaking the silence.

Elric listened quietly, hearing Soran cross the room. He heard the horrifying crack of bone, and the sound of flesh *moving*.

Elric dared a glance around the corner, catching a glimpse of Soran's tortured figure, twisting and cracking in the shadows of the emerald Crystals. The transformation was horrifying to watch; Soran's figure bent and turned, the snapping bones and shifting flesh settling into his new form.

It stopped, a brief second of silence falling over the chamber.

A wretched scream tore through the cave. Elric threw his hands over his ears, the terrible, screeching sound thrashing through the room. Elric's ears thundered, his mind bending beneath the sound. Just when he thought it was about to stop, it got *louder.* Elric cried out, the sound drowned out by the scream. It raked over his soul, piercing his ears, stabbing his mind. It *burned* in a way that he couldn't explain, fracturing his mind.

Then it stopped.

Elric breathed, feeling hollow.

"A few seconds more—and a little louder—and every Crystal in the room would've been shattered," a deep, booming voice growled. More cracking sounded. "I tested it while I waited for you to return... It works," the Skin-Shaper said, his voice returning to normal.

"Well done," Lucien said, his voice smooth. "Yes... Well done indeed. I look forward to seeing your results." Lucien paused, his footsteps shifting.

Elric froze. *My Crystal.*

He had dropped it when the screeching began.

Elric's eyes slowly, shakily, shifted to the side of the chamber, where a mint-green Crystal lay on the floor. It was cracked. Elric's eyes widened. *That sound... It cracked the Crystal.*

His mind started screaming at him to run, to jump to his feet, grab the Crystal, and dive into the snowy mountains beyond. It was his only chance. They would see the Crystal—his only Crystal—and he would be discovered. But he did not move.

He tried, he truly tried, but he was paralyzed... Not by power, or force, but by fear.

"What is that?" Lucien whispered.

Elric held his breath, sliding up against the back of the passage. His eyes snapped shut, his muscles collapsing beneath themselves. Years of anxiety, terror, and fear came crashing in. He had no chance.

He was going to die.

Footsteps sounded. They grew closer, and stopped. He could sense a shadow leaning over. He could hear his Crystal being picked up. Finally, he felt the slow drag of dark eyes settle on him.

"Well..." Soran took a step forward. "This is... unfortunate."

More footsteps sounded, and another shadow appeared.

"The Cloudwalker?" Lucien asked, his voice low.

Elric's eyes cracked open.

The two monsters stood over him, staring with predatory eyes. Soran nodded.

Elric whimpered, trying to rise to his feet.

His mind screamed, thrashing and tearing at him to get away. It wasn't too late. It wasn't his time to die. He could still *escape*. Yet he did not. He sat there, paralyzed, his muscles trembling, his eyes watering, his body frozen.

"Let me guess," Soran whispered, his voice almost soft. "You were concerned that poor Arthion got lost, hmmm? And you decided to go looking for him... Didn't you?"

Elric didn't move, snapping his eyes shut once again.

"Awfully pitiful for a Master Summoner," Lucien snorted.

"Oh, Lucien, don't be so heartless." Soran knelt down. "Elric's just a little scared, right?" Soran leaned forward, a slight grin breaking across his unfamiliar face. "All that false confidence... The savior complex, the courage... It's all a front, isn't it?"

Elric stayed frozen. His muscles grew rigid, the lack of power, the sheer sense of *dread* in his bones tearing him apart.

"Oh, poor, poor Elric," Soran whispered. "You really should've stayed with the others."

Elric's eyes snapped open, his fingers twitching toward his daggers. It was too late.

The cracking sounded again. Bones moved beneath Soran's skin, their loose shapes worming through his body. Flesh squished and squirmed, sliding around the moving bones.

Soran roared in pain and fury, raising his hands. The extra bones settled into place—arriving at Soran's hands.

The bones shifted again, growing longer, *sharper*. Soran screamed again, the now razor-sharp bones stabbing through his flesh, replacing his fingers with massive, jagged claws.

Lucien stepped back, a smirk on his face as Soran's transformation completed.

Elric could only lie there, frozen in terror as Soran's bladed hands reared back for a single, deadly strike.

His mind cried out, begging him to move, to do something —*anything*. But he remained there, watching with tears in his eyes as Soran's momentum snapped forward, and the wicked bones sliced toward him.

And there, lying on the ground in a secret cave, alone with a monster and murderer, Elric's world went black.

PART III

The Skin-Shaper

CHAPTER THIRTY-SEVEN
TO BE A KING

The marble floor scraped beneath Faelyn Titansworn's chair as he was wheeled down the hallway. He sighed, taking a few deep breaths, preparing for the meeting ahead. Several weeks of being stuck in this damned chair had nearly driven him mad, leaving him with nothing to do other than listen to his servants read his books aloud to him.

The servant grunted, pulling the wheelchair to a halt and rotating it to the left as they reached a turn. Faelyn's training with Idris had progressed considerably, though Idris's remedy for Faelyn's condition was still far too taxing to maintain for more than a few minutes at a time—at least until Faelyn practiced more.

The white stone above was slick with water, which was continually dripping through the cracks in the ceiling—it was still in the process of being repaired. Faelyn wrinkled his nose as a droplet landed on his white vest. He had all but officially changed the royal colors to white and gold, though the guards and soldiers still wore the old red and orange. Yet the shift to white and gold was a change he wanted to make in honor of the Solstice.

Reaching another turn, Faelyn was pushed to the right this time.

The fork that they had reached led to a smaller hallway, one that was lined with doors to the rooms of various nobles. Faelyn held a book firmly in his lap, keeping it in place with his nubs-for-hands. It was an old story, though the book had been reprinted.

Finally, he reached his destination, the chair creaking to a halt beyond the white-painted door.

Guards already stood outside, ensuring that the person within didn't leave without authorization. They nodded to Faelyn, and Faelyn nodded back. These particular guards had carried out his orders without question, and he appreciated that.

"Take me inside," Faelyn said. "Then you may leave us."

His elderly servant nodded and moved his wrinkled hands toward the door handle. Opening it slowly, he moved to wheel Faelyn forward.

Seconds later Faelyn found himself inside the fairly unremarkable rooms, his eyes settling on his former friend as Faelyn was wheeled to a stop.

Reluraun was lying on his bed, moving to sit up as if he had just been awoken from a deep sleep. He gazed at Faelyn, his eyes like daggers.

Faelyn now sat in the center of the carpeted rooms, his eyes settling on the tapestry that hung above Reluraun's beige bed.

The tapestry depicted the Knyvet family tree. He looked to Elric's name.

The servant's dull clothing became an unfocused blob in the corner of Faelyn's vision as the man left, closing the door behind him. He would be back to check on Faelyn in a few moments, though Faelyn doubted he would need much time here. This short conversation served only to ease his conscience.

"I hope you're happy," Reluraun said, his words dripping with bitter disgust.

Faelyn blinked a few times, somehow finding himself surprised at the blatant disrespect. "I trust your time under supervision has been enjoyable?" Faelyn asked. "Our scouts report that the Cyfali are still a few days away, but it will all be over soon enough."

"You've made no preparations, I see," Reluraun said. His emerald eyes burned like jewels in sunlight, glimmering with anger.

Faelyn met his eyes, holding their gaze. "I have simply come to tell you something," Faelyn said. "You've been hiding away in your rooms for quite a while now... I figured you could use a little company."

"You're the one who put me here," Reluraun snorted. "I'd rather you leave me alone, thank you." Reluraun settled back into the bed, closing his eyes.

"This idea was actually inspired by Eithor," Faelyn said, speaking anyway. "His suggestion of reading the fables of Ancient Times led to my realization that my decisions are justified, and that you—in your failed attempts to defy me—have been working for the wrong side."

Reluraun said nothing, though Faelyn could feel his attention.

"It was a story that served as the basis for many tales across the ages... And one that has been manipulated by almost all who tell it. The sheer number of variations that have arisen from this story is proof enough to me that what you expect of an event often doesn't matter. But rather, it is best to let fate run its course and accept the results."

"So this is how you're justifying it?" Reluraun asked, shuffling. "You're going to tell me that you think we should simply surrender to the Cyfali because you think *fate* will protect us?"

"This story, you see, is of a girl who wished to escape an arranged marriage," Faelyn started, ignoring Reluraun's comment. "She had many options to avoid the marriage. She could've run away, for example... She could've insulted the boy's family so gravely that they would change their minds. Beyond that, she could've even hired an assassin to have the boy killed.

"But she didn't do any of that," Faelyn continued. "No, she simply surrendered to her fate, as she knew that any sort of resistance would be more trouble than it was worth. And what happened? She ended up happy. She found that her new husband was far more agreeable than she had once thought. Her life was one of leisure and joy, despite what she had believed."

"Why are you telling me this?" Reluraun grumbled.

"Because you need to understand that there are worse things in the world than surrendering," Faelyn said firmly. "Surrendering will give many of us a chance at survival, whereas resisting will get us all killed."

"The Cyfali will destroy our Monoliths either way," Reluraun said. "Surrendering will do us no good if we're all going to die anyway."

"You do not listen to me," Faelyn said, shaking his head. "Turning our city over to the Cyfali is our *only* chance at survival. You say that we will all die, and that may be true—but only if we resist. Surrendering may not be our best option, but it is the only one that doesn't guarantee the deaths of each and every person within Arvendon."

The servant opened the door and approached Faelyn from behind.

Faelyn motioned forward, waving for himself to be wheeled away.

Reluraun opened his mouth, evidently wanting to speak more.

Faelyn turned away, and was slowly pushed out of the room. He heard Reluraun saying something, but he didn't care. He had tried to explain why he was surrendering the city, but Reluraun hadn't listened. As Faelyn was pushed down the hallway back to the stairs, he felt no guilt for what he was doing. The story had been a good idea. He had hoped that it would make Reluraun realize why he was doing this. But alas, it had not worked.

The door to Reluraun's rooms shut, effectively silencing him. Faelyn would ensure that Reluraun stayed under constant supervision for several more days, at least until the Cyfali arrived. It was a shame, though. Faelyn would've really liked to revive his friendship with the boy before it all ended. *A damned shame.*

The door of his chambers swung open, the loud rumbling of the Storm Gale overhead suddenly overshadowed by the obnoxious presence of the figure who stood behind him.

Faelyn turned, opening his mouth to protest that the carpet was getting wet when he saw *who* had entered his rooms.

Elias Surge, wearing dark Sucharan garments, soaked practically beyond recognition, stood before him. His face was red, and his fists were clenched. Faelyn started, noticing the dried blood around a wound at his stomach.

"General..." Faelyn started. "You're—"

"*You!*" Surge roared. He stumbled forward, removing his right hand from the wound and drawing the greatsword on his back. Surge approached with fury, threatening to rear back for a swing.

"Wait!" Faelyn shouted. He trembled, the sheet of papers in his lap falling to the floor. Faelyn raised his nubs as if to surrender.

Surge paused, taking a step back. He took in Faelyn, noticing the wheeled chair and the wrappings around his arms and legs. "You..." Surge started, his voice gruff. "You're... Izara's Shadow," Surge cursed, lowering the blade. He stopped, his body shaking. His dark eyes were alive with thunder, and his gloved hands shook with both blood and fury.

"Surge," Faelyn breathed. "What happened?"

"What the hell have you done with my city?" Surge growled. He stepped forward once again, raising the tip of the greatsword so that it was mere inches from Faelyn's face.

Faelyn almost shouted for the guards, but thought better of it. *Now's not the time.* "My father," Faelyn started frantically. "He was killed on the Solstice," Faelyn said, trying to keep his voice from shaking. "The Cyfali were responsible for his death, so I made the decision to travel to Cyfalion and—"

"*And what?*" Surge seethed.

"I..." Faelyn stuttered. His mind stumbled, fear suddenly pooling in his stomach. "I wanted to make things right. I wanted to punish them for—"

"Make things right? You *destroyed* a Monolith!" Surge roared. "You've doomed the entire city! And nearly got yourself killed in the process." Surge shook his head. "Calida's Claws, it probably would've been better for all of us if you had died that day."

"I know," Faelyn whimpered. He shut his eyes, an overwhelming warmth rising in his eyelids. He blinked back tears, trying to settle himself. After weeks of numbness, the sudden flood of emotion was finally hitting him.

It was all too much. He could hardly get his thoughts together— let alone speak. *My father is dead. My city is doomed. Reluraun wants to betray me.* The thoughts raced through his mind, scarring and bleeding him as they passed with horrifying fury.

"I need you to listen to me right now," Surge growled, taking Faelyn by the collar of his white-gold vest. Faelyn's crown shook, falling from his golden locks onto the carpeted floor. "The Cyfali army is not alone. Suchara's forces are on their way as well, and they will be here before we know it. We might have been able to handle one army, but two... This is beyond your capabilities." Surge paused. "And from what I hear... you were planning on surrendering the city."

"I—"

"*Listen!*" Surge roared.

Faelyn flinched beneath the shout, and his mouth snapped shut.

Surge's heavy breathing became the only sound over the distant falling rain and the occasional crash of thunder. Faelyn's shirt grew wet from Surge's soaked hands. "You will give me control of the city. You have neither the experience nor the courage to deal with this."

"Guards!" Faelyn shouted, against his better judgment.

"I have already spoken with them," Surge growled. "They obey me, not you. They are just as enraged with your plan to surrender the city as I am, so I suggest that you formally hand over the city *now*." Surge breathed hard, tightening his grip on Faelyn's collar.

Faelyn gasped, struggling to keep his breathing steady. He quivered in Surge's grip, twisting and turning with his useless body to try and escape.

Surge held strong. "You have ten seconds," Surge warned. "If you do not give me control, I will *take* it from you."

"I..." Faelyn coughed. He whimpered, flinching. He finally ceased. "Okay," Faelyn whispered. "I surrender control of the city to you."

The world tilted as Faelyn was thrown back into his chair. Faelyn slammed into the cushioned seats, groaning at the impact. His body shook, his mind running faster than it had in weeks.

He saw Surge lift the crown from the ground. He looked at it for a moment, then hurled it at Faelyn's mirror.

The mirror shattered, glass spraying across the room.

Surge slid his greatsword onto his back and stormed out of Faelyn's rooms.

"You'll receive your orders soon," Surge said to Faelyn, pausing as he reached the doorway.

The guards standing beyond nodded to him, then dropped into a kneel.

"I suggest you obey them." Without a single word more, Surge marched out of the chambers.

CHAPTER THIRTY-EIGHT

THE PLAN

Castien Varic stood, squinting out into the morning Frostfall. Two days had passed. His stomach twisted and turned with each passing second. Elric had not yet returned, and neither had Arthion.

Ilyana stirred behind him, rising from her sleep.

"Still no sign of them?" she asked groggily.

Castien remained silent, staring off into the rising light in the clearing.

"Figures," Ilyana said, shaking her head. "I knew we should've just entered when we found the cave."

"If anything, this proves that Arthion was correct," Luka said from behind them. "Odds are they were both captured by the Blood Sorcerers. This whole thing is probably an elaborate trap of some sort."

"They could've killed all of us in The Highlands back on the first expedition. If they didn't then, why go through all the trouble of capturing us now?" Castien asked, turning back. His heart was beating considerably faster than usual. His anxiety was rising, and though he was using the techniques that Elric had taught him, they weren't exactly helping. He couldn't stop worrying about Elric. True, Elric was one of the most powerful Cloudwalkers on Auris, but he was reckless sometimes... And Castien needed him. Castien *needed* the support that he was offering. Ilyana was good to him, true, but Elric's guidance was different.

Elric had been a beacon of order and hope in a world that was descending into chaos and death.

"We don't even know if the Blood Sorcerers are in there," Castien said after a moment.

"They are," Luka said. "Why else would Elric and Arthion still be gone?" Luka closed his eyes.

"How many do you think there are?" Ilyana asked.

"Your guess is as good as mine," Luka snorted.

Ilyana rolled her eyes and turned back to her supplies.

Castien leaned against a boulder, watching the clearing. *How can they act so casual when two of the five of us are gone?* Castien could hardly keep himself together, while the others were simply going about their business as if nothing were wrong. *Because my mind works differently,* Castien reminded himself. *And not in a good way.*

"Assuming there aren't too many Blood Sorcerers within the mountain, we should be able to figure out what's going on before we actually enter," Luka said after a moment.

"What do you mean?" Ilyana turned to him.

"I still think that they may be on the right side of this whole conflict, and trust me when I say I don't want to be responsible for destroying one of our few true allies in this world," Luka said, continuing to pack up his things. He slipped his sword out of its sheath, examining it. "Velarus made a good case to me, and he helped me escape Freyfall. I think that we should at least give them a chance."

"But if they have Elric or Arthion, we make rescuing them our priority," Castien said reflexively. He blinked a few times, almost feeling startled at his own words.

"Castien's right," Ilyana said. "If we find any evidence of our friends being captured, we need to change our plan."

"Agreed," Luka said, nodding. "While I wouldn't be too surprised if Velarus's whole speech was a lie, the fact that he would go through all of this trouble to help me escape only to have me killed here does seem a little odd."

"We can only wait around for so long," Castien said, pacing back and forth. His muscles shook, his burned arm beginning to tingle with adrenaline. Castien turned, looking around the small shelter under the outstretch of boulders and rocks where they had set up camp. He paced within, staring at the dark stone, wondering what could've happened to his friends.

Something was wrong. If one of them didn't return soon... Well, he wasn't sure what he was going to do. A part of him wanted to wait until they came back, but if they never did... Another part of him feared that they had been captured, and that they were waiting to be rescued.

"We need to figure out a plan," Castien said, stopping his pacing. He took a deep breath. "At this point, I'm starting to think that it may be quite a while before they return—if ever."

"I wouldn't be so sure about that," Luka said slowly.

Castien turned to the Cryostalker, who was staring off into the clearing. The cold air bit at Castien's exposed nose, the bright sun causing him to squint as he tried to see what Luka was looking at.

A shadow stood in the clearing, wandering through the snow. It turned toward their shelter.

Castien's heart jumped.

Arthion stumbled into the camp, brushing snow from his torn robes. They were tattered in places, especially around the back.

Castien's breath caught.

Ilyana cursed.

Arthion looked as if he hadn't slept in days. Small splashes of red dotted his robes, marking the site of an injury.

"Arthion..." Luka stepped forward, his voice firm. "What happened?"

"It was the Blood Sorcerers," Arthion breathed, his voice raspy and frantic. He fell over to the side of the shelter, slumping onto the stone floor. His breathing was heavy.

Luka stepped toward the man. "*What happened?*"

"I was..." Arthion took a deep breath, then another.

Luka sighed and handed him his own canteen of water.

Arthion took it gratefully and drank the entire thing in one gulp.

Castien stood a fair distance away, anxiety crawling wildly in his chest. *Where is Elric? Were they ambushed by the Blood Sorcerers?* Did... *Did Elric get captured?*

"I was listening to the Blood Sorcerers within the fortress," Arthion started, returning the canteen to Luka.

Ilyana knelt beside Arthion, reaching for the small patch of blood near his middle abdomen. She pulled back the torn robes, and peeked beneath the bandages. Ilyana tied some sort of knot and reapplied the bandage that she had moved.

Arthion grimaced, but remained still as she did so. Finally, Arthion was able to continue. "I found what appeared to be another entrance after several hours—on the other side of the mountain. There was a large mouth to the cave, and several Blood Sorcerers were guarding it. But I realized this too late, and they started to see my tracks in the snow. I got stuck hiding higher up the mountain while they sent out guards to look for me," Arthion said, his breathing still coming in shallow pants.

"I didn't know how long they were going to be looking for me, so I kept climbing upward—as high as I could," Arthion continued. "After a few hours, and maybe even a few days, I recall seeing Elric flying overhead. I assume he was looking for me and I—" Arthion stopped, coughing. "It was my fault," he whispered.

Castien's heart sank.

"The Blood Sorcerers spotted Elric, and they attacked him," Arthion said, his voice hollow. "They must've brought him down somehow, because by the time I was low enough to see what was going on, they were carrying him into the fortress." Arthion paused. "I think he's still alive, but... I can't even imagine what they're doing to him."

Castien's breathing grew even faster, his heart pounding. The world started spinning.

Elric had been captured. He was in danger... They were all in danger. Elric was the best fighter out of all of them, and without him...

"Izara's Shadow!" Castien shouted. The others turned to him at the curse, but the moment passed—it was well deserved. Castien slumped against the boulder wall and slid down to the floor. His muscles still twitched, and his head felt heavy. It was as if his body wanted to run, hide, fight, and sleep all at once.

He didn't know what to do, and he didn't know what *not* to do. All he could think about was that he wasn't safe. The cornerstone of Elric's teachings was reminding himself that his environment was safe, but it *wasn't safe*. Without Elric, none of them were safe. The Blood Sorcerers likely outnumbered them twenty to one, if not more. And if Castien's group was without their most powerful Summoner...

Castien cursed again, slamming his free hand into the wall. His fist shook, stinging. Castien cursed, bringing it back. If he were a true Starburner—with access to his powers—he might've actually been able to help. But he didn't have any Crystals, and even if he did, he had no training. All he had was this damned crossbow. He reached to his back and unhooked the device, throwing it across the shelter.

The others watched in silence.

Ilyana looked as if she wanted to say something. But she didn't.

Elric was the one who was supposed to help him. Elric was the one who could make everything feel safe again. Elric was the one who could help them all through this disaster.

But Elric was gone. He had been captured.

"I know everyone's upset about this," Arthion said, breaking

Castien's train of thought. "But we need to retaliate and get Elric back before it's too late."

"And how are we supposed to do that?" Luka asked.

Castien blinked a few times, feeling shaken.

"If they managed to capture our best fighter, how are we going to beat them?" Luka advanced.

"I have a plan," Arthion said, his breathing stabilizing. "I was able to get a glimpse of the inside of the cavern, and I think that I know what's going on here."

Luka and Ilyana shared a look. Ilyana turned to Castien, then back to Arthion.

"I think that the Blood Sorcerers in Celes were telling the truth about the nature of their fortress," Arthion said, his tone grave. "I caught sight of blood-red Crystals growing out of the rocks of the mountains—*that's* where their power comes from."

"So? We already knew that." Luka folded his arms.

"I think I might have a way to even the field," Arthion said. "If I'm correct, I'll have a way to destroy every Crystal in that cave."

"*What?*" Ilyana started. "What good would that do us anyway? That would still put us in a fight of four against what... A hundred?" Ilyana threw her hands up.

"Most of them didn't seem to have any combat experience beyond the usage of their powers," Arthion said, suddenly growing calmer. "I think that—if we catch them off guard, and if my plan works—we might actually be able to take them all out."

"But we—" Luka started. He paused, turning to Castien.

Castien's mind woke from its stunned state.

Luka almost seemed to be asking for Castien's input.

Castien nodded absently, feeling the cold grip of powerlessness and fear in his veins. But it had to be done.

Luka wanted to see if Velarus was telling the truth when he had freed Luka, but it appeared that it had all been a lie. Even most of what Likara had told them appeared to be a lie. The group had agreed that if Elric or Arthion was captured, then they would attack... And Elric *had* been captured.

Who knew if he was even still...

Castien flinched again, his lip quivering. His eyes grew warm and watery, the rising tears fighting hard to reach the surface. Castien pushed them back down with all his might—he couldn't afford to get distracted now. Now was the time for action, not fear. If Elric was gone, then they would mourn him *after* they had their revenge—not before.

"What do you need?" Luka asked, breaking the silence.

"I need you to get me two Blood Sorcerers—dead or alive, it doesn't matter as long as they're unconscious." Arthion turned to the Cryostalker. "We'll make our move at nightfall, when less of them are active. With any luck, we'll have taken out the whole Sect before dawn tomorrow."

Ilyana turned to Castien and approached him. She slid down to the floor, sitting down beside him.

Castien looked away.

"Castien, are you okay?" Ilyana asked. "I know that you and Elric are good friends."

Castien closed his eyes, the warmth finally breaking. A single tear flowed down his cold, frozen cheek. He was scared—no, he was terrified. Without his mentor... Without one of his few true friends in this world... What was he going to do?

But they had a plan.

Castien didn't bother trying to put together what Arthion was going to do—or why he needed two Blood Sorcerers. He trusted Arthion, and he knew that the Whisperer had no reason to lie about any of this, so Castien would do whatever he could to help. All Castien knew was that Elric was gone, and that they were storming the Blood Sorcerers' fortress tonight. And hopefully, when they left, they would be leaving with Elric among them... *Hopefully.*

CHAPTER THIRTY-NINE

INFILTRATION

Night fell quickly, wrapping the mountains in a cloak of darkness. Only the light of the moons guided them across the small clearing. It was a cloudy night—making it darker than most.

But there was nothing to see, not in these barren mountains. Once they were within the fortress... Well, that was a different story. It wouldn't take long for the Blood Sorcerers to catch on to their presence if Arthion was correct. But it didn't matter. Elric had been captured, and they had no choice but to try and rescue him.

Arthion had said that his plan involved forcing the Blood Sorcerers to disable their allies. Yet Arthion had not yet said how he was going to manage that. The Whisperer had no idea how deep the caverns went, or how long it would take for them to actually reach the center of the Blood Sorcerers' fortress. It seemed to be large, for the mountain itself was *at least* several hundred yards in diameter. Castien had no idea how many levels were within the fortress, though Arthion suspected that there were no more than one or two.

He said that the layout of the fortress seemed to have a massive atrium near the front and presumably several hallways in the rear.

According to his assessment of the ways the jagged walls were so perfectly *uncut*, he was willing to bet that the cavern was mostly natural. The entrance Arthion had found was near the massive chamber—which rose several dozen yards in height, and dozens more in width.

After having watched the side they camped at for the better part of several days now, they had determined that the back exit they had been guided to by the red markings was largely unused. No Blood Sorcerers had entered or exited through this way, and nothing so much as a sound had been heard from within the cavern.

Of course, after Elric was captured by the front, there probably wouldn't be too many people looking around this side, Castien thought. Elric's capture had given them a slight advantage, actually, as the Blood Sorcerers likely suspected that the only entrance their attackers knew about was the one at the front.

"It's time," Arthion said, rising to his feet. He stepped forward, drawing his dagger and approaching the small crevice on the other side of the clearing. Castien took a deep breath, looking at Ilyana.

She remained looking forward, coolly focused in the face of this danger.

"Remember, we get in, get Arthion the two Blood Sorcerers, and then get Elric," Luka said. "No one do anything foolish and this will all go off without a hitch. They don't know we're coming."

"And when I enact my plan, they won't know what hit them," Arthion added, his voice low.

The Blood Sorcerers had captured Elric, effectively shattering the group's trust in the Ancient Sect. They had likely orchestrated the Freyfallion march on Arvendon from the start. It wouldn't be long before the whole world was falling apart, and all they could do in this moment was try and stop the Blood Sorcerers who were responsible.

Arthion took the lead, sliding in between the cracks of the rock, producing a small, pale gray Whisperer's Crystal as a dim source of light.

Castien blinked a few times, realizing that this was the first time he had seen Arthion take out a Crystal. Castien nearly went down the path of those thoughts, but brushed them aside. He entered the crevice next, slipping one hand into his pocket to feel the drained Starburner fragment. He hadn't felt the Crystal for quite some time, and he had almost found himself missing its touch. Yet another part of him feared it... Feared what it would eventually do to him.

The inside of the cavern was dark and narrow. It was cramped beyond comfort, and Castien could hear Arthion's shuffling close in front of him—indicating that the cavern didn't get any wider.

He heard Ilyana curse behind him, and could practically feel Luka roll his eyes in return. The narrow passage banked right, and upward —which Castien noted as he bumped his shin on the sudden cleft of rock.

Castien found himself cursing as well, and uttered a quiet warning to Luka and Ilyana.

Arthion continued, the dim glow of his Crystal offering barely enough light to reach Castien, let alone Ilyana and Luka.

"Careful," Arthion whispered.

Castien lowered himself to the ground, then felt ahead with his feet. There was a sudden drop. Castien jumped down it, finding the floor only a few feet lower than where his foot had been reaching.

"This place *is* rather hidden," Ilyana whispered.

"How much further until the main cavern?" Castien whispered.

"Probably a few hundred feet," Arthion replied. "I don't know how far back it went, but hopefully we'll be out of this cramped passage before too long." Arthion paused. "This may be our only escape route, unfortunately."

"It's easily defensible, but it would be difficult to make this trek quickly," Luka said, his voice hushed.

Castien looked back, catching his friend's faces in the pale glow of the Whisperer Crystal.

How many of us will make it out? Castien thought with a shudder.

He pushed the thought from his mind. Four were entering, and five would leave. *I hope.*

"Be quiet," Arthion hushed.

They stopped whispering, and the distant murmur of voices became apparent.

Arthion waved them forward, then lowered the Crystal. The light vanished—the Crystal likely slipped back into his cloak.

Castien reached out, guiding himself with his unburned hand along the side of the jagged wall. Sharp points poked him, sticking out and dragging along the bandage of his burned arm.

This place was not man-made. Castien was sure of that much. *Unless this whole cavern was simply made to* appear *unnatural.*

The murmur grew louder, then faded quickly. *We're near a hallway, then*, Castien thought. They were close—to the back corridors of the fortress, at least.

A dim light became visible in front of Arthion, lighting the dark stone in front of him.

Castien picked up his speed a bit, now able to see the slight tips and points of the jagged rocks to better guide himself through the cramped passage. He grunted, squeezing through a particularly tight area, and then found himself almost bumping into Arthion.

The Whisperer had stopped and stood quietly in the growing light. It was especially bright on the wall ahead, indicating that they were at the end. Arthion's silhouette moved, and Castien saw a hand rise to his ear.

Can't he just use his Whispering to listen for others? Castien thought with a start. Something was off. *Why would Arthion not be using his Whispering?*

Castien opened his mouth, but thought better of it. They still weren't sure if there was anyone beyond the corner of the narrow passage, and Castien wasn't going to risk giving away their position to simply ask Arthion a question.

Arthion motioned them forward, apparently satisfied that there was no one guarding the exit.

Castien turned the corner and found himself standing before yet another jagged hallway. Yet this one was lit.

This corridor was more established, for the hallway's edges were slightly smoother than those of the passage. Castien looked around, staring at the torches that lined the walls every few dozen feet. It was dimly lit, but the stone floor was mostly even—save for a few large rocks here and there.

They were inside.

For all that Castien was expecting of the inside of the Blood Sorcerers' fortress, the one thing that he hadn't predicted was that the first place he would see would be a simple hallway. The others filed out, standing alongside Castien and Arthion as they surveyed the curving hallway.

There was no sound of footsteps on either side, though there were a few doors and curtains lining the hallway further away from them.

"Which way?" Luka whispered.

Arthion didn't answer, instead taking the path that turned to the left. The mostly natural cave walls twisted around, turning forward after a few feet, and then back to the left.

Arthion claimed to have gotten a decent idea of what the inside of the cave was like, and they simply had to trust that he was being truthful. Yet Castien still couldn't shake the thought of Arthion's lack of Whispering from his mind.

Arthion paused at another fork in the hallway, looking to the right and left. He took the right passage after a few seconds, carefully leading the group forward.

How have we not been discovered yet? Castien began to wonder. Were there simply not as many Blood Sorcerers as they had thought? Or were all of them asleep? Either way, something was off, and Castien could tell that he was not the only one who was feeling that way.

"Something's wrong," Ilyana whispered.

Arthion spun, shushing her. "Keep moving."

"Arthion," Ilyana hissed.

The Whisperer whirled and stared at her with daggers in his eyes to match the one in his hand.

"We've been walking for several minutes, and we haven't passed a single person. Given that the Blood Sorcerers just found an attacker outside their fortress, doesn't that strike you as a bit odd?" Ilyana asked lowly.

"We chose to attack at night so that they wouldn't be awake to catch us, remember?" Arthion hissed back. "They have no reason to believe that they are in danger, and their fortress is so hidden that they shouldn't even bother with guards and patrols. Why would they?"

Ilyana remained firm, standing her ground.

For once, Luka looked at her, and then Arthion, and nodded. "She's right," Luka said, his voice a little louder now. "Something's wrong. I can feel it."

Arthion closed his eyes, taking a long, deep breath. He took another, and another, and another.

Castien synced his own heartbeat to his breathing and steadied himself. *Five beats in, six beats out. Hold for three. Repeat.* He gave his Crystal another squeeze, feeling the phantom Starburner energy that had once been within.

"Stick with the plan," Arthion said firmly after a moment.

Castien opened his eyes, staring at Arthion. "What?" Castien asked, stepping forward.

"We have a plan, and we need to follow it. We can't let a simple gut feeling sway us," Arthion said.

"And who put you in charge?" Ilyana challenged.

"I did," Arthion growled. "I put myself in charge when I got a glimpse of the inside of this fortress, because I am the only one out of all of us who knows how to—"

Footsteps interrupted him.

Arthion's mouth shut, his eyes seething.

The footsteps were coming from the hall ahead, and turning

around would only put distance between them and whoever was approaching, doing nothing but delaying the inevitable.

Arthion breathed a curse, and then turned around, pushing past the others and rushing down the hallway on quiet feet. He whipped into a curtained room and disappeared.

Castien and the others followed, keeping their steps quiet as the footfalls grew closer. He brushed through the curtain and entered the small, dark room. The others jumped in after him, staying silent as the footsteps grew closer. A shadow passed under the bottom of the curtain a moment later, and the footsteps slowly grew further away.

A Blood Sorcerer, no doubt.

As if in answer to his thoughts, Ilyana produced a dark blue Dexteris Crystal. The deep, ocean-sapphire light illuminated the room, revealing that they were in some sort of bedroom.

A chest lay on the floor, just along the foot of a small makeshift bed. A few poorly made cabinets and dressers were scattered up against the jagged walls, but the room was largely uninteresting. Strangely, however, there were no Blood Sorcerers in here.

Castien had expected massive chambers and a large fight to be waiting for them within this mountain. Yet, so far, they had simply been wandering through a fairly mundane hallway.

Something seemed very strange about all of this. Even as Arthion motioned for them to go back out into the hallway, Castien felt a pooling sense of dread in his stomach. All of this was *off*. Arthion was acting oddly. Whereas he had normally been quiet and mild mannered, he was suddenly trying to be the leader of the group. He spoke with a hidden ferocity that they had never seen before, and he walked with an unusual sense of determination despite his injuries.

Castien heard the footsteps behind him stop, and turned around to find Ilyana and Luka staring past another curtained room. Castien approached, tilting his head.

"This one's empty too," Luka said.

"Completely empty?" Castien asked.

"That's the strange part…" Luka said. "There's a bed, and it looks as if someone has been living here, but there's no one in there now."

Castien's heart quickened.

Arthion cursed, then turned around.

Castien spun, facing the Whisperer.

Arthion's amber eyes were wide, though they quickly narrowed. A look of anger came into them, followed by something else.

What is going on? Castien advanced. "Arthion," Castien said, reaching out.

Arthion turned away, shrugging off his hand. "We're losing time," Arthion said, quickening his pace. His footsteps were louder now.

"Arthion!" Ilyana hissed. "Be quiet, someone else could be coming!"

"Don't you see?" Arthion whirled. "They knew we were coming!" Arthion's breathing grew ragged with anger.

Castien's stomach fell, the dread pooling ever deeper.

"They must've…" Arthion stopped himself and took a long breath.

Castien moved, his muscles feeling shaky.

There was still no sign of Elric.

"Arthion," Luka stepped forward. "Wouldn't now be a good time to use your Whispering to see if there's a lot of chatter around here?"

Arthion grew still.

Luka noticed too, Castien thought. Of course the Cryostalker would've noticed. It was rather strange that Arthion was still refraining from using his abilities.

"I'm going to assume that this is your way of telling me you're not going to do that?" Luka continued, his voice hard. "How about this then—why don't you tell me what your plan is? *All* of it." Luka leaned forward, reaching out. He placed a hand on Arthion's shoulder, pushing him against the wall.

Arthion stared back blankly. "Is this supposed to intimidate me?" Arthion raised an eyebrow.

"It was supposed to make you realize that we know something is wrong," Luka snarled. "Do you think we're stupid? Do you think we're truly foolish enough to believe that all of these Blood Sorcerers are somehow missing? And Elric's disappearance... I don't suppose you know anything about that, do you? And what about the fact that you just wandered off the very *second* we found the entrance to the fortress, hmmm?" Luka seethed, his eyes burning.

Castien advanced, Ilyana as well. It still didn't make sense, though. If Arthion was going to betray them, he would've done it already; he wouldn't wait until they were inside the fortress.

If he was working with the Blood Sorcerers, he wouldn't have let them find the hideout in the first place, and if he wasn't working with them... Then what reason would he have for lying?

Castien blinked. *Elric.* Arthion was the only one who claimed to know what had happened to Elric, and if Arthion wasn't telling them the whole truth...

"We have to go," Castien said. His voice shook, his lip quivering.

"What?" Ilyana turned.

"Luka, keep Arthion here," Castien said, the firmness of his voice catching him off guard. "Ilyana, come on."

"Where are you going?" Luka spun.

"We're going to find Elric," Castien said, starting down the hallway. "I don't know how much time we have, but we need to move *now.*" He reached onto his back and drew his crossbow. He loaded a bolt, preparing for whatever lay ahead. "I worry we may already be too late."

It wouldn't matter if they ran into one Blood Sorcerer; it wouldn't matter if they ran into twenty. Castien was going to find Elric, and he was going to save him... Because with everything that Elric had taught him, the Cloudwalker had practically saved Castien's life— and it was time for Castien to return the favor.

"Come on," Castien said, storming down the hallway. He held the crossbow with his good hand, using his bandaged arm to prop it up so that it was ready to shoot.

"Castien, slow down," Ilyana said, breaking into a light jog to keep up with him.

Castien increased his speed even further, picking up into a run now. It was loud, but he didn't care.

"We may already be too late to save Elric, but we have to try," Castien said, his voice sounding distant once again. The dread pooled in his stomach, but the feelings of fear and adrenaline brought him back into his body with stunning clarity. He was ready.

There were voices ahead now. As Castien followed the twists and turns of the labyrinth, he only increased his speed. He heard Ilyana unsheathe her butterfly-blades. Castien broke into a run.

He could hear Ilyana getting further and further away, as if she were falling behind.

She must've been conserving her Crystals. She called out his name again, her voice clashing against the rising voices at the other end of the hallway.

He made another turn, seeing a brighter, redder light shining on the far wall. He didn't know what drove him forward in that moment... Perhaps it was courage, perhaps it was determination, or perhaps it was just blatant disregard for all things in the world other than Elric's safety. But he knew that the Cloudwalker would've rescued him, and so he had to rescue Elric.

Ilyana cried out, calling his name one final time as Castien whipped around the hallway.

Castien let out a cry, raising his crossbow as he dashed forward.

Three Blood Sorcerers stood on the other side of the corner. The small group wore dark red robes, though they were lighter in weight than the ones Castien had seen on others.

Castien felt the world slow, the *thwack* of the crossbow sounding through the small corridor.

The bolt flew through the air, crashing into the chest of one Blood Sorcerer in the blink of an eye.

Castien's momentum was halted by the force of the shot, but the crossbow had done its job. The Blood Sorcerer stumbled back, his hand wrapping around the bolt piercing his chest.

Castien started loading another bolt, his heart thundering.

The other Blood Sorcerers finally acted. They raised their hands, red orbs appearing in each of their palms.

Castien's breath caught as he struggled to load the crossbow. *No, no! Not again!*

Another pair of Blood Sorcerers appeared from around a corner, red lights materializing in their palms as well.

Castien stopped. The Blood Sorcerers' power was finally taking effect.

More faces appeared around him, and control of his body was wrenched away from him.

His muscles began to fail, and his eyes began to close. The adrenaline had frozen solid, and Castien was left with a fleeting sense of shame. He had been reckless. He had been foolish.

I am going to die. He had gotten himself killed, and now the others were stuck with Arthion—who was acting more and more suspicious the deeper they got into the fortress... And all Castien had wanted to do was save Elric. *How could I have been so foolish?*

Yet this only offered further proof that he needed the Cloudwalker. Castien needed guidance; he needed someone to show him how to survive in this life. Yet he had acted on an impulse, and now he was going to suffer the consequences.

He awaited the killing blow, but only felt calm as a wave of exhaustion came over him.

The world faded away nonetheless. Castien felt himself falling, the hypnotic power of the Blood Sorcerers taking complete control of his body.

He was unconscious before he hit the ground.

CHAPTER FORTY

DESPERATE TIMES

Faelyn Titansworn sat at the table of Arvendon's Council. General Elias Surge stood beside General Falx, looking over a map of the city.

He watched quietly for the most part as the Generals went over their plans. Estmar stood at the table as well, along with the Scorcher division leader, Ayre, and the city's leading Cloudwalker, Wardell.

Eithor had not been invited to the meeting, despite Faelyn's protests. Surge claimed that given all that had happened as a result of Eithor's advice, the Illusomancer's input would not be valuable to them.

"With both the Cyfali and the Sucharans on their way here as we speak, we don't have much time," Surge said. "I suspect that the Cyfali will wait for the Sucharans to arrive, which will give us a few days at most. We need to start reinforcing the city as soon as possible."

"The simplest place to start would be the walls, right? Especially the main gate," Wardell said. The older man was experienced, but far past his prime. He could still fight, but someone a bit younger would be more effective. *Someone like Elric*, Faelyn thought.

"Not the main gate," Surge said. "The rest of the walls will be fortified, but we leave the main gate as it stands," Surge said firmly.

Wardell opened his mouth to protest.

"If we make the main gate significantly weaker than the rest of the wall, then our invaders will be more inclined to enter through it," Falx said.

"Which, in turn, allows us to funnel them through our streets however we choose to," Surge finished.

"So, we're letting them into the city?" Ayre asked. She was powerful—not nearly as strong as Faelyn, but powerful nonetheless. She had accompanied him to Cyfalion, and she had made it out alive; that alone was proof enough of her fortitude.

"With two invading armies and so little time to prepare, they will get into the city inevitably. At least this way they're coming in on our terms," Surge said. He pointed to the map. "We'll still line the gate with archers and siege weapons, but once it is breached, we will force their armies east—deeper into the city." He dragged his finger further along. "Once we get them to the main plaza, past the market district, we turn them to the south."

"Toward the residential district?" Falx asked, pointing to the area between the current street in question and the sea district.

"We keep their forces focused to the south, hopefully diverting them from the homes—though that area will be evacuated as a precaution," Surge said. His voice was firm, *hard*. It commanded a certain sense of conviction that made one listen to him; it was exactly why Surge was now technically King.

Faelyn was still yet to process that. He had given up the crown. A part of him wanted to protest, but another part was thankful. It was... confusing, to say the least, but he was still alive—and that was what mattered.

"We keep pushing them further south and force them into the second plaza," Surge continued. "By then, they'll be in the old warehouse district." Surge pointed on the map to the area by the shore at the southern end of the city.

The old warehouse district was south of the current sea district and was mostly made up of empty, rotting warehouses that had been converted into shelters for the poor. It was also where Eithor had taken Faelyn after kidnapping him the second time they had met. The fact that Eithor had been able to use one of the warehouses for himself and go unnoticed was a testament to just how abandoned that area was.

"From there, we push them even further toward the shore, and shove them up against the southern walls," Surge said. "We will place reinforcements here." He pointed at a cluster of unused warehouses. "And here." Surge pointed at another cluster. "We'll load the buildings and the insides of the southern walls with Incendiary Cannons and Firesnuffers. And we'll fill the fountain in the plaza with Incendiary as well—to be set off if we start to get overrun."

"And from there?" Wardell asked, his bushy white eyebrows knitting together.

"That's where the fight ends," Surge said. "We send the last of our forces through the residential district and have them serve as a barrier. We separate the invaders who have gone to the old warehouse district from those who are still flooding in by the plaza. We trap and eliminate those at the old warehouse district, and then cut off the grand plaza invaders from their reinforcements."

"How?" Ayre asked.

"Sparkcoils," Surge said, his face grim.

"Sparkcoils?" Faelyn asked, leaning forward in his chair, bringing himself back into the conversation.

"A series of thick metal wires that can be quickly installed and removed," Falx said, looking at Faelyn. "One touch from a Voltarian will electrify the whole wire." Falx turned to Surge. "Are you sure you want to use those? The Sucharans have Voltarians too. They could easily turn the Sparkcoils against us."

"Which is why we'll keep our own soldiers away from the wires,"

Surge said. "We use them to line the blockade that will force the invaders to the south, and we have a small strike force install the Sparkcoils across the main gate once the battle is far enough along. Using those, we can block the next wave out of the city temporarily, allowing us to eliminate anyone inside of our walls and reload our siege weapons."

"And once they inevitably breach the wall again, we push them along the same path... Cutting them off and eliminating them a few hundred soldiers at a time," Falx finished for him. "So we keep them on the streets and away from the sea district and most of the homes, and force them into a loop of getting cut off and slaughtered."

"Most importantly, we keep them away from the Palace," Surge said. "We'll line the hillside with Cloudcatchers and Incendiary Cannons to keep Cloudwalkers and any mobile assassins away from us. Lightning rods and Firesnuffers will also be put in place to ensure that no long-range attacks end up reaching Summerglass."

"But how are we sure that we can win once we trap each force inside the city?" Ayre asked, running a hand through her blonde hair as she leaned forward.

"The streets will be lined with Incendiary Cannons, Firesnuffers, and Sparkcoils," Surge answered. "Those should be enough to give us the upper hand on our attackers."

"And do we have enough of those weapons to keep up with the fight?" Wardell asked.

"Not even close," Falx said. "But I already have nearly every soldier in the army as well as every available carpenter we have working on constructing more."

"We are also having the barricades constructed," Surge added. "They will be made primarily of stone, with Incendiary-filled pots on the inside. If they start to breach a wall, we ignite the Incendiary and explode anyone close enough to be a threat."

"Wouldn't that destroy the barricade though?" Faelyn asked.

"Yes," Surge said. "But the second a barricade is destroyed, it will be replaced with a Sparkcoil, and either Falx, myself, or one of our other Voltarians will be sent to defend it."

"Archers will be positioned on top of the walls and at the top of the Palace hill," Falx continued. "We don't have as many ballistae as we would like, but we have enough to cover the main gate. We'll keep half of them hidden until we cut off their first force—allowing us to stall their next wave long enough for our troops to get the Sparkcoils in place and kill any who have already entered."

"We'll keep them away from the Palace and force them to attack in waves," Surge said. "By isolating and eliminating their forces, it should only take two or three waves, at most, to force them to surrender."

"Assuming we survive that long," Faelyn said, his voice low.

Everyone looked at him for a few seconds, then turned away.

"Cyfalion's army is made up mostly of Cloudwalkers, which we will have to stop with a combination of archers and Cloudcatchers," Surge continued, ignoring Faelyn's comment.

"Suchara's forces are made up largely of Scorchers and Voltarians," Falx added. "Firesnuffers will take care of the Scorchers, and the Voltarians won't be able to use their powers accurately around the Palace due to the lightning rods."

"And the Stormless?" Ayre asked. "What are we going to do with them?"

"We use them like we always have: as distractions," Surge said. "Our scouts tell us that nearly every Summoner and Stormless soldier in Cyfalion and Suchara are on their way here, which means that we will have to use every soldier we have. The Stormless will mostly be manning the siege weapons, but some will be used as foot soldiers as well."

"Finally, we will station our Whisperers in the Palace as a last resort," Falx said. "They will be using their lullabies if they have to, which will knock every soldier who comes near them unconscious." Falx paused. "Due to the Whisperers' lack of precision and our desire to not have our own soldiers incapacitated, they will be kept away from the fight unless they are needed."

"It will also be very taxing for us," Estmar said quietly.

Faelyn flinched, forgetting that the man was there. He hadn't said a word the whole conference. But he had been listening, it seemed.

"We cannot uphold the lullaby for long, and if we are forced to do it several times in a row, the resulting Breakdown may take more lives than the act of Whispering saves," Estmar said, his voice grim.

"Understood, thank you, sir," Falx said. His eyes were dark, and the scar on his face only made him look more menacing.

"What about the Monoliths?" Ayre asked. "We destroyed one of the Cyfali's. Who's to say that they won't destroy one of ours?"

"We can't afford to protect our Monoliths," Surge said grimly. "They're too far outside of the city walls to be easily defensible, and once they inevitably fall, the troops we've stationed there will be slaughtered."

"So we're just going to leave them open and pray for the best?" Ayre stepped forward.

"We will deal with the problem of the Monoliths if we survive the attack," Falx grunted. "Right now, the Monoliths are the least of our problems."

A heavy silence fell over the group. It was a fair point, but it was a harrowing realization nonetheless.

Surge turned to Faelyn.

"Why are you looking at me?" Faelyn asked, his voice hollow.

"Because you're the one who got us into this mess, and you're going to help us get out of it," Surge said. "We've put this plan together in less than a day... But this should be enough to give us a chance. *However*, I need your word that you will do everything in your power to help us win."

"With what body?" Faelyn asked, holding up his nubs.

"Just because you've lost a few limbs doesn't mean you've lost your Summoning," Surge said. "Besides, with your weapon conjuration, you should be able to make up for what you've lost."

"I've been working on that with Idris. We think I'll be able to do it—for a short time," Faelyn said, feeling weak.

"You'll hold it for as long as you can, understand?" Surge commanded.

Faelyn flinched. He nodded, his gaze falling to the floor.

"You're still one of our most powerful Summoners, Faelyn. I don't care how injured you are, you are going to help us even if it kills you," Surge said.

"If it weren't for our plan, he'd be doomed to die anyway," Falx grumbled. "He'd better give it his all."

"I will," Faelyn whispered. He closed his eyes, feeling the weight of the dead pushing upon him. The lights seemed to grow darker, leaving him alone with his thoughts. All that he had been through... All that he had lost. It was for this. It had all been for Arvendon, and if they lost this city...

Eithor had tried to reason that the city was doomed, and that sparing the citizens was more important than sparing Faelyn's pride. Yet Faelyn realized now that Eithor had been wrong. The fables spoke of the rise and fall of cities, yet they never once told of one letting their nation fall and going on to conclude that it was for the best.

Nothing lasts forever. All cities and empires fall eventually, but what if one didn't? What if one city survived assault after assault, and grew to become one of the greatest powers in history? What if it restored order around the world and quieted the dangerous tensions that plagued these lands? What if...

What if that city were Arvendon?

CHAPTER FORTY-ONE

THE PERFECT PITCH

His head was heavy. His limbs were numb and limp. It took several minutes for him to even become aware of the restraints placed around his wrists. It took several more minutes for him to realize that he was on his knees, with his arms raised over his head, held by iron chains.

Castien Varic looked around, trying to open his *impossibly* heavy eyelids. From the second he stirred, he got a reaction.

Someone said something, speaking in a thick and pointed tongue. *Utryan?*

Castien blinked a few times, still struggling to keep his eyes open. The world felt as if it were spinning... Twisting and turning with the sways of his head with no apparent pattern.

"Oh, for Helionn's sake," a voice said. Footsteps rushed over to him.

Castien tried to look up but found only a hazy mass standing before him. Something shook his left arm.

He flinched. His hand suddenly fell to his side. Castien felt his heartbeat, dull and quiet. His other arm came down shortly after, leaving him kneeling on the hard floor.

Am I free? Castien threaded the thoughts through his sedated mind, piecing together what had happened to him. He lifted one arm, and then lifted the other. Whoever had approached had undone his restraints.

"You finally find Serissa's son and this is what you do?" the voice said, sounding angry.

Castien flinched. He blinked a few times, his eyes still heavy. *What?* That name... He knew that name... *How do they know my mother's name?*

Castien lifted his head, feeling heavy. *Serissa... Serissa.*

"He shot one of us," another voice said, sounding distant.

"And we will be alright," the first voice responded. "Visit whoever he shot and do what you can to accelerate their healing," the voice said.

His memories started trickling in, and he slowly remembered where he was.

The first thing he noticed was that he wasn't dead. That in itself was surprising enough. But as he connected his mother's name to the Blood Sorcerers, and then remembered his reckless impulse to try and save Elric... Nothing seemed to make sense.

He opened his hazy eyes, taking in the iridescent glow of the blood-red Crystals around him.

"He's waking up," the voice said. It was female.

Castien's eyes focused, and the world became clear.

A woman sat before him, leaning forward on a wooden stool. Her long black hair cascaded down her shoulders, running over the slim, dark red robes that she wore. Yet the most intoxicating thing about this woman's appearance was her garnet-colored eyes.

"Are you able to speak yet?" she asked.

"I..." Castien murmured. "I think—I think... so."

"Good," the woman said, leaning back. Her face was cast in a combination of the red Crystal light and the ordinary torchlight.

Castien stared at her, his eyesight still slightly hazy.

"It at least seems like you can understand me—that should be enough for now," she said.

Castien watched as she rose from her seat, standing up and pacing. He noticed the room for the first time, finding it to be a small circular chamber with two exits that led into jagged hallways on both his left and right sides. This room was fairly imperfect, and though it was lined with torches on either side of him, the red Crystals hanging on the wall drew his eyes.

His crossbow was hanging on the wall a few feet away, his quiver of bolts next to it.

"I've been waiting to meet you for a long time, Castien," the woman said. She spoke with a powerful tone, conveying a sense of confidence and conviction. She motioned to the guards and waved them off.

Castien was now alone with the woman. He looked down, noticing the stone floor that he was kneeling on.

"I'm sure you've been waiting to meet me as well," the woman said. Her deep red eyes glittered in the torchlight, practically glowing with intrigue.

"Who..." Castien muttered. "Who are you?"

"My name is Tsarra Selic," the woman said, twisting into a low bow. "But you may know me as the Blood Empress." She continued pacing. "I'm sure that you have many questions—and I would too if I were in your position—but I am afraid that we don't have much time."

"Wha..." Castien breathed. "What?"

"Your friends escaped, and we aren't entirely sure how they got in here in the first place," the woman—Tsarra—said. "They are likely planning a counterattack and a rescue mission, so I fear that our conversation will be cut short."

"How long was I out?" Castien asked, his words stringing together now.

"Several hours, though from what I can tell that is more than enough time for your friends to regroup and re-infiltrate," Tsarra said. "I can hardly blame them. You are quite a valuable asset."

"Is that why you haven't killed me? Because I'm an asset to you?"

"I haven't killed you because I have no intention of doing so," Tsarra said, continuing to pace. Her slim robes trailed her a bit. "My goal is to help you reach your full potential—just as your mother would've wanted you to."

"How do you know my mother?" Castien narrowed his eyes.

"Serissa? Well... I don't know her—but Velarus does," Tsarra said.

"Don't say her name," Castien growled.

Tsarra stared at him.

Castien held her gaze, his anger rising.

"Interesting," Tsarra mused. She continued pacing. "I wish Velarus was here to see Serissa's son in all his glory, but... I'm afraid that he left some time ago."

"Left?" Castien frowned.

"He..." Tsarra paused. She carefully considered her words. "He took a collection of our Blood Sorcerers—almost thirty—to make good on a promise." Tsarra paused, turning to Castien. "I would tell you more, but I'm afraid I don't quite know if I can trust you yet."

"You don't know if *you* can trust *me*?" Castien seethed. "How can I trust you? Your guards knocked me out and tied me up!"

"And I freed you the second you were awake," Tsarra said calmly. "I don't expect you to trust me, Castien, but I do expect you to listen." Tsarra leaned forward, her garnet eyes burning.

Castien blinked a few times, leaning back. "Okay," he said quietly.

"I need to explain something to you—something that I don't think you and your friends understand despite Velarus's conversation with your Cryostalker," Tsarra said, resuming her pacing. "I suspect that one of the others in your group was pushing for an attack, either that or you and your friends are simply ignorant."

"We wouldn't have attacked if you hadn't imprisoned one of our own," Castien snapped.

Tsarra paused, watching him with curious eyes.

Castien recoiled, suddenly feeling even more uncomfortable than before. *That stare... Zephyr's Watch.*

"You weren't in our custody until this evening," Tsarra said, stepping forward. "We have not taken any other captives."

"Then what do you suppose happened to Elric?" Castien tilted his head. "You expect me to believe that one of the most powerful Cloudwalkers on Auris simply disappeared?"

"I expect you to believe me when I say that he is not in this hideout," Tsarra said. Her voice was harsh.

Castien shuddered beneath it, struggling to find the strength to keep up his defenses while this woman talked. "But—" he started.

"We don't have time for this," Tsarra snapped. "Some of our Blood Sorcerers went missing yesterday... We were preparing a search party when *you* interrupted us. Whoever took our Blood Sorcerers likely took your friend as well. Either way, I can promise your friend's disappearance had nothing to do with us."

"I—"

"You need to listen to me, *right now*," Tsarra growled. "If I had time to talk about this with you, I would. But your friends could attack at any moment, and I will be needed when that happens." Tsarra looked away, staring down one of the hallways. Castien followed her gaze from his spot on the floor, seeing nothing but a stone passage.

"Here's the situation," Tsarra started, speaking quickly. "There is no such thing as a Stormless. There never was. Every Stormless is just a Summoner who had their Crystals—and their Tempest— taken away from them."

"I—" Castien started, feeling a pooling sense of dread in his stomach. "I know, your agents in Celes told us."

"What I don't think they told you was this: The Vanishing wasn't the destruction of the other Sects," Tsarra said. "It was the action of pulling the Tempests from the sky and displacing the energy elsewhere. You understand the nature of energy accumulation to form

Crystals? Well, the Vanishing took place in The Highlands, and the lost energies were displaced to various mountains throughout the region…" Tsarra trailed off. "That's where we are now. We are inside the mountain where the Blood Sorcerers' energy was displaced."

They did tell us that… Some of it, at least. But what was that about pulling the Tempests from the skies? "How did—" Castien started.

"Almost a year ago, a group of Shadow-Swifts started the Resurgence," Tsarra continued. "I was with them, though I had no powers myself. I was a scholar. A few months prior, they uncovered the secrets of how the Vanishing was accomplished, and they wanted to replicate it for every Sect but their own. Instead, they ended up accidentally weakening the bonds that kept the Vanished energies trapped within their mountains. The result?" Tsarra paused. "I felt a *pull* to this mountain. It didn't take me long to find it, and every Blood Sorcerer I've recruited has felt the same thing.

"The Shadow-Swifts have since resumed their operations," Tsarra continued. "Meanwhile, I have spent the last several months gathering my allies and tracking down the other members of Velarus's organization: the Sons of the Storm." Tsarra turned to Castien. "That was how Velarus knew your mother. She was part of the group as well."

"What?" Castien breathed.

"Your mother was part of a secretive group that tracked the lineages of the lost Sects, doing what they could to keep their bloodlines pure as the generations passed in preparation for the Resurgence," Tsarra said. "Don't you wonder why we are so interested in you? It's because you're a Starburner… Not just any Starburner, but you're the closest living thing to a pure-blooded Starburner. And now that your powers are unlocked, you could be the key to stopping the Shadow-Swifts."

"And why are we stopping them?" Castien asked, trying to be forceful. "What are they doing?"

"I don't know," Tsarra admitted. "From what we have gathered, they are trying to replace the Tempests with one single storm: the

Silver Sun—Dyvnire, as they call it." Tsarra paused. "But something has changed. Their leader is currently... inactive. And the man who has taken his place, well, he is far more dangerous, to say the least." Tsarra turned to Castien. "I had two other scholars with me in that group—Eithor and Soran. Similar to myself, their Summoning powers were brought to life. But *unlike* me, both have since become so drunk on their power that they've turned themselves into terrible monsters of murder and deceit." Tsarra turned away.

Castien looked down, slowly regaining some strength in his legs. *My mother... A secret organization of Stormless?*

"How large was my mother's group?" Castien asked.

"It includes several hundred members," Tsarra said. "They are stretched all across Auris, and they are searching every corner of the world for more pure-blooded Stormless."

"Just Starburners?"

"Blood Sorcerers, Stonemasters, Skin-Shapers... and every other Sect as well," Tsarra said. "Velarus is my cousin, and after freeing him from imprisonment, he only told me so much..." Tsarra trailed off once again. "He had been acting unusually aggressive and far more inquisitive than normal for several years, yet all it took was a few red Crystals and he was back to his normal self once again.

"He told me where to find the other Sons of the Storm—at least the others who would be Blood Sorcerers," Tsarra continued. "Yet, when he found you that day in The Highlands so many weeks ago, he knew who you were. He was very close with Serissa, and he knew someone of your power could only have come from her bloodline."

Castien sat, his jaw set. *All this time...* And his mother had never even so much as hinted that she was part of this group. *Did Father even know?*

A letter flashed into his mind, memories of muffled shouting flooding his thoughts. He pushed them away. *He didn't know... Not at first, anyway,* Castien realized.

"Where did Velarus go?" Castien asked, raising his eyes.

"He—" Tsarra paused. "You may recall hearing of the recent movements of Freyfall's army, as well as—"

Footsteps cut her off. Tsarra turned, facing the hallway to the left. A Blood Sorcerer came dashing in, clad in dark red robes. He was out of breath. There was shouting coming from somewhere distant.

"Empress," the Blood Sorcerer panted. His puffy Utryan face twisted into a panicked frown. "They're back. They've entered through the back passage."

Tsarra stepped forward. "Direct the active guards toward them. Send everyone else to the main cavern."

"But, ma'am—"

"Now!" Tsarra commanded. "We don't know what their plan is, but if we can get them out into the open, it would give us the advantage." Tsarra reached out along the wall, taking the fragile red Crystals in her hands and shoving them into her slim robes.

The messenger turned away, running back down the hallway where he had come from.

Tsarra made to follow him.

"Wait!" Castien cried out. His muscles felt less heavy, but he could still hardly stand, let alone run.

She stopped, turning back. Sighing, she approached Castien. "Listen," she started. "I know that you want to help your friends, and I know that you want to do what's right. Unfortunately, you can't do both right now."

Castien felt his heart drop, the dread rising. She was right.

There would be no swaying Arthion. Even if Castien somehow escaped and explained what was going on, the Whisperer wouldn't listen. Luka maybe, but not Arthion. Castien closed his eyes, looking away.

"We'll try not to kill them, I promise," Tsarra said, rising to her feet. "But you and I both know that if you truly want to do what's best, you'll obey my orders," Tsarra said, turning back slightly.

Castien met her eyes.

"Please, stay here. I know you could escape if you wanted. I know you could fight if you wanted to... But please, stay here—it's the only place you'll be safe." Tsarra took off running without another word, leaving Castien sitting alone in the small circular chamber.

He wanted to get up. He wanted to run; he wanted to fight. But who was he going to fight for? *Whose side am I on?*

Maybe he should get up, but... Tsarra had told him not to. Every single time he tried to think for himself and act on his own decisions, he made things worse. His anxiety rose like a sun at dawn, blinding him, paralyzing him.

His pulse quickened, his chest tightening. *No, not here.* Castien took a deep breath, but his breathing became shallow. It was too late. He was not safe. At any moment, any one of the Blood Sorcerers —or even his friends—could come through that door and kill him.

It became hard to breathe. His mind quickened, his palms becoming sweaty. His head grew heavy once again, and everything suddenly felt too loud. The silence was deafening, and the battle between his rapid pulse and panicked breathing threatened to drive him mad.

Nothing was right. Everything was wrong. Elric was missing. His mother had been part of a secret organization that had tracked the lineages of Lost Sects. *Nothing makes sense.*

And he was apparently supposed to be one of the strongest Star-burners alive.

But he couldn't fight. He couldn't do *anything*. Anytime things got *real*, he simply shut down. His friends were fighting and dying on the other side of these walls, and he was doing nothing.

He should've gotten up, grabbed the crossbow that was hanging on the wall next to him, and saved his friends.... saved Ilyana. He should've done it, but he did not. The moment he began to move, his burned arm flared once again.

It reminded him of something... something that he had tried to forget: The last time he had trusted his friends—trusted Ilyana—it had nearly gotten him killed. He had been tricked into betraying his country in the worst way possible.

And finally, what had been weighing on him for weeks finally came crashing in. He had no home. He had no true friends. He had no real allies... Only the word of a stranger and the false trust of people whom he thought he could rely on.

He had been an accessory to the assassination of his own King. Perhaps he deserved this fate. Perhaps he deserved to be paralyzed by fear like this. *You couldn't even save your own family.* Castien's eyes snapped shut. *You blame yourself for the King's death, only to distract yourself from your true failures.*

His thoughts only grew louder, shouting the horrors of his past into his mind—the things that he refused to face. He could not do this. He could not be here right now.

Castien started rising to his feet, his mind racing, his heart thundering. His limbs shook as he tried to move. Adrenaline was flooding his veins, but it did nothing other than unsteady his motions. He had been captured due to his own stupidity. His friends were probably dead already, and the Blood Sorcerers had likely already decided that he wasn't worth protecting. They had probably—

"Castien?" a familiar voice called. Footsteps followed, a shadow appearing in the hallway to the left.

Castien turned, cowering away from the figure. He flinched, stumbling to the floor, staggering toward his crossbow. It took him all of a second to recognize the blue-gray cloak.

"Castien!" Ilyana gasped. She sprinted to him, and he rose to meet her.

In that instant, everything felt calm.

He wasn't sure what it was, or what he was feeling. But seeing those curved Elosian features and those beautiful gray eyes... He couldn't explain it—he wasn't even sure why—but those eyes felt like *home*.

Ilyana had been the only constant over the last few weeks. Ever since that moment on the expedition, she had been there. True, at times he had hated her, but she had stayed by his side. Even after betraying him, she had risked her own life to ensure that he found safety. Somehow, despite everything that happened, she was still here... still fighting to protect him.

Memories flashed through his mind. Waking up on that beach... talking at Fairfrost... laughing in the Celesian library together... All of his best memories from the last few weeks—the bright spots in the sea of darkness that had become his life—those memories were with *her*.

And there, standing in that small room, Castien realized something: She *was* his home. He wasn't sure why, or how, but just *thinking it* felt right. It was impossible to explain. The trauma of the last few weeks had nearly destroyed him, and Ilyana was the only reason he had made it out alive. He had been moving from place to place for so long, and he had finally found somewhere he belonged... He belonged with *her*.

She stared at him, tears in her eyes. She wrapped him in an embrace.

Castien melted into Ilyana's touch, collapsing in her arms, tears running down his face.

"I thought you were dead," Ilyana breathed, pulling him into her body.

Everything was too much. The world... The Summoners... *Everything*. Yet here, wrapped in Ilyana's arms, he felt safe. His tears ran freely, and he let them. He knew that he couldn't hold it in any longer, and he knew that there was a good chance he would've stayed here paralyzed if she hadn't found him.

But she was here.

He buried his face in her collarbone, her warm Celesian cloak wrapping around his very soul.

This woman knew him better than anyone. She knew—within seconds—what was going through his mind. She knew what he was thinking. She knew that his mind had run off to a faraway fantasy of nightmares... And she was the only one who knew how to bring him back.

"I'm..." Castien stuttered. "I'm sorry. I—"

"Shh." Ilyana stroked his hair, holding him against her chest. "It's okay." She took a long, shaky breath. "It's okay," she repeated. "You're *okay*." She pulled back, locking eyes with him.

Castien breathed, slowly and shakily. He hardly got the breath in without collapsing back into her touch.

"I thought I had lost you," she whispered, squeezing him.

He squeezed back. Though after a moment Castien pulled back, a sudden lucidity coming over him. The turmoil in his mind had receded, leaving only clarity. He knew what he had to do. There was only one way that they were going to get out of this alive—and it was together.

"We have to go," Castien said.

Shouts sounded in the distance, followed by the *swish* of blood energy.

Ilyana's eyes steeled as she nodded. "Come on." She turned away.

"Wait," Castien said. "I—" The words slid to a stop on his tongue. He froze, the feeling lost within his mind. "Arthion's been lying," Castien blurted, changing his course of words.

Ilyana opened her mouth, her eyes falling slightly. "What do you mean?"

"Elric wasn't captured by the Blood Sorcerers, and Arthion is the only one who claims to know what happened to him," Castien said quickly. "And if Elric is missing..."

"Then Arthion must be responsible," Ilyana whispered. Her eyes grew distant. She reached onto her back, unsheathing her butterfly-blades. "He and Luka are nearly to the grand chamber by now," Ilyana said, picking up into a run. "If Arthion was lying about Elric, then he must be lying about the Blood Sorcerers too."

"Which means that—"

"We've been fighting for the wrong side all along," Ilyana finished. "Come on!" She sprinted down the hallway, nearly scraping the jagged walls of the passage with her blades.

Castien grabbed the crossbow and his quiver of bolts. Without a second thought, he took off running after her. He instantly fell behind.

A dark blue essence echoed Ilyana's figure—she was using her Dexteris Crystals.

Castien grunted, picking up his pace. His sore muscles ached, burning with each step, but he continued.

Ilyana whipped around a turn, going to the left.

Castien followed, trying to keep up with her.

She spun again, turning down another hallway.

Torches zipped past Castien, dancing and flashing in the phantom winds at their passing. Castien pushed on.

The shouting was growing closer, the sounds of battle echoing through the chamber walls.

Seconds later, Ilyana made one final turn and screeched to a halt.

Castien's lungs burned, and his muscles were still unsteady enough that he nearly fell when he reached Ilyana's side.

Awe struck him once again.

The grand chamber was *colossal.* It was several hundred feet in width, and even greater in length. Massive blood-red Crystals hung down from the high ceiling. Hundreds of red Crystal chunks grew from the jagged floors and walls of the chamber.

To the right was another turn, accompanied by a cold breeze. And to the left, several hundred feet away, the battle was raging.

Luka's ice shards sprayed out in every direction, knocking Blood Sorcerers across the huge atrium.

Ilyana sprinted toward the fight, crossing several dozen feet in the blink of an eye.

Castien bolted into a sprint, the distant flashes of red growing closer and brighter as he neared. He weaved between the massive boulders that rose throughout the chamber, making his way to the distant battle.

His muscles were weak, and his head heavy, but he had no choice. He needed to save the others.

Castien zipped around another boulder, laying eyes on the center of the fight.

Luka was sliding across the clearing, shooting ice in every direction—keeping the Blood Sorcerers at bay.

Beams of red energy shot through the air, narrowly avoiding Luka's elusive figure. Yet Arthion was nowhere to be seen.

Ilyana was a few feet in front of him, standing atop a small boulder. She extended her blades and opened her mouth. "*Stop!*" she roared.

No one listened.

Castien sprinted behind her, his arms and legs aching in protest. "Ilyana!" Castien shouted over the clash of ice and the swish of energy. "We have to stop them before—"

A deafening crack sounded through the chamber.

Castien and Ilyana spun, searching for the source.

On the opposite side of the fight, on a slightly raised platform, a figure moved. Hallways were attached to the raised portion of stone, though they lay empty. Castien didn't have to look twice to know who was standing atop the landing.

Arthion's shape changed, twisting and cracking with wicked bones that were not his. It clicked into place. Arthion never using his Whispering... Always wearing gloves to hide his hands... His strange behavior... His disappearance the moment they found the cave... Arthion wasn't a Whisperer at all—he was a *Skin-Shaper* all along.

Two corpses lay at Arthion's sides—Blood Sorcerers. Their flesh pulled away from their bones, sliding along their figures and into Arthion's form. Castien realized what Arthion had needed the bodies for: He needed extra flesh and bone to grow his body.

Castien watched in horror, the cracking sounding once again as Arthion grew to twice his height, and then *beyond*. His arms extended, claws growing from protruding bones. His sternum expanded, lengthening and widening.

Someone shouted below—Tsarra.

Castien looked at Ilyana, hoping for guidance, a sign, anything.

But she was as entranced as him. Castien turned back, watching as the creature that was Arthion—now standing at over fourteen feet tall, with razor-sharp elongated limbs, wicked claws, and dark, almost plated flesh—rose to its full glory.

It paused, recoiling... and then, it screamed.

Castien fell to the ground, the sound practically knocking him from his feet. He threw his hands over his ears, his eyes slamming shut.

The sound grew louder. It stabbed through his ears, stunning his soul, piercing his mind, scarring his body with its horrific noise.

Castien screamed as well, his body shaking beneath the force of the awful sound.

And then, the shattering began.

Castien's eyes snapped open just in time to see a massive chunk of an overhanging Crystal fall from the ceiling. Castien dove out of the way, his crossbow clanking on his back.

The Crystal crashed to the ground, shattering in a blast of red, almost liquid energy.

Castien spun, the shrieking growing even louder. Crystals fell all over the cave, breaking in massive explosions of red, blood-like energy. Castien searched for Ilyana and saw the horror on her face as the Dexteris Crystals at her waist shattered into thousands of pieces.

He dove out of the way of another falling Crystal.

The Blood Sorcerers started to run. The massive Crystals above fell and shattered, crushing those unfortunate enough to be caught beneath them.

Finally, the screaming stopped.

Castien whirled, finding Arthion's inhuman figure standing above the rivers of blood-red energy flowing among the rubble of the cave. Dozens of Blood Sorcerers still stood around him—their Crystals shattered. They were powerless now... Everyone was.

It was then that Castien realized what Arthion's plan was.

This was not going to be a fight. This was going to be a *massacre*.

Arthion lunged, diving at his first victim. He opened his gaping jaws, letting out a vile roar and exposing rows of razor-sharp teeth. Arthion tore through the first Blood Sorcerer with a terrible bite, then turned to the next. He slashed through the man, cutting him in half with his wicked claws.

Castien screamed, watching as the Skin-Shaper tore apart the powerless Blood Sorcerers.

Arthion didn't so much as flinch as arrows and swords flew into his seemingly impenetrable armor-like flesh. Some of the Blood Sorcerers had regrouped and grabbed weapons while others fled, but it was too late.

Ilyana charged, her blades extended. She reached Arthion in seconds and was tossed to the ground with a single blow from the backside of one of his wicked claws.

Castien cried out, drawing his crossbow. He fumbled around with it, reaching for a bolt. His fingers closed around one, which he hastily pulled from the quiver.

Panicked, he tried to load the crossbow as he had done so many times. His fingers shook, struggling to slide the bolt into place. *No. No. NO! Not again!*

A female voice screamed.

Castien turned, finding Tsarra wailing in anguish and rage as her Sect was destroyed. She carried a small dagger in her hands and sprinted atop the landing. Without her Crystals, she was powerless... The dagger was all she had left.

Arthion wreaked havoc below, ripping apart the surviving Blood Sorcerers one by one. Tsarra cried out, leaping from the raised landing with her dagger raised.

Arthion turned as she fell, raising a sinewy arm to block her attack.

Tsarra's cloak fluttered as she flew, and her dagger met its mark.

The creature screeched, throwing its head back as Tsarra's dagger dug into one of its massive eyes.

Castien stopped, dumbfounded as the Skin-Shaper clawed at its own face, trying to tear the knife from his body.

Tsarra had done it. But with a sinking feeling, Castien realized that it was not enough.

Arthion recovered, whirling around and knocking Tsarra away with one of his limbs.

The Blood Empress crashed into the stone wall, unconscious.

Castien's eyes shot to the left, his fingers slowing as he locked the bolt in place.

Luka was stuck under a fallen chunk of the ceiling a few dozen feet away, trying to free himself.

Arthion cut through another Blood Sorcerer.

Castien knew what he needed to do. *You've spent your whole life running*, Castien thought to himself. His parents, the army, the assassination... And now his destiny. *Not anymore.*

He stepped forward, the world seeming to slow as Arthion's wicked mouth opened to tear apart another Blood Sorcerer. Castien jumped, landing atop a large section of fallen rock. He advanced with ease, his hands steadying as he pulled the latch back. It was time— time for him to show the world what he was capable of.

Castien reached the top of the boulder, dropping into a kneel.

Arthion ripped apart another Blood Sorcerer. He turned, as if sensing Castien. The beast turned across the small clearing, facing him.

Raising the crossbow, Castien felt calm. He would only have time to fire one shot. This was his only chance.

Tsarra was knocked out, but her attack had shown Castien *exactly* where to hit the Skin-Shaper.

Arthion charged, letting out a guttural roar.

Castien closed one eye, aligning the other with the sight of the crossbow.

For my mother... Castien hesitated. *For Elric.*

The beast drew closer, leaping into the air and raising his massive claw-like hands for a single deadly slash.

No...

For ME!

Castien pulled the trigger.

The launcher snapped forward. The bolt flew through the air with blinding speed. It slid into the creature's eye socket, cutting directly into the cursed monster's brain.

The Skin-Shaper froze in midair, suddenly going limp. It tilted downward, then fell, crashing into the base of the boulder on which Castien knelt. It did not move.

A loud thump sounded as Luka freed himself from the debris.

Ilyana rose to her feet slowly, rubbing her side as she surveyed her surroundings.

Castien's breathing was heavy, but his mind was light. He looked down, staring at the dead monster that had once been Arthion.

It was over.

CHAPTER FORTY-TWO
DESPERATE MEASURES

Faelyn was wheeled down the white hallway for the second time in as many days. He waited patiently as he was turned to the left, and then back to the right as they reached another hall. A slow smile crept across his face as he reached the white door a few moments later.

The guards stationed at the door nodded to him, still holding their positions even after Surge's takeover.

"Knock, please," Faelyn instructed.

One of the guards nodded and dutifully rapped on the door.

"Come in," Reluraun said after a few seconds.

Faelyn's servant opened the door and started pushing him inside. He positioned Faelyn in the center of the carpeted rooms, promptly leaving to give Faelyn some privacy.

Reluraun was sitting in a chair beside his table. He set his book down, surveying Faelyn. "You seem to have taken Surge's return in stride."

"You haven't yet requested to be freed," Faelyn said softly. "Does the General even know I've been keeping you here?"

"I doubt it," Reluraun said.

"Why have you not sent for him?" Faelyn asked, tilting his head.

"You ordered me *not* to prepare our defenses; I am simply obeying you," Reluraun said, waving his hand.

Faelyn leaned forward. "You've still got your honor, Rel. I'll admit that much."

Reluraun nodded, his face firm.

"For what it's worth, I'm sorry," Faelyn said, steeling himself. "I know that I hurt you, and I know that what I did was wrong. If you do not wish to forgive me, I will respect that—just as you have respected me."

Reluraun stared at him, his piercing emerald gaze burning into Faelyn's mind. He stood up, pacing over to Faelyn with an air of confidence. Awkwardly, Reluraun leaned down and wrapped Faelyn in an embrace.

Faelyn found himself shocked. *This is unexpected.* Faelyn hesitantly put his too-short arms around Reluraun's back, doing his best to return the embrace.

"I know these last few weeks have been hard on you," Reluraun said, pulling back. "I can't blame you for what you've done, even if you did take things a little too far."

Feeling a warmth in his eyes that had become all too familiar these past few weeks, Faelyn nodded. "I'm sorry."

"I know you are," Reluraun said, forming a slight smile.

"We have a plan," Faelyn said. "And I think it's a good one. But I want you to help."

"You know I will," Reluraun said. He stepped back, running a hand through his messy auburn hair.

"We will need Cloudwalkers to defend the Palace," Faelyn said. "Hopefully, we will be able to keep most of the invading troops away from Summerglass, but some will undoubtedly get through."

"Mostly Summoners, I presume?"

Faelyn nodded. "We will need powerful Summoners of our own to keep them at bay."

"I can help you there," Reluraun said. "I may not be as strong as my father, but I'll do what I can."

"Thank you," Faelyn said, closing his eyes. "To be honest, I wasn't sure if you'd even forgive me."

"Eh." Reluraun shrugged. "It's for Arvendon, right? Besides, I've known you since we were toddlers—it takes a little more than a few guards stationed outside my rooms to turn me against you." Reluraun laughed a little.

Faelyn opened his eyes, wanting to laugh as well. "I'm glad this went the way it did, Rel," Faelyn said. "This conversation, I mean... Everything before this—"

"You don't have to say it, Faelyn," Reluraun said, cutting him off. "I know."

Faelyn met his eyes once again. "Thank you."

"Of course."

"I need to go, I'm afraid. I'm sorry this was so brief," Faelyn said. "But we have many more preparations to make. I suggest you find Surge and Falx and see where around the Palace you can best be stationed."

"Right." Reluraun nodded. "I'll see you out there."

Faelyn called for his attendant, who came in to wheel him away a few seconds later. As Faelyn was pushed down the marble hallway, away from Reluraun's rooms, he found himself smiling. Reluraun was a good friend—a better one than Faelyn deserved. It felt good to have him back.

The Blazeday shined brightly despite the darkness on the horizon. Cyfalion's troops were visible now. Soldiers wearing dark, forest-green armor filled the western lands now—marking their slow approach. If Faelyn squinted, he could almost see the gold and black armor of Suchara's forces behind them. The sun was blinding, but it felt good on Faelyn's ghostly pale skin. He had hardly been outside over the last few days, and this was a welcome return to the world beyond the walls of that damned palace.

His smile dropped, his mind flashing to his father. Faelyn forced the thoughts out of his head the second that they appeared; he couldn't think about that anymore.

The Cloudcatchers were being constructed and locked into place. The massive ballistae looked like a cross between a crossbow and a catapult. Their large wooden arms were being drawn back, tightening the thick ropes that connected them to their central apparatus. There was a large gap in the center of the four-armed ballista, which was where the majority of the net was placed for launch.

Cloudcatchers fired a large net with four weights—one on each corner—and were meant to bring down any approaching Cloudwalkers. The weights were heavy, meaning that one could not shoot the Cloudcatcher until the attacker was very close. However, the added weight was necessary so that the nets could effectively bring down the Cloudwalkers. It wasn't a perfect device—hell, it didn't even work half of the time—but it was all that they had.

"I take it you're satisfied with the battlements?" Surge asked, approaching from behind. He nodded a greeting to Faelyn's servant, who stood ready to push Faelyn to wherever he requested to go.

Faelyn tilted his head slightly, watching him out of the corner of his eye. "Everything is coming together nicely," Faelyn said.

"Your advisor—Eithor—has been put in charge of filling the fountain in the old warehouse district with Incendiary," Surge said. "He insisted on helping, though I still don't entirely trust him."

"He has guided me through these difficult times," Faelyn said. "I trust him with my life."

Surge grunted. He watched as another Cloudcatcher was locked into place. "Are you confident in our plan?"

"It's a long shot," Faelyn said, his voice low. He looked down, staring at his ankles. He took a deep breath in, the ashen tickle of his lungs shooting through his body. Faelyn winced. The Ashwither didn't affect his breathing often, but when it did... The sensation was unnerving, to say the least.

"If everything goes as we hope, we will hold them off long enough to force them to surrender," Surge said, folding his arms and stepping up beside Faelyn. The General wore a bright red vest, looking menacing and commanding as always.

Faelyn made a point of sticking to the white and gold, despite Surge's disapproval. "How are we organizing the troops?" Faelyn asked.

"We have only around a dozen Cloudwalkers, and even fewer Voltarians," Surge started. "We will position the Cloudwalkers by the Firesnuffers, and station the Voltarians near the points where the Sparkcoils will be placed. We have more Scorchers than we know what to do with, so the ones who aren't busy manning an Incendiary Cannon will be on the front lines. Our Dexterises—while few in number—will make for effective reinforcements hidden within the warehouses."

"And the Whisperers stay in the Palace, I assume?" Faelyn asked.

"They will stay within Summerglass." Surge nodded. "The Stormless will be split up between the warehouses and the main streets. The Cyfali and Sucharans will most likely lead their assault with their Summoners and have another squadron of them backing up the rear—placing most of their Stormless in the center of their forces."

"And if we time things right, we'll catch their Stormless with our Summoners," Faelyn said.

"No, if we time things right, our Stormless will be fighting theirs," Surge corrected. He glared at Faelyn. "Don't forget our ways, Faelyn. Just because this is war doesn't mean that—"

"If I have to choose between upholding the proper treatment of our inferiors or saving this city, then I will choose the latter," Faelyn said. "Is that really a decision that you would disagree with?"

Surge leveled his gaze, staring back at him. "I don't know what's been going on in that mind of yours for the past few weeks, but let me tell you something," Surge said, stepping forward. "I am in charge now, and I am the one you will take orders from. You've clearly all but gone mad since we last spoke, and as a result, I can no longer trust you to make the right decisions. So listen to me here and now, because we need to get one thing down: You are to listen to me, and only me. If your own mind tells you to do something other than what I tell you, disobey it. You cannot trust yourself in this state—prioritize my orders over your own instincts."

"So I'm just supposed to—" Faelyn started.

"I don't want to hear another word out of you on this matter," Surge growled. "Understand?"

Faelyn stared at him, blinking a few times. He took a deep breath and nodded. He turned back to the battlements, trying to ignore the sinking feeling in his stomach. It wasn't that Surge had been too harsh; it was that Surge was right.

"After finding out how you've treated Reluraun, I wanted to make a point of telling you this," Surge said.

Faelyn started. "You knew about that?"

"Yes," Surge grunted. "I only learned of his situation *after* you freed him from his rooms." He turned to Faelyn. "The fact that you released him yourself is... encouraging, I suppose."

Faelyn tried to say something, but couldn't manage to put the words together.

"What happened to Elric?" Surge asked. "I know that Luka was heading north, but if I remember correctly, Elric was supposed to return to the city."

"He was supposed to—and he did," Faelyn said quietly. "But he disappeared a few days later. We weren't worried, for he said he was simply following a lead that he had on my father's assassins."

"Then let us hope that he has been successful in tracking them down," Surge grunted.

Faelyn's eyes settled on the Firesnuffer that was being set up below the Palace hill. The contraption was smaller than a Cloud-catcher and consisted of a large metal cylinder with a set of turbines inside. All it took was a Cloudwalker manning it—pushing air through the back end—and air would come flying out the front, diverting any stray Scorcher flames and snuffing the weaker ones out.

There was an Incendiary Cannon next to it. The Cannon was fairly small as well, and was more directed toward dealing with Stormless rather than Summoners. It worked by some sort of chemical reaction that created a small explosion—which pushed a skull-sized metal ball out of the front at a blinding speed when heated. Scorchers controlled these most of the time since it took a much greater heat than any single torch could produce to light the Cannons.

The Cannons and Firesnuffers were positioned within the barricades that isolated the main street from the rest of the city. From the Palace hill, Faelyn could see the entire plan laid out before him.

The workers and soldiers had quickly constructed dozens of the stone walls that Surge had requested. They were all poorly made, of course, and the Incendiary pots inside seemed dangerously close to combusting at any given moment, but that was not something that they had time to worry about.

Faelyn turned to the wall, which would be lined with hundreds of archers in a few hours' time. The armies were still several hours away, and they would likely wait until everyone had arrived before they attacked. But Arvendon needed to be ready nonetheless.

Half of the ballistae were safely hidden behind the walls—which they had determined could not be fortified in time. Surge had instead directed the available carpenters and soldiers toward the barricades in the streets.

Faelyn could see the path now and knew that Surge was right. Thousands of soldiers and builders milled about. The funnel they would force their invaders through started at the main gate, then led straight toward the sea and into the market district. From there, they would move through the main plaza and be forced toward the old sea district to the south—where the old plaza waited in the distance.

The barricades cut off the invaders from the large number of residential areas to the east and kept them even further away from the shipping ports on the far end of the city. If Arvendon were to sustain itself after this battle, they would need to be able to ship supplies in and out.

Finally, Faelyn could barely see—if he squinted—the old plaza, where countless empty, rotting warehouses were being filled with soldiers. There was a small fountain there, which was currently being filled with Incendiary at Eithor's direction.

Faelyn looked over to the side, watching as a large metal stake was planted in the ground beside the castle. *Lightning rod.*

Falx shouted orders somewhere down below, as did Wardell and Ayre. The three of them plus Surge were the only ones who fully grasped the plan, though they had been incredibly efficient in implementing it—under Surge's leadership, of course.

"You're sure that the method you practiced with Idris will work?" Surge asked, bringing the peaceful lack of conversation to an end. "I am aware that weapon conjuration is a specialty of the Scorchers, but I've never heard of something like this."

"It will work," Faelyn said, lowering his head. He closed his eyes and took a deep breath. He suddenly found himself overcome with a desire to see his father.

His father would know what to do. He would know how to save the city. Despite all that was going on, he would be able to make him feel safe. Perhaps it was something about the way his father boomed with laughter after telling one of his silly jokes... The way that...

Faelyn blinked a few times, trying to stop the rising tears. He failed. He sniffled, bringing his arm to his face to try and wipe the tears away.

Surge grunted and turned away.

Faelyn lowered his head again, any hope of comfort fading from his mind. Surge had never been the type to give reassurance. Surge was a good leader, sure. But Surge... Surge could never compare to Faelyn's father.

The King would have done everything in his power to save this city, and his family. Faelyn's father would never have even let something like this happen. He had a certain way about him... A certain aura that somehow allowed him to talk and bargain his way out of a war. And even when it came down to it, his father found a way to minimize casualties on both sides.

He somehow maintained sight of the fact that, during war, both sides were simply trying to prove that their ideals were superior to those of their adversary. His father understood that any war could be solved with diplomacy, but sometimes the people of this world simply wouldn't listen until a little blood had been spilled.

That was where his father excelled. Where others may have instigated slaughters and massacres, he would opt for small-scale skirmishes—like those in The Highlands. After enough of these, he would use his words to convince his opponents that the fighting should stop, and he would find a way to satisfy both himself and whomever Arvendon was facing.

But Avenos was gone.

Another tear slid down Faelyn's cheek. He blinked a few times, sniffling again.

Surge had walked away now, leaving Faelyn alone in his grieving.

All these years living in that palace, and Faelyn had never thought that his father would be taken from him so soon. If he were still alive, then Cyfalion would've never been attacked. The Cyfali wouldn't be marching toward them right now, and the Sucharans wouldn't be close behind... All would be well.

Faelyn raised his eyes, blinking away the tears. His father would've given his life for this city. And if Faelyn needed to, he would do the same.

Faelyn sat on the balcony of the highest floor of Summerglass Palace. He sat alone, and that was the way he wanted it. Faelyn had sent his attendant inside to give himself some privacy a few moments before.

The lights of the Cyfali torches were all too close now in the dim evening sunset. The first lines of them were even beginning to settle a few hundred yards away from Arvendon's walls. They were outside of the wards, and staying there for long would be difficult.

The darkness of night closed in around him. Everything seemed to have gone to hell when that Blood Sorcerer showed up in his father's throne room, and now... Now all of *this* was happening. It was strange how such a small event had created such a massive, disastrous chain of events that led to this *exact* moment.

Footsteps sounded behind him. Faelyn flinched, startled by the approach of someone.

"We've just received word from the scouts," a voice said.

Faelyn didn't have to turn to know who it was.

"There's another army on the horizon," Eithor said. "We can't be certain, but we think that Freyfall's forces plan to march on the city as well."

Faelyn lowered his head, the weight of the situation pressing down upon him. The Freyfallion army had a large number of Cryostalkers and Whisperers—two things that Arvendon had not prepared for.

Night settled, the sun finally vanishing, taking the heat of the Blazeday with it. The stars began to poke through the darkening night sky, and the shadow of the Palace finally aligned with the darkness of the surrounding landscape.

Faelyn couldn't find the words to speak. Freyfall's arrival had solidified their fate. Perhaps they had stood a chance against two armies... but *three*? He could hear distant shouts as the soldiers undoubtedly tried to make last-minute preparations in light of the news.

He thought he could even hear Surge's voice among them. Faelyn shook his head. The General was good—the best there was—but even he could do nothing in the face of this threat.

Faelyn's original plan of surrendering the city now sounded almost pleasant, actually. But Surge would never do that—and Surge was the one who held the power now.

They had been doomed to fail all along, he supposed. Faelyn looked to the sky, almost praying to Niventia.

He had never put much time toward the Gods—perhaps this was his punishment for not doing so. There had never been much of a reason for him to pray. He had always been given everything he wanted, and, in his short life, he never recalled being in true danger —until the last six weeks, at least.

Faelyn felt a sudden presence of energy.

He sat up, hearing the slight clinking of the fragile Crystals that Eithor now pulled from his robes. Faelyn turned, staring at the bright orange light of the Scorcher Crystals.

"Faelyn," Eithor said, his voice low.

Faelyn met his ice-blue eyes with both hardness and defeat. He had accepted his fate, but he would not go down easily.

"We both know that it's time," Eithor said.

"I know," Faelyn said, lowering his head. "It won't be long before they advance."

"I've had a ship prepared. It leaves from the dock in under an hour," Eithor said "I know that it's dangerous, and I know that it's last minute, but if we're able to find somewhere we can—"

"Are you truly asking me to run away right now?" Faelyn asked. He kicked his legs to the side, turning the chair slightly. He grunted in pain, but did it again, now fully facing Eithor.

"Your Grace, you know that I wouldn't ask you to do this unless—"

"This is my city." Faelyn leaned forward. "I'm the one who

brought us to this point, and now you're asking me to abandon Arvendon when it needs me most?"

"Faelyn, you—" Eithor started.

"You have been a good mentor to me, but I think we both know that what you're asking me to do is wrong," Faelyn said, his voice low. "And what? You fill a fountain with Incendiary and you think your work is done? You've hardly done *anything* to help us prepare, and now you're asking me to come with you while you run away from this fight? You could help us, Eithor. You're a powerful Summoner, and I know that it's well within your abilities to at least cause a distraction or two."

"You destroyed a Monolith in a blind rage the last time you took up arms," Eithor said, his eyes stuck on Faelyn. "You truly think that entering another fight is the best decision?"

"When I did that, I was acting out of rage and fear," Faelyn said. "I face the events of tomorrow with the knowledge that death is a very likely possibility. I know that many of my people will die— maybe even all of us—but I also know that it is for good reason."

"You're dooming yourselves, Faelyn." Eithor's voice rose. "You and I both know that you need to leave... It is the only way."

"The only way to do what, Eithor?" Faelyn asked, tilting his head. He kept his voice calm, even. "The only way for me to survive? Or the only way for *you* to survive?" Faelyn leaned forward.

Eithor took a step back, lowering the Crystals. "Faelyn," he started.

"When the fight begins, help us if you want," Faelyn said, turning away. "If you choose not to, then do both of us a favor and *get out of my city*." Faelyn's eyes settled on the distant torches as they approached. "You are dismissed."

Faelyn reached down, hitting the bell with his nub of a hand. The doors opened quickly and Eithor backed away from the balcony.

As Faelyn was wheeled to his chambers, he felt no fear. Whatever happened when he awoke... Well, it would happen, and that was that.

He had done everything that he wished to. He had made his final amends, *mostly*. Sure, he wished that the last couple of weeks hadn't gone the way they did, but... What could he do now?

He was finished, and he was alright with that.

When he finally reached his rooms, and was laid into bed by the servants, Faelyn felt a wave of calmness wash over him. There was nothing left to do now except enjoy one final sleep.

CHAPTER FORTY-THREE

THE FIRE KING PART II

Faelyn Titansworn was dreaming of his father when the bells rang. He woke at the second strike. He was sitting up by the third.

It wasn't long before he knew what was happening. The shouting beyond his rooms was telling enough, and the lights beyond his windows only made it more obvious.

The Cyfali had not waited until morning to attack.

Faelyn twisted, sighting the moons in the sky beyond his window. The Sucharans would likely have arrived by now, which explained why the Cyfali had initiated the assault.

The Freyfallion army would still be at least an hour away—hopefully—though Faelyn wasn't even sure if the city would still be standing by the time they arrived.

A servant burst through the door to his chambers, accompanied by two guards. The servant grabbed the chair by Faelyn's bed and shouted for him to get in.

"No," Faelyn said softly. "I don't need it."

The servant looked at him, perplexed. The guards exchanged

glances. Bells continued to ring overhead, their sounds echoing through the city.

A loud crash sounded somewhere beyond the walls of the castle, likely the sound of a catapult shell landing nearby.

Faelyn had made up his mind. If this city fell, he was going to fall with it.

He reached out, the bandages on his hands searing off at the appearance of bright orange flames. The nubs of his arms were exposed now, bright shining fires burning atop his forearms. Faelyn grunted as he pushed with all of his might, concentrating the flames into solid forms and shoving them forward. He roared, his arms burning with the heat of Helionn's Sun as the edges of his night clothing singed off.

Slowly, the heat built itself into a thin, wrist-sized column. It pressed onward, burning through Faelyn's skin and lungs. It *hurt*, but he kept pushing. He couldn't stop now. Hours of working with Idris had prepared him for this.

Weeks spent rolling around in that blasted chair, and here he was, Summoning a pair of hands made of pure fire for himself.

The guards jumped back, bewildered.

Faelyn continued roaring, the pain becoming almost unbearable as his phantom limbs extended, and bright orange transparent hands began to form at the ends of his conjured wrists.

Faelyn could suddenly feel the air on his fingertips once again. He could feel the slight breeze coming through the open door. He could feel the vibrations of the battle beyond the Palace.

He reached down, leaning forward. He began the same process in his legs. Faelyn grunted again, holding out his hand.

"More Crystals!" Faelyn roared.

The servant and guards cried out. The lead guard tore off his chestplate, producing a small set of Scorcher Crystals.

Another of Faelyn's Crystals burned out. He was using them up quickly, but he would have enough. He *had* to have enough. His ankles formed, twisting and turning in swirling torrents of flame until they finally solidified, a small pair of spectral feet beneath them.

Faelyn rose, finding himself slightly uneven on his Summoned limbs. He snapped his fire-fingers, pointing to the closet. A white-gold sliver of his armor peeked out from the cracked door. It was a replica of the armor he had worn for the Cyfalion attack. The Crystals had been filled the night before, and now that Faelyn could walk again he could use the armor for his final fight.

Faelyn staggered over to the armor, leaving cinders and patches of burned carpet behind him as he walked. He took the armor in his flaming hands, feeling it warm beneath his sun-blessed grasp. The last time he had worn this, he had used it to destroy a city. And now... Now, he was going to use it to save one.

"Fire!" Elias Surge roared, hoisting his greatsword to the sky. The Incendiary Cannons fired, sending massive chunks of flaming metal toward the invaders. Arvendon's troops had been standing atop the walls when they had started falling to arrows in the night.

The invaders had struck quietly, and without warning.

Arvendon had responded with haste. Surge had never gone to sleep. Neither had most of the soldiers.

Falx stood by his side, barking orders from the top of Summerglass's hill.

Another wave of ballistae fired, sending huge bolts into the night sky.

Endless rows of torches lined the outskirts of Arvendon, just beyond the wall. There was shouting and screaming beneath them, far below at the main gate. Arrows whisked through the air. Swords swung in the night, cutting through flesh and bone. Wind whistled, pushed by Cloudwalkers and ignited by Scorchers as they stormed the gates.

"Reinforcements down to the main gate!" Falx shouted, running over to the side. "We can't let them through yet. Our troops are still getting into place!"

Surge grunted, the thrill of the fight rising within his veins. He turned to the west, where the thousands of troops now marched on the city. The Cyfali were in the front, the Sucharans just behind them, and the Freyfallion army a few miles back.

Izara's Shadow... Three armies... Two might have been beatable, but not three. But it was too late now. Surge looked down, his eyes settling on the flaming walls of the main gate.

Incendiary Cannons fired, alternating shots with ballistae.

Something whistled to his right.

Surge spun, catching sight of something moving in the dark sky above. He opened his mouth, preparing to shout orders when a sudden *force* collided with him.

Surge lurched backward, thrown by the invisible push of a Cloudwalker.

"Fire the Cloudcatchers!" Falx commanded.

The soldiers shouted, cranking the massive launcher to the side, trying to angle it correctly. It was too late.

Surge rolled to the side, pushing himself to his feet and shrugging off the impact of the hit.

Four Cloudwalkers dashed through the sky, charging Surge and Falx's group.

The Voltarian Crystals within Surge's armor crackled to life, bringing his body alive with electricity.

It was time.

Soldiers screamed, their bodies torn apart by the flying swords of the attacking Cloudwalkers. They had gone straight for the Palace, opting to eliminate the guards and go for the nobles. It was smart, except for one thing: Surge was there.

Lightning cracked, arcing through the air. It raced through the sky in the blink of an eye and struck one of the Cloudwalkers square in the chest. The Summoner cried out for a quarter of a second before he was thrown to the ground by the violent force of the strike.

Surge had to fight to keep the lightning on target due to the lightning rods, but he was the strongest Voltarian in the *world*; he could manage it.

Surge roared, charging forward. His sword glowed with lightning, electricity radiating from the metal as Surge sprinted forward.

Somewhere to the side, Falx brought down one of the Cloudwalkers with his own strike.

A Cloudwalker zipped by, cutting down another Arvendi soldier before returning to the skies. He looped around, preparing for another strafe, but Surge was ready.

Leaping into the air, Surge shot a bolt of lightning beneath himself, launching into the sky with a blinding speed. His battle cry rang through the night as he plunged his greatsword into the Cloudwalker's body. Surge roared with delight, digging the blade deep into the Cloudwalker's side and bringing him down. Surge twisted, and the pair slammed into the ground.

He stepped back, remaining perfectly upright after the fall; the Cloudwalker had taken most of the impact. Surge's greatsword still impaled the man's chest, electricity sparking through the now sizzling sockets of the Cloudwalker's eyes.

Surge tore the blade from the man's corpse.

Turning to the side, Surge charged the last Cloudwalker. The man slid to the ground, reaching out with twin silver blades and cutting down a pair of Arvendi soldiers.

The Cloudwalker dove to the side and threw his blades forward. The swords crashed into one of the ballistae, shattering the cranks and switches at the back.

Surge growled and charged.

The Cloudwalker spun, pulling his blades back to his hands. He cried out with fury and threw his hands forward.

Surge ducked into a slide, dodging the flying blades of the Cyfali

Cloudwalker. Surge rose to his feet mid-slide, and continued forward.

A stray arrow soared through the air toward the Cloudwalker. A simple wave of the man's hand threw it out of his path.

Rising into the air with another blast of lightning, Surge readied his blade. He sensed something behind him—a whistling in the air.

He twisted, flipping around in midair and preparing his blade.

The Cloudwalker's blades slammed into his greatsword, a strong gust pushing them.

Surge cried out, twisting in the air as he knocked the flying blades to the ground. He landed on his feet, sending out a pulse of lightning to steady himself. He was still several yards away from the Cloudwalker, who was raising his hands for another phantom push of his swords.

Surge readied himself.

One of the Cloudwalker's blades flipped around, the blade twisting toward the Cloudwalker.

The sword zipped forward, pushed by an invisible wind. It stabbed the Cloudwalker in the throat, effectively killing him.

Surge spun around.

Reluraun stood behind him, his hands still raised, a grim frown on his face. "You're welcome," he mumbled, turning to face the armies below.

"You know what to do," Surge said to Reluraun. "Defend the Palace with everything you've got." Surge turned to the others. "Soldiers, avenge the fallen! Launch the Cloudcatchers!"

The remaining soldiers scattered, running across the large surrounding area of the Palace"They won't be able to hold the gate for much longer," Falx said over the shouting soldiers.

Surge met his hard face in the flickering torchlight.

"Go," Reluraun said. "I'll do what I can up here... But the two of you are needed down below."

Surge nodded curtly. The boy was stronger than he looked; he would be able to defend the Palace. Surge stepped forward, marching toward the edge of the plateau. The battle raged below. The soldiers were indeed getting close to breaching the main gate.

He reached upward, calling upon the electricity hidden within his veins, readying a bolt from above. Thunder rumbled.

Falx mirrored him, the Master Summoner running beside him. "Just like old times, eh?" Falx snorted.

Surge grunted in response.

Lightning came crashing down from above, launching them forward through the night sky. The city below became a blur, the hundred-foot drop passing in an instant. Air whistled in his ears, the growing charge in his chest continuing to rise.

It was time to show the Cyfali that they had picked the wrong city.

Surge and Falx crashed to the ground just beyond the wall in the blink of an eye. An explosion of electricity followed their landing, ravaging Surge's Crystal stores in the process. Surge spun, watching as dozens of bodies sizzled around him.

The Cyfali were backing away, readying their weapons hesitantly.

Good, Surge thought. *They're afraid.* Surge spun, drawing his massive greatsword. Some distance away, he heard Falx do the same. Only a few dozen Arvendi soldiers remained beyond the walls, but that would be enough.

Surge was all they needed to hold the Cyfali back.

Wind slammed into him, knocking him from his feet once again. He grunted, twisting in midair and sliding to a stop, landing with his feet on the ground. A swath of flame spun toward him, followed by a crack of lightning.

Surge jumped over the flame and dove directly into the lightning. The electricity swelled in his chest, pooling in his veins for a brief second before he redirected it at the now charging Cyfali.

The first row of soldiers fell from the blast.

Thunder clapped, sounding through the air as an echo to his attack. Surge grinned, and this time, *he* charged.

The Cyfali soldiers, clad in their forest-green armor, cowered beneath his assault.

Surge rose into the air, pushing himself with lightning and draining yet another Crystal. He raised his greatsword over his head, directing lightning into the blade as he slammed it into the ground before him. The movement sent a massive shockwave of electricity through the rocky soil, knocking down the next row of soldiers.

He would need to swap out his Crystals soon. *But not yet.*

Surge spun, swinging his electrified blade through a squad of soldiers. He reached out with his free hand and blasted away another attacker with a simple bolt of lightning.

His lungs burned. His aging muscles were already starting to ache. But he lived for it. This feeling, this *rush*! It was what reminded him that he was still alive.

Surge roared, slamming his blade into the chest of a charging soldier and turning to the surrounding men. He extended his hands and slammed them into the ground. Electricity arced across the soil, dancing through the dirt and into the feet of the charging men.

They fell instantly.

Surge pulled his bloody blade from the dead soldier and leaped back into the air. He was down to one Crystal, and he was likely already getting close to Breakdown. He neared the main gate, sighting Falx adjacent to him.

The General was likely running low on his Crystals as well. They wouldn't have long before they were forced to return. Falx caught his line of sight and nodded.

Surge jumped into the air, sending a massive pulse of lightning through his feet and hurdling the wall with a single movement.

Falx landed at his side on the inside of the wall, where the ballistae once again fired.

"Where are the Crystals?" Falx shouted over the roar of the battle. Hundreds of their soldiers stood at the ready in the streets, preparing for the gate to fall. Even now, Surge saw it start to rattle.

"Back there, atop the gray building," Surge shouted. He pointed, and jumped into the air once again, burning through his last Crystal. Landing atop the small shop building, he tore open the small chest that sat on the roof. It was loaded with Voltarian Crystals—just as many of the roofs had been loaded with various Crystal types to serve as resupply stations for the Arvendi Summoners.

A deafening crash sounded. Surge flinched. He was in the middle of swapping the Crystals deep within the folds of his armor for new, charged ones when he heard a soldier confirm what he suspected.

"The gate has fallen!" a soldier shouted below.

Surge cursed, trying to regain his focus, putting the Crystals in his vermillion armor.

Battle cries of the Cyfali sounded.

Surge could hear the Firesnuffers spinning. He could hear the crash of the Incendiary Cannons as they mowed down soldiers. And he could hear the crashes and *swishes* of the enemy Summoners as they tore through Arvendon's ranks.

The battle had started not moments before, and the main gate had already fallen.

"Izara's Shadow," Falx cursed, turning to Surge. "We really are doomed, aren't we?"

Something sounded above.

Surge spun, catching sight of strange lights in the sky. Dozens upon dozens of arrows flew through the night. *No*, Surge realized. *Not arrows. Firebolts.*

He turned, his jaw setting as he watched the bolts near the Cyfali soldiers.

The fire rained down, burning through the invading army. Pitiful spurts of air, flame, and thunder rose from the Cyfali, trying to block the strikes. But it did no good.

A greater light in the sky became visible, growing closer with each second. In an instant, the massive fireball was hurtling toward the streets.

It crashed to the ground, leaving a deep crater in the stone streets of Arvendon. Flames exploded in all directions, fires spreading through the night sky—even toward Arvendon's own troops.

Then the flames *moved.*

The fires turned, twisting in midair as if controlled by unseen hands. They curled, then flew toward the Cyfali, *scorching* through their ranks. Screams of the dying filled the night.

The smoke cleared, revealing the glowing figure of Faelyn Titansworn—flaming crown atop his head—standing in a crater of his own making. He raised his hands—which seemed to be made of flames themselves—toward the attackers once again, preparing another blast.

"No..." Surge breathed. "No, Falx, I don't think we are."

Faelyn Titansworn was death. He was pain, suffering, and cruelty. He was everything that this world had made him to be... And he was *powerful.*

His Summoned hands flashed up, sending an explosion of flames toward the charging group of Stormless. They were wrapped in fire an instant later, leaving only screams in their wake.

The smoke and dust from the main gate's fall cleared, and more Cyfali charged through without hesitation.

Faelyn raised his hands, taking a step forward on his still unsteady feet, and prepared for the next wave.

Their army was speckled with soldiers of gold and black. *Sucharans.*

Someone sprinted toward him—a Cyfali—with an almost unbelievable speed. A dark blue essence trailed the Cyfali soldier. *Dexteris.*

At their back, a Sucharan launched into the air, pushed by a bolt of lightning.

Faelyn cursed, willing his hands to change into spectral blades.

The Dexteris slid toward him, raising a large mace and swinging for his head.

Faelyn reached out with his right hand, watching as the flaming energy transformed into a pointed blade.

The top half of the mace fell over, clanking to the ground—severed by Faelyn's hand of flame.

The Dexteris cursed, wide-eyed.

Faelyn raised his hand again.

A bolt of lightning slammed into him from the side. Faelyn flew through the air, his limbs disappearing as he lost his focus. Faelyn cursed, tumbling and rolling against the hard stone— plowing into dozens of his own men—until he finally came to a stop.

Faelyn growled, blinking. His phantom limbs regrew, and he rose to his feet. His armor clanked heavily. The massive suit simmered with heat, as did the Summoned crown atop his head.

The soldiers milled around him, charging their invaders in ignorance of their King. They parted, diving away from the charging Dexteris and Voltarian.

Jumping to his spectral feet, Faelyn prepared twin blades of fire —one in each hand.

The Dexteris charged first, while the Voltarian pressed her hands together, readying another bolt.

Faelyn reached out with both hands, channeling the blades into long pillars of flame. They concentrated, then shot forward.

The Dexteris gasped, but Faelyn wasn't going for him. The beams of fire wove around the Dexteris, sliding in between the passing ranks of Arvendi soldiers, until they reached the Voltarian.

Faelyn expanded the flame.

A blast of flame and a puff of smoke sounded over the deafening roar of the fight. Faelyn's heart thundered as the smoke cleared, revealing the ashes of the Voltarian floating to the ground.

Azamar's Blast, Faelyn thought, grinning. He reached out, keeping the shape of his hand as the Dexteris approached.

Faelyn dodged the swing of the severed mace and grappled the man with his hands. He threw the man to the side, then dove on top of him. Faelyn *pushed* fire through both of his hands as he grabbed onto the top of the man's green and silver armor.

The Dexteris screamed, burned alive within his own armor.

Lorkah's Hand. Faelyn grinned. There was nothing that could stop him. He turned back to the fight as hundreds of Arvendi soldiers pushed past him.

Faelyn charged once again, hearing the roar and crack of the Incendiary Cannons and ballistae. He raised his hands, pushing past his men and reaching the front lines. Faelyn threw out his hands of flame.

A strong gust of wind blew behind him, and the fires shot forward with blinding speed. Faelyn spun, the thrill of the fight rising within him.

A Cloudwalker stood behind him and nodded in his direction.

Faelyn recognized the figure—Wardell. Faelyn nodded back, then turned around once again.

He slid across the stones as if they were a dance floor, reaching out with both hands. Following the motions of the spell, he made an "X" with his arms. He swung, directing all of the *heat* within his draining Crystals toward the invaders.

An X-shaped arc of flame dashed forward, knocking down a few dozen men. He was *obliterating* squadron after squadron, but his Crystals were getting low. He didn't have much time before he would have to refill.

A blast of flame slammed into him, burning into his scalding-hot armor. Faelyn cried out, trying to hold and redirect the flame. He couldn't gather his focus before the heat scorched through his armor.

Something else crashed into him—a gust of wind. Faelyn fell to the ground, knocked from his feet once again. He raised his head, catching sight of the charging Scorcher and Cloudwalker.

Faelyn growled. He tried to rise, but fell. His muscles were tiring so fast that he could hardly even stand. He cursed, trying to redirect the flames to fortify his limbs. His heart thundered. His breathing was ragged, and he was practically drenched in sweat, blood, and soot.

No. Faelyn looked around, raising his eyes as the pair of Summoners neared him. They both raised their hands, preparing another joint strike.

Twin pillars of flame shot into the air from behind, twisting and turning with beautiful elegance until they crashed down atop the charging Summoners, felling them both instantly.

Faelyn coughed, looking to the right where the flames had come from. He saw the distant figure of Idris nod to him, then turn back to the fight beyond. Faelyn tried to smile, but could not.

A pair of Arvendi Scorchers charged past him, glowing Sunspears raised and ready. They burned with a heat that few metals could reach, and tore through the skin and flesh of the men that they collided with seconds later.

Faelyn breathed, raising his head.

Screams. Pain. Death.

There was nothing else on these once friendly streets. Fires burned, thunder cracked. Blood poured into the cobblestones below, drenching the feet of friend and foe alike.

Faelyn watched as the pair of Arvendi Scorchers charged the invaders. One of them raised their spear and hurled it at the nearest Cyfali.

Thunder cracked, and the Arvendi Scorcher fell to the ground not a second later. A Sucharan Voltarian grinned on the other side of the battle lines, then raised his hands again.

The remaining Scorcher—now covered in his friend's blood—raised his spear defensively.

Lightning arced from the Voltarian, crashing into the Arvendi Scorcher. Faelyn watched in horror as an Incendiary Cannon fired, and the Sucharan Voltarian was crushed by a flaming hunk of metal.

Faelyn's eyes shifted to the left. A squadron of Stormless Arvendi charged.

A Cyfali Cloudwalker threw his hands forward, then twisted them together. Fallen swords rose from the ground, then lurched forward at the command of the Cyfali.

A dozen Arvendi soldiers fell to the ground, killed by the flying swords. *A dozen.* Faelyn felt sick. *A dozen of my people, dead... just like that.* Faelyn felt sick.

The stench of burning flesh and blood reached his nose, mixing with the deafening screams of the dying. A disquieting realization settled over Faelyn. This was different from his fight in Cyfalion... That had been a small ambush. This? This was war. All his life, he had pictured glorious battles between two foreign powers. He had imagined beautiful fights with grace and dignity, but this... This was *horrifying.*

Faelyn looked up, feeling the winds of a Firesnuffer blowing behind him. He watched as Surge and Falx reentered the battle, ripping through ranks of Cyfali and Sucharan soldiers as if they were nothing.

Faelyn fell to the ground once again, not even bothering to Summon his feet and hands. It didn't matter whether they won or lost, because this... This was losing. Even if the city still stood at dawn, they had already lost too much. He had failed.

Someone ran by him, tossing a satchel of Scorcher Crystals in his direction. Faelyn let them hit his nub of a hand and watched as they fell to the ground.

Several of them cracked, releasing small puffs of heat. Orange energy drifted through the air, begging to be used as it curled into the night.

Someone shouted, and the lines drew closer to Faelyn. The Arvendi were being pushed back. It wouldn't be long before they were thrown all the way back to the old sea district, and it wouldn't be long before their ambush failed.

Strong hands grabbed Faelyn, ripping him from his spot on the ground and pulling him into the air. He found himself lifted to the roof of the nearest building. His eyes slipped shut, and his head smacked against the roof of the building. He blinked a few times, noticing someone standing over him, rifling through a chest that seemed to contain orange lights.

Elias Surge turned around, shoving a dozen Scorcher Crystals onto Faelyn's chest.

Faelyn cursed, bringing himself back to life as the energy flooded his veins.

Surge leaned down, picking Faelyn up by the collar.

"You said you would fight," Surge growled, his bloodstained face hollow and taut. "So *fight!*" Surge released him, turning to the battle once again.

Faelyn remembered Surge's words: *Prioritize my orders over your own instincts.* Faelyn had made a promise to the General, and he would uphold it. He had promised that he would obey any command, and that was what he was going to do. Faelyn raised his head, crying out as he forced his feet and hands to reform.

Pushing himself to his feet, Faelyn started switching out the drained Crystals for the new ones in his armor. He became aware of a loud cranking noise to the side. Faelyn looked up.

The cannons and ballistae atop the stone barricades were turning... turning toward... *the sea?*

Faelyn spun, following Surge's line of sight.

Dark masses in the sea had appeared, seemingly out of nowhere.

"The Cyfali Fleet!" Surge roared, turning around. "Fire! Don't let them draw close enough to shoot!"

But it was already too late. Torches began to appear on the ships, and lights began to spark. Faelyn watched in horror as the ships drew closer, the dark masses nearing the shore.

The Arvendi cannons and ballistae finally finished turning.

A volley of shots rose into the night sky, soaring toward the ships. Faelyn and Surge cursed, watching as the flaming metal and masses of arrows flew upon the fleet.

Most missed, but some hit their marks. Faelyn squinted,

watching one particularly hard-hit ship. It remained still, its lights flickering slightly.

Another massive ballista bolt soared toward it, and flew through it. A distant turquoise light flickered, and the ship remained unchanged.

"Oh no," Faelyn breathed. He spun, facing the dozens of soldiers who operated the weapons—which were now pointed toward the ships. "Hold your fire!" Faelyn shouted, his voice hoarse. "The ships aren't real!"

"What?" Surge growled, grabbing Faelyn by the collar once again.

Faelyn squirmed beneath the man's hard grasp.

Surge held him close to his face. "What is going on?"

"The ships..." Faelyn breathed. "They aren't real." Faelyn paused, turning back to the dozen ships that floated in the bay. "They're projections, generated by an Illusomancer."

"Illusomancer..." Surge took a deep breath. "Calida's Claws, we didn't anticipate them having one!"

"I know," Faelyn whispered. He turned around, facing the fight behind them. The siege weapons were bombarded with arrows and swords. Bolts of lightning arced through the air, destroying the cannons and ballistae.

The distraction with the ships had cost them over a dozen weapons and many more men.

Surge cursed again, nearing the edge of the roof. They watched as the Arvendi were pushed around the corner, falling back to the next phase of the fight.

They fought half-heartedly, trying not to lose too many as they fell back to the old sea district. Some even turned and ran, letting their fear get the best of them.

Faelyn turned to the main streets, watching as hundreds of Cyfali and Sucharan soldiers marched over the countless corpses that littered the shattered stone streets. Finally, Faelyn raised his head.

The lines of soldiers were endless, continuing on for miles beyond the Arvendi walls.

Surge stepped up, rising to the edge of the roof. "You head to the old sea district. I'll send Falx with you," Surge said, his voice firm.

Faelyn turned to him, wiping blood and sweat from his brow. "Where are you going?" he shouted over the roar of the fight.

"I'm going to cut off our invaders from their reinforcements," Surge said. "I need you to make sure that we wipe out every single one of those who have already made it inside the city. The Sparkcoils will keep any more from entering, but not for long." Surge paused. "It's time to initiate the second phase of our plan."

"Surge," Faelyn started. "We don't even—"

"Do not speak!" Surge roared, cutting him off. "*Obey.*" Surge turned away and leaped off into the night with a blast of lightning.

Faelyn watched as the retreating Arvendi neared the old sea district. He turned, catching sight of a small amount of fighting near the Palace—likely a few stray Cloudwalkers. The Palace would hopefully remain unharmed thanks to Reluraun and the soldiers stationed there... And so long as the Palace stood, Arvendon had a chance.

Faelyn whirled and sprinted along the rooftops, pushing past the market district and the main plaza—where the invaders were currently marching. They were tearing through the Arvendi that had been stationed there effortlessly, following the retreating troops toward the old plaza to the south.

He jumped to the next one, and then the next, fires catching around his Summoned feet as he picked up speed. The armies looked up, firing a few arrows and blasts of flame at him, but Faelyn ignored them.

Thunder crackled, and General Falx crashed down in the center of the old plaza—their destination. He stood next to the Incendiary-filled fountain, preparing for the arrival of the next wave of troops.

Something moved in the distance to the south. Dark masses

sneaking through the back alleys. Faelyn tilted his head. *Weren't the reinforcements supposed to be hiding in the warehouses?*

Unless... Those were not Arvendi reinforcements. Faelyn started, lifting his gaze. Smoke rose from the southern wall. The Sucharans and Cyfali had punched a hole through the wall and were coming in from *behind* Arvendon's hidden reinforcements.

"To the south!" Faelyn screamed.

Almost every soldier on the battlefield spun to face the southern walls. Seconds later, Falx gave the order.

Hundreds of Arvendi soldiers charged out of the warehouses, while the main force of Cyfali and Sucharans remained around fifty yards from the old plaza itself.

The invaders jumped back, cursing at the sudden flood of Arvendi troops.

No, no, no, NO! It hadn't worked. The troops had come out too early because of the ambush.

The Cyfali and Sucharans retreated slightly, keeping themselves in the street rather than advancing to the plaza where they would have been surrounded.

Faelyn's heart plummeted. Their ambush had failed. Just at that very moment, bolts of lightning lit up the battlefield to the northeast. Faelyn spun.

Surge was activating the Sparkcoils, but it wouldn't matter. They had planned to repeat this plan for several waves of invaders, yet they had failed on the *first one*.

Faelyn could only watch as the Arvendi reached the southern ambushers. He blinked a few times as the Arvendi swung straight through the soldiers.

Turquoise frost flickered where each of the enemy soldiers had been standing.

"Izara's Shadow!" Faelyn cursed. They had been tricked again. The smoke from the south instantly vanished.

More Sparkcoils lit up, activated by Falx. Yet they did no good. The invading force to the south didn't even exist.

Illusomancer. Faelyn fell to his knees, watching as the confused troops spun, trying to figure out what had happened as their enemies suddenly vanished into thin air.

Their plan had failed. The battle would be over before it had even truly begun.

A few minutes earlier...

Elias Surge leaped from building to building, ignoring the charging invaders below. He opened his mouth, channeling the power of thunder into his voice.

"Arm the coils!" Surge roared, his voice booming through the streets. "Three across the gate, one bordering the plaza!" Surge called out. He grunted, leaping to the next set of rooftops.

His muscles ached from carrying the weight of his massive armor and sword, but he pushed on. This wasn't his first extended fight, but it *was* the first fight that he had ever seen on this scale. He couldn't afford to think about that right now. He shoved the thoughts from his mind, replacing them with a cold focus.

Finally, as if in response to his focus, the hidden ballistae rose from behind the wall, rapidly assembled by the soldiers who had been hiding within. In unison, they let out their war cries, and Arvendon started to take back some of its lost ground.

Surge took this as his signal and leaped from the building directly into the fray of hostile soldiers tearing through the streets.

He landed with a small explosion, sending a burst of electricity through his legs. Drawing his sword, Surge took down the nearest soldier with a single swipe of his blade.

The others turned to him, forming a small ring around Surge. The ring expanded, and continued doing so until it encompassed several dozen soldiers.

Fire lashed out toward him. Surge ducked, letting the blast burn through the soldiers on the other side of him. A Cloudwalker wove a block of air and hurled it toward Surge.

Surge raised his sword, electrifying it and swinging it directly into the invisible block. His sword connected with something, and the wind dissipated.

He just needed to wait.

The soldiers charged at that moment... Yet they had *no idea* what he was capable of.

NOW! Surge imbued his sword with lightning, commanding the power to stay *within* the blade. He took a deep breath, then let out a vicious roar, pushing every bit of his power into the tip of the blade.

Thunder cracked through the night. His ears rang as lightning exploded from the tip of the sword, shooting outward in a continuous beam of destruction, disintegrating the charging soldiers.

He spun, bringing the sword in a full arc around himself, wiping out every single one of his attackers. Surge collapsed, feeling the fearful tingling in his fingertips. Lightning trickled through his veins, itching his hands with its dangerous grasp.

Breakdown.

It didn't matter. Surge staggered to his feet, using his massive sword as a crutch while he surveyed the land around him. His eyes settled on the gate, whose opening was now being wrapped with three sets of Sparkcoils.

Enemy soldiers were already charging the gate, swords raised to cut down the wires.

Surge grunted, sheathing his sword and slamming his fists together. Breakdown or not, he would never surrender. He leaped forward, lightning arcing across the stones as he flew. He reached the gate within seconds and threw both of his hands up against the wires.

Just as the soldiers were beginning to reach the gate, Surge pushed his lightning through the Sparkcoils.

Somewhere deep within the thin metal wires, Surge felt the reaction trigger.

Brilliant lightning exploded across the wires, perfectly covering the entrance to the city in a mesmerizing, crisscrossing pattern.

Surge spun as a group of Arvendi soldiers filed out from their posts behind him to defend him while he held the gate.

Already, he could feel the shaking of the wall elsewhere as the invaders tried to break through. The Sparkcoils would be severed before too long, but they would hold for now. Surge could only hope that it would be long enough for Faelyn and Falx to wipe out the others.

Faelyn Titansworn jumped from the building he stood atop, landing among the enemy soldiers. They spun in surprise, raising their curved swords and longblades.

Faelyn's face was fixed in a tight frown. The plan they'd worked so hard on was ruined, and he was in no mood for games or fancy tricks. If Arvendon was going down, he was going to take some of its invaders down with him. Faelyn threw out both hands and began concentrating his energies into his palms.

The soldiers shied away as lights appeared around Faelyn's glowing, spectral hands. He Summoned several flames, growing and cultivating them with a careful, focused mind.

He expanded them, feeling the rush of the wind and the quiver of the bow in the distance. Faelyn ducked, his enhanced senses making him aware of the arrow that was presently flying toward him.

A small volley of arrows from Cyfali soldiers flew past him, crashing into the men on the other side of Faelyn.

The attacks snapped the Cyfali and Sucharans out of their trance, and they charged.

Faelyn growled, twisting the tapestry of fire that he had made and *throwing* it into the ground. The cracks in the street suddenly began to glow. Faelyn planted his feet, holding his ground as he pushed out with both hands. The ground grew unsteady, and the soldiers started to stumble.

The glowing cracks in the stone spread, crawling and expanding to encompass more and more enemy soldiers.

Now. Faelyn threw his hands to the sky, bringing the fire up *through* the stones and incinerating the soldiers who had been standing around him. He closed his eyes, shielding himself from the blinding display of fire.

He heard the flames wash through the soldiers and felt their warmth float through his skin. He cracked his eyes open, sighting the remnants of the flames around him.

He lowered his hands, the blazing inferno that he had Summoned from below falling back beneath the surface and dissipating. It was a dangerous spell, one that he had learned very recently, but it was effective.

Faelyn leaped into the air once again, then landed with a crash a few dozen feet away. He bolted through the streets, fire trailing his still shaky conjured feet.

Naturally, the invading soldiers followed the man who had killed their allies and charged behind him, punching through the Arvendi lines and pouring into the old plaza.

Yes... YES! The soldiers were charging the plaza anyway. His plan to bait them into the ambush had worked—even if the Arvendi reinforcements were already drawn out.

Faelyn jumped back, watching as row after row of Arvendi Scorchers sprinted toward the approaching threat, glowing Sunspears held at the ready.

Flames burst out of nowhere. Lightning cracked through the enemy lines. Phantom winds tossed soldiers like leaves in the wind. Faelyn took a few deep breaths, trying to resettle himself.

His ashen breathing returned, his haunted lungs feeling empty. Faelyn struggled to get another breath. He was getting close to Breakdown once again. And if he went as far as he did last time, he wasn't sure he would survive.

Faelyn stumbled back as a brilliant explosion of electricity grabbed his attention. He spotted General Falx standing to the side, holding the edge of a set of Sparkcoils. The long metal wires were laid across the ground and had been firmly embedded in the cracks of the cobblestone streets throughout the northern half of the plaza. Falx had electrified them, bringing down almost a hundred soldiers in a single second.

A few Voltarians stood in the electrified street—the lightning flowing harmlessly through them. They charged Falx, knocking him from the wires.

Faelyn shouted, sprinting toward them. He passed the fountain and felt a strange *pull*. Faelyn stopped. *Incendiary.*

There were still nearly a hundred soldiers left in the plaza, and the Arvendi soldiers were falling fast. Faelyn shouted his commands and then turned to the Cyfali soldiers, who were armed with their vicious longswords.

"You want revenge for your Monolith?" Faelyn roared. "Come and get me!"

The soldiers turned to him, charging almost instantly.

Faelyn grinned, taking a few steps back, standing right beside the stone fountain.

The soldiers started to reach the edges of the fountain, their battle cries becoming deafening as they plowed past the Arvendi soldiers who had stood between them and Faelyn.

Faelyn jumped back and sent a single bolt of flame toward the fountain.

He was thrown from his feet in an instant.

A deafening explosion rocked the city. Stone rubble shot in all directions, crushing Arvendi and invaders alike. Faelyn rolled to a stop somewhere in the streets, feeling the crushing weight of the heat around him.

Faelyn turned to his phantom feet, trying to Summon them once again as the ash started to fall.

No. It was like... It was like... *NO!*

Ash swirled around him, falling lightly on the endless piles of corpses and rubble around him. The Incendiary... *How much had there been?* Faelyn rose to his feet, Summoning them once again. *What has Eithor done?*

His breath caught as he took in the entirety of what he had done. Hundreds of bodies littered the plaza. Survivors—General Falx among them—tried to rise to their feet, pushing aside the rubble that had fallen.

Faelyn recognized the female Scorcher he stepped over. *Ayre.* Faelyn took another step. The woman was dead.

Faelyn looked down to his armor—now coated black. He brought his spectral hands to his face, a scream rising in the depths of his haunted soul when another explosion sounded across the city.

He spun, raising his eyes to the sky, where a pillar of smoke rose steadily.

Shards of ice began twisting into the air to the north—by the main gate. A *force* pressed against his brain, bringing distraction and discomfort. *Whisperers.*

Whisperers and Cryostalkers could only mean one thing: The Freyfallion army had arrived.

Elias Surge stumbled back, the trap of wires finally falling.

Cryostalkers slid over the walls, cutting down Arvendi archers and ballistae as they went.

Surge cursed, sprinting back and waving for the small squadron of soldiers that had been covering him to follow.

An explosion sounded to the south.

Surge stumbled, nearly falling to the ground. He cursed again, scanning the sky as a plume of black smoke rose into the night. *What is going on?*

Another explosion sounded as fire was set to the next barricade.

Surge roared with fury, leaping into the air with an electric blast as he watched the Freyfallion Summoners—clad in black armor—rip apart the Arvendi soldiers... *his* soldiers.

Surge screamed. He landed with a small explosion, grabbing a Freyfallion Cryostalker and throwing him to the ground with an electric grapple.

The Summoner's skull cracked from the impact.

Another barricade exploded, now fully opening the path to the northern half of the city. Surge cursed, grabbing another Freyfallion Cryostalker and throwing a firm, electrified punch deep into the man's skull, killing him instantly.

Now was not the time for mercy. His men were dying, and they were dying fast.

Another explosion sounded to the *west*, beyond the wall. *No,* The explosion was some distance away, meaning...

The barely visible white film in the sky above weakened, fading slightly. *The ward.*

The invaders had destroyed one of Arvendon's Monoliths.

A weight crashed into his mind, weakening his muscles before he could react. Surge gasped, moving to draw his greatsword.

Surge started, stumbling to the ground.

Whisperers.

Another explosion sounded to the west, the ward overhead weakening even further.

They're going to destroy every last Monolith, Surge realized, his stomach sinking. Some of Arvendon's Monoliths were underwater—to the east—but those alone wouldn't be enough to protect the city. Even if Arvendon somehow survived this battle, it would be destroyed by the first Storm Gale that blew through.

Surge only had one option left... He wasn't sure what had happened at the old plaza; all he knew was that what he was going to do next would finally seal their fate.

"Fall back!" Surge commanded, enhancing his shouts. "Fall back to the Palace!"

"Fall back!" Surge shouted from across the city. "Fall back to the Palace!" His calls rang out through their shattered forces.

Faelyn had seen the ward weakening overhead, and he had heard the explosions to the west. It was over. Regardless of the outcome of this battle, Arvendon would be destroyed.

An Illusomancer had tricked them into giving away their ambush, and the resulting fight had led to many of their forces falling. Eithor had overfilled the fountain with Incendiary... It didn't take Faelyn long to put together that Eithor was the one behind these illusions.

He had betrayed them. But Faelyn couldn't worry about that now; he would deal with Eithor if he made it out of this alive.

Faelyn realized that it didn't even matter that the Monoliths were being destroyed—the Arvendi would all be dead by morning anyway. He was out of options. The least he could do was give everything he had to this one *final* stand.

Faelyn dashed through the streets, then launched himself up to the rooftops with a thick, ashen breath. He landed with a grunt and took off in a sprint across the tops of the warehouses and homes.

Summerglass Palace loomed in the distance. A heavy shadow fell over the city, signaling that they were entering the darkest part of the night.

As Faelyn passed by the main plaza, he understood.

Lotius and Oria had slipped behind a pair of clouds, hiding their radiant lights. Fires still burned in the streets, scorching the bodies of the dead. Fighting still rang out in some places, filling Faelyn's ears with sounds of steel and death.

And at the center of it all, the Freyfallion army marched through Arvendon's streets—heading for the Palace. Their Cryostalkers Summoned Iceblades, cutting through any Arvendi who remained.

Whisperers chanted, weaving their hands in practiced motions as they cast a curse of discomfort over the city.

Faelyn looked away, feeling the numbness return to his body. It was not the same numbness from before. The apathy that he had felt over the last several weeks had been a result of denial. This... This was acceptance.

He had made mistakes, and now his city was paying the price.

Faelyn jumped to the next set of rooftops, his heavy, blood-stained armor clanking against itself. The Crystals rattled within their compartments, half empty.

He leaped to the ground with a grunt, turning up toward the Palace hill.

Faelyn sprinted up the street—just ahead of the marching Frey-fallions—fire coating his phantom steps. A few dozen Arvendi ran in front of him. Faelyn sped past them, shouting at them to move quickly. But it wouldn't matter.

Faelyn reached the top of the steep hill moments later and sprinted for the massive doors to the Palace. He found General Surge standing atop their steps, shouting orders to those both inside and outside of the Palace.

"Whisperers, prepare yourselves!" Surge was shouting. "When they get within range, knock them out... Take down as many as you can—this is our last stand."

"General," Faelyn called, slowing to a stop. He took a few deep breaths, trying to recenter himself before he spoke. He peered inside the massive doors to the Palace, seeing the Whisperers and guards within as they hurried to get into position. The grand entry hall had never looked so small... so pitiful.

"Faelyn," Surge started, descending the steps. He brushed past a squadron of Arvendi soldiers rushing inside. "You're still alive. After that explosion, I—"

"I know," Faelyn panted, cutting him off. "But there's no time for this now—the three armies are on their way, and they've likely put their Summoners at the front. I don't know about you, but I'm getting dangerously close to Breakdown. I'm not even sure how much longer I'll be able to fight."

"I know," Surge said, his voice firm. He raised his gauntleted fingers. They twitched. "I'm close too," Surge said. He narrowed his eyes, watching the edge of the hill. "We won't be able to hold them off for very long."

"Izara's Shadow," a voice cursed from behind Surge. Reluraun limped forward, clutching his side. Blood dripped from a wound near his stomach. "This is it."

Faelyn turned to his friend, his eyes weak. "Reluraun, I'm—"

"It doesn't matter anymore, Faelyn," Reluraun said softly. "We did what we could."

Faelyn opened his mouth. "Rel—"

He was cut off by the sound of steel hitting steel. Faelyn spun, his eyes settling on the front lines at the edge of the hill.

The Freyfallion army was leading the charge, and they had finally reached the top of the path.

It was too late.

"Izara's Shadow," Faelyn cursed.

Surge raised his head, a cold focus coming over his vision. He grunted. "All of this because of that damned Blood Sorcerer six weeks ago." Surge cursed, drawing his sword. He stormed forward, unleashing a vicious battle cry.

Faelyn started. *Six weeks...* It had been six weeks. Velarus had given them six weeks to surrender the city before he returned, and now... Now, he hadn't even bothered to show up and deliver on his threat.

The irony of it all was not lost on him. All of this had started because of a threat, and the Blood Sorcerers hadn't even followed through. Faelyn sighed. It didn't matter.

Faelyn extended both hands, twisting them into swords of solid flame. He charged past the few remaining Arvendi soldiers, sprinting toward the Freyfallions.

Lightning cracked through the soldiers. Ice exploded with it, and, above all, the oppressive Whispering weighed over his head. Faelyn caught a glimpse of the legions of soldiers still filing into Arvendon.

All that they had done, and they hadn't even destroyed half of the force that was invading them. Even now, a large group of a few dozen dark figures wearing Summoner cloaks were charging through the city—likely reinforcements. Faelyn let out a battle cry and leaped into the air with both hands extended.

His wrists began to burn even further, signaling that his body was finally beginning to surrender to Ashwither yet again. It seemed that the large expenditures of his power over the past few weeks—both through the battle in Cyfalion and his training with Idris—had raised his limits, though he had broken them once again.

He reached out, cutting through a Freyfallion Cryostalker and a Sucharan Stormless. Faelyn spun, extending both hands and severing the spines of two more soldiers.

He jumped back, avoiding the swings of a few Freyfallion soldiers. Faelyn retaliated with a blast of fire, burning them to ash. Even with Breakdown setting in, Faelyn was still a force to be reckoned with. As he cut down another soldier, he vowed that he would not fall easily.

Lightning exploded to his right, signaling that Surge was holding strong as well.

Something slammed into Faelyn's abdomen. Faelyn gasped, lurching back. His eyes shifted downward, settling on the thin shaft of metal that stood between him and a Freyfallion Stormless.

The Freyfallion spear impaled his left side.

Faelyn screamed, the shock giving way to an explosion of pain.

Shards of ice slammed into his spectral hands, knocking away his Summoned limbs. Faelyn fell to the ground—the spear still sticking out of his stomach.

He screamed, wailing against the deafening cry of battle. It was over. It had finally happened.

All that he had been through, all that he had fought for... It was ending now. All it had taken was a single spear.

Faelyn gasped for air, his side screaming in pain as he struggled against his body's demands for life. He used his nubs to crawl backward, the spear jutting from his side awkwardly.

Soldiers reached for him, but Faelyn continued trying to crawl. He hit loose stones in the ground, another burst of the shock wearing off.

Faelyn screamed. Furious pain stabbed through his body, ripping apart his nerves, tearing through his limbs and splitting his mind.

Soldiers began to stumble and then fall around him. Invaders as well as Arvendi collapsed, succumbing to the Arvendi Whisperers' spell.

Even Faelyn began to feel a new weight pressing against his mind. He leaned back, taking a short breath before continuing to crawl. The last of his Crystals burned out, leaving him completely alone in his body.

Surge took a hit to his right—a deep cut to his leg. Another soldier approached the General, stabbing Surge's right arm. The General did not scream. He *roared* with fury, using his free hand to bash in his attacker's skull.

Faelyn finally stopped, his ashen lungs now weak with wet blood. His body felt hot. His throat tightened as he coughed. He wheezed, feeling the blood pouring out of his stomach.

His eyes started to close. His breaths became violent gasps. Convulsions took over his body, begging for Faelyn to save himself. But there was nothing he could do.

The invaders charged past him, storming the Palace.

Faelyn could hear the slaughter beginning in the entry hall. The weight on his mind disappeared. The Arvendi Whisperers were either dead or disabled.

It was over.

His eyes slid shut, and he finally surrendered to his fate.

Surge continued fighting somewhere near him, shouting orders to try and save the Palace, but it was no use.

Faelyn lay there, letting the exhaustion take over his weak, dying body. He could almost hear his father speaking to him over the roar of the battle. Faelyn smiled, feeling a strange rising sensation in his chest.

Red flashed in the darkness.

Blood spattered, and steel crashed to the ground. Bodies fell, twisting and turning against one another.

Faelyn's eyes cracked open.

Bright red lights illuminated the battlefield. Crimson energy exploded through the night, wrapping around the invading soldiers. It froze their bodies, dropping them instantly. People started twitching, stumbling and struggling against themselves as they were forced to move against their own minds.

The brilliant red energies were beautiful.

Faelyn was certain that he had died, and that this was somehow his transition to the Afterworld. He closed his eyes once again, but not before catching sight of one of the dark-robed figures that he had seen storming the city a few moments before.

Their robes were not black, but instead a deep, blood red.

A hand slammed into Faelyn's stomach, and the spear was ripped from his body.

Faelyn screamed in agony. Thrashing pain tore through his nerves, shredding his spirit and—

It vanished.

A warm feeling washed over him. He felt his flesh start to meld together, bending and twisting until it reformed.

He opened his eyes, a bald head leaning over him. The man's dark eyes curved as he smiled. Faelyn lowered his eyes, staring at the dark red energy that hovered above his wound.

The skin was knitting itself back together. The man—the Blood Sorcerer—was *healing* Faelyn's wound. Faelyn shifted slightly, a sudden awareness settling over his mind.

Dozens of Blood Sorcerers stood around him, hands raised. They were weaving waves of blood-red energy, disabling each and every Freyfallion, Sucharan, and Cyfali on the hill.

Where had they come from?

"What..." Faelyn wheezed. "What's happening?"

The Blood Sorcerer smiled. "It's been six weeks, prince." The Blood Sorcerer winked.

Faelyn leaned back. He heard horns far below as he closed his eyes once again—horns of surrender from their invaders. They were retreating.

The Blood Sorcerers had snuck into the city, behind enemy lines, and were now using their powers to take control of their foes' bodies. There couldn't have been more than a few dozen Blood Sorcerers, but it seemed that was enough.

Faelyn felt weakness take over his body once again, but not before the shock washed away. The Blood Sorcerers had single-handedly turned the tide of the battle and forced Arvendon's invaders into surrendering.

This Sect was not ordinary. *No...* The Blood Sorcerers were something *far* greater. Faelyn finally understood why his father had been so terrified when Velarus had arrived on Arvendon's doorstep six weeks ago, and now... Now, the very same Summoner who had turned his entire world upside down had just saved his life.

Faelyn's mind went blank, and he succumbed to sleep once again.

CHAPTER FORTY-FOUR
FLAME HAS A SHADOW

Faelyn Titansworn sat in his chambers, feeling the stark light of the moons shining down through the open window. The night was warm, and the air was thick.

Smoke still lingered in parts of the city, though the fires had all been extinguished. His body had survived the next level of Breakdown, and he had only lost a few more inches of skin and bone on his forearms and legs.

After an extended conversation with the Blood Sorcerers, Faelyn and Surge had learned that the Shadow-Swifts were apparently on a mission to conquer the world, and that the people of Auris had become their pawns. Seeing as the Blood Sorcerers had traveled all the way from their fortress in The Highlands to save Arvendon once they received word that Freyfall was going to attack, Faelyn felt that they had no choice but to believe them.

The Blood Sorcerers had planned to return to take command of the city either way, but upon learning of Arvendon's situation, their course of action had changed. They had snuck in through Freyfallion lines and used a unified spell of corporikinesis to take down the front lines of the invaders and consequently force them to retreat. The invaders had done enough damage by that point anyway; they had no reason to stay and fight after what they had done.

Faelyn breathed in the pleasant night air, sighing.

Thousands of Arvendi had been killed. Thousands more of the invaders, true, but that wasn't exactly the greatest of Faelyn's worries at the moment. Bodies were piled to the height of a person throughout Arvendon's streets.

The fires and explosions had destroyed much of their infrastructure. It was, of course, an utter disaster. All of that paled in comparison to their true problem: Four of the eight Monoliths surrounding the city had been destroyed. The entire western half of the ward had been rendered useless, meaning that all it would take was one Storm Gale or Cyclone to tear Arvendon apart. Today had been a Mistveil, fortunately, but it was only a matter of time...

His city was in ruins, and while many of their people had survived, their entire army—save for a few dozen soldiers—had been wiped out.

Had the Blood Sorcerers not rescued them, they all would have perished that night.

Perhaps if the walls had held longer, or if the Incendiary had not been overfilled in the old plaza's fountain, things might have been better. Maybe if Freyfall had taken a few hours longer to arrive, things might have been better. But those worries were not at the top of Faelyn's mind either, for he was awaiting an arrival at the moment.

He heard soft footsteps outside of his chambers. Faelyn turned slightly, hearing the door creak open. The guards had been instructed to let his guest in, and it seemed that they had done so.

Faelyn caught a glimpse of the paper that he had set out on his desk. He was still facing the window, feeling the soft midnight breeze, watching the stars collide with the waves on the distant horizon.

There was something peaceful about tonight. It was a night of realization, and understanding. It was a night of reckoning... A night of justice. He could still smell the stench of burning flesh and blood in his nostrils. He could still hear the screams of the dying in the back of his mind, the clash of the steel, the crack of the thunder. Images of ruined bodies tore through his thoughts, ripping a hole in his very being. Soldiers, citizens... friends. They were gone. Those who had been fortunate enough to survive the assault were not without their scars, and Faelyn acknowledged with a heavy heart that each and every one of the Arvendi had lost someone important to them.

And it was all because of the man standing right behind him.

"You may recognize the letter sitting on the desk," Faelyn said softly, keeping his eyes forward. "You did write it, after all."

Silence filled the room. It was broken by the soft whistling of the evening winds. Faelyn took a slow breath, listening carefully as the man behind him stared at the letter—the short note that had been addressed to the "Fire King."

"Moments after I read that note, I went to sleep," Faelyn said. "And moments after that, you kidnapped me." Faelyn reached down, kicking his chair to the side. He turned it slowly and painfully, but it was worth it. He wanted to see this man's face as he spoke. "I didn't realize it then, but you revealed what you truly were that night." Faelyn paused. "I didn't even notice that you had addressed me as 'Fire King.' Yet, by stumbling upon it once again, I now have all of the evidence that I need.

"You have been working against me all along," Faelyn continued, his voice low. "Since the moment we first met, your only goal has been to sabotage my city and cause me pain. You facilitated an elaborate plan that ultimately led to my father's demise. Then you framed the Cyfali by carrying out an illusory interrogation—in which you made it sound as if Hallan confessed. I saw the flicker of your illusions flash across Hallan's face as I entered that cell, and I realize now that I killed him before he could explain what had happened." Faelyn spoke slowly, and with carefulness. He was not speaking out of rage, no... *Not yet.*

"But you were just getting started," Faelyn continued, nodding to himself. "You manipulated me into storming Cyfalion, knowing that I would likely destroy one of the Monoliths in a blind rage. You encouraged me to kill Adresin Jastira, thus eliminating yet another of Auris's monarchs." Faelyn stared at the man's ice-blue eyes, watching them for any reaction.

He was yet to show any, for he simply stood there as Faelyn listed off his crimes.

"You once again pretended to be my ally and guided me home from those jungles. Yet, when we reached Arvendon once again, you convinced me that the only way out of this was to surrender. I had thought that you were on our side, and I still did at that point. But you finally gave yourself away last night, during the assault." Faelyn paused, the words dripping from his lips. "You conjured an illusory fleet, drawing our cannons away from the fight, and then Summoned an illusory attack force at the southern end of the city, therefore forcing our hidden ambush crew out from their hiding spots and ruining our plan. And finally, you had the fountain overfilled with Incendiary so that it would obliterate our forces when ignited."

Faelyn took another deep breath. He kept his eyes firm.

"You are almost single-handedly responsible for the destruction of my entire city, and can be blamed for the tens of thousands of lives that were lost in the conflict. Did I miss anything?" Faelyn raised an eyebrow. "I summoned you here tonight bearing both an order and a warning: You, Eithor Vassellet, are to leave Arvendon and never return. I know you are not foolish enough to have come here in your true form, and as a result of that, I have chosen to spare your life," Faelyn said. Even if he had been able to kill Eithor, he wasn't sure if he would have. Killing was something that Eithor would've wanted him to do, and Faelyn was trying to repair the damage that Eithor had done to him. Eithor had made Faelyn into a monstrous killer, and now... Now, Faelyn was trying to change for the better.

He paused, raising his too-short, bandaged arm. A small bolt of flame shot forward, passing through Eithor's figure and leaving a flurry of turquoise frost in its place.

Faelyn nodded to himself. "*But*, if I *ever* see you again, I will personally burn every single inch of your skin, nerve by nerve, until you are begging for the mercy of death. And when I am finally done with you, you will be put in a cell, where you will live out the rest of your miserable life, starved and beaten until you die a slow and painful death." Faelyn paused, his eyes illuminating with bright orange flames as he drew from the Crystals on his nightstand. "Am I clear?"

Eithor remained perfectly still, his illusory figure unmoving. He shifted, turning his eyes to the open window. Eithor had to be somewhere nearby. His true form would be near enough to hear Faelyn's words. Yet the Illusomancer's real body was likely hidden by an illusion, thus making him impossible to find—even if Faelyn had wanted to capture him.

The projection of Eithor turned back to Faelyn. "We suspected that you would catch on sooner or later," Eithor said, his voice low. A slight breeze caused him to raise his gaze once again. It settled on Faelyn after a moment, those lifelike illusory eyes staring right back into him. "I will leave Arvendon, as you have requested, though there is something I wish for you to understand: This will not be the last you see of me, Faelyn Titansworn." Eithor paused, his wrinkled face folding into an indescribable expression. "You may recall your trip to The Highlands several years ago... You may think nothing of it, but you killed my sons that day," Eithor said calmly. "Our paths are forever crossed in this conflict, and whether you accept it or not, the score is not yet settled. We will meet again."

"You'd best be praying that we don't," Faelyn warned, narrowing his eyes. Fires grew at his arms, extending through his body and sprouting a set of bright orange, spectral arms. Hands followed shortly after, and a small swath of flame formed around Eithor's illusory figure—a threat.

Eithor's face twisted again. "Until then, Fire King." His body dissolved into a flurry of turquoise frost, swirling and dancing in the air as it floated toward the window.

Faelyn turned in his chair, silencing his flames and watching the frost twist into the sky. It drifted a little further, then vanished.

Until then.

CHAPTER FORTY-FIVE
WAYFINDER PART II

Castien Varic picked through the rubble. The crimson energy had escaped through the mouth of the cavern—which was smaller than Castien had expected it to be. But despite the departure of the energy, the rocks and shattered Crystals remained.

He lifted another stone, revealing the crushed face of a Blood Sorcerer. Castien recoiled slightly, lowering the stone once again. This mountain had become the final resting place for nearly eighty Blood Sorcerers. Only a small handful had survived—Tsarra among them.

None of them had spoken to the Blood Empress since the fight. She had taken to burying as many of her comrades as she could with the help of the other survivors.

The massacre here left only a handful of Blood Sorcerers on the continent, so far as they could tell. Velarus and his team's whereabouts were still unknown to them... Tsarra would likely tell them when she was ready, but Castien could already assume that they were very far from this cave. Only a fraction of Tsarra's original clan survived, meaning that they now had a significant disadvantage in their fight against the Shadow-Swifts.

They were all but certain that Arthion had been working with the Shadow-Swifts, as it was the only logical explanation for what he did. Castien suspected that Arthion played some part in Avenos's assassination as well, which would explain the confusion between Ilyana and Callum.

"Any more?" Ilyana called from somewhere a few boulders over.

"Just one," Castien said softly, closing his eyes. He synced his heartbeat to his breathing and continued looking through the remains of the mountain. Castien had been using the last few hours to recount what he had learned. Castien had learned the truth behind his heritage—something that he was still yet to face—and the fight with Arthion all but confirmed that Tsarra was telling the truth about the Shadow-Swifts.

It was a sobering realization. The Shadow-Swifts were by far the most powerful of the Sects. *Although*, Castien thought, *now that all fourteen Sects are back in play, who knows which one is the strongest?*

Worst of all, Castien had no idea what his next move was. They could return to Arvendon and try to explain that the man they knew as Arthion had been replaced by a Skin-Shaper at some point a few months ago, and that he had proceeded to trick Ilyana into assassinating the King and eventually went on to wipe out most of the Blood Sorcerers.

Castien snorted. That didn't exactly sound very believable—even though it was true. Regardless, returning to Arvendon seemed to be their only option. They could move to Celes, true, but the city was hardly powerful enough to be considered a true force on Auris.

The unfortunate truth was that Arthion had likely told the Shadow-Swifts when he found the Blood Sorcerers' fortress, which meant that Castien and the others wouldn't be able to stay for long. Castien wanted to be long gone if one of the Shadow-Swifts came to finish the job.

"Castien! Ilyana!" Luka shouted from across the cave.

Castien turned, Ilyana appearing from around the corner of a fallen rock.

They shared a look, a strange connection still binding him.

That feeling hadn't gone away. Whatever it was that he felt when she rescued him in that chamber was still there.

He could still feel the words getting caught in his throat.

"What is it?" Ilyana asked, breaking the moment.

"Come to the entrance," Luka said. "I think the sun is rising."

Castien and Ilyana shared another glance, then turned toward the distant cave entrance.

"You holding up okay?" Ilyana asked, walking alongside him as they wove through the fallen rubble.

"Yeah," Castien said, his voice soft.

"I know Elric meant a lot to you," Ilyana started. "I promise that we'll look for him but... After what Arthion did, I fear the odds aren't in our favor."

"I know," Castien whispered. He could feel Ilyana's eyes on him. Castien blinked, keeping his emotions in check. He took a deep, shaky breath, syncing his heart and lungs once again. "But Arthion's dead now, so if he did... kill Elric, then at least justice has been served."

"Did you know that Arthion was a Skin-Shaper?" Ilyana asked, sidestepping a stone.

"I had no idea," Castien said, shaking his head. "I started to grow suspicious toward the end—when he refused to use his powers. But I guess I didn't think it was because he was a Skin-Shaper."

"So I suppose it was him who replaced Callum and told me to kill Avenos, then," Ilyana said. She shook her head. "Who knows how long he's been sabotaging Auris."

"I still don't fully understand why the Shadow-Swifts are doing all of this," Castien said.

"Neither do I." Ilyana shook her head. "But we'll get to the bottom of this, together."

"Yeah," Castien said, his voice sounding distant. He cursed himself for not knowing what to say.

"Luka, what is it?" Ilyana called as they passed by another massive, broken Crystal. The shards were spread all throughout the small area of impact, the dull red coloration looking pitiful.

Castien looked over his shoulder, hearing footsteps behind him.

Tsarra jogged toward them, catching up. She slowed beside them, not saying a word.

Castien stole a glance at her haunted eyes, then instantly regretted it. She bore the look of someone who had lost everything—because she *had* lost everything.

"Over here," Luka said from around the corner.

Castien peered across the small part of the cavern that they had left, noticing that Luka was standing in the mouth of the cave. The ceiling was lower here, and the walls began to close in around the eventual opening around the corner.

He could practically feel the twisting flood of red energy that had flown through this area, escaping the night before. It was finally dawn now. He stepped into the smaller passage that led to the entrance, joining Luka. Castien took the lead, Ilyana and Tsarra slightly behind him as they took the small steps to the entrance. Something about Luka's expression was... off, though.

Turning the corner, Castien realized why Luka had called them over.

Stepping up to the mouth of the cave, Castien paused.

Ilyana stopped next to him, cursing. The entrance faced east, giving them a perfect view of the sunrise... and how *wrong* it was.

A red haze hung over the sky, turning the sun a bright scarlet. Red mists blanketed The Highlands, rising and falling like the fog of a Mistveil—only this was different. These mists were thicker, with seemingly more water and substance... And they flowed almost like... *blood.*

Castien stepped forward, his boots crunching on the snow. He reached out a hand as a swath of mist passed. It floated through his hand, dampening his glove and leaving it slightly red. He turned back, his attention settling on the scarlet sun that was slowly rising over the mountains.

A new Tempest, he thought. *Not something you see every day.*

"The Scarlet Sky," a voice said.

Castien cursed, stumbling back as two figures floated down from the air above.

Luka drew his blade, as did Ilyana. They were without their Crystals now, though they were still dangerous warriors.

Tsarra only watched, dejected.

Castien jumped back, standing before Luka, Ilyana, and Tsarra as he faced the two figures levitating before them. They landed softly on the ground, and let the red mists wash over them.

The first wore white wrappings, almost coming together to form a robe. They covered his face, leaving only a small opening for his eyes. He pulled down his hood, revealing a bald head and strangely smooth skin. His gold-brown eyes sparkled in the red sun as he turned to Castien and smiled. A faint, yellow-gold glow came from a pouch in his wrappings. *Crystals?*

"Despite my foresight, I still find myself in awe of the reborn Tempest," the man in the white wrappings said. His clothing was already stained a faint red by the scarlet mists. He approached, holding his hands up to show that he bore no weapons. "You have no need to fear us. We come only to offer our assistance."

"He..." Luka started. "That's a Shadow-Swift." He pointed at the man standing beside the white-wrapped figure.

The other man wore a white cloak over black armor, coalesced with strange mists of darkness.

Castien's heart dropped. Tsarra had said that the Shadow-Swifts were behind all of this—and there was a Shadow-Swift right in front of him.

"He is," the white-wrapped man said calmly.

"Which means that you and your kind are responsible for all of this," Ilyana said through gritted teeth, motioning to the mountain.

"You are mistaken, Ilyana," the man said.

Castien gasped. *The yellow Crystals in his wrappings... Wayfinder Crystals?*

"How do you know my name?" Ilyana growled, her voice rough.

"A Wayfinder always knows," the man said.

Ilyana shared a glance with Luka. They nodded to one another. It didn't take long for Castien to follow their thought process. A Shadow-Swift and a Wayfinder—both of whom had done nothing to prevent the massacre of the Blood Sorcerers, despite seemingly knowing about it.

Ilyana turned, and then charged.

The other man—the Shadow-Swift—drew his blade.

The Wayfinder placed a hand on the Shadow-Swift's chest, motioning for him to remain still.

"Allow me, Keries," the Wayfinder said. He advanced, his steps smooth and fluid... almost like he was floating.

Ilyana swung, her butterfly-blade slicing diagonally through the air, making to cut across the Wayfinder's face.

The Wayfinder raised both hands, his eyes calm.

The blade stopped.

Ilyana gasped.

A faint golden glow emanated from the Wayfinder's hands, coating the covered skin where he held the blade.

"Only a Wayfinder possesses abilities like this," the man said, his voice even. He looked Ilyana in the eyes. "We are not here to hurt you; we are only here to help... both you and the Blood Sorcerers."

"Well, you're about eight hours too late," Ilyana said sharply, lowering her blade.

The golden glow faded from the man's hands. "I know," the man said, coming to a stop. His soft eyes grew distant. "We knew we would arrive too late to save them, no matter what we did."

"How did you know we were here?" Luka advanced.

The man smiled once again and paced closer. He waved the Shadow-Swift over as well. "I suppose I should introduce myself," the man said. "I apologize for not doing so earlier, but I have grown to know the four of you so well... I sometimes forget that you do not yet know me."

"What are you talking about?" Ilyana demanded.

"My name is Enzo," the man in the white wrappings said. He motioned back to the Shadow-Swift. "And this... This is Keries." Enzo turned back to the four of them.

Castien opened his mouth.

"Don't worry, Castien. I already know your name." Enzo winked again.

Castien frowned. *A Wayfinder indeed... Niventia's Light.*

"We have much to discuss," Enzo said, motioning toward the mouth of the cave. "Shall we?"

No one moved.

Tsarra stepped forward. "Keries can be trusted," she said softly. "He should be dead... But we can trust him. He isn't with the rest of the Shadow-Swifts."

"Thank you, Tsarra." The Shadow-Swift—Keries—nodded. "It's good to see you again."

Tsarra nodded back. She turned to Luka, Ilyana and Castien. "We might as well see what they have to say. Besides, it's not like we have a lot of options right now."

Luka and Ilyana hesitantly backed toward the cave.

Enzo advanced, following calmly.

They kept their blades drawn, though Enzo hardly paid them any mind.

The Wayfinder looked down, examining his damp clothing. It was still stained a slight red, even as Enzo entered the cave.

Keries stayed silent and followed Enzo without a word.

I've never seen such a docile Shadow-Swift, Castien thought, following behind them.

"Tsarra," Enzo said as he approached the Blood Empress. "I would like to offer my sincerest apologies. You have sacrificed much for our cause without even knowing it, and I will do everything in my power to ensure that your efforts do not go to waste." He paused, turning to the rest of them. "I suppose I should start by explaining how I found you," Enzo began as they walked. "I am a Wayfinder, and I was led here by my visions of the future."

Castien turned sideways, observing him.

"As your friend said, Keries can be trusted," Enzo said. "Though I must warn you, the rest of Auris's Shadow-Swifts are not on our side."

"*Our* side?" Luka asked, his grip on his blade tightening.

"Yes," Enzo said. "Our side. My order has been working to stop the Shadow-Swifts for many months now," Enzo continued as they turned the corner of the cavern. They entered the grand atrium, where the jagged mess of rubble and corpses lay quietly. "Though clearly, we have thus far been unsuccessful."

"If you've had a Shadow-Swift on your side all this time, then why are we only just now seeing you?" Luka asked.

"Keries was in Arvendon the night of Avenos's assassination. He did what he could to prevent the King's death, but another Shadow-Swift interfered," Enzo answered.

Castien looked to Ilyana. *She did say she saw two Shadow-Swifts that night.*

"I am aware that isn't enough proof for you to believe that we are all allies here, but I have something that might change your mind," Enzo said. He started unwrapping a section of his robes.

Luka and Ilyana held their weapons tighter, flinching.

Enzo reached into his pockets and pulled out two Crystals. One was a Dexteris Crystal, and the other a Cryostalker Crystal.

"I offer these to you as a show of my allegiance," Enzo said. "I know that you have lost your Crystals due to the recent... *conflict.* But I have come bearing a new set for you, should you choose to accept my help."

"A set? Where are the rest?" Luka asked, taking the Cryostalker Crystal and staring at it. His eyes seemed to glow as he held it.

"There are a dozen of each in a small cache a few miles from here

—which I will lead you to *after* you agree to let us help each other," Enzo said, rewrapping his clothing.

Ilyana, Castien, and Luka stared at each other for several seconds, as if trying to gauge one another's reactions to the proposal.

Castien stepped forward. *It's time for me to make my own decisions.* "We are listening," Castien said firmly.

Enzo smiled, then blinked a few times. His face fell, his eyes growing slightly distant. He looked around again, surveying their surroundings. His smile returned to his strangely smooth face.

"My apologies," Enzo said, looking each of them in the eye. "My Splinter ended here. I am just as ignorant to the rest of this conversation as you are now." Enzo motioned to the room around them. "I don't suppose you could tell me what happened here? I was able to gather that the Blood Sorcerers were largely destroyed, and that their Crystals have been broken, but I was not able to discover how."

"You first," Ilyana said. "You said something about the new Tempest. What do you know about it?"

"The Scarlet Sky," Enzo said. "It is the lost—or formerly lost—Tempest of the Blood Sorcerers." He paused, as if waiting for a reaction.

If the Blood Sorcerers had a Tempest, then... "So every Lost Sect truly does have a Tempest," Castien breathed.

"Indeed." Enzo nodded, confirming his suspicions.

"Calida's Claws..." Luka cursed.

"The Tempests have been here since the dawn of Auris," Enzo said. "The notion that they arrived with the Vanishing was a fabrication created by the Revenants and Shadow-Swifts—who were responsible for the Vanishing in the first place."

Castien nodded slowly. "I think Tsarra started to tell me as much, just before the attack."

"The Vanishing, from what my Sect can gather, was brought upon us by a group of Revenants who intended to erase the other Sects," Enzo continued. "They were led to some sort of artifact—one that somehow captures the energies of Summoning. This artifact pulled the Tempests from the skies and even from the very Crystals in which they were held. It then displaced them, hiding the energies in the mountains near the artifact. These mountains are spread throughout The Highlands... With one of them being the mountain we stand in now." Enzo paused. "My Sect was the first to return, as my ancestors had discovered the location of our stolen energies before the Vanishing even began through our Divination... Thus allowing us to retake our Crystals within a few days.

"Yet something has changed," Enzo continued. "There was a... *force* keeping the energies trapped, but that force has since been weakened. It allowed the Blood Sorcerers to find their mountain, and I suspect that it will soon lead you to yours," Enzo said to Castien.

"What do you know about the return of the Skin-Shapers?" Ilyana interrupted.

"Skin-Shapers?" Enzo raised an eyebrow. He turned past the maze of boulders. "There was one here, wasn't there?" He looked back, surveying their reactions. "Interesting... In all of our Splinters, there was never a Skin-Shaper with the Shadow-Swifts."

"That's probably because Castien killed it yesterday," Luka said. He gave Castien a nod.

"Ah," Enzo said, nodding. "Yes, that would explain it."

"I have a question," Castien said, stepping forward once again.

"Go ahead, dear boy." Enzo smiled.

Keries stared at him curiously, as if he were a scholar studying a subject.

Castien shifted uncomfortably beneath his gaze. "Why did the Shadow-Swifts want to destroy the Blood Sorcerers? Why are they doing all of this?" Castien asked.

Enzo turned to Keries.

"I don't know," Keries said softly. He turned to Castien. "I defected from my order before the Resurgence had fully begun, and —at least during my time with them—no one mentioned the Blood Sorcerers."

"The Blood Sorcerers have long been an enemy of the Shadow-

Swifts and Revenants," Enzo said. "I can only surmise that Tsarra's order was deemed a threat to the Shadow-Swifts' plan, which is why Lucien sent someone to destroy them.

"What's more, from what I can gather, the Shadow-Swifts believe that my Sect is the root of Auris's struggles," Enzo continued. "They believe that the Wayfinders have control over the future, and that we have robbed Auris of its free will... This is incorrect, for while we can *see* events that have not yet come to pass, we have no control over them." Enzo paused. "Though our adversaries seem to have trouble believing that."

"You said a name..." Ilyana raised an eyebrow. "Who's Lucien?"

"The leader of the Shadow-Swifts," Enzo said. "He's Elosian... much like yourself."

"Though he wasn't always our leader," Keries said quietly. "Our former master, Asteros, has vanished. I've been looking for signs of his presence across Auris, but I've found nothing."

"So, the Shadow-Swifts truly are behind all of this," Castien said softly. "Tsarra knew this," Castien said, looking to the Blood Empress.

She remained silent, her mournful gaze unfocused.

Enzo sighed. "There is something beyond any of us involved here... There are *much* greater forces at play."

"What do you mean?" Castien advanced.

Enzo turned back to him, meeting his eyes. "There is yet another... force, of some kind," Enzo said. "Something that changes our future so radically that even I have trouble looking ahead at times—and it may be related to the force that was behind the Vanishing." Enzo paused. "This force is something that changes people—corrupts them. I do not know how it works, nor what it is, but this much is clear: Any who come in contact with it have the most terrible parts of their souls brought to the surface. Whether you really do trust me or not, this force must be stopped... I suspect it is related to Izara's return—she may even be behind it—though I do not know for certain."

"Wait," Castien started.

"Did you say... *Izara*?" Ilyana breathed.

"As in... the Goddess?" Castien finished. "You're saying that she's real?"

"Oh, my friends..." Enzo grinned. "You didn't think that the Six Gods of Auris were just myths, did you?"

A stunned silence fell over the group.

"The Six Gods of our world are more than just smoke and mirrors. They are as real as you and I... And I fear that they are making themselves heard in our Realms once again," Enzo said.

"What do you mean?" Luka asked.

"The Gods watch over Auris, but they do not live on this plane of reality," Enzo said, his voice low. "They are from a distant land, one known as Katauriel."

"But..." Castien breathed, at a loss.

"The Gods have descended from Katauriel once before, in the distant past." Enzo fell silent, staring at each of them individually. "Either way, our course of action is clear."

"*What?*" Ilyana stepped forward. "You just told us that the Gods are real, and now you expect us to think—"

"The Gods are powerful, but the four of you have the potential to gain enough power to match them," Enzo said. "Though I must warn you, the powers of the Harbingers will not be easy to find."

Castien's jaw dropped. He blinked, his eyes fixed on Enzo.

"Harbingers are not singular people," Enzo said. "Harbingers are better described as transferrable powers, rather than individuals... Meaning that once the current carrier of a power dies, that power can be claimed by another of their Sect." Enzo paused. "I have had several Splinters of an event in the Blazing Circlet, on the Southern coast of Auris. As I understand it, most of the former Harbingers' Sepulchers are there—or at least the ones that we need.

"Our adversaries will have Izara on their side," Enzo continued. "It would be beneficial to have a Harbinger fighting for us as well."

"But…" Castien breathed. "The Blazing Circlet is on the other side of the continent."

"I know," Enzo said softly. "The journey will not be easy, and it will not be quick, but it is a trip that you must make." Enzo paused again, his eyes growing distant. "The four of you have a great task ahead of you, and I am afraid that I will not be of much help. I will assist you where I can, but my knowledge is needed elsewhere… There is but one who can help you: a girl with bright orange eyes that shine like embers. Without her, I fear none of you will become Harbingers.

"I know that this is a lot to take in," Enzo continued. "But trust me when I say that it is all *absolutely* necessary." He paused, once again meeting each of their eyes.

"Why should we listen to you?" Castien asked. "Do you expect us to do all of this just because you told us to?"

"A fair question." Enzo nodded. "But the way I see it, whether you believe me or not, your course of action would be the same. I intend to point you, Castien, toward the Starburner mountain so that you may regain your powers—something that will benefit you regardless of who you align with. And now that you all know of the Harbingers' powers in the Blazing Circlet, you will head there either way, will you not?"

They fell silent.

"The world is falling into chaos," Enzo continued. "The four of you are undoubtedly searching for direction, and that is what I am offering. Now, why don't you start by telling me how this Skin-Shaper destroyed almost an entire Sect, hm?"

Castien Varic stood quietly, watching as the red sun fell behind the horizon, ending the Scarlet Sky's first appearance in centuries. He closed his eyes, feeling the red mists dissipate.

The last few days had been... a lot. Starting with his capture, and now ending with the flood of knowledge that Enzo had imparted. It seemed that, in Castien's random misfortune, he had ended up in the middle of a rising war between the Gods themselves. Not only that, but he was apparently meant to be a key player.

It didn't seem right. He was Castien Varic, a Stormless from a family of innkeepers. He had no place in this conflict. He had no place among the company of Summoners such as these.

Castien took a deep breath, watching the radiant lights of the northern sky come out as the day waned. He blinked a few times, remembering that Elric was still missing—not necessarily dead. Castien would look for the Cloudwalker. He wasn't sure where Elric had gone, or what Arthion had done to him, but Castien would try to find him.

Arvendon had likely fallen. Enzo had told them that several armies had attacked the city at the Shadow-Swifts' direction. By now it had almost certainly been destroyed, leaving the world without its greatest capital. Who knew how many soldiers were lost on both sides of the conflict, leaving Auris's forces severely weakened against the rising threat.

He understood the tactics of the Shadow-Swifts now. They were turning Auris against itself, causing chaos and destruction so that no one would ever think to turn a blade in their direction.

The Shadow-Swifts were growing stronger with each passing day, and they were likely coming closer to uncovering the powers of their own Harbinger.

That was something that Castien still had trouble processing. The Harbingers' powers were not limited to the person who carried them. If the carrier died, another of their Sect could claim the power for themselves. Castien had always thought that the Harbingers were ancient demi-gods of the past who would never come into play again, yet he was wrong—just as he and the rest of the world had been wrong about the temple of Elan Taesi and the Wispwinds. What they had assumed was a small temple of devout Navesians was actually the sanctuary of the Wayfinders, and what they had assumed was a useless Tempest was the secret Sect's source of power.

Castien was beginning to learn something as he put all of the pieces of this puzzle together. Between Arthion's lack of Whispering, the presence of two Shadow-Swifts at the Solstice, and now the discovery that Elan Taesi and the Wispwinds were not as they seemed, Castien was realizing that this world was far more complicated than he had assumed.

This, coupled with the discovery that the Gods were real and that they lived in an entirely different Realm, led Castien to even more questions.

Because if they now knew that the Gods were real... did that even make them Gods at all? When one finds confirmation of a deity, does their divine power lose some of its influence? With the knowledge that the Gods had some shred of mortality, Castien no longer feared that his every action was being watched. If this knowledge spread to the rest of the world, chaos would ensue.

Navesians and atheists alike spent their lives searching for proof —or lack thereof—of the Gods. Now that there was proof, what would become of these beliefs?

Perhaps the point of religions, and of the concept of Gods themselves, was that there *was* no proof. For, if such things were confirmed, they would no longer be considered religious; they would merely be a fact of the universe.

Was there some other force above all of it? Castien had inquired about the Afterworld—given that Enzo had confirmed Izara's existence. Yet even Enzo had said that he had no knowledge of such a place. Castien, for the first time in his life, was finding comfort in the unknown.

Enzo's Wayfinding implied that they were on a set path... that their future was predetermined. But he had said that free will did still exist, despite saying that *everything* that he saw eventually came to pass, no matter what. Even more curiously, Enzo insisted on only telling them what they needed to know about their own futures. He claimed that if he told them more, they would risk tampering with the fundamental forces that made up the Realms themselves.

Castien rubbed his temples, syncing his heartbeat to his breathing. His brain could hardly handle these sorts of thoughts. What was clear was that they needed to travel south, and that he needed to somehow unlock his powers along the way. Enzo had said the Starburner mountain was several miles to the south of the Blood Sorcerer mountain. Yet Castien was well aware that finding his mountain and figuring out how to use his powers were two very different things. How, exactly, Castien would learn to Summon, he didn't know. But it needed to be done, one way or another.

Castien heard the soft crunch of snow behind him as someone approached. He listened carefully to the pace—a pace he now knew by heart.

Ilyana stopped beside him, leaning against the side of the cave. She said nothing for several moments, simply standing there with him.

Castien suddenly became very aware of his hands. He felt tempted to reach out to Ilyana. He looked back, trying to read her face. Even now, it was sometimes hard to tell what the Elosian was thinking.

She stared out at the mountains, watching silently.

Castien followed her gaze, turning back to the mouth of the cave.

The red mists had now fully disappeared, leaving nothing but the ordinary silence of dusk in their wake. The darkness was growing with each passing second, and with it, the lights of the mountain sky grew brighter.

Stars began to appear, materializing as if out of nothing in the vast black sky. Castien stared, watching the stars pierce through the heavens above.

Ilyana snickered, shaking her head.

"What are you laughing at?" Castien asked, his voice soft and light.

Ilyana laughed again. "It's just funny, you know?" Ilyana said, stepping out. "We're still alive."

"What do you mean?"

"Think of all that's happened these past few weeks," Ilyana said. "The expedition, the assassination, the journey to Celes, and then everything that's happened here in The Highlands... It's a miracle we're still here, honestly."

"And you find this funny?" Castien cracked a smile.

"It's just kind of strange, I guess," Ilyana said. "Do you think it's just luck that we're still here?"

Castien closed his eyes. "I'm really not sure at this point." He wasn't surprised that *she* had survived all of this. As far as himself? That was a shock. But Ilyana? The woman before him was something unlike anything he had ever seen. Ilyana was intelligent, cunning, and wise. And her soul somehow held more layers than he ever thought possible for a single human being.

He had watched her go from a narcissistic, snobby undercover spy to a bloodthirsty assassin. And from that, he had seen her transform into a haunted, guilt-ridden criminal, and finally into... something else.

Someone he trusted.

Someone he cared about.

"We have a lot ahead of us," Castien said after a moment. "It won't be easy."

"No, it won't."

"Even Enzo doesn't *really* know how to open the Sepulchers."

"I know," Ilyana said.

The darkness grew stronger, waves of green and blue shimmering above as night fell.

"It's going to get pretty rough out there," she said. "You sure you're ready for this?"

"I'm sure," Castien said, letting his eyes settle on her face. "We've made it this far, haven't we?"

"If we stick together, I think we can make it a hell of a lot further too," Ilyana said, smirking. "And lucky for you, I don't plan on going anywhere." She winked.

Castien smiled. "Neither do I."

Luka, Tsarra, and Keries would be inside with Enzo, plotting their next moves. The world's Summoners and Stormless alike would be panicking at the arrival of the Scarlet Sky. And the Shadow-Swifts would be putting their plans into action, one step at a time.

Yet, in that moment, none of it mattered. Despite all the horrors and wars that lay ahead, Castien was not afraid. There was nothing he and Ilyana couldn't do so long as they were together—and they *were* together.

And finally, Castien realized something. Standing here, watching the stars come out far above, he felt something come over him. It was a sensation he hadn't felt in years... For the first time in a *very* long time, Castien was happy.

EPILOGUE

Waves washed against the shore, running up the sandy beach like nrekuma across The Wastelands. Stars shined brightly overhead, their wondrous radiance illuminating the night sky. Lotius and Oria twinkled above, looming like a pair of celestial eyes, watching over Auris.

Faelyn Titansworn sat in his chair, breathing in the cool, wet air of the Salarin Sea. His father had come down to the shore whenever everything became... too much.

He felt mildly sorry for the quartet of attendants that he had tasked with carrying him all the way down from the Palace, but he shrugged off his guilt. He planned on staying here for much of the night, and he doubted that the servants would mind spending a few hours lounging on the beach.

The steady beat of the waves washing against the sand made for a calming melody. The quiet hum of the night accompanied it, coupling with Faelyn's heartbeat to forge what Faelyn believed was the sound of life itself.

His breathing slowed, a yawn coming over him.

One large battle and thousands of deaths later, and he was still here. Now an orphan, and a disgraced King with a tarnished reputation. Eithor had been rather effective in ruining his life, though now that Faelyn knew his motivations, everything made a bit more sense.

None of it mattered anymore though. Eithor was gone. He claimed that they would cross paths again, and if they did... Faelyn would be ready. Even now, he realized that he had let the Illusomancer off easy, but perhaps that was the point.

Had he killed Eithor, he would've just added another name to the list of those whom he had murdered. The satisfaction would've been brief and fleeting. Niventia's Light, it would've been completely gone by the time he finished disposing of the corpse.

He did not regret his decision, though he did wish that he could know where Eithor had gone. He was still dangerous, and keeping tabs on him wouldn't have been the worst idea.

Turning his head to the right, Faelyn's eyes settled on the bright glow of Summerglass Palace. It was still standing. Despite the Solstice and the assault of three armies, it was still standing. His city had not fallen, against all odds. And the foe who had set all of this into motion had returned to save them. It was poetic, in a strange way. Velarus had demanded control of the city, and Surge had agreed to co-lead Arvendon with the Blood Sorcerer.

The ward was severely weakened, and it would only be a matter of time before a Storm Gale or Cyclone blew in. But that was a problem for tomorrow. Surge and Velarus were devising plans to ensure that the Arvendi survived, and hopefully at least one of their ideas would work.

Six weeks had changed Faelyn's life in immeasurable ways. While there were a great many things that he wished he could change, he was at peace with the way things had happened. Overcoming grief and regret was not about becoming indifferent toward the tragedies, but instead learning to accept what had happened. Faelyn knew that he would be mourning the loss of his father for the rest of his life. And he knew that the weight of thousands of dead

Arvendi soldiers would be pressing upon his conscience until his final days.

But he accepted these things. He had made mistakes, and that was okay. Of course, he wished that those events had never come to pass, but who was he to demand that such actions be undone? Besides, acceptance was not about longing for what could have been, but growing to appreciate that which you still have.

The sister moons reflected off the waves of the ocean, shining into Faelyn's tired eyes. Something passed over their reflection, blocking them.

Faelyn tilted his head, leaning forward slightly. It passed, and the reflections returned. *Curious.*

It appeared again, resurfacing closer to the shore. Faelyn started, squinting through the night. Something was floating in the water, and it was nearing the shore.

It appeared to be a piece of driftwood, perhaps from a distant ship, but he couldn't be certain. Faelyn made to scoot himself forward, then realized that his chair was sitting on sand. He whistled, then waved two of the attendants forward to carry his chair to the edge of the beach.

The tired servants stepped up and got into position. Faelyn sat back as his chair was lifted and carried the short distance down the water, bringing him to the sea's edge.

"Do you see that?" Faelyn asked as they set him down. He pointed forward with his right nub.

The servants stepped to his side, squinting.

The lump in the water disappeared.

"See what, Your Majesty?" One of the servants stepped farther forward, still squinting.

Faelyn fell silent, staring into the black waters of the ocean.

Water sloshed as something moved toward the shore. One of the attendants cursed, jumping back. A particularly strong wave pushed forward, driving up the beach and almost soaking Faelyn's chair.

The wave receded, leaving in its place a limp, humanoid figure. That mass wasn't a piece of driftwood. It was a *person.*

"Tarathiel's Stones! Help them!" Faelyn cursed. The servants rushed forward, grabbing the person's dark, wet cloak and pulling them up the beach. They pulled the man to Faelyn's feet, only for him to realize that it was not a man at all, but a woman.

Barely older than me.

Faelyn gasped at the paleness of the woman's skin, and the youth in her features. It was then that he realized she was likely dying.

"Save her!" Faelyn commanded.

One of the servants leaned down and started pressing on her chest. He periodically pressed his mouth against hers, blowing air deep into her lungs.

Faelyn watched, a strange sense of both anticipation and fear in his chest. An ashen breath passed over him. He watched as the seconds ticked by.

The attendant held strong, continuing to try and save the woman.

Is she from Freyfall? Faelyn wondered, noticing her black cloak. But no, there were hints of brown in the cloak, though it appeared black from the water. The closer he looked, the more he realized that her clothing was unlike anything he had ever seen.

The woman gasped for air, her eyes flying open. She lurched forward, coughing up more water than she had any right to take in, taking a large breath and then falling back to the sand.

"Calida's Claws," Faelyn cursed, leaning over her as the attendants backed away. "Are you alright?"

She coughed a few times, then laid her head back into the sand again. She closed her eyes, groaning.

"I'm alive," she grunted. Her words were stunted slightly. She had an accent, yet Faelyn couldn't place where it was from. She opened her eyes again, turning them toward the ocean. "Where... Where am I?"

"You're on the shores of Arvendon," Faelyn said softly. "You washed up—coming straight from the ocean." Faelyn watched her reaction carefully.

She laid her head back, groaning.

"How did you end up here?" Faelyn asked.

The woman's eyes stayed shut. "I don't remember," she said.

Great, Faelyn thought. "What do you remember?" Faelyn asked, studying her.

"Not much," the woman said, her eyes cracking open once again.

"Hmmm," Faelyn grunted. "Either way, we need to get you to a doctor. Do you think you can walk?" Faelyn tilted his head.

The woman nodded slightly.

"Good, then follow if you can. The servants can aid you if necessary."

"Wait," the woman said, slowly sitting up. She coughed again, little spurts of water coming from her mouth. She turned to him. "Who are you?"

Faelyn met her eyes. "I am King Faelyn Titansworn," he said. Then he lowered his head. "Or at least, I was."

"I'm Maven," she said, rising to her feet. She extended her hand. Her gaze settled on Faelyn's wheelchair. She blinked a few times, stepping back.

At least she remembers her name. Faelyn studied the woman's face, taking in her odd clothing and pale skin. Yet the most curious thing about her was not her cloak, or her face, but her eyes.

They were not of an ordinary color. While most people's eyes were some shade of brown or blue, hers were a bright, almost radiant orange. Almost like...

Embers.

<u>To Be Continued...</u>

REFERENCE GUIDE

TEMPESTS

Auris does not experience ordinary weather patterns... Instead, there is a collection of seven Tempests that blow across the land (switching daily) dominating the sky and dictating many aspects of life on the continent. The Tempests are deadly, violent storms, and most will not survive if caught in one unprotected. Due to this, roughly a thousand years before our story begins, one of the Lost Sects known as the Rune-Writers created wards to dampen the effects of the Tempests. These wards cover only a small portion of Auris, and all of the continent's cities have been built within their protection. However, the Tempests do not come without their advantages... Each Tempest (save for one) serves to recharge the Crystals of one of the Sects. The Tempests are listed below.

- **BLAZEDAYS:** Blazedays are the warmest of the Tempests, and are characterized by intense heat, a blinding sun, and the presence of sunbeams.

- **CYCLONES:** Similar to Cyclones in our Realm, Cyclones on Auris are dangerous windstorms that consist of breezes and gusts strong enough to knock many off their feet.
- **FROSTFALLS:** While similar to snowfalls in our Realm, Frostfalls can range from violent blizzards to light ice-rains.
- **MISTVEILS:** Mistveils are a form of *very* heavy fog in which many are unable to see more than a few feet in front of themselves.
- **SLICK-DAYS:** Slick-Days are a mixture of moderate rain and high winds, leading to many surfaces becoming "slick."
- **STORM GALES:** Storm Gales are rather similar to thunderstorms in our Realm, though Storm Gales are far more dangerous. They consist of powerful winds, heavy rain, and frequent lightning strikes.
- **WISPWINDS:** Wispwinds are the only one of the seven Tempests that does not recharge a Sect's Crystals. These are characterized by swarming (yet harmless) orbs of white energy with thick, immaterial tails. Visibility is drastically reduced on these days, though the Wisps cause no harm to people or animals.

THE SEVEN SECTS OF AURIS

Auris has ordinary humans—called Stormless—though the land is also inhabited by Summoners, humans who possess magical abilities. Summoning is passed on genetically, with the potency of each parent's bloodline dictating the Sect that the child will belong to as well as how powerful they will be. Though two parents could be of different Sects, their offspring will only possess one Sect's powers (usually whichever Sect runs more strongly in one's blood).

Each Sect was founded by one of the Ancient Harbingers. The Harbingers were Ancient beings from the Planes of Genesis who came to Auris bearing the gifts of Summoning. These demigods held incredible power, and were responsible for founding each of their individual Sects.

All Summoners gain their power from Crystals, which they typically carry with them. These Crystals serve as vessels of the power offered to Auris by the Tempests, and are capable of absorbing the energy released by the Tempests and allowing Summoners to use said energy to power their abilities. These Crystals grow outside of the wards, though only very rarely. They refill slowly, over the course of the day. They also transfer one Tempest's energy into a usable form for Summoners, as Summoners cannot draw power directly from the Tempests themselves. The Sects, their abilities, and their corresponding Tempests are listed below.

- **CLOUDWALKERS:** Telekinesis, Wind Shaping, Flight - Cyclones
- **CRYOSTALKERS:** Cryokinesis, Greater Weapon Conjuration - Frostfalls
- **DEXTERIS:** Enhanced Physical Speed, Reaction Time, Strength, and Coordination - Slick-Days
- **SCORCHERS:** Pyrokinesis, Lesser Weapon Conjuration - Blazedays
- **SHADOW-SWIFTS:** Umbrakinesis (Ability to Manipulate Darkness), Transcendence (Ability to temporarily remove themselves from their current Realm, transporting themselves to an underlying one) - ???
- **VOLTARIANS:** Electrokinesis, Storm Conjuration (On a small scale) - Storm Gales
- **WHISPERERS:** Limited Thought Reading, Emotional Manipulation - Mistveils

THE EIGHT LOST SECTS

Around a millennia ago, eight of the fifteen original Sects disappeared alongside the arrival of the Tempests in an event known as "the Vanishing" for unknown reasons. The eight Lost Sects were known to be extraordinarily powerful, even when compared to the seven remaining Sects. The eight Lost Sects are listed below.

- **BLOOD SORCERERS:** Sanguimancy (Blood Manipulation), Corporikinesis (Control over one's own body, and others)
- **ILLUSOMANCERS:** Hallucikinesis (Ability to create and control illusions)
- **REVENANTS:** Unbinding, Necromancy, Tainted Umbrakinesis, Greater Weapon Conjuration
- **RUNE-WRITERS:** Rune-Writing (The ability to imbue written letters with divine power that can serve various purposes, such as locking, warding, trapping, etc.)
- **SKIN-SHAPERS:** Shapeshifting
- **STARBURNERS:** Dynamokinesis (Energy Manipulation), Lumokinesis (Light Manipulation), Starfire Summoning
- **STONEMASTERS:** Terrakinesis (Ability to control most elements of the earth, including rocks and the ground itself)
- **WAYFINDERS:** Divination (Ability to predict the future), Very Limited Dynamokinesis

GLOSSARY

ARVENDON: Capital of Etherus

ASARI: Country in the Southwest of Auris

ASHOS: Volcanic island in the middle of The Archipelago

AURIS: Continent where most of the story takes place

AYRIA: Small city in the South of Asari

BAREHOLDE: Mountain in The Highlands

BLAZECREST: A medium-sized flying creature famous for its ability to ignite its own feathers

CALIDA: The Goddess of deception and transformation

CELES: Capital of Elos

CLOUDCATCHERS: Siege weapons capable of shooting large, weighted nets to bring down Cloudwalkers

CRYSTALS: Vessels of power that absorb and transform energy from the Tempests into usable energy for Summoners

CYFALION: Capital of Jaskye

DESERTSPINES: A plant with a sharp outer shell, and a sweet fruit inside native to Asari - edible

DIVEBRISKS: A species of fish native to the Salarin Sea, these fish tend to leap from the water and flash their reflective wing-like scales before diving back into the ocean

DUNESAILS: A new, revolutionary vehicle created in Suchara to make crossing the Dunes of Despair easier.

ELAN TAESI: Island-sanctuary of reclusive Navesian monks

ELOS: Country in the northeast of Auris

ERYDON: Shadow-Swift fortress in The Highlands

ETHERUS: Central country of Auris

FIRESNUFFERS: Arvendi device operated by Cloudwalkers used to extinguish or redirect incoming flames

FREYFALL: Capital of Utrya

GOLDENLEAF: Small town in southeast Etherus

GREENBRANCHES: Trees native to Jaskye

GREENVINES: Rapidly growing vines native to Jaskye... They often grow on Greenbranches

GREYFUR: A four-eyed, four-legged predator native to the North. Its thick, gray fur protects it from the bitter cold of the Ice Fields

HARBINGERS: Ancient Summoners of Divine Power who came from the Planes of Genesis, bringing magic to Auris. Each of the fifteen founded a Sect, passing on their gifts before returning to Genesis

HELIONN: The God of the sun

HERQEN: Mountain in The Highlands

HIRANE: Small city in southern Utrya

HYTHE: Small town in northwest Etherus, on the border of The Highlands

ICE-BLADE: Commonly conjured weapon of Cryostalkers

ICEBLOOMS: Plant grown in northern Auris - edible

INCENDIARY: A flammable mixture of liquids used as fuel for most lamps and torches

INCENDIARY CANNONS: Powerful weapons capable of shooting flaming hunks of metal toward targets

IZARA: The Goddess of death, darkness, and decay

JASKYE: Country in the Southeast of Auris

KRELLIN: A twelve-legged insect with a hard shell... they are very common in the Northern part of Auris

LESSER SUMMONER: A half-blooded Summoner, or a Summoner whose bloodline is weaker than that of a Master Summoner's.

LOTIUS: One of Auris' Moons, it has a pale gray coloration

MASTER SUMMONER: Pure-blooded Summoner who comes from two parents of the same Sect ... they are considerably more powerful than Lesser Summoners

NAVESIAN: The primary religion of Auris, mostly followed by those in the North and the East of the continent

NIVENTIA: The Goddess of life, light, and prosperity

NREKUMAS: Scaled beast of The Wastelands

ORIA: The Second of Auris' Moons, it has a blue-green coloration

ORRINSHIRE: Small town in northern Elos

PHASING: Another word for shifting

RUNES: An ancient language created by the Rune-Writers that allows written letters to be imbued with unparalleled power

RUNE-LOCKS: Rune based locks that are virtually impossible to bypass

SANDWORMS: A species of worm that live in the deserts of Asari - edible

SHIFTING: The switching of a person (usually a Shadow-Swift) from Auris to the Unbound

SECT: A class or "order" of Summoners characterized by specific abilities

SHADOW-SAND: Sand-like material from the Unbound... the only substance capable of shifting with Shadow-Swifts (can be condensed and forged into weapons and armor)

SHOREBEANS: A plant grown in southern Auris - edible

SNOWFIN: A large, thick-skinned fish native to the Northwest of Auris

SNOWPROWLER: A large, aggressive snow cat that dwells primarily in The Highlands

SPARKCOILS: Electricity-conducting wire systems usable by Voltarians.

STONEBLOSSOMS: A plant grown in central Auris - edible

STORMLESS: Ordinary people that are not Summoners

STORMROOTS: A bitter plant that grows in central Auris– edible

SUCHARA: Capital of Asari

SUNBEAMS: Harmless wisps of heat-energy that float through the air on Blazedays

SUNBIRD: A type of bird with eight angelic, luminous wings. These birds are said to be the children of Niventia

Tᴀʀᴀᴛʜɪᴇʟ: God of the land, stone, and the mountains

Tᴇʟᴇɴᴀʀɪs: The mountain in which Erydon is hidden

Tʜᴇ Aʀᴄʜɪᴘᴇʟᴀɢᴏ: An island chain surrounding the volcano: Ashos on the southern tip of Auris

Tʜᴇ Hɪɢʜʟᴀɴᴅs: A massive region of mountains in the central-northern part of Auris consisting of virtually inhabitable, treacherous mountains

Tʜᴇ Pʟᴀɴᴇs ᴏғ Gᴇɴᴇsɪs: A mythical Realm from which all powers of creation and Summoning began

Tʜᴇ Uɴʙᴏᴜɴᴅ: A parallel/underlying Realm to Auris that is still partially connected to Auris

Tʜᴇ Vᴀɴɪsʜɪɴɢ: The unexplained event that led to the disappearance of The eight Lost Sects and the arrival of the Tempests

Uᴛʀʏᴀ: Country in the Northwest of Auris

Uᴍʙʀᴀᴋɪɴᴇsɪs: Manipulation of dark energies

Wᴀʀᴅs: Rune-powered shields that serve a various purpose

Zᴇᴘʜʏʀ: The God of time

ACKNOWLEDGMENTS

Creating The Fire King, and transforming it from a messy first draft into a finished novel was an incredibly exciting experience, and I couldn't have done it without a lot of help. My parents have continued to be my biggest supporters, offering feedback and encouragement even when I didn't know I needed it. I want to thank my mom for reading countless drafts of this story and always working with me to make this book the best it could be. I want to thank my dad for helping me bring this story to life, and for guiding me through the complicated publishing process. I also want to thank my brother Lukas for always supporting me and for making each and every day fun and entertaining.

I would also like to thank my editors: P.J. (Tricia) Hoover and Samantha Wekstien. Your feedback helped make both Stormless and The Fire King as amazing as they are now. Thank you to my website designer: Daniel Berkowitz, and my cover artist: Jeff Brown. I want to thank Shaun Loftus and her entire team for their help with the publication and marketing of The Fire King.

Thank you to my grandma Linda, who provided some very helpful feedback on the early versions of this story. I want to thank all of my friends and classmates who put up with me constantly talking about my writing. Finally, I want to thank all of you: my readers. Without you, the Stormless Series wouldn't be all that it is today. This journey has been the most incredible experience of my life, and I hope that my stories continue to entertain you for many years to come.

ABOUT THE AUTHOR

Nick is eighteen years old. He lives in Indiana with his mom, dad, older brother, and two dogs. His writing career began in sixth grade, when Nick started writing fantasy stories for fun in his free time. As he learned and grew as a student, his writing also improved. He connected with other readers and writers in his grade, compelling him to work even harder on his stories.

As Nick started high school, he began to take writing more seriously. Following an injury during his sophomore year that forced him to take a step back from his tennis career, Nick began writing the first pages of the Stormless Series.

He woke up early every day to work on the project before school, and by May 2022, he was finished with the first draft of Stormless. He was paired with an editor on Reedsy, and after spending the next year editing and revising his work, Nick published Stormless.

Now, with both Stormless and The Fire King completed, Nick has started to work on the next entry of the Stormless Series. He doesn't plan to stop writing stories. Writing is his passion, and even after releasing two novels as a teenager, his journey as a writer is just beginning.

facebook.com/nickstitleauthor
instagram.com/nickstitle_author
amazon.com/stores/Nick-Stitle/author/B0BZQ8KFCN

ALSO BY NICK STITLE

STORMLESS SERIES

1. Stormless

2. The Fire King

3. Summoner (forthcoming)

4. TBD (forthcoming)